Rescuing Hope

A Novel

Heidi M. Thomas

SunCatcher Publications

Praise for *Rescuing Hope*

"Sometimes in rescuing others, we rescue ourselves without knowing that's what happened. Sam has more than her fair share of trials and tribulations, but she never gives up and always continues to rescue others along the way. Friends, animals, total strangers, her young ward ... the list goes on. She's a go-getter and a hard-working woman with a set of goals that would choke some men down. But she prevails ... somehow ... some way. Read how in the pages of *Rescuing Hope*." –Sally Bates, award-winning author of western women's fiction and poetry

~~~

"If you like the show, Heartland, you'll love this book! Good characters in real-life situations." —Laura Drake, award-winning women's fiction author

~~~

"Samantha Moser has a heart as big as Montana and it seems everyone knows it. Injured dogs, spooked horses, damaged veterans, troubled teens—they all find their way to Sam for nurturing and healing by her compassion and generosity. She sometimes wonders in the quiet of the midnight darkness if there will ever be anyone to love and nurture her and help her achieve her dream of buying her grandparents ranch."—Leta McCurry, author of *Dancing to the Silence*

~~~

"A compelling tale of a young woman's dream to own the Montana ranch her great-grandparents once owned. She hopes to raise thoroughbreds using income from her as-yet unrealized equestrian center. But obstacles abound. Colossal snowstorms, financial woes. Big Game developers gobbling up good ranch land, misunderstood love interests. None throw her so far off course as her own self-doubt. A host of characters—good, bad, and just plain mean—show her how to find her way to a dream come true. This book stands to renew one's faith in the goodness of ordinary people."—Karen Casey-Fitzjerrell, award-winning author of *Forgiving Effie Beck*

~~~

"The story of a young woman who doubts herself in the face of tragedy. Running through all of the "what-ifs," she bounces back to hope in spite of the odds."—Brenda Whitesite, award-winning women's suspense author of The MacKenzie Chronicles

Other books by Heidi M. Thomas

Cowgirl Dreams series
Cowgirl Dreams
Follow the Dream
Dare to Dream

American Dream series
Seeking the American Dream
Finding True Home

Rescue series
Rescuing Samantha
Rescuing Hope

Nonfiction
Cowgirl Up! A History of Rodeo Women

Children's
The Secret of the Ice Castle & Other Inspirational Tales

Praise for Heidi M. Thomas Books

Cowgirl Dreams: "…Brings heart, verve and knowledge to her depiction of the intrepid Nettie. A lively look at the ranch women of an almost forgotten West." —Deirdre McNamer, MFA English Professor, University of Montana, *Red Rover, My Russian,* and *One Sweet Quarrel*

Follow the Dream: "I enjoyed this bittersweet novel with its accurate depiction of the lives of cowgirls in 1930s Montana and its tender portrait of a marriage." Mary Clearman Blew, award-winning author of *All but the Waltz: A Memoir of Five Generations in the Life of a Montana Family*

Dare to Dream: "Finding our place and following our hearts is the moving theme of *Dare to Dream,* a finely-tuned finish to Heidi Thomas's trilogy inspired by the life of her grandmother, an early rodeo-rider. With crisp dialogue and singular scenes, we're not only invited into the middle of a western experience of rough stock, riders and generations of ranch tradition, but we're deftly taken into a family drama. This family story takes place beginning in 1941 but it could be happening to families anywhere—and is. Nettie, Jake, and Neil struggle to find their place and discover what we all must: life is filled with sorrow and joy; faith, family and friends see us through and give meaning to it all. Nettie, or as Jake calls her, 'Little Gal' will stay in your heart and make you want to re-read the first books just to keep her close. A very satisfying read."—Jane Kirkpatrick, an award-winning, *New York Times* Bestselling author

Cowgirl Up: A History of Rodeo Women: "The best kind of history lesson; Informative and entertaining. Thomas does a great job of showing the lifestyles of these women in a very male dominated world, and how through hard work and determination they gained the respect of many people not only in the U.S., but throughout the world. You can't help but be impressed with the toughness of these women, who competed even with broken bones and other injuries. An eye-opening look at the world of rodeo, and the accomplishments of these women. –John J. Rust, author of *Arizona's All-Time Baseball Team* and the "Fallen Eagle" series

Seeking the American Dream: "Heidi Thomas's novel grips the reader from the first opening sentence, as her nurse-protagonist struggles to face the wretched suffering in war-torn Hamburg during the final days of WWII. From there, her sweeping saga takes her away from Europe's lurching efforts to rebuild, and into building her own new life in America. From the perspective of a hard-working, and still bright-eyed young woman, we participate in America's own next chapter." –Mara Purl, best-selling author of the Milford-Haven Novels

Finding True Home: "This sequel to *Seeking the American Dream* continues Heidi Thomas' heart-tugging saga of the life of a World War II war bride as she struggles to adjust to life on a Montana ranch, where family is everything and neighbor helps neighbor through the toughest situations. Struggling through isolation, prejudice, and self-doubt, Anna Moser finally finds peace, acceptance, and her true home through a lifetime of love and sacrifice." – Donis Casey, author of the Alafair Tucker series

Rescuing Samantha: "Heidi Thomas brings us a story about a young woman facing life's trials in rugged Montana. But "Sam" has the gumption of her grandmother and great-grandmother, to persevere and overcome. She is also compelled to rescue horses and young people.

There is drama and true-to-life dialogue in Thomas' smooth writing and the reader will become immersed. It is a joy to watch along with the characters how God brings "mysterious" blessings to their predicaments.

This is also a story of rural America that many of us long for—neighborhood rodeo, BBQ, homemade ice cream, reverence for the Star-Spangled Banner, fiddles and dancing, and (mostly) friendly neighbors. Readers will love this story." ~ Denise F. McAllister, MAPW, Atlanta, GA. Freelance editor, Member of Western Writers of America and Women Writing the West.

Rescuing Hope

A SunCatcher Publications book

Cover Design by Jason McIntyre

www.TheFarthestReaches.com

Library of Congress Cataloguing-in-Publication data is available on file.

ISBN: 978-0-9990663-4-8

Printed in the United States of America

10 9 8 7 6 5 4 3 2 1

ACKNOWLEDGMENTS

So many have been involved in making my books a reality. I thank God for the gift of the writing gene, my family for their continued support and encouragement, the teachers and editors who believed in me, my fellow Women Writing the West members, my Word Spinners critique group, and my Chino Valley critique group who have given me such valuable feedback: Sally Bates, Leta McCurry, and John J. Rust. Thank you also to my beta reader, Karen Casey-Fitzjerrel, and Brenda Whiteside, critique partner and editor, for helping make my work better. And, of course, thank you to all my readers for supporting my writing habit.

"...those who hope in the Lord will renew their strength. They will soar on wings like eagles; they will run and not grow weary, they will walk and not be faint." Isaiah 40:31

CHAPTER ONE

An empty ache tugged at Samantha Moser as Electra and her mother Alberta Lucci boarded the plane for New York. An hour earlier, her best friend from childhood, Jace, had headed back to Phoenix. Another image flashed through her mind of former fiancé, Kenny, unable to face the harsh winters and tough life of Montana, flying away two years ago. *Why do people I love always leave me?*

She took a deep breath. *Okay, buck up, girl. You're not entirely alone. You have three rescued horses to care for and great neighbors. And... Brad is still in your life.* Her heart tripped a happy beat.

Turning from the window in the Billings airport, she strode toward the parking lot. Places to go, people to see. She had an appointment with her employer's accountant.

It had been an eventful summer—going to work for Clyde Bruckner on his dude ranch. There, she'd met her teen friend Electra who morphed from sullen Goth girl to a lovely young woman totally obsessed with horses. And she'd met Brad, a free-lance videographer.

She giggled. Boy, had she misjudged him at first. Because he'd been hired to do a documentary for a group trying to buy up ranches to form "The Big Open"—a wildlife refuge in eastern Montana—she immediately pegged him as one of the "enemy." But he'd won her over by doing another documentary about her rescue horses, Apache and Trixi, and the troubled kids she worked with.

Because of that film, she'd received enough money to take care of her horses and... what else? That part she wasn't sure of yet.

Sam found a parking spot downtown and then took the elevator to the office of Duncan Soto, CPA. She glanced at her blue jeans and short-sleeved western shirt and bit her lip. *Maybe I should've worn a dress and heels.* She shrugged. *Oh well, too late now.* As she entered the modest but comfortable lobby, butterflies engaged in a vigorous tennis match in her stomach. Memories of approaching bankers a year ago about getting a loan to breed her Thoroughbred mare, Sugar, lobbed balls of defeat. She squared her shoulders. She could do this. It wasn't about being rejected. Clyde had assured her that Soto was a good guy and would help her with her investment decisions.

The receptionist showed her into the office, and the accountant stood up from his desk. "Miss Moser? I'm Duncan." He gestured toward a gray-padded chair. "Clyde told me a little about your situation. How can I help?"

"Well, Clyde probably told you I received donations from Brad's documentary, and I don't know what to do with the money. Putting it in savings won't earn any interest, and I'm afraid it'll be too easy to spend." She shrugged. "Some kind of investment, maybe? Clyde suggested we go into partnership, using my rescue horses to work with teens. We've already been doing that on his dude ranch."

"That would be an option." Soto steepled his fingers. After half an hour of talk about stocks and bonds, examples of non-profits, articles of incorporation, bylaws, and IRS forms, Sam's head spun.

She gathered up the papers the CPA had given her. "Okay, this is a lot to chew on. I'm going to have to study these and think about what to do." She stood. "Thank you for your suggestions. I'll get back to you on what I decide."

Outside, she blinked in the late summer sunshine as a warm breeze blew strands of chestnut hair from her ponytail. *What on earth was he talking about?* The hopeful buoyancy she'd felt when she went in had shriveled to a hard lump in her stomach. She didn't have any more of a clue what to do now than when she went in. Sam pulled out her cell phone and hit Brad's number.

"Hi," she said when he answered. "I'm ready for you to buy me lunch now."

"Great!" His smooth baritone rumbled in her ear. "Meet you at Jaker's in five."

She walked a few blocks down the street to the popular restaurant and entered its cool dimness. The rich wood columns and area dividers gleamed under a pressed copper ceiling. The hostess showed her to a table, where she studied the menu. More decisions.

"Hi, gorgeous." Brad leaned down and brushed the corner of her mouth with a kiss before he sat across from her. "How'd the meeting go?" White teeth flashed in his tanned, clean-cut face.

Warmth grew and rippled across her chest, remembering their first "real" kiss a week ago at the ranch barbecue. She hoped this was the beginning of a more serious relationship. "Am I glad to see you." She waved the folder from Soto. "I'm totally overwhelmed. I can't even decide what I want for lunch."

Brad chuckled. "Well, I can help you with that. Their burgers are the best in town, and the steak taco is my favorite."

Her stomach rumbled. "The taco sounds good to me."

When the waiter came by, Brad ordered and then shifted his attention back to her. "Electra and her mom take off okay?"

The ache in her heart returned. "Yes. From a houseful of chattering women—especially that girl—I don't know. It's going to be so terribly quiet now."

Brad reached over and took her hand. "You'll miss her, won't you?"

"Yeah." She forced a smile. "I never would've thought it when she first came to stay with me. My, oh my. I thought I'd bit off much more than I could ever chew."

Electra and her mom had come to the dude ranch to get away from the city and the tragedy of losing her brother in a car accident. Her dad had been driving, he couldn't deal with the death, and he abandoned them. *What a sad thing to have happen.*

The young teen had been so broken.

Brad's voice brought her back. "She was a handful, all right. But, as you always say, 'A girl and a horse is a healing combination.'" He brushed his perpetually wayward lock of dark hair off his forehead. "She sure didn't like me at first though. Thought I was there to steal your affections away from her."

"I think she's changed her mind about you now. But you're right, rescuing Apache from that horrible situation turned her completely around." She sighed. "I hope she can come back and help again next summer when school's out."

Their food arrived, and while they ate, Sam related some of what she'd talked about with the CPA. "So much paperwork and regulation to forming a non-profit. I really don't think I'm up for that. I simply want to work with my horses and the kids from the group home and help Clyde on the dude ranch. It's so hard to visualize the future, especially out there in the middle of nowhere at Ingomar."

"Yes, but look at what has happened already—people from all over the country are hearing about Bruckner's ranch, and now because of my documentary skills..." he grinned as he blew on his fingernails and polished them on his green plaid shirt with great exaggeration, "people have heard about you and your horse and kid miracles."

She laughed and reached across the small table to cuff his shoulder. "Yes, you've made me somewhat famous, or maybe 'infamous', at least in Montana. But seriously, thank you again for that. It has changed my life."

"Pfft. All in a day's work, m'lady." His face flushed. "Speaking of work... I have to head back to Wyoming to do more filming on that kangaroo introduction project."

Sam snorted. "Kangaroos in Wyoming. Who knew? But now I know they were serious when they proposed exotic animals, like lions and elephants, for 'The Big Open'." She took a sip of her soda. "When are you leaving?"

He looked down at the table and then up at her through

lowered lashes. "Day after tomorrow. Probably be gone several weeks again."

A lead balloon dropped to the bottom of her stomach. "Everybody's left me. Now you are too."

He pulled his face into a grimace. "I'm sorry. I'm not leaving you forever. I'll be back as soon as I can." He covered her hand with his.

She dropped her gaze to their hands. Would he be like Kenny, making promises he wouldn't keep?

***

Sam barely registered the two-hour drive home, her thoughts chasing one after another like kittens in the barn. She drove up to the two-story ranch house and stumbled up the steps to her wrap-around porch. As if weighted with a cement block, her purse slipped from her fingers to the floor, and she sank heavily onto the swing. Her head ached with the pounding of a hundred drums.

Just a couple of days ago, she'd been on top of the world, surrounded by her friends, with a new romance, and finally, a few extra dollars in the bank. Now, all this new information and decisions to be made—all alone—paralyzed her. The old dark cloud settled heavily on her shoulders. She was only leasing this ranch; her dream of raising Thoroughbreds had dried up with the sunburned prairie, and she was still only an employee at a dude ranch. Was she really any better off?

A hot breeze blew a tumbleweed across the yard. Sure, she had some money now and could do something... but what? Winter would be here before she was ready, and there would be no more dudes—or few, anyway—for several months. She couldn't imagine people from California or New York coming to Montana to traipse around in four-foot snowdrifts. The group home in Billings surely wouldn't be braving icy roads to bring the kids out regularly. Besides, it would be too cold to ride.

Shadows lengthened across the rolling hills. Sam slumped deeper on the swing, absently pushing it with the toe of her boot. Her mind flashed to the cabinet above the refrigerator. A nice stiff drink would taste so good right now. She shook her head abruptly. No. She'd dumped out what was left of the vodka in front of her friends, vowing she no longer needed that crutch.

Alcohol—that's what had come between her and her best friend. That's what put Jace in a wheelchair for life. That's what nearly killed her friend a second time when she spiraled into a life of drinking, drugs, and homelessness. But Jace overcame it. Sam could do that too. Drowning her sorrow, even occasionally, could lead to dependence, and she didn't want to go there.

A horse whinnied from the pasture, startling her. *Oh gee, I almost forgot about my babies.* Sam rose from the swing and trudged down the incline toward the barn. Hanging her head over the fence was Sugar, her first rescue—a racehorse scheduled to be put down because of a serious leg injury. Her grandparents, Anna and Neil Moser, had put up the money to buy the mare.

Sam grabbed a handful of grain pellets from the barn and held one out for the mare to lip softly from her palm. She rubbed the horse's head and ears as her two other rescue horses gathered beside them, nudging each other and nosing her arm for a treat too. Running her fingers through Trixi's blonde mane, she pulled out a cocklebur and fed her a pellet. Then she gave one to Apache.

"I need another arm to pet you all at the same time." She chortled at their antics and headed to the barn to get a bit of hay for them. The grass in the pasture was pretty much dried up, so she needed to give them a little supplemental feed.

After making sure the galvanized water tank was full, Sam leaned against the corral fence, taking in the peaceful sight of her horses munching their hay. Simply being near them made her headache subside, and the heaviness on her shoulders eased.

She and Electra had found Apache emaciated and dejected

near Forsyth and went to court to gain custody. The buckskin gelding filled out nicely and looked strong and healthy now. He was the love of Electra's life.

And Trixi. She was the beloved trick horse of Montana's famous Miss Ellie, who because of declining health, had to move to a retirement facility. They'd hit it off and Ellie was adamant she wanted to sell the light-colored chestnut to her. But Sam didn't have enough money to buy the horse, and it was slated to go to auction and probably to slaughter. After Brad's documentary, Ellie had gifted her with the beautiful mare. She smiled, more relaxed now than she had been all day.

The image of Trixi kneeling so Jace could mount brought the sting of happy tears. "For the first time in a long time, I feel normal," Jace had declared, beaming.

Sam strolled back to the house to prepare a light supper. While she cooked, a motion picture of images moved through her mind: each child who had responded to a horse and come out of a shell, from Electra to troubled kids from the group home, Goth-girl Sapphire and shy Wendy. Even the boys who abandoned a disinterested slouch to brush and care for a horse.

As she swallowed her last bite of supper, the phone rang. "Hi, Sam, ohmygosh we're finally home!" Electra's voice echoed over the line. "We had a long layover in Salt Lake and then the flight was delayed because of something wrong with the plane, and we had to wait for another one to come in, and I was so tired, I just wanted to be home, and we finally got on the plane, and now we're home, and ohmygosh I miss Apache so much, I want to come back!" The girl finally stopped with a sob. "I miss you too."

Sam wanted to laugh and cry at the same time. This breathless litany was signature Electra. "Oh, my dear, I miss you as well. The house is so empty and so quiet. I don't know what to do!"

"Is Apache okay? Does he miss me?"

"I think he does. I just fed and watered the horses, and he

seemed to need some extra petting."

A long shuddering sigh came over the phone. "Well, give him a big kiss for me, okay? Here's my mom. She wants to talk to you."

Alberta's voice sounded tired. "Hi, Sam. I wanted to thank you again for the wonderful time we had and for all you've done for Electra. She is a totally different girl, and I appreciate you so much."

"It was my pleasure. We really did have a wonderful time together, and I'm missing her already. You guys will have to come visit again, soon."

"We will. Electra is already talking about when." Alberta laughed. "Take care now. We'll be in touch."

CHAPTER TWO

Thursday evening before the Labor Day weekend, Sam stopped by Horace Jones' ranch to borrow his horse trailer. The Bruckners were expecting two more families plus the group home kids, and she wanted to take Trixi and Sugar to supplement the dude string.

Her elderly neighbor shuffled out of his house as she drove up. "Howdy there, little gal."

"Hi. You know, I need to buy my own horse trailer and quit mooching off you. I've been looking for ways to invest my money, and that would be a good start."

"That's a great idea." The older man ran his hand over his short-cropped silver hair. "Say, why don't I sell you mine. I don't use it that often anymore, and when I need it, I could come borrow it from you." He chuckled. "Then you can pay the repair bills."

Sam grinned. "All right." She grabbed her checkbook from the pickup. "Let's do it."

They chatted for a while, and she told him about her visit to the accountant and her continuing dilemma.

Horace nodded. "Yeah, you'll most likely want to put most of it aside in some kind of investment, so it'll grow."

Sam widened her eyes. The old rancher sounded much savvier than she'd thought. That was better than what the accountant told her. "What should I do? Is there something you'd recommend?"

He leaned against the pickup. "What's your dream now? What do you want to do—stay here, keep workin' with horses and kids, or what?"

Her insides churned. "Well...that's part of my indecision. Maybe if I were thirty instead of twenty-four, I'd have better insight. When I first moved here with Kenny, my dream—our dream, I thought—was to raise Thoroughbreds. You know how expensive that would be, and how unrealistic in this isolated, dry country."

Horace snickered. "Yeah. I thought at the time you were pretty ambitious. But you're young and smart and a hard worker. Whatever you set your mind to, you can do 'er."

"I have loved seeing the results of putting kids and horses together. Electra is the biggest and best example. What a difference."

"Night 'n' day." Her neighbor kicked his boot toe against a dirt clod. "So, what're you thinkin'? Gonna stay with Clyde or go off on your own?"

She leaned over the side of the pickup and stared at wisps of hay scattered in the bed. "Well, Clyde has the facilities for his dude ranch—the cabins and barn and corrals. I love working with the Bruckners, but that's pretty seasonal. After hunting season, there might be a few hardy souls who will come out for snowmobiling, but I don't see a big role for me from now till next spring."

She reached down, picked up a sprig of straw, and traced patterns in the dusty truck bed. "I barely had room for Electra in my house, and with three horses now, my barn is getting pretty crowded. I can't see me hosting kids there. Besides, I'm only leasing the place."

Horace grabbed a straw and stuck it in his mouth. "Yup. That's true."

A light exploded in Sam's brain, like the old-fashioned flashbulbs her grandpa used to have on his camera. She looked up at him, her lips tugging upward. "That's it! I'll buy the ranch, my great-grandparents' place! I can afford to do that now." A giggle erupted. "Why didn't I think of that before?"

He laughed, a deep belly rumble. "I was wonderin' how long it'd take ya." He squeezed her arm. "I think that's a super idea."

***

The weekend whirled by like a dust devil. At Bruckners', Sam took the dude wives on horseback, worked with group home kids to make them comfortable around the horses, and took the more adventurous ones on rides. From all sides came requests: "Sam, would you help me saddle?" "I need help getting up there!" "I'm tired of brushing horses, can I ride now?"—until she felt like barbed wire being stretched between two fence posts.

She sank onto a picnic bench at the end of the day. "Oh, I miss Electra!" she blurted. At least the teen had been a big help with the more-reticent kids. She gratefully accepted an iced tea from Irene Bruckner.

"I know you do, dear, and so do I." The motherly woman patted her hand. "Tomorrow is the rodeo, and then you can rest."

"I'm looking forward to that." Sam sighed. "But this is pretty much the end of the dude season. What will I do then?"

Irene sipped from her tea. "I'm sure Clyde will find things to keep you busy during the winter."

Sam stared off toward the corral. Out of the shadows stepped a small form. Benjy from the group home slouched closer to where Sugar hung her head over the low fence, once again her nostrils fluttering softly in his direction. Whereas the first time he met the horse, he had hung back, too frightened to get near, this time he rested his palm on her nose and then gently caressed it. A smile blossomed on his face, and he rested his cheek against Sugar's.

Sam bit her lip to keep tears at bay. "Oh my," she breathed. "Where's Robin? I wish she could see this." She pointed, and Irene turned to watch.

She scanned the yard and corral area. The counselor stood

in the shade of a cottonwood tree near the corral. Her hands covered her mouth. Sam's pulse throbbed with the sight of Benjy, and she understood the joy and wonder the other woman must be feeling.

Benjy and Sugar stood in their hug for long minutes. Then he drew back to pat her face and neck and run his fingers through her mane. Sugar stood patiently, her head and neck curved to enfold the boy.

The women remained silent and enraptured.

Finally, Benjy swiveled toward Robin, his head straight and the smile still on his face. "Nice horse," he said.

***

Early the next day, people gathered for the rodeo—from the neighborhood, from Forsyth, Miles City, and Billings. Sam helped Irene prepare food for the barbecue and organize the potluck dishes visitors brought.

Group home kids, Sapphire and Wendy, hung out near the corral to catch glimpses of the barrel racers. "Oooh, look at her outfit." Sapphire turned to Robin and Sam. "Do you think we could get blue satin shirts like that? I bet Electra would want one too!"

Sam smirked.

Robin rolled her eyes. "Well, I suppose you could, if you can think of ways to earn money for them."

"Oooh, or red ones, like that!" The young girls ran off to talk to the contestants. Robin shook her head. "I think I've opened a Pandora's box with those two."

The girls returned to watch the racers put their mounts to the test, running figure three-leaf cloverleaf patterns, leaning far to the side as they rounded the barrels, and then urging the horse in a fast gallop back to the gate. The two young teens gasped and applauded each one.

"I wanna do that!" they shrieked. Sam and Robin chuckled, shaking their heads.

Clyde announced the first event on his megaphone, and the first few team ropers executed their moves. Afterward, Sam went back to the house to help Irene, occasionally catching one of the events. She paused when a bronc rider came into view. *To think my great-grandma Nettie used to do that.* Pride coursed through her. And she was living on her great-grandparents' ranch, maybe to stay.

Toward the end of the afternoon, as the women set up food on long plank tables, Clyde announced the winners and gave out ribbons and trophies. Then the crowd descended for the succulent beef that had been roasting all afternoon and the myriad salads, rolls, and other side dishes.

Despite wanting to drop over at any moment from sheer exhaustion, Sam forged on with a smile on her face. "You're welcome, enjoy," she repeated like a robot, barely noticing who came through the line.

"Golly, are you a sight for sore eyes!" A familiar rich baritone brought her attention up sharply. The dark, wayward lock fell onto his forehead, and he brushed it back.

"Brad!" Sam's face warmed, her heartbeat sped up, and she dropped the forkful of beef she held. "Where did you come from? I wasn't expecting you!"

His boyish face erupted into a huge grin. "I know. I wanted to surprise you. Can you take a break and come eat with me?"

Clyde, slicing meat nearby, boomed out, "Of course she can. She's been workin' harder than a one-armed paper hanger all weekend." He made shooing motions. "Go on, Sam, have something to eat."

She grabbed a paper plate, filled it, and followed Brad to a vacant spot at a picnic table. "I thought you were going to be gone for several weeks."

He finished his bite. "Well, yes, I did too. But the weekend came up and we weren't doing any filming—most everybody took time off—so I thought, what the heck, I'll come back and see my favorite girl, even if it's just for one day."

His girl? Sam's face heated again, and she lowered her eyes to her plate. Then she looked up. "I'm glad. I've missed you. Although…" she gazed around at the crowd, "I've been so busy this weekend I think I met myself coming back."

Brad laughed. "You've got a great turn-out. The last hurrah of summer, huh?"

She sobered. "Yeah, I'm afraid so. Hunting season is next, and I'm not a hunting guide, so things are going to slow down considerably. I've got to make some decisions soon." Then she smiled. "But I have made one decision. I'm going to go talk to Jack Murdoch about buying the ranch."

Brad grabbed her hand. "Awesome! That's a terrific plan."

She raised her eyebrows. *I hope it's a terrific plan.*

CHAPTER THREE

After helping with clean-up at Clyde's the next day, Sam went home early. On the way, while she still had cell reception, she called her friend and real estate agent, Teresa Knudson. "Hey, girl. You want to come over for supper tonight? I have an idea I want to run by you."

"Absolutely. I'd love to. Sorry I didn't make it to the rodeo yesterday. I was out of town."

"I missed you, but that's okay. Guess who showed up?"

"Who? Brad?" Teresa gave a little squeal. "That's fantastic."

"Yeah, but he had to leave again right away. Anyhow, I'll see you after a bit." Sam clicked off.

Back at the ranch, she fed the three horses, spending a few extra minutes with each one, stroking noses and finger-combing manes. Apache snorted and ran circles around the corral, kicking up his heels. Sam laughed. "You're glad the girls are back, aren't you, boy."

She walked up the slight incline to the house, where she prepared burgers and salad. Gazing out the kitchen window, she allowed herself a moment of reflection—how she and her ex-fiancé Kenny had arrived here two years ago, full of plans and dreams. Together they'd remodeled the sagging house and barn, working side by side. *Just like great-grandma Nettie and Jake did when they moved to this place.*

It hadn't worked out with Kenny, but... she paused chopping vegetables. This ranch was a family legacy, even though it had been sold several times since the 1960s. It was pure luck that she'd seen the ad to lease the place. She raised her eyes to the pristine blue sky. Or maybe it was meant to come back into the family. Every time she rode the undulating prairie, she sensed Grandma Nettie galloping alongside her, their horses running in tandem, the wind blowing through their hair, reveling in the freedom of the wide-open spaces.

Her sight blurred and she brushed away a tear. *I have to buy this place. I don't know what I'll do if I don't. There is no Plan B.*

At that moment she saw Teresa roar up the lane in her black SUV. She jumped out, carrying a grocery bag, and trotted up the steps to the porch. Sam opened the door and gave her a hug. "Thanks for coming."

"It's my pleasure. And I brought Rocky Road ice cream for dessert." Her friend strode to the refrigerator and deposited the treat in the freezer. She leaned a hip against the counter. "So, dish. How was Brad?"

Heat spread through Sam's chest to her hairline. "He's fine. Working on that documentary in Wyoming, you know, about introducing kangaroos there."

Teresa waved a hand. "Yeah, yeah, I know. The documentary. I mean HOW was Brad?"

Sam snickered. "I had no idea he was coming. He surprised me toward the end of the rodeo. I was so excited to see him, and we had a nice time at the barbecue and fireworks. But then he had to leave, had to be back at work today." She pushed her lower lip out in a sad pout.

"He is *so* cute. And to drive all that way, just to see you for a short while… Hmm…" Her friend waggled her eyebrows. "I think he likes you."

Sam imagined her face was as red as Teresa's T-shirt. She ducked her head and tossed the lettuce.

"C'mon, you like him too."

"Yeah. I do. He treats me really nice—he's so polite and sweet and makes me feel special. Not like a certain someone we shall not name but begins with 'K.'" *That jerk.* "And, after all, Brad's photos and documentary helped me get Apache and Trixi and the donations that I…" She peered into Teresa's face.

"That's what I want to talk to you about. I want to buy this ranch."

"But of course!" The blonde woman pushed her long hair over her shoulder. "You signed a lease with an option to buy. You have the right of first refusal. That's been the plan all along, right?"

"Yes, and now I have enough for a down payment. But I need your advice in how to approach Jack Murdoch. You know how stinky he was with those 'Big Open' guys, how he tried to sell the place out from under me."

Teresa's eyes narrowed. "Yeah. But they're long gone, and I can't see that he'd have any other plans for it now."

"Let's eat, and then I'll get the lease papers out, and we can go over all that."

The women ate the grilled burgers, Teresa teasing her more about Brad. Sam dished up the ice cream, and they went to sit on the porch. "So, what about you—who were *you* visiting this weekend?"

It was Teresa's turn to blush. "Oh, I just went up to Flathead Lake and went sailing with some friends."

"Some friends, huh?" She pointed her spoonful of Rocky Road toward her friend's face. "Any *one* in particular?"

"W-e-l-l, kind of." Teresa stirred her ice cream. "Allen Richardson. I met him at a conference in Billings this summer. He's a real estate agent too."

"Aha. And he has a sailboat?"

Her friend smirked. "Yes, and it is *sweet*. We all had a lot of fun. Maybe you and Brad could come with us sometime."

"I dunno. Brad is gone so much, with his work. I have no idea when I'll see him next... or even if there's really a relationship yet." Sam shrugged, but her lips tingled with the memory of his kiss.

"Oh, there is. I just know it."

"Anyway, enough about my romance. Let me go get my papers, and we can strategize."

They went through her lease, and Teresa suggested a price

for Sam's offer. "Based on other ranch properties in this area, that's what I would start with."

Anticipation clutched at her throat. Even though this dry-land area was worth much less than land in other areas of Montana, the number still hit her as huge. "Okay."

"Do you want me to meet you at his office or even submit the offer for you?"

That was generous of her friend, but... "No. As much as I would love your support, I think I need to go talk to him myself, clear the air about the past, and see if we can start off on a better foot. But thank you."

"Sure. My office is just down the street from his, so if you want to stop by after, give me a call."

***

The next morning, Sam called to make an appointment with Murdock. His secretary said he was available that afternoon, so she drove the forty miles to Forsyth. Her hands gripped the wheel with cold clamminess, and her pulse beat in the back of her throat. Last summer, her landlord had tried to sell the ranch out from under her when he became involved with "The Big Open" group trying to create an exotic wildlife refuge in the area. He'd tried to bully her into giving in. Maybe she was making a mistake in turning down Teresa's offer to come along. Strength in numbers. She sneaked a look at her cell phone on the seat beside her. She could always change her mind and call.

"No. You have to cowgirl up and do this on your own." Sam spoke firmly to herself as though she were ten years old.

She angled into a parking spot in front of the office building, and with shaky knees, walked up the steps and through a mahogany-paneled hall to Murdock's door. The middle-aged secretary rose from her sleek modern desk, welcomed her with a smile, and ushered her into his plush office.

The tall, forty-something businessman, dark hair showing threads of silver, stood from behind a huge cherrywood desk and put out his hand to shake. "Hello, Sam. Good to see you again. Please sit down."

After shaking his hand, she eased herself onto the burgundy velvet-covered chair and inhaled deeply. "Well, I…" her voice came out in a strange squeak.

"What can I do for you today? Everything going all right on the ranch? Cows doing good?"

She cleared her throat and tried again. "Yes. Yes, everything is fine. The cows and calves are looking good, and I think you'll get a decent price this fall. I…uh…" she blurted the rest out before she could change her mind. "I would like to exercise my option and buy the ranch."

Murdock's eyebrows arched, and he steepled fingers with manicured nails. Silence grew long as he stared at her.

Sam's heart drummed, and she forced herself to breathe evenly. *Why is he doing this, making me sweat?* When she couldn't stand the quiet any longer, she named the price per acre Teresa had suggested.

"Hmm." He nodded slowly, then picked up a pen and tapped it on the desk. After a few seconds, he punched the intercom button. "Susie, bring in the Samantha Moser file."

The secretary brought in a manila folder. Murdock made a big show of pulling a pair of reading glasses out of his pocket and cleaning them with a soft cloth from his desk drawer. Then he opened the folder and peered at the paperwork.

With her insides turned to jelly, she clasped her hands tightly to keep them from shaking. If he delayed speaking for another minute, she might throw up.

Finally, he leaned back in his chair and took off the readers. "Well… I see that you signed a five-year lease. So, you have three more years to go before it comes up for renewal."

She tried to swallow, her throat as parched as a dry creek bed.

"I mean, it's a very nice offer. But… I don't think I'm quite ready to sell just yet."

The words hit her like a kick to the solar plexus. She blinked rapidly, and her mouth opened. *What did he just say? Not ready to sell?* She honestly had not expected that. The room swirled as if in the middle of a giant black dust devil. She sat, mute, for the longest minute.

Then red-hot lava rose from within her. She stood and flattened her palms on his desk. "You certainly were ready to sell it out from under me just a few short months ago!" She spat the words as if she had a mouth full of horse manure.

Murdock shrugged. "That didn't work out so well, did it? Thanks to your buddies showing up with guns locked and loaded when we came to the Jersey Lilly to talk in good faith."

Her heart plummeted like a chunk of granite. The slick New York "Big Open" developers had been warned not to return, and when they did, the entire neighborhood was lined up on the street, waiting.

Murdock's holding a grudge.

She wanted to grab his neck and twist it like a tom turkey, but she forced herself to take a step back. "I am sorry for the intimidation tactics on the part of the ranchers." She paused.

Of course your guys worked plenty of intimidation themselves, trying to buy up land in the area. "But I had nothing to do with that. I came here to make peace with you and to negotiate a sale in the gentlemanly manner of my great-grandparents. I would like to buy the ranch, and I hope we can shake hands and make a deal that will benefit us both."

Murdock stood. "I appreciate the apology and your effort. But I think we need to revisit this issue in three years." He stepped to the door and opened it. "Have a good day, Miss Moser."

Sam wasn't sure how she made it out of the building onto the street. Her whole body shook. Her feet were like cement. Her mind swirled. She leaned against the hood of her truck. *Now what?* Everything she had come up with in terms of her future rode on buying the ranch.

As if in a trance, she got into the vehicle and drove the few blocks to Teresa's modest office.

Her friend stepped out from behind her desk. "Hey there,

how'd it go…? Oh my. You look like you've seen a ghost." Her forehead puckered, and she gestured. "C'mon in, sit down."

Sam stumbled in and sat.

Teresa grabbed a bottle of water from a small fridge near her desk and offered it to her. "What happened?"

"He said no. I truly did not expect that. He was so eager to sell to those New York guys. But now…" She still couldn't quite process what had transpired.

"Really!" Teresa's eyes were wide. "That is a surprise."

Tears stung her eyes. "He's still ticked about being run out of town, losing face with the developers."

"Ah." Teresa nodded. "I see."

"He wouldn't listen to reason, wouldn't discuss anything. Said we'd revisit it when the lease is up in three years." She drew a hiccupy breath. "I was thinking of building an indoor arena, so I could still have clients in the winter. Everything hinged on buying the ranch. What am I going to do now?"

Teresa leaned forward and gently clasped Sam's arm. "We'll figure something out. Maybe I can find you a place that's more suitable, even better."

Tears flowed freely now. "This is the ranch my grandparents built up. *My* ranch. It's *this* ranch or none."

***

Sam drove home, a boulder in her stomach, her body numb. She chewed her chapped lower lip. It seemed like this was her perpetual state anymore—doomed for failure. Alone. She automatically shifted, slowed for turns, sped up on the straights, and somehow made it home before she realized she'd arrived.

After parking the truck, she trudged down the hill to the barn. The three horses saw her coming and whickered a greeting. They trotted up to the fence, waiting for a treat and a head scratch. Sam fed them each a couple of cake pellets from her hand, stroked their faces, and then went to the barn where she grabbed a bridle.

She caught Sugar, swung up on her bare back, and headed out onto the dry, faded prairie dotted with silver sagebrush. A gray grouse flew up from the brush, wings whirring as she fluttered from their path. Sam inhaled in the scent of dusty grass and spicy bushes and allowed her body to meld with the horse's rhythm as they loped through a coulee and up a rolling hill. The breeze she and Sugar generated evaporated the sweat on her face and neck. Gradually her tight shoulders relaxed.

She reined in the horse on a bluff overlooking the reservoir where white-faced Hereford cows and calves lingered by the water. These fifty head were Murdock's, and under the lease, Sam took care of them, feeding hay in the winter and helping gather for branding and shipping. She loved working the cattle and allowed herself a satisfied smile at their good condition. She'd always hoped they would be hers someday, along with the ranch. The smile evaporated and her back tightened again with a shiver when she thought of winter coming. She'd be on her own. How would she manage feeding them without Kenny to help? She hated asking Horace all the time. Sure, Murdock had given her a break on the lease payments for doing this, but if anything happened to any animal, she was sure there would be hell to pay.

Sugar snorted and bobbed her head. "Okay, let's head back." Sam turned the mare around and galloped home. Apache and Trixi needed to be exercised too, but she couldn't bring herself to do any more than give them extra feed and check their water. Thoughts of being alone in the winter, lack of finances, and her defeat with Murdock hovered over her like a dark storm cloud.

Sometimes, riding gave her clarity and provided answers, but today she had more questions than answers. She dragged herself back to the house, where she heated leftovers for her supper, and then chewed without tasting.

The phone rang and she jumped, dropping her fork. She picked up the receiver to hear Electra's voice. "Hey, Sam."

"Good to hear you, Electra. How are things?"

"Oh, Sam, I... I don't like it here." Her voice quavered. "I want to come back to you... and Apache."

"What's wrong, honey? Why?"

"School sucks." A long, drawn-out sigh. "My friends... they don't understand. They're still, like, stuck. They're still into Goth, kinda like I was when you first met me." She sniffed loudly. "They make fun of me, call me names, call me 'hayseed' and 'cowherder.'"

Sam swallowed. "I'm so sorry. But you know how much better you feel. You've simply grown past that stage. You are much more mature than they are. I'm sure they can see that, and they're probably jealous."

"Yeah."

She heard the defeat in her young friend's voice. Probably little comfort being "more mature" when she felt so lonely. "Have you been able to ride since you've been home?"

"Mom's taken me to the riding stables a couple of times." Electra spoke in a small, hushed voice, not like her usual run-on, excited jumble. "But it's not the same. It's really lame, like 'equestrian' style—so 'prim and proper'—not like riding with you. Not Apache." She choked out a sob. "I miss Apache."

Sam hunched over the kitchen counter. What could she say to make the girl feel better? *I can't think.* "I know you do, honey. I wish I could help you somehow. All I can do is say, hang in there. It *will* get better. And before you know, it'll be summer, and I think your mom is willing to have you come out here again and help me." She tried to make her words sound cheerful, but Electra's term *lame* stuck in her mind.

"Yeah, but that's...like...for*ever* away!"

"No, no. It'll go quickly, I promise. Keep working hard at your schoolwork, and don't let your friends get you down. Do you think they'd go riding with you sometime? Maybe they'd like it."

The teen snorted. "I doubt it. Anyway, gotta go. Mom just came home."

"Wait. Let me talk to your mom."

"Okay. Here she is. 'Bye, Sam." Her mournful, little girl voice made Sam want to cry.

"Sam?" Alberta came on the line. "What's going on?"

"Electra sounds so unhappy, with school and her friends, and missing Apache. I didn't know how to encourage her..." She sighed. "I feel at a loss."

"I know. Me too. I'm not sure what to do either. She doesn't like the riding stables, she's not into school, and she's started to wear black again."

Sam winced. "Oh dear." A sick feeling washed over her.

"Yeah. I'm afraid her friends are going to drag her back into that Goth thing again."

"Well, we can't let that happen." She straightened, her mood suddenly brightening. "What about the two of you coming out for Christmas?"

A moment of silence. "Well...I'd have to think about that, financially and all. But..." Alberta paused again. "You know, it might give her something to look forward to."

"Yes, I think it would. Maybe perk up her mood a little."

"All right. I'll look into airline tickets and see what I can work out. Thank you, Sam, that's a good idea."

She ended the call with excited anticipation. She didn't know about Electra, but she felt better, having their visit to look forward to. *Well, that's one problem I could help with, for the moment.*

CHAPTER FOUR

Even though Murdock's attitude hung like a gray cloud in her periphery, the sky seemed a little bluer with the prospect of Electra and Alberta's visit. As Sam drove up to the dude ranch, Clyde oiled tack in the shade of the barn. He looked up, brows arched. "Mornin', Sam. How'd it go?"

She closed the pickup door with a resolute thump. "It didn't."

Clyde paused his work and frowned. "What? Why? What happened?"

"He's still ticked about the stand-off at the Jersey Lilly. He said I have three years left on the lease, and we'd revisit it then."

The rancher took off his hat and swiped a hand over his hair. "That snake in the grass."

"Yeah. And I was already making plans to build an indoor arena at the ranch so I could continue working with the kids during the winter." Disappointment shrouded her again. "Now... I don't know what to do. You're not going to need me here much longer, and..."

"Aw, no. Don't you be worryin' about that." Clyde gazed into her face. "I still need you to help me keep the string ridden down, there's lots of tack to repair and maintain, and Irene can use your help cookin' for the hunters."

"Thank you. I appreciate that." Her voice caught. "A lot."

He held his palms out. "No problem. You're such a big help to me. And, you know, my offer still stands. I'd be willing to go halves with you and build an arena here."

"I know. That probably makes the most logical sense, since you already have facilities." She worried her lower lip. "But I have this idea, this dream, that someday I'll own that ranch and I really want to do my own…thing."

"Yeah. I understand that. But if I can help, just say the word. I'm here for ya." He patted her back. "Anyhow, we've still got guests booked for the weekends through September, and then hunting season in October and November. Snowmobiling was popular last winter too. So, there'll be stuff for you to do."

"Great. I'd better get busy then." Sam smiled. "Oh, by the way, Electra and Alberta might be coming for a visit at Christmas."

"All right! That'd be super. I know you miss that little gal." He grinned. "And I kinda do too. It's a little too quiet without her."

They both laughed.

On her way home that evening, Sam stopped at the Jersey Lilly and got a couple of burgers and fries to go. She pulled into Horace's place and took the bags to the house.

"Hey, Sam. Good to see ya." He sniffed. "Mmm, that smells mighty good. I was just about to rustle up some grub. C'mon in."

He cleared newspapers and books off his kitchen table, poured cups of coffee, and they sat. She told him what had happened with Murdock, Clyde's offer and her dilemma, and her worries about taking care of Murdock's cattle in the winter.

The older man scrunched his mustache to the side and growled something about "unscrupulous sonuva…."

Horace—in his seventies—and Clyde, his fifties, were like fathers, immediately jumping to her defense. Her chest filled with gratitude.

His face softened. "I'm here for ya, little gal. You know I'll help you feed the cows. No sweat."

She patted his hand. "Thank you, Horace. And I'll help you

feed yours."

He nodded. "Clyde's a good guy. He'll be there for ya too. But I understand how you want to do this on your own. If there's anything I can do..."

"You're the best." She cleared the table and tossed the sacks in the garbage. "I love this place... and my neighbors."

Horace winked. He stood in his doorway and waved as she drove away.

After feeding and taking Apache and Trixi for short rides, Sam settled into her rocking chair with a book. The heavy cloud of disappointment had lifted, and the rocking motion sent a rhythm of peace through her body. The winter wasn't going to be easy, but she still had employment, and she wouldn't have to fight the snowdrifts by herself to feed the cattle.

Her landline rang, startling her out of a half-doze. It was Teresa. "Hey, girl, how're you doing?"

"Much better." Sam told her what had transpired in the last couple of days.

"That's awesome! I hope Electra will be able to come visit. That'd be fun. Hey, I met a guy the other day in Miles City, and we got to talking. He's a veteran, struggling with PTSD, and he's taking some classes at the college."

"O-kay." Sam frowned. What was Teresa getting at? *Is she trying to fix me up?*

"I just got to thinking, with the marvelous results you've had with the group home kids, that maybe he would benefit from being around horses too. He's from here and rode a little as a kid, but mostly has been a town guy."

"Oh. Okay." She took a breath. "I can certainly try working with him, if he's willing. Did you mention it to him?"

"No, not yet. Thought I'd run it by you first."

"Well, yeah. See what he thinks, if he's willing to come out here, and we'll see what happens."

"Great! I'll get back to you."

Working with kids was one thing, but a PTSD veteran? Sam shook her head to clear her jumbled thoughts. *Well, I won't know until I try, will I?*

***

The next week on a pleasantly warm fall day, Teresa roared up the driveway with a passenger. Sam stepped out on the porch to meet them, her hands clammy. *What am I doing? I don't know anything about this.*

Teresa made the introduction as she hopped out of her car. "Sam, this is Garrett Webb. He'd like to meet your horses."

The sandy-haired man dipped his head. He looked to be in his late twenties or early thirties, about five to ten years older than Sam. He put one foot on the bottom step and climbed up awkwardly. He stuck out his hand. "Nice t' meet you, Sam."

Her throat seized up. *Oh dear, he's an amputee.* She swallowed and shook his hand. "Hi, Garrett. I'm sorry." With a heated face, she squinted at his prosthetic foot. "I should've come down."

"Naw. It's okay. I do this all the time." He shrugged. "It's my new normal."

"Shall we go down to the corral?" Sam glanced at Teresa who gave her a smile and a thumbs-up.

"Sure." Garrett turned and limped back down the steps.

Sam stifled an urge to reach out and help. "Have you ridden before?"

"Not since I was a kid. My grandpa had a horse." He gave a nervous chuckle. "But it bucked me off."

Hmm. He's going to be a bit gun shy then. I'll have to take it easy with him. Sam whistled for the horses who trotted up to the fence. "Well, mine won't do that. But you don't have to get on one today." She handed him a cake pellet. "Just get acquainted for now."

The first one to stick a head over the railing was Sugar. "This is my Thoroughbred rescue, and she does love her treats."

Garrett put out a flat-palmed hand and the mare lipped it

gently. His Adam's apple bobbed, and one side of his mouth curved upward, just a little.

Good, he does know how to feed a horse. Apache was next in line and the young veteran fed the gelding a treat. Last was Trixi. She blew softly, took the pellet, and still crunching, extended her neck so her head rubbed against his arm. He flinched when she moved but stood still, his face tight-lipped.

"That's okay." Sam spoke in a low voice. "She won't bite. She likes you. If you want to scratch her head, you can."

His hand trembled, but he massaged her forehead. Trixi leaned into his touch and closed her eyes. Garrett tilted his head slightly toward Sam. "I think she likes this."

"Yeah." Sam grinned. "She really does."

His face softened, and he moved up to scratch her ears and then combed her blonde mane with his fingers.

"Would you like to go inside the fence and maybe brush her?"

Garrett shook his head, a quick jerky movement, and he pulled his hand back.

"That's okay." She reached out and patted his rock-hard shoulder. "You just do whatever feels right for today." She offered him another pellet, and he started the process again, feeding Trixi, rubbing her nose and face up to the ears and this time farther down her neck.

Teresa kept Apache and Sugar occupied with the attention they wanted, and Sam merely stood beside Garrett, while he tentatively caressed Trixi's soft coat. His short, shallow breathing gradually slowed, and his shoulders visibly lowered.

Sam let out her own breath and relaxed. This was a process. No need to hurry. He would get used to the horse in his own time.

After about half an hour, Garrett stepped back. "Thanks. I think I'm done... for now."

"Okay. That's fine. Would you like to come up to the house and have a glass of iced tea?"

He hesitated. "Sure."

Sam patted Trixi's neck. "Good girl." She slipped her another pellet, and the trio headed for the house, where they sat on the porch overlooking the barn, corrals, and horses in the pasture.

She poured icy glasses of tea and brought out a plate of chocolate chip cookies. "You did very well for your first encounter since you got dumped."

Garrett took a couple of cookies. "Yeah. It... was a little intense. I'm sorry I didn't..." He stared down at the wood floor, still holding the cookies in the same position.

"Oh. No." She set the plate on the side table between them. "You don't need to apologize. Not everyone can jump on a horse the first time they meet and go riding off into the sunset." She tried for a bit of levity.

"Sam's absolutely right." Teresa spoke up. "You did awesome. I could tell Trixi likes you. She's a very gentle horse."

Garrett finally raised his head and gazed out toward the pasture. "They're just so huge." He snorted a laugh. "Here I am, the big, tough Marine who drove tanks and... and I'm afraid of a nice, gentle horse." He turned his face toward Sam, his eyes glistening. "You must think I'm a total wimp."

Sam swallowed around a lump in her throat. "No way. Not at all." She fought to find words to encourage, to comfort this man who was in such pain. "It's something new, something different, and we are wired to be mistrustful of the unknown."

She put a hand on his arm. "Give it time. It'll get easier."

He gave her a lopsided grin. Then he gestured to Teresa. "If I could impose, I probably should be getting back."

"Of course." She stood and took their glasses to the sink.

Sam followed them to Teresa's car. "Come back anytime."

Garrett gave a curt nod and swung into the seat.

"Thanks, Sam." Teresa gave her a little wave and drove off.

She stood on the porch as the black SUV disappeared down the dirt road, a plume of dust rising behind. Tears stung her eyes. "Well, was that a bust or what was it?" She spoke out loud to the magpie sitting on the fence.

Sam slumped in the chair on her porch for a long time after they left. The growing dusk seeped over the prairie and into her bones. What had made her think she could work with a veteran? Just because a couple of kids had experienced miraculous turnarounds didn't mean adults would respond in the same way. Especially someone who had experienced the horrors of war and had lost part of his leg. Especially someone who'd had a bad experience with a horse. She wasn't a psychologist, just a cowgirl who loved her rescue horses, and hoped she could do a tiny bit of good in this world.

There's more to this than simply being bucked off. The man's pain radiated from deep inside and her heart ached for him. *But something did happen between him and Trixi for a moment.* Even though the session hadn't been entirely successful at first blush, she still had a tingle of excitement. *Maybe I can help him... if he comes back.*

She jumped as the phone jangled inside.

"How's the horse rescuer extraordinaire on this fine day?" Brad's cheery voice sang over the line.

Sam huffed a laugh. "Not so 'extra' today. Pretty ordinary, actually."

"Your voice sounds a little down. Something wrong?"

"Aw, it's nothing." She tried to sound more upbeat.

"I don't hear 'nothing.'" Brad persisted.

"Okay, then. I guess I do need to talk to somebody." She told him about Garrett and trying to introduce him to her horses and her doubts about her ability to work with a veteran.

"So, the girl who, against all odds, rescued Apache from an abuse situation; who, against more odds turned a Goth girl into a cowgirl; and again, against even more odds, rescued a fantastic trick horse from the slaughterhouse—this girl is now a failure because the guy didn't jump on the horse and gallop over the hills? No. I don't think so!"

Sam burst out laughing. "Well, when you put it that way. But," she sobered, "I also got shot down by Murdock when I made an offer on the ranch. I know I can't win them all. I'm going to fall and fail sometimes. It hurts, and I do feel at a loss right now."

Brad's voice was gentle. "Geez, yeah. I know you do. And I'm not trying to make light of the situation. I know you well enough by now to know you're not going to give up. You're going to persevere, and you'll find a way."

"I sure hope so." Sam blew out a breath.

"I know so. I wish I was there to give you a hug." Brad sighed now. "I miss ya, girl."

Her pulse skipped a beat. *He does?* "I miss you too."

"I'll be back in Montana in a week or so. We'll make up for lost time."

"It'll be nice to see you again. How are the 'roos doing?"

Brad laughed. "Well, that was a big fail, actually more of an April Fool's joke. These easterners were trying to do that, but their contacts kept putting them off and delaying shipment, all that kind of stuff, and it never materialized."

"What about your documentary?"

"Oh, I'm still working on it, just not from the same angle. I'll tell you all about it when I come home."

Her heart paused for an anticipatory moment. *Home? Here? Does he think this is home?* "Hmm. Interesting. Well, thanks for the pep-talk. I needed that."

"You bet. Anytime. See you soon." Brad clicked off.

Sam headed for the fridge for something to eat. *Serves those jerks right if they were duped by this kangaroo transplant.* She giggled, feeling lighter than she had in several days. Brad had such supportive words for her. *Maybe I'm better than I think I am.*

CHAPTER FIVE

Clyde kept Sam busy for the next few days, preparing for hunting season along with the group home kids who came for the last weekend in September. Nights were getting crisp and cool, but the days still summer-like.

One evening at the end of the week, she got a call from Teresa. "Hey, girl. I've been meaning to call you all day. Garrett wants to come back out."

"Really?" Sam blinked. "Wow. I thought he totally hated it and would never be back."

"Well, I thought so too, at first. He withdrew and hardly talked on the ride home that day. But last night he called and wants to try again."

"Oh wow, Teresa. That's awesome. I thought I'd failed for sure on this one. I mean, I'm not a counselor. I don't know how to deal with stuff like this. All I've ever done is put someone together with a horse, and they seemed to figure it out on their own."

"I think that's exactly the right approach, no matter who it is. Sam, give yourself more credit. You have a gift. Don't take that lightly."

"Hmm, never thought about it like that either. Thanks!" They set a date and Sam hung up, warm fuzzies fluttering from her core. What a surprise. She hadn't thought he'd be back.

***

Sam woke early with a jolt of adrenaline. Teresa would be arriving later today with Garrett. Her stomach too tense for breakfast, she grabbed a cup of coffee and hurried to the pasture to let the horses into the corral. She fed them a bit of grain and a healthy flake of hay and checked their water.

When she checked her watch, it was still early, so she went back up to the house and forced herself to eat a slice of toast with peanut butter and jelly. Then she washed up the dishes. Another glance at her watch. Still an hour before they were to arrive. The coffee and toast warred in her stomach.

Sam paced the porch. What should she do differently this time? Maybe show him how Trixi can kneel. Maybe force the issue, see if he'd get on the horse. No. Not a good idea. She wiped sweaty palms on her jeans. *This is ridiculous.*

She strode back to the corral, grabbed her bridle, led Sugar back out to the pasture, and jumped on her bare back. "C'mon, girl, let's run off some steam."

The mare lengthened her stride until they were galloping over the prairie. Sam tightened her knees against the horse's sides, leaned forward on her neck, and let the speed and the wind blow through her mind. Her chestnut hair came loose from her ponytail, and she laughed with the pleasure of a child.

She reined in Sugar atop a bluff, where she could see the ranch in the distance below. Panting as if she'd done the running, patted her horse's neck. "This is more like it. We don't do this often enough anymore."

Sugar snorted and blew.

Worries and dread of the unknown had taken over her pleasure of working with horses and riding for sheer joy. Since when did she obsess over putting someone together with a horse? It had to happen naturally, or it wouldn't happen at all. She couldn't force anything. That wouldn't help Garrett or the horse.

She trotted Sugar back to the barn and brushed her down. When she heard Teresa's SUV pull up the drive, she swallowed a flutter. The two got out of the vehicle and walked toward the corral, Garrett with a stiff gait.

How to deal with that prosthetic foot. She bit her lip. Just like with Jace, her paraplegic friend, of course. "Hi, guys." Sam greeted them with a big smile, as confident as she could make it.

Garrett's gazed flickered from her to the horses, and he licked his lips. "Hi, Sam." His voice held a slight quaver.

"I'm glad you came back."

"Hey, girl." Teresa gave her a hug, and her face reflected cheerfulness. "I thought maybe I'd borrow one of your horses and go for a ride while you two work here, if that's okay."

"That'd be great. I just took Sugar for a ride, but Apache could use a little trot-out." She turned to Garrett. "Trixi seemed to like you, and she has some special abilities that could benefit you."

"Okay."

Sam led them to the barn, showed Teresa where the tack was, and grabbed a handful of cake pellets. She gave Garrett several for his pockets. "Are you ready? Do you want to feed her?"

He swallowed and peered at the horse standing with her head over the fence, anticipating the treat. Limping slowly, he approached, his arm outstretched, pellet in his palm. Trixi bobbed her head as he came closer, then gently took the offering. Garrett's mouth rose slightly at the corners. He stroked her nose and glanced at Sam. "I'd forgotten how soft their noses are... like velvet."

That gets 'em every time. She smiled. "Yes, they are."

The veteran continued scratching the horse's forehead up to her ears and down her neck, as far as he could reach over the fence. Like on his last visit, his tense shoulders visibly came down a notch.

Sam stood back. She wanted to make suggestions, to show him the mare's trick, hurry things along, but she made herself wait.

"Good girl," he murmured and with a gradual, slow motion, leaned his forehead against the mare's. Trixi stayed still. His breathing deepened.

After several moments, he drew back. "I... think... I'd like to go inside the fence." He bit his lower lip. "Will it be okay?"

"Yes. It'll be fine." She led the way to the small gate, opened it, and let him step through. She walked beside him to Trixi and patted her neck. "You like Garrett, don't you, girl? Okay, be good now." She faced him. "Go ahead. Whatever you're comfortable with."

His Adam's apple bobbed, and his shoulders raised again, but he approached with another pellet. Trixi took it and crunched. He caressed her nose, forehead, and neck again, running his fingers through her mane. The horse rubbed her head against his arm. He flinched, but then continued the combing.

This slow back and forth, tensing and relaxing, rubbing and combing, continued for endless minutes. Sam forced herself to simply watch, not making any sudden moves or speaking for fear she'd frighten him.

Then Garrett buried his face in Trixi's neck. His body trembled. The horse stood patiently, quietly. Sam hardly dared breathe. Her chest was tight, her eyes full.

Finally, the young man lifted his head, passed a hand over his face, and seemed to shake himself. He turned in slow motion toward her. Then he walked out of the corral back to the car.

Sam stood, frozen. What should she do now? Go after him? If he wanted to talk, he would've said something. If he wanted company, he would've stayed in the corral. *This is awkward.* She stepped to Trixi's side and patted her back. "You are such a good girl." She scratched the soft ears and gave the mare a pellet. "Thank you. You are so special."

Teresa trotted back on Apache and dismounted. "I see the session is over. How did it go?" She loosened the cinch.

Sam helped her unsaddle. "Okay. I think. We got a little farther than last time. He was in here, right next to her." She flashed her gaze toward the vehicle. "But I think he got to a certain point and had enough."

"Well, it sounds like progress. Thank you. It may not seem

like it, but you are helping." She gave Sam a hug and headed to the car. "See you soon.

A glow suffused from her core. Maybe there was hope for next time.

***

October brought crisp nights and golden leaves on the cottonwood trees. Sam's days filled with helping Irene Bruckner cook and prepare meals for the hunters to pack in. She helped Clyde oil and repair tack and packs and kept the horse string ridden down. "Wouldn't want 'em to go buckin' with a dude first time out," Clyde quipped.

Garrett came several times, at first with Teresa and then alone. He continued the slow process with Trixi, each time seeming to start from scratch. He approached her slowly, fed her a pellet or two, stroked her face and neck, and jerked if she moved quickly.

With great difficulty, Sam restrained herself from jumping in and trying to move things along. "I'm not sure what I should be doing to encourage him," she confided in Irene and Clyde.

Clyde moved the chaw of tobacco inside his cheek and shrugged. "Can't rush a man."

Irene patted Sam's arm in her motherly way. "It sounds like you're doing fine, just letting him be. He keeps coming back, right?"

"Yes, there is that." As long as he did, there was hope.

Finally, one day she brought out the brushes. "Would you like to try this?"

Garrett tensed and ran a hand over his sandy crewcut. Finally, he nodded. Swallowing hard, he took the brush and tentatively moved it along Trixi's creamy-gold neck. He glanced at Sam.

"You want me to show you?"

"Okay."

Sam demonstrated the technique, moving along Trixi's withers and over her back. "Ready to try?"

He copied what she had done, but his shoulders grew rigid

as he brushed over her back. Trixi blew softly.

"See, she likes it." Sam smiled. "It's like getting a massage, very relaxing for her."

"Okay." Garrett continued to brush, and his shoulders lowered, his strokes more confident.

He stayed a little longer that day, and instead of leaving abruptly as usual, he gave Sam a grin. "It's easier today. Thanks."

She took a deep, satisfied breath as he drove off. *Well, it is extremely slow, but he has made some progress.*

The next week, when Sam came back from a morning ride on Sugar, Garrett was there, wearing a blue plaid western shirt, already brushing Trixi. His face beamed. "Hi, Sam. I hope this is okay. I just decided at the last minute to come out."

"Of course it is. You're doing great. I think she looks forward to your visits." She unsaddled Sugar and joined him, brushing her mare.

After a long silence, he shifted his eyes toward her. "This is relaxing."

"Great. I find it is too." She tapped her lips. *Should I broach the subject?* "The best part for me is riding out onto the prairie. It's so freeing to feel the breeze and smell the sage and see the birds..." She flicked a glance in his direction. "It makes the whole world and all its troubles just kind of melt away."

His jaws worked and he remained silent.

"But there's no hurry. If you ever feel like it... I'll be right here." She sneaked a peek at his feet. The left foot was the prosthesis. His mounting foot. Okay. Trixi could help with that.

Sam let Sugar go and came back to the pair. *Here goes nothing.* "I don't want to scare you, but I want to show you something that could be very helpful... when the time is right."

Garrett stood back, mouth tight, the brush hanging from his hand.

She gave Trixi her signal, and the mare bent her front legs to bring herself into the resting position on the ground. Sam slid onto her back, the horse rose, and they rode around the corral.

Garrett's eyes were wide in a pale face. His prominent Adam's apple bobbed up and down as he swallowed repeatedly.

Sam dismounted. "Please don't feel any pressure. If and when you're ready, you'll know."

He let out a long sigh. "Okay." As he strode toward his truck, he stopped and half-turned. "Thanks for showing me."

***

For the next couple of weeks, Sam heard nothing from Garrett. *I must have scared him off.*

She did receive a call from Jack Murdoch, however. "Hello, Samantha. It's time for shipping, and I've got a buyer coming next Friday. Can you get the cows rounded up then?"

Rolling her eyes, she bit back a sarcastic reply. "Um, yeah, sure. I'll have to ask for the day off from the dude ranch earlier in the week and get a couple of riders to help me."

"That'd be great. We'll be there at 10 a.m." With that cheerful reply, he clicked off.

Sam slammed down the receiver and ground her teeth. *Presumptuous twit!* She paced the house, trying to wrest control over her anger. Then she called Clyde.

"You bet. Take Wednesday and Thursday off." He paused. "Say, you need some help gathering? I don't have an any hunters coming until Saturday. I can come over."

"Thanks, Clyde. I would appreciate that." After they hung up, she called Horace to ask if he could help too.

"Of course, little gal, I'd be most pleased to help out my favorite neighbor. I'll ride over bright and early."

Before the late October sun peeked its tangerine head over the eastern horizon, Sam, Clyde, and Horace rode out to the pasture. Some of the cows and their calves were at the reservoir, but Sam and Clyde checked the far corners to gather the sleepy remnants.

The small herd of fifty head moseyed along easily toward the ranch, with no sudden dashes to round up a runaway calf. The lead cow knew where she was going, and they arrived at the corrals without incident.

The men separated the calves into a smaller pen for weaning and let the cows out. The next couple of days and nights were filled with the cacophony of calves bawling for their mothers, and the cows' answers echoed from the far pasture as the weaning process went on. Sam winced—*poor babies*—and put in ear plugs at night so she could sleep.

Friday morning when Horace arrived and Sam went to the barn, a stock truck was already backed up to the chutes and Jack's vehicle was parked nearby. He and the buyer stood by the fence, chatting.

Sam strode over to the waiting pair. "Hello, Jack. Let us know which ones you want to ship and which ones to keep."

He nodded and climbed into the corral. The mamas still milled around outside bawling for their white-faced babies, and the calves bellered for their mothers.

A twinge of sympathy spiked through Sam. This was always a difficult time of year, but a necessity in making a living at ranching—selling the steer calves and keeping the heifers for replacement stock. She enjoyed working with cattle, remembering when she used to ride out as a kid of about ten with Grandpa Neil for gatherings. *Maybe one day I'll have a herd of my own.* She peeked at Murdock. *If he'll ever let me buy this place.*

As the process continued, another vehicle pulled up beside the corral. Garrett got out of the driver's side and went around to the bed of the pickup, where he hefted out a wheelchair. Then he opened the passenger side and helped another man, who appeared a little older than he, out and into the chair. They approached the corral.

Garrett tipped his head at her. "Hi, Sam. Shipping time, huh?"

"Yeah. I lease this place from Jack Murdock and take care of his cows." She shifted her attention toward the other man.

"Sorry I didn't call. This is my friend, Del Conner. He wanted to see the thing you do with Trixi."

She held out a hand, and the dark-haired man shook it with a strong grip. "Nice to meet you," he said, "but it looks like bad timing. Like Garrett said, we should've called first."

"Um… yeah, things are a little busy right now, but I'd be happy to introduce you to the horses another time. Did you used to ride?"

"Yeah, before I went… overseas… I did a little roping in the rodeo." He looked down at his leg stumps and then up at Sam. "Well, anyway, it's probably a moot point. I was just curious, is all."

"Hello, Garrett, Del." Murdock's voice behind Sam startled her. "How are things going at the VA center?"

Sam widened her eyes. *Jack knows these guys?*

Del shook Jack's hand. "Oh, you know, same ol', same ol'. One day at a time and all that."

Murdock glanced at Sam and then back to the guys. "So what brings you out here—come to watch the shipping process?"

"No, Sam's been working with me… to get used to her horses, and um…Del wanted to see… what that was all about." Garrett spoke in a low voice.

"Well, I'll be…" Jack's eyebrows rose, and he tipped his head to the side. "I didn't know you were working with the vets, Sam."

CHAPTER SIX

Sam blinked and simply stared at Murdock. *Working with vets?* She opened her mouth, but nothing came out.

"Hey, Jack, we're ready to load up," the buyer yelled from the chute.

"I'll be interested in hearing more about this sometime." Murdock touched a finger to his hat. "Good to see you all." He changed direction and walked away.

Sam's mouth closed and opened like a fish out of water. *What just happened here?* She tried to blink away the confusion and faced the guys. "Well, I… you…" *Good grief, Samantha, get a grip!* "How do you know Jack?"

Del smiled. "Oh, he comes to the vet center once in a while, gives us these motivational talks and whatnot." He scratched his head. "I believe I heard he's donated to the center, and he's hired a few of us from time to time."

Garrett nodded. "His dad was a veteran, I think."

"I had no idea." She gave herself a mental shake to clear her head. "Hey, you know what, they're going to be loaded up in a short time. If you want to stick around, after they're gone, I can get Trixi out and introduce you. Show you what she can do."

Garrett stared at the ground, but Del spoke up. "Sure. That'd be great." He shrugged at the younger man. "As long as we're here."

When the last of the calves were loaded, the buyer hopped in the cattle truck, waved, and drove off. Jack helped her let the heifer calves he'd decided to keep out of the corral into a separate pasture, and then he left, with no more mention of the veterans.

Sam filled her pockets with cake pellets and whistled for her horses. They came running to the fence, snorting, and tossing their manes. Garrett hung back, but Del wheeled closer. She gave each horse a treat and then offered a handful to Del. "This is Trixi. Do you want to feed her?" The mare hung her head over the fence and fluttered her lips.

He held a pellet flat-palmed between the fence rails and beamed as she took it. "She sure is beautiful—a palomino?"

"No, she's a light-colored chestnut. She was Miss Ellie's trick horse, named after Trixi McCormick, the famous trick rider from the forties and fifties. Miss Ellie was a pretty well-known rider too in her prime, but she recently had to move to an assisted living situation. That's how I ended up with her horse."

"Yeah, I've heard of Miss Ellie." Del gave the mare another pellet. He reached to touch her face, and his expression softened.

Sam fed Apache a treat too and ruffled his mane. Out of the corner of her eye, she saw Garrett take a pellet from Del and step to the fence to feed Sugar. She smiled. *Good.*

"Shall I show you what she can do?"

Del's face brightened. "Yeah."

She went inside the fence, put a halter on Trixi, and gave her the hand signal. When the horse kneeled and Sam mounted, she heard a soft "Whoa!" from Del. Trixi rose and they rode around the pen and back to the guys.

"Anybody want to try?" Sam swung her gaze from Garrett to Del.

The men exchanged glances. "You go ahead, you've been around here the most," Del offered.

Garrett stiffened and stood frozen, staring at Sam and Trixi.

"C'mon, man, you can do it." Del's voice was soft.

Her breath stopped in her throat. She could only imagine how Garrett's heart must be pounding, his hands sweating. Dismounting, she signaled Trixi to kneel again.

"Okay." Garrett spoke in a hoarse whisper. He entered

through the small gate and approached.

"I'll help you if you want. Take your time. I'm right here." Sam gently touched his shoulder, rock hard with tension.

"I can do it." Slowly, gingerly, he swung his good leg up over Trixi's back and eased himself into a sitting position. Trixi moved slightly. His face went ashen. "No. Don't get her up yet."

"Okay. You don't have to at all. We can just stay here for a while." Sam tried to keep her voice even and soft. "Stay, Trixi, good girl."

He sat for a minute, taking deep, shuddering breaths. He finally met her gaze. "I'm getting off."

"All right." She stood close by in case he wanted a hand, but he dismounted by himself.

He stood for a moment, staring at Trixi, and reached out a hand to stroke her neck. "Good horse." As he walked back toward Del, he flashed a momentary grin. "Your turn."

To Sam's surprise, Del shook his head. "Naw. Maybe another time."

She signaled Trixi to stand and then walked with the men back to their truck. "Garrett, you did great. You've made real progress."

He ducked his head and looked at the ground. But she saw the corners of his mouth curl upward.

An inner smile buoyed her. Although small, today was a success. She waved at the men as they drove away. Strange day, with the revelation about Murdock. *Wonder what that's all about?*

***

The November frost brushed the tips of the golden prairie grass with silver filaments that glinted like giant spider webs in the early morning sun as Sam drove to the dude ranch to help with a group of hunters. This time, the men had brought their wives, so she and Irene were in charge of feeding and entertaining them.

After a hearty breakfast, Sam took the women to the corral to introduce them to the horses. A couple of the wives had some riding experience, but she started out having them feed treats. She followed with brushing and then saddling and bridling.

The women warmed to the adventure and were soon relaxed, laughing and chatting. "Mrs. Bruckner told us how you work with group home kids and rescue horses," one rider named Jill commented.

"That's so brave of you," said another. "I can barely keep my own kids in line."

They all laughed, and Sam joined in. "It's not easy, but there's something very healing about a horse for kids with problems. For anyone, really." Her thoughts flashed to Garrett and Del, wondering if they would ever feel as comfortable with horses as Electra and Sapphire.

After lunch, the women went off to their cabins to rest, and Sam helped Irene wash dishes and start supper preparations. She was wiping the last plate when her cell phone rang.

"Sam!" Jace's voice sounded panicked.

"What's wrong?" Her stomach tumbled.

"Oh dear, I didn't know who to call, but maybe you can help. I hope. I have a friend who sold her horse, she thought to a reputable buyer, but she just found out it's been sold to a kill pen." Jace sounded near tears.

"A kill pen?"

"It's going to be sent to Mexico... for meat! Sylvia—my friend—found a site online where they get donations to rescue these horses, but so far we haven't been able to raise enough money to save Toby. He's only eight years old and in good shape. Not ready to die. They're going to be shipping a load tomorrow, and he's scheduled on that truck."

Sam tried to swallow. She'd known vaguely that old horses sometimes were used for dog food or to feed zoo animals, but not healthy, young horses. "Oh no, Jace, that is terrible."

"I know you have plans for the money you got, but maybe... if you could donate a little, maybe we could rescue this horse. Sylvia is distraught. She's not eating or sleeping, and she can't stop crying. She blames herself."

Tears stung Sam's eyes, remembering how she'd felt when she had found Apache in a bare pasture with no water, skin and bones, hanging his head in defeat. And how helpless when the owner had his hired thugs run her off the place so she couldn't help the horse.

"I know how she must feel." Sam swallowed, decision made. "I want to help. What can I do? How much do you need to get the horse back?"

"We're short about nine hundred dollars." Jace told her the online address and how to pledge a donation. "Oh, Sam, you are a life-saver! Thank you so much."

"Will Sylvia be able to take him back home?"

Jace sighed. "Um, no. She had to sell him because she lost her acreage and had to move to an apartment in the city."

Sam frowned. "So where will he go?"

"Well…" Silence hummed over the miles. "Since you're putting up most of the money, you'll be the new owner, so…"

Her mouth dropped open. "Oh my goodness." Thoughts cascaded through her head. How to get the horse from Arizona to Montana? Now she'd have four horses. Where to put him when he got here? The barn only had three stalls. That wouldn't do for winter.

She took a deep breath. "Okay. I'll make the donation. I'll call you back when I have confirmation of the rescue. We'll figure it all out."

Jace sobbed now. "Thank you, Sam, thank you, thank you, thank you!"

"Of course, hon. It'll be all right. Don't worry." Sam disconnected and sank into a kitchen chair, her legs too wobbly to stand. *Don't worry… ha.*

Irene Bruckner stepped back from the countertop she'd been wiping and stood beside her, creases of concern on her forehead.

Sam said, "I need to use your computer to rescue a horse."

Wavering between excitement and trepidation, she spent the

rest of the afternoon on the computer and the phone—back and forth between the rescue site and her bank and Jace. Then there were the questions of who would pick up Toby from the kill pen and how she would get him to Montana.

Irene kept her supplied with coffee until she finally waved her away, her hands shaking. "No more caffeine. I'm so nervous I think I could take off and fly."

Irene massaged Sam's neck for a few minutes. "It's okay, dear. You're doing the right thing."

She found another site online, Equine Voices Rescue and Sanctuary in Green Valley, Arizona, and called them. After explaining her situation, the manager agreed to go get Toby and hold him there until Sam could arrange for transport. "This is a wonderful thing you're doing, Sam. We primarily rescue mares and foals, otherwise we'd be right there to take him."

She hung up, hands shaking. "Whew! I need to go out and get some fresh air." She gave Irene a hug. "Thanks for your moral support. That helped so much. I'll be back in a little while to give you a hand with supper. Sorry I abandoned you this afternoon."

Irene made a face. "Pshaw. This horse rescue is more important than a little food. Even if we have to open a couple cans of pork and beans, we're just fine."

"Yeah, right." Sam snorted. "I can see you feeding your clients from a can."

She stepped outside and breathed in the crisp air. The purple shadows were lengthening from the rolling hills, the sky changing from azure to gold as the sun settled on the horizon. The horses saw her and whinnied from the corral. Sam strolled to the fence and leaned into Ginger's neck, drawing strength and serenity from the mare.

"You are one amazing lady." The woman's voice startled Sam, and she stood for a moment, blinking. Turning, she saw Jill, one of the wives, standing behind her.

"No, really. Irene just told me what you did today. That's a wonderful thing, for your friend and her friend, and for the horse. I didn't know such things went on in the horse world." Jill held her palms up. "What an eye-opener. I am in awe of you."

Heat rose to her cheeks, and she scuffed her boot toe in the dirt. "Oh, gee. Thanks. I don't know about that..." She looked up at the woman. "But it seemed like the right thing to do. I hope." *How am I going to get the horse here and where am I going to put him?* "Well, I need to go back and help Irene with supper. I think we'll be ready to eat soon."

Jill smiled. "Okay. Sounds good. We'll be in shortly."

That evening when Sam got home, she went directly to the pasture next to the barn. Her three horses galloped up to the fence for their cake pellet treats. "So, guys, are you going to welcome another horse?" She rubbed each one's ears and neck, sighing. "I have too much on my plate already. And not enough room in the barn." She fed them a couple flakes of hay, checked their water, and headed back to the house.

As she trudged up the incline, she heard a pickup engine grinding up the driveway. She stopped by the house and waved as Horace got out of his truck, carrying a large cooking pot.

"Hey there, little gal. I made a big mess of chili, and I thought you might like some to put in your fridge for when you don't feel like cookin'."

"Thank you, Horace. You're a sweetheart. I already had supper tonight, but what about you?"

He chuckled. "Yeah, I had to sample it, make sure it was edible."

"C'mon in. I'll make you a cup of coffee."

"Coffee sounds great." The older man followed her into the kitchen. "So how are the hunters?"

"I don't know if the guys are having any luck. I didn't see them come back before I left. But I took the wives riding. They seemed to enjoy themselves." She measured out the grounds and poured water into the coffee maker. Then she sat at the table to wait for it to brew.

"And..." she snorted a little laugh, "I rescued another horse."

"You did?" Horace cocked his head. "How did that come about?"

Sam told him about the phone call from Jace and her frantic afternoon, trying to save Toby from being shipped to Mexico.

Horace ran his fingers through his hair. "Well, I'll be... You're one amazing gal."

Funny. That's almost exactly what Jill said. "Naw. I just happen to have a little extra money right now and there was a need and..." She shrugged. "Nothing amazing about that."

"You do sell yourself short, Miss Samantha." He held out his cup. "Think that coffee's done yet?"

She got up and poured him a cup. "I had way too much coffee today, so I'm not joining you. If I was still drinking vodka, I'd have a good stiff one." She blew out a shuddering breath. "So now I have to figure out how to get Toby here. And when he gets here, he'll be fine in the pasture once the others get used to him, but this winter when it's blizzarding, I need another stall in the barn."

"Dunno if I can help you with the transportation. If I was ten years younger, I'd borrow my trailer back and drive down myself, but I jes' don't do those long drives anymore." He stood. "But let's go down to the barn and take a look. Might be able to help ya there."

Sam and her neighbor walked to the small barn and stood in the doorway. It had three stalls, perfect for Sugar, Trixi, and Apache. The larger area held tack and feed grain and pellets, while hay bales were stored in the loft.

"I would very much like to build on or simply build a bigger one, but..." she held out upraised palms, "since Murdock won't sell, why would I do that?"

"Understood. Understood." He strolled around inside, looking in every nook and cranny and studying the layout. "W-e-l-l, it is a little cramped... but what if we moved those feed bins out of this corner? And we could mount some stacking rails for saddles and add more hooks for bridles. I think we could squeeze in another stall, what d'you think?"

Sam raised her eyebrows. "Now who's the amazing one? That's a fantastic idea. I think it'll work." A lighter-than-air sensation lifted her to hopefulness.

"All right then. I'll be back bright and early tomorrow and take some measurements. Then I'll run in to Miles and get the materials."

Gratitude swelled like a fountain. "Oh, Horace." She gave him a hug. "Thank you."

After Horace left, Sam settled in her rocking chair with a book and a cup of hot chocolate. What a day! If only she had someone to simply sit with and share the jumble of ideas, doubts, and fears that raced through her mind. If only Brad was back, or even Electra. Loneliness enveloped her like a cloud.

Every time she thought she had a handle on which direction she wanted to go, a detour popped up. More horses? Did she want to continue to work with the kids? What about Garrett and Del?

She took a sip of cocoa, nearly sloshing it in her lap when the phone rang. When she heard Brad's voice, her heart jumped. "Hi, stranger, what are you up to?"

"Missing you." His soft baritone gave her goosebumps.

"Yeah, me too. It's been two months since I've seen you. Are you ever coming back to Montana?"

Brad chuckled. "I am. Heading back in about a week and I'll be around for the Thanksgiving holiday, maybe even through the end of the year."

"Fantastic." Excitement zinged through her nerves. "I can't wait to see you. Oh, we have so much to catch up on." She told him what had happened that day.

"Wow. My horse rescuer extraordinaire, at it again! That's great. I guess I don't know a lot about that business."

"I may just have to hook up my horse trailer and drive down to get him. But we're looking at possible snow in the mountain passes pretty soon, and I'm not that experienced in pulling a trailer in those conditions. I might have to learn real quick though."

Brad paused before speaking again. "Listen... I'm in Wyoming, my truck has a hitch, and I think I can borrow a trailer from some people here. Why don't I drive to Arizona and pick up your horse?"

"What? Really?" Sam blinked. "You would do that?"

"Sure. Why not? I'd be happy to contribute to this rescue."

"W-wow." Sam was at a loss for words. "That is so generous of you. I... "

"In fact, why don't you come with me?"

"Oh." *How fun would that be!* Then her mind flashed to her horses in the barn, her job at Clyde's, and the cows that would need to be fed extra soon.

"That would be awesome... if I could." She gave a little laugh. "But I am kind of tied down here with ranch stuff and clients at the dude ranch, so if I don't have to be away, that would help out so much. Thanks, Brad. You are an answer to prayer."

He laughed quietly. "It's my pleasure, Miss Rescuer Sam. I'll firm up the details and let you know when to expect your new horse."

She hung up, all smiles, the weight of the cloud lifted.

CHAPTER SEVEN

The next morning as Sam was about to leave for the dude ranch, Horace arrived. "I'll go to town today, get all the materials, and get started tomorrow."

"Bring me the receipts, and I'll write you a check." She gave him a kiss on the cheek. "Thanks again."

"You have a good day now, ya hear." He waved her off down the road.

At the Bruckners, the women were finishing breakfast, visiting over coffee at the large round table in Irene's kitchen. "Morning, Sam." Irene poured her a cup of coffee. "Sit down and join us."

"It's a nice, sunny morning. Do you ladies want to go for another ride today?" Sam took a sip.

"Absolutely, we would." Jill smiled at her and then glanced at the other women who nodded. Jill stood and retrieved her purse from a side table. "We, um, we all feel so badly about those horses going to Mexico to be killed, and so impressed with you and what you did yesterday." She reached into her purse and took out a thick envelope. "We talked to our husbands last night and the whole group wanted to donate to your cause."

Sam's breath caught in her throat. "What? You do? You did?" Disbelief, wonder, and gratitude swirled around her like a dust devil. Dizziness pressed her back in her chair. She felt her mouth gaping open and tried to speak but nothing came out. Tears stung her eyes and dripped down her cheeks.

The women stood from their seats and gathered around her

in a group hug.

"Th-thank... you." She finally managed to stutter.

"Thank *you* for what you do." Jill squeezed her upper arm. "You and the Bruckners here have restored my faith in humanity. Before we came out here, I was beginning to wonder if there were any decent people left in the world." She grinned. "Now I know. There are. And you are number one on my list."

Through her tears, Sam absorbed their kindness. *Yes, there are good people in my world.*

Horace started the stall project in the barn, and after the hunters left, Sam had a few days off to help. She handed him tools and nails and held lumber while he measured, sawed, and hammered. Their easy camaraderie took her back to when she and her former fiancé Kenny had remodeled the house and fixed up the barn when they first moved here two years ago. They had worked well together—for a while. A sigh rose, threatening to choke her. Oh well. That was in the past and no going back.

"Ready for some lunch? I'll go up to the house and fix us some soup and sandwiches."

"You bet. I think my stomach is starting to gnaw on my backbone."

Her landline phone was ringing when she walked into the kitchen. Del's voice greeted her. "Hey, Sam. We thought we'd call this time instead of just dropping in on you. Is it okay if we drive out this afternoon and visit with Trixi a while?"

"Of course. I'm home today, so that would work just fine. Looking forward to seeing you."

In the early afternoon, Sam stepped out of the barn as Garrett's truck pulled up beside the building, and he went through the process of helping Del transfer to the wheelchair.

"Hi, guys." She turned to Horace who had followed her out. "You remember Garrett and Del from shipping day, don't you?"

The older man put out a hand and shook with the two. "Shore do. Gonna do a little riding today?"

Garrett's face changed to a paler shade, but Del spoke up. "Maybe. Who knows?"

Trixi and Sugar whinnied from the pasture and approached the fence at a lope. Apache, not to be left out, followed a moment later. Sam went into the barn and came back with a small bucket of pellets for each man. "Okay. Ready?"

Del wheeled toward the fence, Garrett behind, pushing the chair when it stalled over ruts and dirt clods. They fed the horses their treats. Then Sam gave them each a brush. "You want to go inside the corral?"

The men exchanged a quick look. "Yeah." Del nodded.

Sam let Trixi and Sugar into the small corral and opened a gate for the guys to enter. She forced herself to stand back and allow them to take their own time approaching the mares, petting them, and finally brushing. The minutes crawled by in agonizing slowness. She looked at Horace who shrugged and went back into the barn to continue his work.

Sam itched to hurry along the process but forced herself to stand back. It had taken a couple of visits at times for the group home kids to warm up to the horses, but even withdrawn little Benjy had come around a lot quicker than these two grown men. *I wish I knew how to deal with their fears, but that's something for a trained counselor. I'm not, that's for sure.* But on the other hand, they kept coming back. And each time, they made a bit of progress. And that certainly was encouraging.

Del's voice broke into her thoughts. "...your turn. I did it last time."

"Yeah, but you didn't get up and ride. You need to do that first."

"I will if you get on her back at least."

Sam snickered at their argument. Like a couple of ten-year-old boys. She signaled Trixi who knelt. "Okay, guys, who is going to do this?"

Garrett's Adam's apple bobbed, and he stepped back.

Del threw out his hands, palms up. "All right. I'll get on her." He wheeled close to the horse and laboriously lifted himself out of the chair to slide onto her bare back. Sam stood close by in case he needed help. Finally, he sat upright, breathing heavily. "Whew. That was some fun." He gave her a shaky grin. "If it's okay, I'd like to just sit like this for a bit."

"Sure, that's fine, Del, you did great getting on her." She patted Trixi's neck. "Good girl. Stay still now."

Del reached down and patted the mare as well. After a few minutes, he inhaled audibly. "Okay, here goes nothing. I'm ready for her to get up."

"All right. I'm going to give her a signal, and she'll get to her knees and then all the way up. It'll be a little jerky at first, so I'm going to hang on to you in case you lose your balance. I want you to feel her muscles and movement, so I didn't saddle her. Try to clench your thighs against her and hang on to her mane. Ready?"

"Yup."

Sam signaled, grabbing hold of Del's belt, and Trixi gathered her legs under her. Del slipped to one side, letting out a howl of anguish and a guttural oath.

Sam's heartbeat thrashed in her ears. Holding back a yell of her own, she managed to steady him, and pulled him back to center as the horse stood. "Okay. Good. You're doing fine."

"Oh crap." He panted, trying to catch his breath. "I'm sorry, ma'am. I didn't mean to…"

"It's okay. Don't worry about it."

He looked all around. "Wow. What a great vantage point."

The sound of slow clapping came from behind them. Horace stood there with a huge grin on his face. Then Garrett joined him. Inside, Sam leaped and yelled with joy, but on the outside, she simply smiled and patted his back. "You did it, Del. You did it."

His face lit up. "Yeah. I did."

"Do you want her to walk a little?"

He grabbed her mane tighter. "Sure. Okay."

Sam led Trixi slowly around the corral. When they completed the circle back to where the others stood, Del gave a joyful laugh. "This is cool. Garrett, you've got to try this. But first, a couple more times around, please. I'm a real cowboy now. Yeehaw!"

Sam's pulse returned to normal and her limbs relaxed.

After riding around the corral several times, he was ready to dismount. As he sat in his chair, he raised his gaze to Sam's. "That... was the most normal I have felt since..." He gestured to his stumps and swallowed hard. His eyes glistened.

A lump formed in her throat. Almost the same words Jace had used. *Maybe I'm doing something right after all.*

Del found his voice. "Okay, Garrett. This is the most fun you can have with your clothes on."

Horace guffawed, and Sam giggled. Even Garrett gave a little snort of laughter. "All right, Del. You can't one-up me now." He turned to Sam. "Let's roll."

She gave Trixi the signal to kneel, and Garrett maneuvered onto her back. "Up. Before I change my mind." Sam grabbed hold and signaled the horse again. The mare rose with a slight jerk. Before Sam could gather her wits, Garrett was sliding to the other side, away from her. His belt came loose. She lost her grip. A pain-filled yell accompanied a hard thud.

"No!" She raced around the mare and knelt beside him. "Garrett, are you all right? Garrett, talk to me!"

"Aarrgghh." He curled into the fetal position. "Incoming! No! Stop!" His body curled tighter. "Make it stop!"

Sam's core turned to ice. "What's happening? What's wrong? Garrett?" Her greatest fear had just come to pass. *It's only a nightmare. I'm going to wake up any moment.* "Del! What do I do?"

Horace loped up beside them, and Del wheeled himself to his downed friend. "He's having a flashback. PTSD." He leaned forward and yelled out, "Sergeant Webb! At ease!"

Garrett opened his eyes, and his gaze shifted wildly from side to side. His breaths came in short gasps. Then his eyes settled on Del, and he stilled. "Oh."

"You're okay," his friend spoke calmly. "Just had a bit of a horse wreck."

Garrett started to straighten his legs, grimaced, and grabbed his knee.

"Deep breaths now." Horace felt along the leg.

Garrett groaned. "Ow!"

"I don't feel any broken bones, but then I'm not a doctor." Horace stood. "We'd better get you in to see one though. Can you stand?"

Garrett pushed himself to a sitting position. "Oh man, it hurts. My good leg. Twisted when I landed."

Del offered a hand. "Here, lean on the chair." Horace and Sam grabbed him under the arms and lifted him to his feet. "Aarrgghh!" He screamed in pain, swore, and sank back to the ground.

Sam fought back her tears. "Garrett, I'm so sorry. I'm so sorry."

He shook his head. "Not… your… fault."

She drew a sharp inhale that hurt her lungs. *Yes, it was.*

"Okay, help me get back in the truck, and then you can use my chair to get him there," Del offered.

"Good idea." Horace pushed him to the pickup and brought the wheelchair back to Garrett. Together, he and Sam lifted the injured man into the chair and to his vehicle. "You okay to drive?" He gave Sam a piercing look.

"I think so."

"Head in to Forsyth, and I'll follow you in Garrett's truck."

Her hands trembled as she slid onto the driver's seat and started the engine. Clasping the wheel until her knuckles went pale, she gunned the vehicle down the driveway and over the rutted road toward the highway. Garrett moaned in the back seat, and Del swiveled to talk calmly to him.

She hunched over the wheel and stared straight ahead, her body cold, her pulse racing. *Oh my word. What just happened? I should've put the saddle on. Why didn't I do that? Why? What was I thinking?* She wheezed, trying to get air. *You weren't thinking, you idiot.* An old, critical voice came back to answer. *You never do anything right.*

She squeezed one eye shut and then the other, trying to stop the stinging tears. *Do* NOT *cry. I will* NOT *cry.*

Not sure how they'd made the forty miles, Sam pulled up to the emergency entrance at the Rosebud Health Care Center. Horace parked behind her and then ran inside to get help. An orderly came out with a wheelchair, gathered Garrett, and took him inside. Sam and Horace helped Del into his chair and they followed.

The clock on the wall ticked in slow motion. Sam fidgeted in the hard plastic chair, staring at but not seeing a magazine in her lap. The scene at the corral kept replaying in a continuous loop, but every time she tried to change the ending, Garrett's belt came loose again, and she felt him slip away from her grasp. *Why wasn't I more careful? Why did this have to happen—just when he found the confidence to get on Trixi's back. I ruined everything! I wonder if he has insurance. Or will I be liable?* She covered her face in her hands and pressed the tears back into her eyes.

"Are you Garrett Webb's friends?" A voice broke into Sam's misery. She looked up at the doctor.

"Yes," Del answered for them. "How is he?"

"He's doing fine. Has a bad knee sprain, but with rest and ice, he'll be good as new in no time."

Through her haze of worry, she found her breath. *Oh, thank you, Lord.*

"That's great!" Del broke into a big smile, and Horace stood to shake the doctor's hand.

"He'll be ready to go home in just a few minutes. The nurse will finish up his paperwork and bring him out." The physician strode back down the hall, checking his pager.

Horace looked down at her. "That's good news, little gal, isn't it?"

Still rooted to her chair, she gulped. "Yeah. Yeah, it is. Good. I'm glad."

"Well, I'm assuming Garrett won't be able to drive his pickup, so we'll make sure you guys get home." Horace stepped to Del's side.

"No, that's okay. I can call a friend at the Vet Center and he'll come get us. I don't want to put you out any more."

"It's no bother." Sam's voice came out squeaky, like an old gate hinge. "It's the least I can do."

An older nurse in blue scrubs wheeled Garrett out to the waiting room. She looked at Del and then at Horace and Sam. "I assume one of you can drive him home?"

"We've got friends coming to get us." Del gave his friend a playful punch on the arm. "Hey, man, now you're at my level."

Garrett snorted. "Yeah."

His pain-filled face wrenched at her conscience. "Garrett, I'm so sorry this happened."

His gaze remained on the floor. "Yeah."

A stone dropped to the pit of her stomach.

Sam stared out the passenger window, not seeing the landscape. Only Garrett's anguished pain and then his cold, hard face as he sat in the wheelchair beside Del, waiting for their friends to arrive.

"I know you're blaming yourself." Horace finally broke the silence. "But it wasn't your fault. It was just one of those fluke things—his belt came loose."

"No. It was my fault. I should've put the saddle on." She gritted her teeth. "With Del, I thought he would benefit by being able to feel the horse with his thighs. Then Garrett decided so quickly to try and I… didn't think. He's been so hesitant, and now…" She shook her head. "I blew it."

"You didn't blow it. These things happen." He tried again to reason with her and offer comfort.

She turned her head away. Talking about it wouldn't take away the hurt. Her heart felt like it was caught in a vise. Horace was being kind and fatherly, but she couldn't handle his platitudes. It *was* her fault and she had caused Garrett's accident.

When he finally came to a stop in front of her house, he patted her shoulder. "I'm just down the road, if you want to talk."

"Thanks. I'm fine. See you." She trudged up the steps and into the house, dropping her jacket on a chair. Tremors overtook her hands. *What have I done?* She had ruined any chance of working with veterans. And if that happened with an adult, something as bad or worse could happen with kids. She wasn't meant to do this. Another failure. Another dream swirling down the drain.

She could sure use a drink, just one to numb this pain, to forget what had happened today. Squaring her shoulders, she strode to the coffee pot. *That was the old me. I don't need that.*

CHAPTER EIGHT

A shrill jangle pierced Sam's sleep. She lifted her head. *Wha...?* She let her head fall back onto the pillow. The noise persisted. The phone. Sam groaned, rolled to one side, and fumbled on the night table for the handset. "'Lo." Her voice croaked like an old bullfrog.

Brad's voice came over the line, sounding somewhat breathless. "Oh, hi, Sam. Sorry if I woke you. Just got the horse trailer hooked up and everything packed and ready to go. Wanted to let you know I'm on my way to Phoenix to get your horse."

"O-o-kay." She tried to clear her throat to sound more awake. "Um. Good." Her head kept up its Tom-Tom beat.

"You all right? You sound—"

"No, 'm fine. Rough day yesterday. But 'sall good."

"Okay. Well, I'm getting a bit of a later start than I thought, so I'd better get going." He did sound frazzled.

Sam fidgeted with the phone cord. "Yeah. Safe travels. Thank you, Brad. You're a good friend."

Silence filled the airwaves for a beat. He let out a long sigh. "Friend? I... thought we were more than just friends..." Another exasperated-sounding exhale. "But I guess I was wrong. Well, you have yourself a good day. I'll let you know how things go."

"Brad, wait! I—" Sam heard a click. He'd hung up on her. *What the heck just happened?* She squeezed her eyes shut. *He didn't like me calling him a friend. But why? What's wrong with that?*

She burrowed under her covers, shutting the world away.

Nightmares chased each other through restless sleep.

Wheelchairs, wrecked cars, and leg prosthetics. Garrett slipping from her grasp, his pained, angry face that morphed into Brad's.

Sam awoke, bathed in sweat. Nearly noon. She eased herself into a sitting position against the headboard. A colossal failure. She imagined a giant eraser, rubbing out the mistakes of yesterday. If only she could go back and do it over.

Finally, she made it to the bathroom and plunged under a cold shower, letting the water flow over her head, mingling with her tears, trying to wash away the negative thoughts. "Okay, Samantha Moser, today is a new day, a clean slate. You can do this! Cowgirl up, like Great-Grandma Nettie would say."

She got dressed, made a pot of strong coffee, and choked down a piece of dry toast. Past time to take care of the horses. And then she remembered, Murdock was having a load of hay delivered this afternoon.

Out in the cold November day, the air smelled of snow, sharp and damp. Heavy gray clouds covered the sky from one horizon to the other. She pulled her coat collar up and tucked her hands into her pockets as she headed to the barn.

The horses lifted their heads and tails and galloped around the small pasture, blowing mini clouds of steam. "Hi, guys. I'm sorry I'm so late." Sam let them into the corral and spent a couple of minutes rubbing faces and finger-combing manes. "I'm a bad mom, I know." She gave them each several grain pellets as treats and then threw out a few flakes of hay. It was a good thing that delivery was coming in. Thanksgiving might be a white one, and she would probably have to start feeding the cows soon.

The semi rumbled up the driveway mid-afternoon, with Horace's pickup following. "Hey, little gal." He got out and touched a finger to his hat brim. "Thought you might need a hand unloading."

"Thanks! That'd be great. Looks like we might be feeding this out all too soon."

Sam and Horace helped the delivery men unload and stack

the small bales in the area behind the barn. Since she didn't have the equipment to unroll the big round bales, she appreciated Jack getting the forty-pound ones that she could handle on her own.

Panting, Sam stopped as a wave of dizziness passed over her.

"You look a little gray around the edges." Horace peered at her from under his hat brim. "You okay?

"Yeah, I'm fine. Haven't had much to eat today." She took a couple of deep breaths. "When we're done here, come on up to the house. I'll scramble some eggs for us."

"Sure." Horace's brow remained furrowed as he studied her a moment longer. Then he went back to the task at hand.

After the hay was taken care of and the truck left, they ambled up to the house. Sam poured her friend a cup of coffee and took eggs and bacon out of the refrigerator.

"So, what's up?" Horace tipped the cream into his java.

"Nothin'." Turning her back to her neighbor, she tried to ignore the pain and anger and disappointment flooding back. Her hands shook, and she dropped an egg on the floor. "Crap! This is my life." She grabbed a roll of paper towels and bent to clean up the mess. A cry of anguish burst from her throat.

Horace was by her side in a heartbeat, draping an arm around her. "Hey, hey." He pulled her to her feet. "Come, sit. I'll clean this up in a minute. Tell me what's wrong. Is it what happened yesterday?"

"Y-yeah... N-no... ohhh!" Hiccupping sobs punctured her words. "Everything... is wrong. I blew it..."

"No-no. You didn't." Horace shook his head emphatically. "It was just the luck of the draw. Just circumstances. It'll be okay."

"I failed those guys, and Garrett got hurt." She looked at Horace through bleary eyes. "And then this morning when Brad called I told him he is a good friend, and he didn't like that and he hung up on me. I've tried calling his cell several times, but it goes straight to voicemail." She burst into a fresh spate of tears.

Horace patted her arm clumsily, muttering, "It's okay, little gal, it's okay."

After Horace left, Sam saddled up, and one by one, took each of her horses on a short ride to exercise them. She left Sugar for last and galloped her out to the butte that overlooked the ranch. The air was crisp, and she shivered when she pulled the mare to a stop, but her head felt clearer. She slipped off the horse's back and squatted in the dirt, looking out on the vast prairie that ran for miles in all directions with few hints of civilization. Peace folded around her like angel wings. She belonged here. This ranch was in her blood. If she couldn't buy this place, and if she wasn't able to continue working with kids and people who needed that special bonding with these animals, what would she do? Horses were all she knew.

Sugar fluttered her nostrils beside her. Sam looked up at her pal, stood, and stroked her face. "Oh, Sugar." Tears streamed down her cheeks again. "Dang it! I thought I was done with these." She swiped them away with the back of her hand. "I'm stronger than this!"

A snowflake floated lazily from the slate sky and another followed. Sam shivered again. "Okay, girl. I'm getting cold. Let's go home." She mounted, and they raced the snow toward home.

After she finished her chores, she ate a light supper and then curled up in her chair by the stove with her book. Outside, snow fell, coating the ground. She tried to read, but negative images kept flashing before her, interrupting the story in the book. Finally, she gave up and went to bed. The what-if scenarios kept repeating endlessly, and she tangled herself in the bedclothes as she tried to find a comfortable position.

Around midnight she got up, pulled on a fleecy robe, and went to the window. The snow had stopped, and the moon peeked between clouds to illuminate the white dusting below. Sam breathed in the beauty, and she sank to her knees, her legs suddenly weak. Lifting her face toward the moon, she whispered, "Hey, God, it's me, Samantha. Again. I know it's been a while, and I only seem to talk to you when I'm in the deep stuff. I'm sorry, and I'm sorry for all the things I've messed up lately. I can't seem to get a handle on what I'm supposed to do, and I keep failing at everything. I can't do this by myself. Can you sit with me a while and tell me what to do. I need your help. Please."

She buried her face in her arms, kneeling at the windowsill until a chill forced her back to bed where she curled up, warmth and peace at last allowing sleep to overcome her.

***

The next morning, the clouds had parted enough to allow brief appearances of sunlight that glinted on the skiff of snow. Enough grass still poked through that there was no need to feed the herd extra hay yet, so Sam took care of her horses. Then she checked her tack, setting aside what needed to be repaired or oiled. She worked by rote, thankful that she could concentrate on the task and not have the regrets and sorries running through her head.

At lunchtime, she walked up to the house, heated a can of tomato soup, and made a toasted cheese sandwich. As she lifted a spoonful of hot soup, the phone rang. Startled, she dropped the spoon and splashed its contents on the table. "Darn it!" She tossed her napkin over the mess and got up to answer.

"Hi, Sam, it's Del."

"Oh, hi." She gulped. "How...?" She couldn't bring herself to finish the question.

"How's Garrett? He's good. Yeah. He's been resting, icing, and elevating." He chuckled. "He'll be fine. He's... just... um, embarrassed."

"Oh, gee, *I'm* embarrassed. And I'm so sorry. He was making such good progress." Sam's eyes stung. "I messed this up. I'm afraid I've ruined everything for him... for you both."

"No-no. Not at all. If anyone's to blame, it's me for egging

65

him on when maybe he wasn't quite ready. But... I can't wait to come out and try again." Del's voice held a note of excitement. "And, believe it or not, Garrett wants to try again too."

"What? Really?" Sam couldn't believe what she'd heard.

"Yeah. No kidding. As soon as his knee heals up. Of course, now that winter is coming, I know it's going to be hard to do out at your place."

"Yes, that is a problem I've mulled over without an answer." Sam still couldn't quite comprehend Del's news.

"Well... I think we may have a solution."

"Oh?" Sam puckered her brow.

"Yeah. I don't know if you know, Garrett and I have been taking some classes at Miles Community College."

"Yes, I remember Teresa telling me that."

"Well, they have an agriculture center with an indoor arena. I know one of the instructors, and I've told him about what you've been doing with us, and he's eager to talk to you about some kind of program."

Sam stood in shocked silence for several heartbeats.

"Um... Sam? You still there?"

She drew a sharp breath. "Yeah. I'm here. I'm... stunned. I don't know what to say."

"How about 'yes'?" Del laughed. "I can set up a meeting with him next week, if you want to."

"Okay. Yes. Sure. Why not?"

After she hung up, she remained standing, staring at the phone. *What just happened? Is this an answer to prayer?*

Thanksgiving morning, Sam went out to the pasture early to check on the horses. She lifted her face to the bright sunlight and inhaled the frosty air. "What a beautiful day! Thank you!" She smiled into the cloudless blue sky.

Sugar whinnied from the fence, and the others joined her as Sam approached. She scratched and petted and gave each one a few pellet treats. Then she went to the water tank and broke the skim of ice on top so they could drink more easily.

Still smiling a couple of hours later, she grabbed the bowl of fruit salad she'd made the day before, hopped into her pickup, and headed to the Bruckners' who had invited her and Horace for the holiday meal.

Clyde opened the front door as she got out of the vehicle. "Hey there, Sam. Happy Thanksgiving."

"Hi, Clyde. Beautiful day, huh?"

"C'mon in. Irene's been slavin' away over the hot stove for the last two days."

The aroma of roasting turkey wafted over Sam when she stepped into the large old-fashioned country kitchen with blue checked gingham curtains at the windows.

"It smells wonderful in here." She set the fruit salad on the counter and gave the pleasantly plump, motherly woman a big hug. "Tell me what I can do to help."

"Thank you, dear. It won't be long now until we eat. As soon as Horace gets here and our ranch guests come over." Her graying brown curls bounced as she gestured with her head. "If you'd like, you can put out the plates and silverware."

Sam set out plates and silverware on the festive table, already decorated with a horn-of-plenty centerpiece and fall-colored placemats. Horace arrived, bringing olives, pickles, and a cranberry relish. He gave her a one-armed squeeze. "How ya doin', little gal?"

"Good, thanks, really good. It's a great day." She hugged him back.

A knock came at the door and a middle-aged couple came in. Clyde introduced them. "Sam, Horace, this is Lillian and John, our guests for the weekend from San Diego." They shook hands all around.

"What brings you to chilly Montana this time of year?" Sam grinned at the hazel-eyed woman who shivered as she took off her down-filled coat.

"Oh, we decided we wanted a 'real' ranch experience, something different for our Thanksgiving get-away this year."

Sam raised her eyebrows. "It's a little cold for riding."

"Oh, that didn't stop us yesterday. We bundled up and had a great time." Lillian was dressed in a western shirt, jeans, and boots. "I can see why this is called 'Big Sky Country.' It is just stupendous. That sunset last night. Wow."

"We do get the most beautiful ones in the country, I think."

Lillian produced a bag. "If I could get a bowl from you, Irene. We brought some of our famous saltwater taffy."

Soon they all sat around the large dining table, a beautiful, browned turkey in front of Clyde for carving. "I want to say how thankful I am for my husband, this ranch, and all of you." Irene started the round-robin of thanks.

Sam chimed in last. "I'm so thankful for you, my friends; for giving me a job here and the opportunities to work with horses and kids; for your help, Horace, and for your friendship. And here's to new friends." She raised her glass of apple cider to Lillian and John.

Clyde bowed his salt-and-peppered head and concluded with a short prayer. Then with a flourish, he carved the turkey, and momentary silence fell as everyone tucked into their dinner.

"Mmm, this turkey is fabulous." Lillian broke the lull. "We're going to have to get a smoker and try this sometime."

John spoke around a bite. "Yeah, best I've ever eaten."

"And your fruit salad is so delicious." Lillian looked at Sam. "There's something different about it."

"It's called '24-hour Fruit Salad.' The secret is in the sauce—egg yolks, vinegar, and butter." Sam smiled. "But it's not a secret recipe. I'm happy to share. My grandma Anna always made it, my aunt Monica continued the practice, and now I'm following this tradition for holidays in our family." A pang of loneliness shot through her, remembering the good times they all once had together. What was Brad doing today? Had he stopped along the way to visit friends or was he having a lonely meal at a truck stop somewhere in the middle of nowhere?

"That's wonderful." The California woman beamed. "I love hearing about family traditions. Irene said you're living on the ranch your great-grandparents once owned?"

Sam told them about her rodeo-riding grandmother, which sparked a lively conversation.

"But you didn't follow along in that particular tradition," Lillian remarked.

"No, I love horses and riding, but I don't want to get on anything that's going to buck me off—on purpose, that is." Sam giggled.

"Sam's been working with group home kids here on the ranch during the summer, and she's also started working with a couple of veterans with PTSD." Irene passed the stuffing around for second helpings.

"Wow. You are a very accomplished young lady." Lillian spooned more food onto her plate.

John nodded. "Working with vets. That's a big undertaking. Do you have a background in psychology?"

Her face grew warm. "No. Unfortunately, I don't. And it has been difficult." She glanced at Horace. "But... I had a bit of good news the other day." She told him about her call from Del and the possibility of working at the ag college in Miles City.

His mouth dropped open and then he gave her a toothy grin. "Hey, that's great. I knew it'd turn out okay."

As the three women cleaned up after dinner, Horace went out to his truck and fetched his fiddle. Clyde brought out a guitar, and toe-tapping notes of "Turkey in the Straw" filled the living room. When the dishes were packed in the dishwasher, Irene went to the piano, pulled out several songbooks, and chorded along with the men. Sam and Lillian joined the singing, John following along slightly off-beat and off-key.

Toward evening, she drove home, her heart overflowing with the music and camaraderie of the day. She stopped first at the corral and fed the horses a bit of hay. "This has been one of the best days," she stroked Sugar's neck, "and I'm thankful for you three in my life."

The answering machine light blinked when she stepped into the kitchen. The first was from Electra. "Hey, Sam. I just wanted to call and tell you Happy Thanksgiving and I'm so excited to come see you at Christmas, I can hardly stand it. I can't wait! Love you!"

Sam cracked up. A relatively short outburst from the girl, but she agreed. She looked forward to seeing her young friend again.

"Hi, Sam, it's Brad. Letting you know I'm having Thanksgiving at the Green River Ranch and I'll be heading out tomorrow with Toby. Should be there sometime Monday. We need to talk."

Oh, thank goodness he wasn't alone today. A twinge of guilt clutched at her stomach over their last conversation and the ominous 'need to talk' statement. He'd obviously not wanted to talk to her, otherwise he would have called her cell phone. An aching sigh moaned through her. And it had been such a good day.

CHAPTER NINE

The next morning Sam rode Apache out to the pasture to check on the cows. Another turquoise sky filled the horizon bowl, with only a few frothy clouds floating lazily overhead. She had bundled up against the chill, and the gelding moved with an easy gait—no lingering effects from his near-starvation. He seemed to relish the opportunity to run, and she let him have his head.

She still didn't know what to think of Brad's terse message, and it replayed in her mind throughout the morning. Her stomach butterflies shook out their wings. *Well, no use fretting about it. I'll find out soon enough.* She took a deep breath of the cold air and focused on the scene ahead.

The red and white Hereford cows hung out near the reservoir where a grove of cottonwood trees stood. She had seen pictures from Great-Grandma Nettie's day when there was only one tree to provide a smidgeon of shade in the summer.

Slowing Apache's pace, she rode near the bunch and counted, making sure they were all there. They were, and appeared no worse for having had their babies taken away just a couple of short weeks ago.

Sam turned the horse back toward home. Might as well make sure the barn was ready for Toby and work on cleaning and oiling tack. If she finished that, there was always housework. She made a face and snorted. "We can always find something else to do, huh, Apache?" His ears flicked back. "Electra will be here in no time. Are you going to remember her?" The gelding bobbed his head and picked up his pace. She smiled. "I think you will."

The next couple of days continued in the same vein. The ag instructor from Miles City called, and they set up an appointment for the following week. "I'm excited to talk to you about this potential program," Nick Seward told her. "Del seemed quite enthusiastic about you and your trick horse."

"Thank you. I'm looking forward to talking with you too." Inwardly, she cringed. Had Del told the man about Garrett's fall? Must not have, otherwise... *Cross that bridge when I come to it.*

Sunday morning, dark gray, heavy clouds gathered on the horizon like pregnant elephants. They grew to block out the sun by afternoon and the temperature dropped.

"Looks like snow again." Horace had dropped by to check on the new stall.

A sharp worry-arrow pierced her gut. "Yeah, I was afraid of that. Brad is supposed to be coming in tomorrow. Sure hope he doesn't have trouble along the way."

"Aw, he'll be fine. The graders and sanders are out on the highways as soon as it starts to accumulate." He kicked at a mud clod. "Got any hot coffee?"

"Sure. C'mon up to the house." Sam led the way and served fresh chocolate chip cookies she'd baked, along with the java.

Horace guffawed. "I knew there was a reason I stopped by today."

The two passed a pleasant hour by the fire, munching on cookies and sipping coffee. Horace told her how his great-granddad had homesteaded his place, his father took over the reins, and Horace continued the Jones ranch legacy. "So, I can understand you wantin' to buy this place. Hope it works out for ya."

"Me too." She gazed out the window at the prairie beyond, contentment filling the formerly-empty spot in her heart. "There's just something about it. I feel like I belong here— more than anywhere I've ever been."

"Yup. I get that. I do." He stood. "Well, best be gettin' home, get my chores done before it snows."

After her neighbor left, Sam brought the horses into the corral, fed them, and let them in the barn for the night. She thawed and heated a bowl of chili from the freezer and read an old Zane Grey novel while she ate.

By the time she went to bed, snowflakes were drifting down as if someone had opened a huge feather pillow high in the sky. She bit her lip and whispered a prayer for travel safety for Brad.

Sam awoke to banshee wails, as wind gusts shook the ranch house. She leaped up, her pulse hammering in her throat. "Oh no! It's a blizzard!" Wrapping herself in her fleecy robe, she went out to the living room, turned up the heat, and then started a pot of coffee. She tapped her fingers on the counter while she waited. When it had brewed, she clasped her hands around the cup and went to stand in front of the window. The outline of the barn was barely visible across the yard. *Sure glad I put the horses inside last night.*

She paced from one window to the next, refilled her cup in the kitchen, and walked back to the living room. She gulped a cold, anxious lump. *Brad is on the road in this.* She tried not to let her mind go to worst-case scenario. Air caught in her chest. No, surely he holed up somewhere in Wyoming last night and boarded Toby. *Yes, of course, that's what he did.* She was able to breathe again, picturing him lying in bed watching TV all day while the snow fell and the wind blew.

She wouldn't be able to get out to feed the cows until the storm let up but might as well go check on the horses. She dressed in her heavy coveralls, down coat, hat and mittens, and stepped out into the maelstrom. Her nose hairs froze immediately, and the wind nearly took her breath away. She put her head down and slogged through the drifts to the barn.

Pulling the door open, Sam stepped into the warm, moist hay- and manure-scented interior. The horses whickered when they saw her. "You guys are so lucky to have this space out of the wind." She stopped to pet each one and give them a bucket of grain pellets and added hay to their troughs. Then she doled out flakes of hay and took their water buckets out to the well to refill. The wind blew even stronger now, almost enough to blow the water out of the pail. "Yikes! I've got to get a pipe installed into the barn."

Whirling around, she stared through the white-out in the direction of the barn. She had heard horror stories of ranchers getting disoriented and lost within a few feet of their barn or house and freezing to death. *I know it's there.*

The chill that ran through her was not from the storm.

The barn created a faint dark outline just ahead. Sam carried the buckets back to the horses. Once finished, she headed toward the exit. "Well, here goes nothing." With a deep breath to brace herself, she opened the door again and stepped outside. She knew the direction of the house and set off up the incline, catching glimpses of the silhouette through the swirling snow. Aunt Monica had written about her great-grandparents stringing a rope between the house and barn so they wouldn't get lost in the storm. Wishing she'd remembered that earlier, she hitched her scarf higher over her nose and mouth.

Heart pounding, she shivered and trudged through the drifts. "Please help me find my way," she prayed. "I'm not ready to freeze to death right in front of my house."

After eons, Sam stumbled up the steps to the porch. In the kitchen, she shoved the door shut against the wind and collapsed against the wall. "Thank you," she whispered. Teeth chattering, she took off her outerwear and hurried to the living room to stand in front of the propane stove. Thank goodness she didn't have to feed it wood or coal, like her great-grandparents did.

Finally, the tingling pain and itching in her fingers indicated she was thawing out. While she rubbed her hands, worried thoughts fluttered through her mind. *I sure hope the cows are all right. I have to get out there to feed them soon.* Usually, cattle would find shelter in the bottom of a coulee, but she'd heard that once in a while the wind would drive them into a fence corner where they would freeze to death. She gulped. Jack Murdock would have her hide if that happened.

Sam crossed her fingers. *They'll be in the coulee.*

But where was Brad? She strode to the kitchen, grabbed the phone, and dialed his cell number. Incessant ringing went to voicemail. *Oh no. Why doesn't he pick up?* If he was waiting out the blizzard in a motel somewhere, surely he would answer his phone. She paced back to the living room and spread her palms out over the stove. Maybe the storm had knocked out communications somehow. Or maybe he was in an area without cell service, like she was at the ranch. That had to be it.

Sam sat in her rocking chair and picked up her book, stared at the page a moment, and then stood again. She went to the window, scratched a hole in the frost, and peered out. The wind continued to howl and the snow still swirled. The view from the kitchen was no better, nor was the scene outside her bedroom window. Her stomach knotted like a tangled lariat.

Finally, about noon the wind let up somewhat. She heated soup and forced herself to eat, all the while staring at the silent phone. The clock on the wall ticked off slow seconds.

She cleaned up her few dishes, washed down the counters, and then tackled the kitchen floor on hands and knees, scrubbing as though she could wash away her worries.

The phone's shrill jangle startled her, and she banged against the mop bucket as she jumped up, sloshing water on the floor. Panting, she grabbed up the receiver. "Brad?"

"No, sorry, little gal, just me." Horace's voice boomed over the wire. "Wanted to check and see how you're doing."

She slumped against the wall and fought the urge to cry. "Oh. I'm fine."

"Nasty storm, huh?"

"Yeah. I got down to the barn to feed and water the horses, but almost couldn't see my way back to the house." Sam's voice caught as she stared out the window at the snowstorm. "I'm worried about the cows."

"I knew you would be. But they'll be all right. I'm sure they're holed up in that coulee east of the reservoir. If this lifts enough this afternoon, I'll come over, and we can drive out to check on them and throw out a few bales of hay. If not, I'm sure it'll be okay by morning." His calm voice soothed her somewhat.

"I haven't heard from Brad, though, and I've tried calling several times but only get his voicemail." The fear rose again, and for a moment she thought she would throw up the soup she'd eaten.

"Well, I know cell service is pretty iffy in parts of Wyoming anyway, and with the wind, I'll bet some tower's been knocked out. He's a big boy; he knows to get the horse somewhere and wait it out. He's fine."

Sam let out a long sigh. "I sure hope so. Sorry I'm such a worrywart, but I feel so helpless."

"I know, I know. You're a good gal. Always thinkin' of others before yourself. Now, just curl up with one a them books by the fire and enjoy your forced day off." Horace chuckled.

"Okay. I'll try. And you too." She disconnected, mopped the spilled water, and put away her cleaning supplies. Back in her chair by the stove, she picked up her book again. This time she was able to read a couple of sentences, then a paragraph or two, and as the wind stopped wailing, she found herself immersed in Zane Grey's world.

As the room darkened with evening approaching, she switched on a lamp and continued to read. When the phone rang again, she dropped the book and sprinted to the kitchen. "Hello?"

"Hello. Is this Samantha Moser?"

"Yes." Her voice squeaked.

"Ms. Moser, this is Trooper Emmet Zimmer with the Wyoming State Patrol."

Sam's throat closed, and she could barely breathe. "Yes?"

"We're on the scene of an accident, and papers we've located indicate that you are the owner of a horse named Toby?"

"Yes..." Now fear raked its claws through her innards. "Is

he…? Is Brad…?

"The horse seems to be okay. A local veterinarian was first on the scene and took the horse to his clinic to check him out. Um…" Papers rustled in the background, "the driver, a Brad… Ashton? Yeah, Mr. Ashton. He's been taken to the hospital in Billings."

"No!" Darkness descended. She dropped the receiver and slumped to the floor.

She blinked, trying to clear the fuzzy, dark images and sounds swirling around her. A disembodied voice came from nearby. She shifted her attention to the phone receiver. "Hello? Ms. Moser? Hello?" *Oh yes, the trooper. The accident.*

With a shaky voice, she answered. "H-hello…"

"Are you all right, Ms. Moser?" The officer's baritone voice spread over her like a blanket.

"Y-yes. I think so." She cleared her throat. "Do you know how badly Brad is hurt… and where they took him?"

"Sorry, I don't know the extent of his injuries, ma'am. But I believe the ambulance took him to the Billings Clinic trauma center."

Another wave of dizziness washed over her. "T-trauma center?" *Oh my word, he must be hurt bad.*

"It's only a precaution, ma'am, with an accident. I'm sure they just want to check him out."

"Oh. Okay." Sam tried to swallow past a hard object in her throat. "And Toby? Where is he?"

"Well, likewise. The vet, Dr. Palmer, said he'd take the horse to his clinic." Papers rustled again in the background. "I have the phone number here, if you are ready to copy."

"Ah… Yes, just a second." She rose on jellied legs and stumbled to the counter where her pad and pen lay. "Okay, go ahead."

The trooper gave her the number. "Also, do you know if Mr. Ashton has family in the area?"

Brad's family? Her mind went blank. She'd never met them, but she searched her memory bank for what he'd told her.

Livingston. He grew up on a ranch in Livingston. But wait… no, they'd lost the ranch. *Think, Sam, think!*

"I'm not sure, but I think they live in Billings." The realization of how little she knew about Brad hit her like a riding whip. If she'd thought they had a chance at a relationship, why hadn't she talked to him more, asked more questions? *Oh dear, I've been so caught up in my own selfish problems, I couldn't see beyond my barn.*

"Thank you, Ms. Moser. I'll locate them. Do you have someone there with you? Are you sure you're okay?"

No, I'm not sure I'm okay. "I'll be fine," she lied. "I have a close neighbor I can call. Thank you, officer."

After he disconnected, Sam slumped into a kitchen chair, holding the receiver with shaking hands. What could she do? The snow was still coming down, too deep to go anywhere. The hospital wasn't likely to give her any information on Brad. How would she get Toby home? Thoughts and questions spider-webbed from her brain like shattered ice on the horse tank.

Hanging up the phone, she stared at the frost-covered window and the blackness beyond. Chills ran through her from the inside, her chest tightened, and her breaths came in short gasps. Weakness paralyzed her. *There's nothing I can do!*

When the phone rang again, she shrieked and grabbed for it, dropping the receiver. She leaned over to pick it up and answered with a quavery, watered-down voice.

"Sam?" Teresa's tone exuded concern. "You sound terrible. What's wrong?"

"Oh, Teresa. Everything! The storm… Brad… Toby… Oh, dear Lord." She collapsed into sobs.

Her friend's concerned voice came over the line, soothing, comforting. "It's okay, Sam, it's okay. I'm here. I'm listening. Can you tell me what happened? Are you all right?"

Sam's breath stuttered as she tried to inhale and calm herself. "Brad's been in a bad accident in Wyoming."

"Oh no. Do you know how he is?"

"No. The trooper couldn't tell me anything except they took him to the t-trauma center in Billings."

A sharp intake of air from the other end.

Her heart hammered. She had no idea what that meant. *Broken bones? Head injury? He must be hurt bad.* "And I don't know anything about his family. I don't know who to call. Oh, Teresa, I don't know what to do!"

"Oh, sweetie, I'm sorry. I know you are feeling so helpless right now, with the storm and all. Me too. I wish I could come be with you right now. Do you think Horace could make it over?"

"I don't know." That thin, reedy voice didn't belong to her, did it?

"Listen. I can make some phone calls. I'll see what I can find out, okay? Is Toby all right?"

Sam told her about the veterinarian who'd come upon the accident and taken the horse to his clinic.

"Okay. That's some good news in all this. Hang on to that. I'll call you back shortly."

"Thank you, Teresa. You're the best." Sam hiccupped, disconnected, and scrubbed her hands over her face. More than anything, she wanted to jump in her truck and drive to Billings. But the storm. There was nothing she could do but wait. *Oh dear God, please help me. Please let Brad be all right.*

CHAPTER TEN

Sam sat slumped in the dark kitchen until her stomach growled. A chill shuddered through her, and she rose to turn up the thermostat. Heating a bowl of chili, she forced herself to eat the hot food while she stared at the dark, frosty window as if she could will away the snow. Her hands shook when she lifted the spoon to her mouth, and no amount of heat disbursed the cold that coursed through her. Her gaze strayed to the silent phone. *C'mon, Teresa, call! I need some news!*

When it did ring finally, Horace's voice boomed over the line. "How're you holding up there, little gal? Keepin' warm enough?"

She spoke haltingly between gulping breaths and told him the news.

"Oh no. I'll come over, keep you company."

"No-no-no. I can't let you do that. The snow's too deep, and it's too late. I'm fine. Really." She chewed on her lower lip.

"I got the chains on and the snow blade hooked up. I can make it fine."

She blinked against the sting of tears. "That is so nice of you, Horace, but it's not necessary. It's too dark, the snow is too deep, and I don't want you out in the cold." She swallowed. If something would happen to him too… "There's nothing we can do tonight anyway. Just wait."

"Well, that's probably true. Sounds like Brad and Toby are both in good hands, and I'm sure things will look brighter in the mornin'. I'll be over to help you feed. But if you change your mind about company, give me a ring."

"Okay. But I'll be fine. Honest. Thank you."

Sam spent the night tossing in her bed, nightmares and worst-case scenarios looping through her fitful snippets of sleep. She awoke to sunlight streaming through her bedroom window and the growling sound of an engine outside. *Oh no, I've overslept!*

She leaped out of bed and threw on her long johns, jeans, and a sweatshirt. Horace's big diesel truck pushed mounds of snow aside, creating a pathway from the road to her place. She opened the kitchen door, shivering with the blast of frigid air, and waved to him to come in. Then she started the coffee maker and took out eggs and bacon from the refrigerator.

Shuffling and stomping on the porch announced her neighbor's arrival. Sam handed him a broom to sweep the snow from his pant legs, and he came in, sniffing. "Mmm, coffee. Don't mind if I do."

"Sorry I'm late this morning, didn't sleep well last night." She poured him a cup of hot brew and then lay bacon slices in the pan.

He inhaled the steam appreciatively. "You're not late. Not much we could do till the sun came out anyway." He took a sip. "Got the road plowed between my place and yours. After we fuel up our bellies, I'll help you load the hay, and we'll go find Murdock's cows."

"Sure hope they're all right." She dished up their plates and sat at the table across from the older man.

He peered at her from under bushy white eyebrows. "No news?"

She glanced at the phone. No blinking light. "Nope."

"Well, you know what they say—no news is good news."

His attempt at humor fell like a flat rock in a pond as she attempted a smile but failed. Her bite of egg and bacon wouldn't go down, and she sipped coffee to wash away the congealed lump.

After he polished off his meal, Sam put her half-eaten breakfast plate on the counter and donned her coveralls, hat, scarf, and gloves. "Okay, let's get this done."

Horace plowed a swath to the barn, where she first chopped ice in the tank, fed, and let the horses out into the corral to water. They whickered and blew in what sounded like appreciation. Then Sam climbed into the loft and threw hay bales into the back of the truck while her neighbor arranged them.

The vehicle ground slowly out to the pasture as he plowed a road to the reservoir. As they approached the watering hole, Sam spotted the cows lumbering out of the coulee, wading through the deep snowdrifts toward them.

Horace chortled. "They know breakfast has arrived."

Sam counted and offered a small prayer of thanks. "Looks like they're all here."

"Told ya they'd be smart enough to hole up out of the wind." He winked at her. "Okay, you wanna drive this rig while I throw out the hay?"

"No. I don't want to get us stuck. I'll go up top."

"Well, jes' thump on the roof when you've had enough."

"Okay." She got out and climbed on top of the load of bales. Her eyes watered in the sub-zero temperature, and the tears froze on her cheeks. She pulled the scarf up over her mouth and nose and fished out her pocketknife. As Horace inched slowly in a large circle, she cut the twine and threw down flakes of hay, her fingers quickly growing numb. The cows crowded the truck, grabbing a few bites from each bunch, and then running ahead to catch the first of the next offering. Sam laughed. "You're as greedy as some people I know."

When the hay was all distributed, Horace circled again, and she dribbled out cake pellets from a sack. "Your dessert, ladies." Again, the Herefords chased the truck to grab the first nuggets.

Sam got back in the cab, pounding her gloved fists together to speed up her circulation. Horace turned up the heater. "Good job, little gal."

She snickered. "It never ceases to amaze me how cows

stumble over each other to get to the food first."

"Yeah, me too, and I've been doin' this a long time."

Back at the house, Sam opened the truck door. "I want to check my messages. Do you want some lunch before we go over and feed your cows?"

"Sure. It's been a while since breakfast, and I've worked purty hard this mornin'." He patted his stomach and shot her a grin.

"All right then, c'mon in." She hurried inside, glancing at the message machine as she kicked off her overboots and peeled down the coveralls. Sure enough, the light was blinking.

She nearly stumbled over the coveralls as she dashed for the phone. The message was from Teresa. "I know you're probably out feeding. Call me when you get in."

Fingers shaking, she punched in her friend's number.

"Hey, Sam. Everything go okay with feeding?"

"Yeah, yeah, everything's fine. Horace is here and helped me. Did you find anything out about Brad?" She grimaced. Her tone was a bit on the impatient side.

"Well, a little. I found his folks' number but wasn't able to get a hold of them last night. Finally, this morning, his dad answered. He wasn't too forthcoming at first, not knowing me, of course. But apparently Brad had told them about you, and they probably also watched his documentary, so…"

Sam fidgeted with the phone cord. "Yeah? And?"

Teresa inhaled audibly. "Well, when I said I was your friend, he told me that Brad is in a coma. They're not sure the extent of his injuries, but the doctors are watching him for brain swelling and so forth."

"Oh man." Sam's knees would no longer hold her, and she slid down the wall to the floor.

"I'm sorry, my dear. I know this is hard for you, being stuck out there in the snow and all." Teresa's voice lowered to a comforting tone. "I'll come out if you need some company."

Sam gulped. "Um… yeah. No. Horace is here, and we need to go feed his cows now." The weight on her chest crushed her lungs, and she heaved short, shallow pants. "I need to get into Billings... I need to see him... Oh-man-oh-man, what can I do? What's happening?"

Horace had come in during the conversation and knelt beside her. His big hand patted her arm. Gently, taking the receiver from her trembling hand, he spoke to Teresa. "I'm here with her. I'll make sure she's all right." He hung up and cradled her shoulders with one arm. His normally gruff voice softened. "It's okay, little gal, it's okay. C'mon, let's sit and make a plan."

As if her body was a limp piece of rope, he lifted her to her feet and led her to a chair at the table. He stuck the coffee carafe in the microwave to reheat and then put the steaming cup in her icy hands. Her whole body was a block of ice—she could barely breathe, she couldn't think, she couldn't cry. She focused on her neighbor. "I need to go."

"Yes, you do. I'll drive you in."

"But your cows... we have to feed them first... And tomorrow... I have to be back to feed here..." Her words came in starts and stutters.

"Don't worry about all that. I'll call Jim Gardiner—he's got a ranch hand, and I'm sure they can handle both our chores for a couple of days."

Sam stood on trembly legs. "Gotta go change." She stopped halfway to the door. "I can't ask you to do this, Horace." He'd already done so much. "I can drive myself in. I'm fine. Seriously."

The older man lowered his brows to half-mast. "No arguments now. Go get changed. I'm taking you to Billings. Besides, I want to see him too."

She blinked against the familiar prickling behind her eyelids and walked into her bedroom. Grabbing a clean pair of jeans, a turtleneck, and sweater, she shrugged into them as quickly as she could and strode back into the kitchen with her purse. Horace already had his coat on and was pulling on his overshoes.

"Oh." She stopped short. "I'm sorry. I forgot I was going to give you some lunch."

"No, no, I'm fine." He fished a napkin-wrapped cookie from his pocket. "Stole a couple of these. That'll hold me a while." He winked at her but then frowned. "What about you? You worked pretty hard this morning. You probably need a little fuel."

Her stomach roiled. "No. I'm not hungry. Let's just get going."

The hour and a half drive to Billings seemed interminable. Had someone come along and stretched the road farther? Suddenly the thought of Brad not being in her life froze Sam's insides like one of the chunks of ice she chopped out of the stock tank each morning. Would it be his steady friendship she missed? *Or do I love him?* She looked down at her hands, clenched into tight fists on a knee that bounced on its own volition.

Horace glanced over at her periodically with a smile or a word of distraction, but she turned away from him. She appreciated what he tried to do but couldn't respond to him. She stared out the window at the white, undulating prairie. Stalks of maize-colored grasses poked their heads through the snow where the wind had swept it away into drifts against the pewter sagebrush.

Her last conversation with Brad... he'd been upset with her and hung up abruptly. Because she called him a friend? The blinding snowstorm... icy roads... She pictured the horse trailer swaying and sliding and pulling Brad's truck into the ditch. He must have hit his head. Wasn't he belted in? Didn't the airbag inflate? A coma. How did Toby avoid injury? *Oh my, I need to call the vet and find out about the horse.*

She bit her lip to keep from screaming. Only Horace's presence kept her quiet. Thoughts, images, worries all balled into a heavy, dark cloud around her.

***

As they entered the hospital, Sam paused a moment to

steady her shaking legs. A sharp antiseptic smell mingled with the perfumes of scented candles for sale in the gift shop right inside the door. She exhaled and stepped up to the information desk, asking for Brad Ashton.

"He's in ICU. Are you family?" The receptionist peered at her over half-glasses.

"No. I'm his g… a close friend."

"I'm sorry, but only family is allowed to visit and only for a few minutes at a time."

Her shoulders slumped. "Oh no. We've driven all the way from Ingomar…"

The woman's eyes crinkled in apparent sympathy. "I'm sorry, ma'am. You have to understand. It's hospital policy."

As Horace cleared his throat loudly behind Sam, the receptionist clicked a few keys on her computer. "His family is in the waiting room right outside ICU, second floor. You can go and talk with them."

With a hard swallow, she managed a reply. "Okay, th-thank you." She turned to Horace for support. He took her arm and escorted her to the elevator. As the car swooped upward, she tamped down her stomach butterflies. Would the family blame her?

They got out on level two and followed the signs. ICU was closed off with metal double doors, but Horace steered her into the open waiting room across the hall. Half a dozen people sat in easy chairs, a couple of men thumbing mindlessly through magazines, some women looking at cell phones despite signs to the contrary, and others pacing.

Sam looked around the room, trying to figure out who might be Brad's family. Her perusal stopped on an older gentleman with thick graying dark hair, a wayward lock falling over his forehead.

"Mr. Ashton?"

"Yes?" He pushed the hair back with his fingers as his gaze met hers.

"I…I'm Samantha Moser, a friend—"

"Oh yes. Sam!" The elder Ashton stood, his hand outstretched. His rumpled, checked shirt and jeans looked like they'd been slept in. "Brad has talked about you."

She blinked. "He has?"

An attractive brunette with streaks of gray, dressed in a shapeless blue sweater, rose to stand beside him. "Yes, he certainly has. And of course, we've seen his documentary about you." The woman stepped forward and gave her a hug. "I'm sorry. I'm Dee Ashton, Brad's mom." She gestured to a younger version of herself, with dark hair, wearing neat khaki slacks and a rust sweatshirt. "And this is his sister, Melissa."

They know me? He talked about me? He has a sister? Her head swam, and she gulped and stammered, "H-hello, it's nice to meet you. I... I'm so sorry... Do you know how... how he is?"

Mrs. Ashton blinked moist eyes. "He's still in a coma, and the doctors want him to stay that way while they watch for brain swelling."

Her husband took her hand. "So far, so good. They only let two of us in to see him about five minutes at a time. It's a waiting game."

"Oh dear. I sure was hoping to be able to see him. We just drove two hours... Oh!" She stopped and gestured to Horace. "I'm sorry, this is my neighbor, Horace Jones. He's been helping me feed the cattle, and he drove me in. He knows Brad too."

They shook hands all around. Horace held his hat in his hands. "I'm sure sorry about your son... ah, and brother. He's a good guy, did Sam here a world of good with that documentary. We owe him a lot of thanks."

Ashton nodded. "Yes, that's the kind of kid he is... He finds the treasure in amongst the horse manure."

Sam covered her mouth with her hand. Mrs. Ashton dabbed at her eyes with a tissue.

Melissa put her hand on Sam's arm, her eyes bright. "Listen, they say nobody but family can go in to ICU, but if you'll come with me, I think maybe we can sneak in for a minute."

"Really?" Her breath came in short spurts. "I would... like to... see him."

"Okay, let's go." Brad's sister guided her across the hall and opened the formidable-looking doors where they were greeted with even stronger medicinal smells and the sounds of multiple machines beeping, keening and whooshing.

Sam's step faltered as they approached Brad. His head was swathed in white bandages, his arm and one leg plastered in casts, and tubes and wires ran from his arms to various drip bags and blinking machines surrounding his bed. Weakness washed through her and her knees went spongy. *No. Get a grip. You're not going to faint!* She stepped forward and took Brad's hand.

"Brad, it's me, Sam. I don't know if you can hear me, but I'm here. Your family is here. Horace is here. I'm pray-praying for you." A sob threatened to rise in her esophagus, and she swallowed it back. "Please, wake up. Please get better. I'm so sorry this happened. It's my fault!" She choked and squeezed his hand tightly. "Please..."

A nurse strode to the bed. "Who are you? You didn't check in. I'm afraid you'll have to leave now."

Melissa wiped tears from her cheeks with the back of her hand and put an arm around Sam. "C'mon, hon. It's okay."

They stumbled from the room and embraced in the hallway, cheek to cheek, their tears mingling.

Back in the waiting room, Sam stepped to Horace's chair. "I'm sorry you weren't able to see him."

He rose. "That's okay, little gal. Are you doing all right?"

She nodded, the surreal image of Brad—so helpless, so hurt—stamped on her brain. "I think... I don't think they'll let me back in there again, so..." She shrugged. "I s'pose we'd better go on home."

Her neighbor patted her arm. "That's up to you. If you want to stay, I'll make sure your horses and the cows will be taken care of. Don't worry about that."

"I know you would. Thanks." She surveyed the sorrowful

people in the room. "But I can't..."

Brad's family gathered around her. "Thank you for coming. It's so nice to finally meet you." Mrs. Ashton brushed her cheek against Sam's.

"We will keep you updated." His dad pushed the signature Ashton lock from his forehead.

Melissa hugged her tightly again. "Come back anytime. I'll sneak you in again, if you want."

CHAPTER ELEVEN

The trip home was another silent, endless drive. The memory of beeps and thumps and groans in the ICU kept time with the rhythm of the truck tires. Sam tucked her hands under her thighs to try to warm them and keep them from shaking. Brad's bruised and swollen face, the stark white bandages, the tubes—everything she'd seen and heard, along with their last conversation and his ominous "talk" message replayed like her own hellish version of *Groundhog Day*. She curled her lip in an ironic half-smile.

Horace downshifted and slowed as he turned off I-94 onto Ingomar Road. "Let's stop in at the Jersey Lilly. I'll buy you supper."

At first, Sam's stomach lurched. "I don't know if I could eat anything." But as they drove along a few more miles, the queasiness settled into a growl.

Horace grinned. "Sounds like someone has a different idea."

She huffed a snort. "Yeah. Maybe I am a little hungry. I guess we didn't get lunch, did we? I'm sorry. I promised you."

"Pfft! No, you are not to be apologizin' for that. Besides, I had a very tasty cardboard snack from the vending machine."

Sam couldn't help but snicker. "I can imagine that would certainly do it for you. Sure, let's stop and get something to eat."

Over juicy burgers and crispy fries, Sam was able to share some of her fears with her neighbor. "It was my fault he was even on this trip. If I hadn't acted so impulsively rescuing that horse... If only I had called him sooner and told him to hold

90

off… If it hadn't stormed…" She choked on a bite of fry.

"Hey, hey, hey." Horace put a large, calloused hand over hers. "You can't be beatin' yourself up with those 'what-ifs.' That's a big, heavy load to carry, and it ain't yours. It is *not* your fault Brad was on the trip—he volunteered. His reaction to your 'friend' comment was a heat of the moment thing that you two will resolve—soon—I know it. And, the storm is certainly not *your* doing."

Sam stared down at her plate, eyes misting over. She bit her lip and then lifted her gaze.

He scrubbed a hand over his iron-gray crewcut. "So what if you're not perfect. None of us are."

Sam smiled through the mist. "Thanks, Horace. You're right. You're absolutely right." *Such a wise man, so like Grampa Neil. I need to stop feeling sorry for myself.*

She pushed her plate aside. "Let's go home. I need to see my ponies."

"Attagirl." The older man threw down some bills on the table and waved at the proprietor. "Thanks, Billy. See you soon."

Back in the barn, Sam breathed in the familiar, soothing aromas of hay, horse sweat, and manure. Her horses nickered as she approached, gave them treats, and neck scratches. Burying her face in Sugar's mane, she absorbed the mare's strength, allowing the horse and barn scents to wash away the sterile, antiseptic experience of the day.

***

The next morning, Sam refilled her coffee cup, and with heart thumping, punched in the number for the Wyoming vet.

"Parmley Veterinarian Clinic, may I help you?" A pleasant alto voice greeted her.

Sam identified herself and explained the purpose of her call. "How is Toby? Was he hurt?"

"Oh yes, Ms. Moser. And Toby. We've been expecting your call. My husband… Dr. Parmley… is on his rounds right now, checking on our patients. Let me get your number and have him call you when he comes in."

"You can't tell me how my horse is?" Sam's voice quavered. *Oh dear, is it worse than I was led to believe?*

"Oh, yes, well, I'd rather he talk to you, since he's the doc. But Toby is doing pretty well, as well as can be expected after such a bad crash."

Sam hung up, no more enlightened than before. She called Melissa Ashton's number. Nothing had changed with Brad. He was still in the coma. Still in ICU. Her insides clenched. *Will he get better?*

She washed up her dishes from the night before and breakfast, went into her room, picked up clothes, and made the bed. The idea of dusting made a brief appearance, but she shrugged it off and stared out the window.

The sun shone brightly again, and the temperature had climbed to above freezing. Water dripped from icicles that hung from the eaves. If the weather continued in this vein, all evidence of the freakish, early snowstorm would be gone in a couple of days. As Grandpa Neil used to say, "If you don't like the weather in Montana, wait five minutes." Her mouth twitched upward, remembering. Her grandparents and great-grandparents had to put up with the fickle whims of mother nature all their lives.

"If they could do it, so can I." With a resolute breath, she forced her shoulders down an inch or two. She itched to get out and take care of her horses, but without cell service, the expected vet's call tethered her to the landline. *Darn.* Oh well, Horace would be there soon to help feed.

She paced to the living room, picked up her book, and tossed it down again. Then to the kitchen to stare at the phone. She grabbed the dishcloth and wiped down the counters and table once again, scrubbing at a stubborn sticky spot.

When the phone rang, she jumped. "This is Sam," she panted into the receiver.

"Dr. Parmley here."

"Oh, good. I'm so glad you called back. Sorry I didn't call you sooner, but Brad—Mr. Ashton, the driver—was badly injured and in a coma, and I was in Billings yesterday to see him." She stopped. *I'm babbling as bad as Electra.* "Anyway, I wanted to find out how Toby is and how I can arrange to get him home."

"I understand. The highway patrol told me a little about the situation, and I'm sorry about Mr. Ashton. I hope he gets better soon." The vet's voice was pleasant. "Yes, Toby. Beautiful gelding, a good horse, I think. He escaped serious injury, thankfully. Has quite a few contusions and abrasions that I've been treating, so he's a bit sore."

Sam let out an audible sigh. Relief lifted the worry weight from her shoulders.

"But… as sometimes happens with a serious accident such as this, Toby was traumatized, and he's quite skittish."

Her heart tumbled into her stomach. "Oh no!"

"I'm sure, with lots of TLC, he'll be fine. Right now, I have him in a separate pen, and I'm keeping a close eye on him."

"Oh my." Sam paced the length of the phone cord and back, twirling it around her wrist. "What…? I'm not sure what to do. I have a horse trailer, but will have to wait until the snow melts and roads clear off to come get him."

"Of course. You don't want a repeat of what happened the other day. Don't worry about it. I'm taking good care of him. Get here when you can."

Sam bit her lip. But the cost of treating and boarding the horse at the clinic… And if he was skittish and traumatized, how would she deal with that?

"Ms. Moser?" The doctor broke the growing silence. "Toby will be fine. You take care of yourself and let me know when you are able to make the trip."

"O-okay. I will. The snow is already starting to melt, so I think it'll only be a couple of days or so."

Dr. Parmley gave her the clinic's address and directions, and they clicked off.

Horace's big diesel roared up. Shrugging on her winter coat and coveralls, she went out to meet him.

"Mornin'." He touched fingers to his hat brim. "Doin' better this morning?"

She blew out a puff of air. "I dunno, Horace. I thought I was…" As they loaded hay bales into his pickup bed, she filled him in on Brad's unchanged condition and the new complications with Toby.

He arranged the bales she threw down from the loft. "Well, you know I'd be happy to drive down and get your horse—"

"Oh no-no! I could never let—"

"Or," he grinned up at her, "at least ride with you when you go."

Sam gave him a half-hearted smile. "Thanks, Horace, I appreciate that. You do too much for me already. But…" she added when he raised his hand, palm facing out, "I'll think on it."

The following day, after feeding the cows in the growing mud, Sam drove to Billings. Her decisions and dilemmas chased each other through her mind like kittens in a barn. Brad. Still in a coma. Would he die? Would he live and be brain-damaged? Would they have a future? Toby. She needed to get him home before the vet bill exceeded her yearly lease payment. And if he was so emotionally injured, how would she deal with him, and her other horses? The drive, pulling a horse trailer on secondary roads. She wasn't experienced, and what if it snowed again?

Her knuckles turned white on the steering wheel, and her neck screamed at her from tension. She rolled her shoulders, trying to relax, and attempted to clear her mind by scanning the biscuit-colored rolling hills, snow still nestling in the higher, north-facing drainages.

"It'll be all right; it'll be all right." She repeated the mantra, as if to convince herself it was true.

***

Teresa phoned while Sam was en route to the hospital. She

answered, clicking on the speaker.

"Just wanted to check on you, see how you're doing." Her calm, concerned voice was almost Sam's undoing.

She swallowed. "Not great." She filled in her friend on Brad's unchanged condition and the situation with Toby. "I'm torn. I really need to get down to Buffalo, Wyoming to get my horse. But I also want to be here for Brad and his family if… when he wakes up."

"I can understand that. I would be feeling the same way." Teresa rustled papers in the background. "Listen, call me when you head home from Billings. Let's get together tonight and talk it out."

"Oh, Teresa, thank you. Yes, let's do that. I'll give you a call." Her shoulders relaxed a little, and she shook out her cramped fingers.

At the hospital, she went directly to the waiting room. This time, Melissa sat alone in the room, hunched over her cell phone. She looked up and smiled when she saw Sam. "Hi. I'm glad you're here." The two hugged. "Sit down. The folks took a break and are out running errands. It's exhausting, just sitting here and waiting, wondering, hoping."

"I know, and I'm sorry you're having to go through this." Her heart contracted. "Wish I could be here more to give you support."

"No, there's no need for you to sit here twiddling your thumbs, feeling helpless. I know you have a ranch to run. And as long as he's in this coma…" Her voice trailed off, and she squeezed her eyes shut.

Sam put a hand on the young woman's arm. "I do feel helpless, and I can't imagine how you're coping. No change?"

"Not really. They actually want him to stay in the coma to keep the swelling down. That apparently decreases the likelihood of brain damage." Melissa bit her lip, eyes glistening. She stood abruptly and went to the door, looking up and down the hall. "Come with me. Let's go see him."

They walked into ICU past the nurses' station, the beeps

and smells enveloping Sam's senses until she thought she might faint. Brad lay on the bed, still swathed in bandages, looking like he hadn't moved since she was there last. His face was mottled blue and black, turning to sickly yellow as the bruises began to fade.

"Oh dear." She took his hand gently. "Brad, it's Sam. Please come back. I want to see you laugh again. I miss you. I need you in my life." Her voice choked. "Dear Lord, please heal Brad."

She squeezed his hand, willing her strength and life force into him, wishing for that "magic wand" to make things all right again.

This time, they stayed for a few minutes and made their way out without interference. "Thank you, Melissa. It means a lot to be able to see him, even if he doesn't know I'm here."

"The nurses say people in comas often are aware of who is there and talking to them, and that's an important part of healing. So that's why we hang out here all day and go in as often as we are allowed, to talk to him and tell him we love him." The young woman's haggard face crumpled.

She put her arms around her, patting Melissa's back as she sobbed into Sam's shoulder. Her eyes stung and her chest cavity ached. She gritted her teeth and blinked rapidly, trying not to join her.

A dark heaviness rode on her neck as she drove home, unable to think of anything but Brad's discolored face against the white gauze. She finally shook it off long enough to call Teresa and let her know she was getting closer to home.

"You want to meet at the Jersey Lilly?"

"Um, yeah, but I'd better go home and do chores first."

"Okay, then let me bring something for supper, and I'll come out to your place."

When Sam drove in, the horses kicked up their heels in the pasture next to the barn, as if they were expecting her. She threw them a few flakes of hay and put out a small bucketful of oats. Her breath puffed white in the cold air. After making sure the barn door was open so they could go inside if they wanted to, she trudged to the house.

Teresa's SUV roared up the incline, and she got out, carrying a large, flat cardboard box. "Pizza delivery," she hollered. "Hope you like sausage and mushroom."

"Sounds good to me. Thank you. I wasn't sure what I had on hand to cook." She took a grocery bag from her friend, and they climbed the steps to the porch and into the kitchen.

Over pizza and salad, Sam related what she'd seen at the hospital. "Oh, Teresa, it just seems hopeless. I don't know if he's going to die. I don't know if he'll live but have brain damage. I care... but I'm not family. I don't know what to do!"

Teresa squeezed her arm. "I'm sure. All we can do is hope and pray."

Sam hiccupped. "I haven't been very good about praying. I try, but I don't know what to say, and I don't know if it's working."

"It does. It actually does. Sometimes it takes a while to get an answer, but don't give up."

They sat, not speaking, for a few moments. Sam stared at the remnants of the pizza, now congealing in the box, and offered up a silent prayer—*healing, for Brad... and for Toby.*

Finally, she rose to clean off the table. "Want some coffee? I have decaf."

"Sure." Teresa grabbed the roll of plastic wrap from a drawer and helped put the leftovers in the fridge.

When the coffee was brewed, Sam poured them both a cup and put a plate of chocolate chip cookies on the table.

"I have an idea. Let's you and I take a road trip to Wyoming and get your horse." Teresa's face shone with a hopeful glow.

Sam raised her brows. "Really? Horace made the same offer, but—"

"No, Horace can oversee your chores. This needs to be just you and me, a girls' adventure."

"Like Thelma and Louise?"

Teresa giggled. "Yeah. But without the cliff."

"Okay." Sam gave her a thumbs-up. "I'm game. Day after tomorrow?"

CHAPTER TWELVE

The morning sun lit up the sky in what felt like a balmy thirty-five degrees when Sam and Teresa hitched up the horse trailer. With Horace's blessing and promise to "take care of things," they hit the road about 8:00.

"Okay, we have cheese sticks and mixed nuts and chips and Cokes to keep us fortified." Teresa indicated the blue insulated bag she'd stowed behind the seats. "And chocolate."

Sam grinned. "It's only about a four-hour drive, so that should keep us from starving until we get there."

Her friend bounced on the seat, looking through a collection of CDs. "Well, you never know, in this country."

"That's for sure." Sam nodded. They'd both thrown in coveralls, overboots, and cold-weather gear. That's simply what a person did in Montana, especially in the winter.

"All right, we're off!" Teresa put in a Garth Brooks CD and turned up the volume. "Let's rock and roll." The women sang along at the top of their lungs, pumped their fists, and laughed at each other.

Thankful the roads were clear, Sam drove conservatively, getting used to the trailer and how it reacted to corners and going up and down hills.

"You're doing well." Teresa popped the CD out when it finished. "Want more music or do you feel like talking?"

Sam groaned. "I don't want to think about... everything, but it all keeps flooding my mind. I'm really scared."

"Yeah, it's the not-knowing that weighs the heaviest."

"That's for sure. Waiting is a killer. I feel so bad for Brad's family. They're in that little family room all day, every day. I should be there with them, but I'm not allowed in to see him, so there's not a lot I can do." She told Teresa how Melissa had sneaked her in a couple of times. "Seeing him lying there so still..." Dread pooled in her belly.

"That has to be hard. But you're right, you can't be sitting there all day. It's best you get on with the things you have to do on the ranch, and this trip, getting your new horse."

"You know, I feel like I'm not dealing with things very well. All this 'stuff' that's been coming my way, and I'm just a hot mess. Only last year I was standing up to Murdoch and his New York crew. I used to be strong, and now... I can't seem to handle a hangnail without dissolving into tears." Sam gave a rueful laugh. "That's no way to 'cowgirl up.' I'm afraid my great-grandma Nettie—or Grandma Anna—wouldn't be very proud of me right now."

"Oh nonsense!" Teresa faced Sam. "They would be very proud of you. Listen. You are a strong woman. But you're young, what are you—twenty-four?—and you're trying to do something that would overwhelm the most experienced and mature person. Besides, Great-Grandma Nettie had Jake right there by her side. And your grandma Anna had your grampa Neil to lean on in her hard times."

Sam shrugged. "Yeah, but..."

"Yeah, but, nothin'. I admire you so much for all you've done already, running a ranch by yourself, rescuing horses, and the kids you've worked with... Good heavens, girl, you've done more in two years than many people do in a lifetime!"

"I dunno, it feels like everything I've tried to do lately has been a big failure. I can't buy the ranch, so I can't expand what I started at Clyde's. And then, Garrett and Del. That just doesn't seem to be working at all. I feel so bad that he was injured, right as he seemed to be warming up to Trixi."

"Hey, that is *not* a failure. You told me about Del's call and maybe working with the college and these vets." Teresa raised her eyebrows. "That's no failure, it's *huge*!"

"Yeah, it does give me hope." Sam allowed herself a smile.

"And that reminds me, I need to call the instructor and set up an appointment. I almost forgot, with everything else going on."

Teresa leaned over and cuffed her playfully on the arm. "That's exciting. It could lead to big things. I. Am. Proud. Of. You. Okay?"

"Thank you. You're a good friend, and I'm glad I met you. You and Horace have both supported me so much. You're like family."

"Aw shucks. Girlfriends are the sisters you choose. And I can't think of anyone else I'd rather be with on a road trip." The other woman giggled. "How about a Coke and some chips?"

"Sounds good. I'll be ready for lunch when we get to Buffalo."

It was just past noon when they pulled into town at the foothills of the Bighorn Mountains, greeted by a huge mural on the side of a tall brick building, depicting elk, antelope, and cattle. It read: "Buffalo Wyoming. A Creek Runs Through It." Sam smirked. A play on the famous line about Montana: "A River Runs Through It." She found a place to park the truck and trailer. The women walked a few blocks to the Breadboard Café where they joined a crowd of locals ordering sandwiches, salads, and soups. While waiting for their order, Sam called Dr. Parmley to let him know they'd arrived.

"Glad to hear the roads were good." The vet gave them directions to his clinic. "I'll be looking for you within the hour then."

After refueling themselves and the truck, Sam drove to Parmley's, a squatty office building, with a medium-sized barn and corrals, surrounded by cottonwood trees and pasture. She backed the trailer up to a chute, where she assumed they'd be loading. "Whew. I did it on the first try." Teresa gave her the thumbs up.

As they got out of the truck, an older man wearing a John

Deere cap approached, a big grin under a white mustache. "Howdy there. I'm Dr. Parmley." He stuck out a hand.

Sam shook it and introduced herself and Teresa. "So, how is Toby doing? How bad are his injuries? Has he calmed down any?" she blurted.

He chuckled, his weathered face creasing. "Well, he's doing pretty good, considering. His injuries are minor, thankfully. A few cuts you'll need to continue to treat, and he may have a knee sprain, but that seems to be getting better." He paused. "But it's going to take a little longer to heal the trauma."

Her heart skipped a beat. *Oh dear.* "What... uh...?"

"C'mon out. I'll let you see him." The vet nodded toward the corrals.

The two women followed him to a round pen, where a bay gelding paced, bobbing his head and snorting. A gasp caught in her throat. The horse was visibly underweight and numerous scratches marred his nut-brown coat. He tossed his head and ran to the opposite side of the corral, his black mane and tail flowing.

Dr. Parmley stuck a booted foot onto the bottom rail. "As you can see, he's pretty skittish. I've had a devil of time treating his wounds, and he raised holy heck in the stall, so I had to let him outside." He turned to Sam. "I'm guessing, but it seems like he may have been mistreated before he was even in the accident."

She took a ragged breath, aching for the horse. "Yes. I rescued him from a kill pen in Arizona. He was scheduled to be shipped to Mexico."

"Ahh. That explains the ribs showing."

Teresa frowned. "But he wasn't there that long, was he, Sam?"

She shrugged. "I'm not sure how long. Long enough to show signs of neglect. Oh dear, poor Toby." She climbed to the top of the corral. "Do you have a few cake pellets? I'm going to see if I can get him to come to me."

Dr. Parmley stepped to the barn and came back, rattling a

bucket. The bay stopped his pacing and raised his head toward the sound. Sam took a handful, entered, and crept toward Toby, holding out her hand with the treat. The horse took a couple of tentative steps closer, but then switched direction and galloped away.

"I don't know how we're going to get him loaded." Sam stood quiet in the middle of the corral, still holding out her hand. "C'mon, Toby. You're okay now, you're going to be safe." She spoke barely above a whisper. "C'mon, boy, come home with me."

The bay continued his frantic circling around the fence, limping slightly. She rotated with him, letting him run. Then as he slowed, she took a bandana from her jacket pocket and waved it in front of him, forcing him to switch direction and run the other way. Each time he slowed his pace, she repeated the action. Time and time again, Toby ran one way, then turned and cantered the other. Back and forth, round and round.

"He oughta be gettin' tired pretty soon," Doc commented from the fence behind Sam.

She had no idea how long they'd been out here doing this and even if this form of "lunging" would work. It had been a couple of years since she'd seen or done any training.

Finally, she sensed Toby was slowing. He stopped, snorting, and watched her. She turned her back on him and walked toward Teresa and the vet, stopping a few feet in front of the fence. Sam stood like a statue and waited. After long minutes, she saw Teresa's eyes widen and Doc's face wrinkle in a smile.

She felt a presence at her shoulder but continued to wait. Then Toby moved his muzzle down the length of her arm. He fluttered his nostrils as she opened her hand, offering the pellets. He nuzzled her palm, gently picking up the treat. Sam swiveled to face him and ran her other hand up his face and along his neck. His muscles quivered, and he looked ready to take off at any moment.

"Good boy, my Toby, good boy," she murmured, caressing his head and running her fingers through his mane. "We're going to make a good team, aren't we, boy?"

As Sam continued to massage the gelding's neck and withers, Dr. Parmley came up beside her. "You got him calmed down nicely. Good job." He handed her a lead rope. "We might want to consider giving him a mild tranquilizer though."

She hooked the lead to Toby's halter. "I'd prefer not to do that, if possible. Let's see how this goes." She led him around the corral several times, all the while speaking in soothing tones. His muscle quivering calmed, and he followed her, watching, tense, but obedient.

"Well, here goes." Glancing at Doc and Teresa, Sam slowly led Toby into the narrow passageway toward the open trailer. "C'mon, boy, you can do this. I know you can. C'mon now."

Before she could take another step, his eyes rolled white and he threw his head back, jerking the lead out of her hand. His front hooves flailed the air. He got himself turned around in the chute and thundered back out into the corral. Blowing and snorting, he ran frantically around the corral with his head high, tail in the air. His whinnies reverberated with terror.

Sam wrapped her arms around her middle, feeling his panic. "Oh, Toby." Her anguished cry joined his.

Doc and Teresa rushed to her side. "It's okay, Sam." Teresa gave her a one-armed squeeze. "It's nothing you did. He's scared from that accident."

"Yeah. This is a natural reaction. I've seen it before. Horses can have PTSD too." Dr. Parmley's voice was soothing. "Why don't we let him calm down a little, and I'll give him a shot."

Sam gulped air. "I don't want him down in the trailer."

"No, that shouldn't happen. This is mild enough just to calm him so we can get him trailered. He'll be all right."

"Okay." Sam walked toward Toby, again going through the steps of offering him pellets and talking to him calmly until she could grab his rope. Once more, she caressed his face and neck, continuing to soothe him. By this time, Doc had returned with a syringe and before the horse could react, injected him with the tranquilizer.

"Why don't we go on up to the office while this takes effect and do up our paperwork." The vet tied Toby's rope to the corral fence, and they headed to the clinic.

Inside, a slender woman with graying curls stood up from her desk and held out her hand. "Hi, you must be Ms. Moser."

"Call me Sam." She shook the woman's hand and introduced Teresa.

The doctor patted his wife's shoulder. "Do you have the papers ready?"

"Just about. I need to make a couple of copies, and then you can sign off." Mrs. Parmley indicated chairs in a waiting area. "Would you like some coffee or tea?"

"No, thank you, we had lunch when we arrived." Sam sat on an orange plastic chair and looked at her watch. "Oh my word, two o'clock! I had no idea we'd take this long."

Teresa perused the animal posters on the walls. "Yeah, me either. Maybe I will have a cup of coffee, ma'am." She stood. "To go, of course."

"Sure thing. If you'd like to help yourself, the kitchen is just around the corner." Mrs. Parmley gestured toward the hallway. "Sam and I can settle up while you're doing that."

"Might as well get me a cup too, Teresa." Sam took out her checkbook, gulping as she looked at the bill. Oh well. She'd known it would be expensive, but it wasn't quite as bad as she'd feared. She wrote out the check and signed the paperwork.

Doc came from the back. "Here are some oral tranqs you can give him in about two hours so he'll stay calm."

"Thank you, doctor." Sam took the bottle. "I can't begin to tell you how much I appreciate what you've done. It was serendipity that you just happened to come upon the accident."

He waved off her comment. "Yup. It was meant to be, all right. I've grown rather fond of the ol' feller. Hope he's going to be a good horse for you."

"I hope so too. I think I may have my work cut out for me though."

"I'm sure he'll be all right, once he gets to his new home and gets used to you and knows he has a stable life."

"Well. Let's go try this loading business again." Sam held out a hand to Mrs. Parmley. "Nice to meet you. Thank you."

"You too, my dear. You gals take care now, drive carefully."

This time, Toby followed Sam through the narrow chute with only a little coaxing. He faltered for a moment when he took his first step into the trailer, but then went in and settled cautiously. She tied his lead to the stall and made sure he had hay and oats to munch on during the trip, and then went out, closing and latching the door. She leaned against the trailer and let out a relieved breath.

"Whew." Teresa grinned at her. "That went a lot smoother, thank goodness."

"Yes. I should've taken your advice the first time, Dr. Parmley. Sorry. I'm a bit of a greenhorn when it comes to this sort of thing. You know what you're doing. I apologize."

The vet waved a hand in the air. "Naw. Don't worry about it. I had hopes too that he'd calmed down enough we wouldn't need to medicate him."

They all shook hands, and the women climbed into the pickup. "Let me know how he does, would you?" Doc patted the window frame. "Safe travels now." He waved as they drove off.

Teresa let out a whoop. "And, we're off, like a herd of turtles."

Sam ground gears as she shifted. "Man. We are running so late. I was not thinking when I planned this. We should've left earlier this morning; we shouldn't have stopped for a sit-down lunch; we should've—"

"Stop! Shoulda, woulda, coulda. It does no good to second-guess yourself. We're fine. We'll get home about 6:30, and that last hour or so driving in the dark, you'll be in familiar territory."

"Yeah, you're right. We'll be home in time for supper." Sam forced herself to switch mental gears. "So, what's up with whatshisname? You haven't mentioned him in a while."

"Allen? Yeah. He lives so far away, we don't get to see each other very often. I don't know if these long-distance relationships can work. We do talk on the phone quite a bit though."

"Well, that's something. You do like him, right?"

"I do. I guess we'll just have to let things progress naturally and see what happens." She looked at Sam. "Kind of like you and Brad."

"Yeah. I haven't seen him for a couple of months. He travels—traveled—so much, it's like a long-distance thing too. And I don't even know... if he wakes up... if he's okay... if we'll still have a relationship. There *is* that 'friend' issue left looming." Confusion swirled inside her heart. "Oh, Teresa, what if he doesn't get better? What if those are the last words between us?"

The other woman patted Sam's arm. "I know, sweetie, it's a huge worry for you, and I know you feel guilty. But it was simply a misunderstanding. Surely, Brad knows you care about him as more than just friends."

"I don't know if he does. We've taken things really slow and have only kissed a couple of times. So maybe he doesn't know. Maybe I don't know... for sure."

"Well, we can't be worrying about things that haven't happened yet. You know, the Bible is full of verses about 'do not worry' and 'do not be afraid.' We just have to trust and believe that Brad is going to be all right, and that your relationship will pick up where you left off last time you saw him."

She blinked away the sting in her eyes. "Thank you. I'm trying to be optimistic. Hey, why don't you find that George Strait CD and let's have a little respite from this 'worry.'"

They drove through Sheridan, Wyoming and about an hour later, through the tiny town of Decker, Montana, where Sam pulled over to check on Toby. He stood calmly in the trailer, as if dozing. "So far, so good." She jumped back into the pickup, and they continued on through Colstrip.

Pulling into a truck stop to stretch and top off the gas tank, s-he checked on the gelding who still seemed calm. "Well, it's been about two hours since we left, but I don't want to overmedicate him. He seems good right now."

Teresa peered through the trailer window. "Yeah, I agree. We can always stop later if we need to. It's only an hour and a half, two at most, till we get home."

Sam drove back onto the highway. "Okay, how about some Toby Keith tunes."

"Comin' right up. Want some chocolate?"

"You bet. And a Coke. Between all that, I should be able to stay awake." She laughed.

Dusk settled over the hills like a blue blanket, and Sam switched on the headlights. They sang along with the CD, shutting out all the worries of the world.

Sam tapped her fingers on the steering wheel in time to the music. Then a loud thump broke through and the wheel twisted. "Yikes!" She grabbed it hard with both hands, wrestling the pickup as the trailer fishtailed and they veered toward the barrow pit. Pressing the brakes, she struggled to keep the vehicle on the road.

Teresa screamed.

CHAPTER THIRTEEN

Darkness closed in. The beam from her headlights veered from side to side. Sam locked her fingers onto the steering wheel. Her arms and shoulders tightened as she fought the overwhelming pull toward the ditch. Her foot automatically pushed harder on the brakes.

Gradually the pickup and trailer slowed. The bizarre road dance diminished. Sam guided the vehicle to a stop on the shoulder. For a long moment she sat, panting, her heart pounding, sweat pooled in her armpits. In slow motion, she turned her head to Teresa whose face was ghost-white in the lights from the dashboard. "You okay?"

Her friend gulped. "Ohboy-ohboy-ohboy!" Her voice squeaked. "Yeah. I'm fine. Are you?"

Sam nodded. She pried her frozen fingers from the wheel. "I think we blew a tire." She opened her door and climbed out on shaky legs. Walking around the pickup, she located the culprit, on the right front. She checked her cell phone. No service.

Teresa stepped out with a flashlight and stared at the shredded mess. "Sheesh, girl, that was some fine driving." She gave the trailer a once-over. "Otherwise, we'd all be upside down in the ditch. Hope you have a spare."

"Yes, I do, thank goodness." Just then a raindrop hit her face. And another. "Oh no. Not what we need right now." She hurried to the pickup bed to retrieve her tools and the spare.

Thumps and squeals came from the trailer, and it rocked as Toby suddenly fought his confinement. Sam groaned. "Crap!" She swiveled her head from the tire to the trailer. "I should've given him that tranq back there. Darn it!" Jumping into the bed, she threw down the tire and handed Teresa the jack and lug wrench. "Sorry, but could you maybe get started on the tire? I've got to see if I can get Toby calmed down."

"Uh... sure." Teresa grabbed the tools and bent beside the truck.

Stopping by the trailer window, Sam spoke in soothing tones to the thrashing horse. He jerked his head up and down and kicked at the walls. She opened the back door and stepped into the empty stall next to him, thankful for the high dividing wall between them.

"Good boy, Toby, c'mon. It's okay now, it's okay," she murmured as she stroked his neck and then massaged his back. He snorted and blew and twitched, but finally stopped kicking and trying to get away. She smoothed her hand over his shivering muscles and continued to talk to him.

Reaching into her pocket, she took out the bottle of pills Dr. Parmley had given her. "Now, how am I going to get you to take these? Huh, Toby? Are you going to be a good boy and take your medicine?" She felt in her other pocket where she found a handful of cake pellets left from earlier. Mixing the pills in with the pellets, Sam held out her palm. "Here, sweetie, have a treat. Mmm. Good stuff. C'mon, boy, c'mon."

Toby sniffed at her hand but turned his head away. With a sigh, she stroked him with her other hand and spoke calmly, continuing to offer the pellets and pills. He shook his head and blew.

Sam clenched her fists, trying to keep from screaming in frustration. *Come ON, Toby!* She heard raindrops on the metal roof and a curse from Teresa. "Oh, dear Lord, we need your help so bad right now." She forced even breathing and continued to stroke and massage the horse.

Gradually the twitching and quivering calmed. Sam kept on petting him, her other palm open. Toby moved his head closer. He sniffed. Then he opened his soft lips and took one pellet, again turning his head away while he crunched. "Good boy,

Toby. Here's some more. Take another one." She hardly dared move as he took another and then a third. Finally, he scooped up the rest of her offering all in one mouthful.

When she was sure he had swallowed everything, she let the air out. "Oh, you are *such* a good boy." She stroked his face and scratched his neck. "Okay, I'm going to make sure you have more oats to munch on, and then I'm going to help Teresa get that tire changed so we can get you home."

Sam stepped out of the trailer into a light drizzle. Teresa grunted and blew out deep breaths at the front of the pickup.

She looked up as Sam approached. "I can't get any of these lug nuts to budge. They use those dad-gummed air wrenches at the tire shop and the average gal can't even change her own tire anymore!" She threw the wrench on the pavement.

"Well, isn't that just a steaming pile of horse apples!" Sam picked up the wrench and tried, but nothing moved. "I've got some WD-40 in the back." She found the can and sprayed the lug nuts liberally. "Okay. Let's both get our weight on this and see what happens."

The women pushed down with all their might. Nothing. Rain and sweat dripped down Sam's forehead into her eyes. Teresa's blonde hair hung wet around her shoulders. They looked at each other, and suddenly Sam burst into laughter. At first, her friend stared at her, one eyebrow cocked. Then a giggle erupted from her. They slid to the ground, holding their stomachs in convulsive laughs and sobs.

Finally, Sam recovered her composure. Wiping her eyes, she stood. "Well, what d'ya think, did the lube have time to work its magic?"

Teresa shook her wet tresses. "Let's give it another try."

Again, they put their combined weight on the handle. Nothing. Then Sam bounced on it. "It moved!" The two women continued to push and bounce, and at last, the nut loosened enough so Sam could get it twisted off. "Yes!" She threw her arms up in a V sign. "One down, three to go."

Grunting, pushing, and bouncing on the wrench handle,

Sam and Teresa had to stop to take a breather and wipe rain and perspiration from their brows. Teresa groaned. "Man oh man, who would've guessed this would be so hard?"

Just as they redoubled their efforts, headlights lit up the rear of the trailer, and red and blue flashers came on.

"Oh good," Sam gasped. Toby kicked the sides of the trailer and whinnied. "It's okay, boy. Be good now." She continued to talk to him in a soothing tone.

A highway patrolman came around the side of the rig to where they were working. "Howdy, ladies. Havin' a little trouble?"

"You could say that." Sam pointed to the tire. "We got one nut off, but the second one is pretty stubborn."

The young officer peered at the wheel. "Yeah, I know how tight they can be. Let me see if I can help." He put muscle to the wrench and with a screech, the nut came free.

Teresa cheered. "Woohoo!"

"You gals loosened it for me." He grinned. "Let's see about the next two." With a few more grunts and pushes, he soon had the tire off.

Sam rolled the spare over. "Thanks. If you want to get out of the rain, I think we can get the rest handled."

"Naw. I'll finish this up and you can be on your way. Good job puttin' out the flares, by the way. Not a lot of traffic on this road, but it's pretty dark, and with this rain..."

The tire on, the women thanked the officer profusely. Sam checked Toby whose eyes rolled back to reveal the whites, but then he sighed and settled into a calmer demeanor. They peeled off their sodden coveralls and jumped back in the pickup. Sam turned up the heat full blast.

The patrolman followed them for a few miles, and then with a burst from his flashers, drove back the other way.

"Whew, that was an adventure." Teresa toweled her wet hair. "Glad we brought our coveralls and these towels."

"No kidding." Shaky laughter escaped her lips. "I'm going to be so glad to get home. I'm starving. Would you hand me a protein bar, please?"

As Teresa unwrapped the bar, Sam slapped the steering wheel. "Oh no!"

"What?"

The rain hitting the windshield had formed into tiny white pellets. "Sleet."

Her friend groaned. "What next?"

Sam slowed, testing the brakes. So far, the road wasn't slippery. They crawled along the remote two-lane highway in less-than-great visibility for about twenty minutes or so before they got on I-94. The sleet had begun to collect along the shoulder and the road appeared white in the headlights. They were on the Interstate for less than a mile and then took the offramp to the two-lane toward Ingomar.

Finally, with a murmur of relief, Sam steered up her driveway. The dashboard clock showed nearly 9 p.m. She maneuvered the trailer up to the chute, and the women got out. The snow had let up, showing only a light dusting in the yard.

Sam opened one of the gates in the trailer and stepped into the empty stall. "Well, Toby, we made it. And you've been such a good boy." She rubbed his head and neck as she untied the rope. "C'mon now, I'll show you your new home." He backed out of the trailer and followed her willingly to the barn.

But when she approached the doorway, he snorted, gave a high-pitched whinny, and pulled the rope out of her hands. Dashing into the corral, the horse ran around the perimeter, kicking and blowing.

Sam's shoulders sagged. She stood watching the gelding, the weight of defeat heavy around her. The drugs were wearing off, and his fear was simply too strong.

Teresa came up beside her. "Just leave him be. He needs to get used to the place. He'll be fine."

The other horses whinnied from the pasture and trotted up to the fence to investigate the new guy. Sam made sure they could get into the barn from the pasture gate if they chose to, and left Toby in the round corral, where a lean-to on the side of the barn would provide shelter. She made sure all the horses had feed and water and then turned to Teresa. "You might as well spend the night. It's getting pretty late, and we're both exhausted."

"Yeah, that actually sounds pretty good. I'll take you up on that offer, as long as it includes a bowl of soup or a sandwich."

"You bet. And some hot chocolate."

"With marshmallows?"

Sam chuckled. "You got it." She parked the trailer, unhooked it, and drove up the incline to the house. "I don't think I've ever had such a white-knuckle trip. I am so glad to be home!"

Sam awoke in the night, listening for whinnies or sounds of commotion from the corral. She didn't hear anything, but still got up and peered out the window at the moonlit yard. Nothing going on. She went back to bed.

Early the next morning, she started a pot of coffee, slipped on her coat and boots, and headed for the barn. Her horses came to the fence, nickering their greetings. Toby stood off to the side near the lean-to. His eyes flickered from her to the corral. Sam pulled out the handful of carrots she'd grabbed and gave Sugar, Trixi, and Apache each a treat and a quick scratch. Then she went into the round corral, holding out her palm to Toby.

His ears pricked forward. He hesitated but then plodded toward Sam, his nostrils flaring, sniffing as he came near. "Good morning, my boy. And how are you this morning? Did you get acquainted with the others?" As the horse lipped the carrots from her palm, she stroked his head and neck with her other hand. "Good boy."

"How's ol' Tobe this morning?" Teresa's voice came from behind.

Sam twisted to greet her friend who met her at the fence with a travel mug of coffee. "Thanks. I need that. I think he's doing okay. I'm sure Sugar and Trixi informed him of his rightful lowly place, but he seems calm." She grinned. "He likes carrots."

"What's not to like?" Teresa went into the barn and came out with cake pellets. "Here, boy. Here, Toby." She reached through the fence with her offering. The gelding approached her cautiously, but the treats won him over. He crunched and then sniffed for more.

Sam laughed. "He is a sucker for cake. Aren't we all?" She finished feeding all the horses and then broke the thin sheet of ice on the water tank. "I think I'll leave them separated for another day. I want to work with Toby again a little later." She opened the gate and stepped through. "Let's go get breakfast."

"Sounds good to me." Teresa fell into step beside her. "He's a beautiful horse, and I think he's going to fit in just fine."

"If I can ever get him over his fear of confined spaces." Sam grimaced. "Just hope I don't have to take him to the vet anytime soon."

The women sat visiting companionably over eggs, bacon, and second and third cups of coffee.

Teresa stirred more cream into her cup. "That trip was pretty doggone hairy, but you know what, I really enjoyed it."

Sam raised an eyebrow. "The blown-up tire and the skidding and the almost landing in the ditch?"

"Well, almost all of it." Teresa grinned. "No. It was just fun being on the road with a girlfriend, seeing different country, meeting the Parmleys and Toby."

"Yeah. That part was fun. And I'm so glad you were with me. You were a big help."

Teresa snorted a laugh. "Yeah, right. I couldn't even get one lug nut loose!"

"Just having your support means a lot. Thank you. We'll have to take another trip sometime, but no horse trailer and not in winter weather."

"Agreed!" Teresa saluted with her cup. "But you are an excellent driver, so I wouldn't hesitate to do it again."

The phone rang, and Sam got up to answer. Horace's cheery voice greeted her. "Hey, little gal. You made it home. How's the horse?"

"Toby is fine, but very traumatized from the accident and scared of trailers and stalls. He's going to need some work." She related the details of their trip.

"Land sakes, you gals had one heckuva time! I should have gone with you."

"No-no. I needed you here. Thank you, by the way." She gave a quiet laugh. "We managed."

"I *guess* you did. Well, you are a very capable young lady, and I'm prouda ya."

Her face warmed with his compliment. That was high praise, coming from the veteran rancher.

As she hung up, she glanced at the calendar hanging on the wall. "Oh gee, I'd almost forgotten. I have an appointment in Miles City tomorrow with that ag instructor."

"That's great. I'm excited for you."

Sam fluttered air through her lips. "I dunno. We'll see. I don't know how I'm going to pull off traveling to Miles and working with more vets and still be able to take care of the horses and cows here, especially in the winter." And then there was Toby—how was he going to fit in to all of this?

"Well, don't go crying over crushed eggs just yet. Wait and see what the guy has to say." Teresa stood. "Let's go play with Toby for a while, and then I need to get home."

CHAPTER FOURTEEN

The next morning, Sam rose early to feed the horses. She checked Toby's healing cuts and bruises, thankful nothing had broken open. He flinched when she applied salve but calmed when she talked softly while brushing him. After finishing, she gave her other charges a few minutes of attention and treats.

Then she headed her truck down the highway for the hour and a half trip to Miles City. Gray wintery clouds spread themselves across the sky, and Sam found herself wishing for the sun and heat of summer. Oh well, it would be Christmas soon, and Electra and Alberta would be coming. She smiled as a ray of sunshine broke momentarily through the clouds, and a ripple of excitement rolled up her back. "Gee, I'd better do some Christmas shopping while I'm in town."

But then the specter of Brad lying in that hospital bed, swathed in bandages, crushed her excitement. Would he wake up? And if he did, would he have brain damage? The clouds closed again, and she shivered.

"No, Sam, don't go there!" She scolded herself like a naughty child. "I've got to stay positive!" Breathing deeply helped calm her mind. "All right. Count your blessings. Christmas is coming and my friends will be here. I have a new horse to work with. I have this opportunity to meet with the ag instructor and maybe work with the vets in an indoor arena."

But like a jumper's course, the obstacles kept looming. How would she manage the ninety-mile trip, with horses, to do that? And how often? She had cattle to care for and chores at home and her job with Clyde. She let out a sigh that sounded more like a groan.

"C'mon, Sam!" She hit the steering wheel. "That's what you're going in to find out today! Quit counting your chickens dead before they're even hatched."

She punched on the radio and sang loudly to cover the negative thoughts that kept threatening her equilibrium.

Cresting the last hill, Sam glimpsed the town nestled in the valley below the rim rocks formed by the Yellowstone River. Although brown and dormant now, the trees in summer provided a lush green oasis in the midst of the eastern Montana prairie. Dubbed the "cow capital of the world," Miles City hosted the nationally-famous Bucking Horse Sale, a huge rodeo, every May.

She drove through town, past historic buildings, to the college, and pulled up in front of a large, white-painted steel building. A two-story entry was painted a contrasting black. Entering, she paused in a small lobby, with a closed concession stand and a stairway to the mezzanine. Photos of historic and modern rodeo riders covered the walls, and glass cases held trophies. It opened to hallways to the left and the right, and in front of her were large double doors, probably to the arena. She hesitated, wondering if she should look for offices down the hall or go through the big doors.

"Good morning." A cheery voice came from behind her.

A dark-haired man in his late thirties to early forties, with a beard and mustache, stuck his hand out. "Nick Seward. You must be Samantha."

She shook it heartily. "You can call me Sam. Are you related to the Sewards who used to own the Jersey Lilly in Ingomar?"

"Yeah. Bob was my great-uncle. Quite the character. Famous for his pinto bean soup."

"I've had it. Billy Cole still uses the same recipe." She chuckled. "Lots of history there. My great-grandparents used to live on the ranch I'm now leasing out there, and they apparently frequented the saloon often."

"Oh yes, the Mosers. That's why your name sounded

familiar. Well, it's good to meet you. Sounds like you're continuing your grandmother's—was it?—tradition of loving horses."

"Great-grandma. I guess I am, although I've never ridden a bucking horse in a rodeo, like she did."

"Pretty amazing." Nick threw his arm out wide. "C'mon, why don't I show you around, and we can talk a little about what each of us has in mind." He pointed out classrooms down the hallway to the right, and offices to the left.

He opened the double doors to the arena, and Sam followed him into the huge open space, her gaze traveling up the bleachers to the high ceiling. "Wow. Beautiful facility."

"Thanks. We're proud of it. We used no government money. It was all funded by a non-profit endowment board. The arena is twenty thousand square feet and holds five hundred people."

"So, you have ag students and a rodeo club too?"

"Yeah, a young farmers and ranchers association and a team in the Intercollegiate Rodeo Association. Our cowboys and cowgirls have done very well over the years." Nick gestured back toward the lobby. "You saw the photos out there."

"Quite impressive."

"Thank you. Let's go to the office, and we can talk."

She followed him back to the lobby and then to a small cubicle office where he cleared a chair of a stack of papers and folders.

"Well, we have several ag students who are veterans and disabled either physically or emotionally with PTSD." He leaned back in his chair. "Personally, I found when I came back from the middle east, the only thing that made sense to me was working with the land, and from that extension, with horses."

Sam raised her eyebrows. "You're a vet too?"

"Yup. I wasn't injured physically, but..." He cleared his throat and looked down at his desk. "Anyway, I've noticed several of the guys—and there's a couple gals too—seemed to be drawn to our horses. I got to talking with Del and Garrett and found out how much they've gained by working with you."

She snorted a laugh. "I'm not so sure about that. Garrett fell the last time he was there. I didn't think he'd ever want to see another horse again—or me."

"No. On the contrary. I've seen a change in him already. He wants to do more."

"Really? Wow. That's great." Sam could hardly believe what she'd just heard.

"Yeah. And I know, in this country, nobody can do much outside in the winter, not for enjoyment anyway." Nick chuckled. "So, I got to thinking, why couldn't we set up some kind of program here for the vets? I think I can get our non-profit on board to pay you."

Sam's mouth dropped open, and she stared at the man across from her. Program? Pay her? *What?* "B-but I'm not a certified trainer. I'm just doing this by the seat of my pants. And it's not always working real great."

"I'll bet you're doing better than you think." He shuffled some papers and brought one out from the stack. "There are programs for vets, like PATH International—stands for Professional Association of Therapeutic Horsemanship International—and they work with the Wounded Warrior Project to get veterans into the program. And, through the VA, there's an instructor certification course you can take."

Sam gave her head a sharp shake. What was he saying? She closed her mouth with a gulp. *I must look like an idiot.* "Uh… gee… I—"

Nick laughed. "I know this is a lot to take in, and you'll probably want to mull it over a while. Let me make some copies of all this stuff for you." He stood and stepped outside the cubicle to a copy machine.

"But I… training? Certification? I don't know…"

"Think about it. I believe this is what you love doing, just from what I've heard from the guys and from that documentary that featured you. This is a great opportunity for you, and for our community." He handed her a folder with the copies. "If the training fee is an obstacle, I'll bet I can find you a scholarship. And, I think we can have on-the-job training while you are completing it."

Sam stood, feeling like she'd been knocked over by a thousand-pound horse. "Oh my word. Thank you. I-I certainly have a lot to think about."

Snippets of their conversation played in Sam's head as she drove toward home. "Pay you... program for vets... scholarship for training... certification..." Warm giddiness alternated with cold rushes of fear. Could she do this? Nick Seward seemed to think so.

More questions arose: would she use her own horses or theirs? How many days a week? What would they pay? Could she still work for Clyde and commute to Miles City for this? She needed to write these down and call Nick to get more details. Funny how her mind simply went blank when he talked about the job.

Oh, I've got to call Brad and tell him the good news! She reached for her cell phone. Her hand stopped in mid-air. Brad. Lying in that hospital bed, unable to communicate. More and more she realized how much she wanted to share with him, talk to him, be with him. A wave of gray sorrow swept through her.

She pulled over on the side of the road, rested her forehead on the steering wheel, and took deep, slow, even breaths. *He* will *come through this. We* will *do all those things together.* She sat until the interior of the cab grew chilly. Life presented one oozing quicksand pit after another. Great-Grandma Nettie and Grandma Anna were able to deal with everything they were thrown, and they didn't have all the advantages Sam did. She sat up straight and squared her shoulders. *Okay, Miss Samantha, you have good news. And good genes. Let yourself enjoy that for a moment.*

A smile twitched at the corners of her mouth. She had to share this with someone, so she grabbed her phone and punched in Teresa's number. "Hey, girl, guess what?"

Teresa shrieked with the news. "That's terrific! This is a wonderful opportunity, and I know you will rise to the occasion. I'm so happy for you."

"Thank you, my friend. I just had to share it with someone. I'm excited and scared at the same time. So much to think about, so many questions still, decisions to make." She stared out over the undulating hills, grass brown, backlit with a skiff of snow. Then she laughed. "Oh my goodness. I was going to do some Christmas shopping while I was in town. I was in such shock, I totally forgot!"

Teresa giggled. "I can see where that would happen. You still have a couple of weeks to get it done though."

"Yeah. And I do need to go to Billings and see if I can sneak in to visit Brad. I'll do my shopping then."

They disconnected, and Sam drove home. Horace was waiting by the corral, hay loaded in the back of his truck. He touched the brim of his hat. "Hi there! Just about to go out and feed the cows."

She grimaced. "Oh good grief, you loaded that by yourself? You should've waited for me."

"Phht. When I get too old to buck a coupla bales, then I need to hang up m'spurs." He thrust his face toward hers. "So. How did it go?"

Sam couldn't stop grinning as she related her conversation with the ag instructor. "I still have a million questions, but it looks like it might be doable."

"Well, yeehaw!" Horace swept his hat in an arc. "Great news! I'm prouda ya!"

The next morning, after doing chores, Sam hopped in her truck and headed for Billings. She made a mental note of who she wanted to buy gifts for and what they might like. When she got into town, she went first to Connolly's Western Wear and Tack on 24th Street. It wasn't too far from the mall, so if she needed to, she could brave that monstrosity and its crowds.

She hummed as she browsed the western clothing racks.

Maybe matching shirts for Electra and Alberta. Would Electra think that was weird? *Naw, I'll bet she'd like that.* Or maybe a hand-tooled belt. Sam agonized over her decisions, finally choosing items for the New York women, something for Teresa, a gift card for Horace and for the Bruckners, and a leather wallet for Brad with his name engraved on it. She would pick that up later.

Her boots barely touched the ground as she carried her packages to the truck. The sky was a brilliant blue, and the sun melted the residual piles of plowed snow in the parking lot. She had her Christmas shopping done, she had a potential job helping veterans, and today she *would* get in to see Brad, and he *would* wake up.

Buoyed by possibility, Sam bounded up the stairs to the family room where the Ashtons waited. She entered with a smile. "Hi, everybody. It's a beautiful day out there. How are you doing?"

Mrs. Ashton looked at her with eyes wide. She pushed herself from her chair slowly, as if with great age, paused for a heartbeat, and then flung her arms around Sam, bursting into tears.

Sam's breath stopped. What? What was this? Oh, dear Lord. Brad. She looked around the woman's head at Melissa's white, drawn face. "Is... Brad...? What happened?" Fear splashed over her like an ice bath.

"Brad... has... pneumonia!" Mrs. Ashton punctuated her words with sobs, ending in a wail.

"Oh." Sam let out the pent-up air. Pneumonia. *Okay. He's not dead. Pneumonia is fixable. Isn't it?*

Melissa encircled both women in a hug, patting their backs. "It's okay, Mom. It'll be okay." They helped Mrs. Ashton back to her chair.

Fear rose in Sam's gut again. "Wh-what do the doctors say? What are they doing?"

"They've put him on a ventilator and are giving him antibiotics, of course, and still have him on sedation to keep him in the coma." Melissa's eyes were red and moist. "They think he'll heal faster that way."

Ventilator. Coma. That was almost dead. Sam bit her lip to keep from joining Mrs. Ashton's sobs. She forced a cheerful tone. "Well, I'm sure they know what they're doing, and you're right. He'll be okay."

She and Melissa tried to enter the ICU, but Nurse Ratchett stopped them at the door with a frown. "Family only, and only for a minute."

Sam hid her disappointment, and stayed a few minutes longer, trying to reassure the Ashton women. "I haven't done a lot of praying in recent years, but I am now."

Fresh tears flowed as Brad's mom grasped Sam's arm. "Thank you so much, my dear. Every one of those prayers is felt and appreciated. We believe in miracles, don't we, honey?" She looked at Melissa who nodded.

With a promise to keep in touch, Sam left the waiting room, her feet heavy as if caked with the sticky gumbo mud of the ranch. She sat in her pickup, her body numb but her mind swirling. *I need to talk to somebody.* Who could she call—Teresa, Horace, Irene Bruckner? *But not on the phone.* Robin, the group home counselor. She had become a friendly acquaintance, someone she could talk to. She would understand. An urge to see her and the kids at the home swept over her. She turned the ignition, put the truck in gear, and drove to the center.

Robin sat behind her paper-cluttered desk in the small office and looked up with a smile as Sam knocked and entered. "Well, hello, stranger. Long time, no see."

Sam lowered herself in the chair Robin indicated on the other side of the desk. Sunlight streamed through a single window, highlighting the woman's auburn hair.

"I know. I've missed seeing you and working with the kids."

The other woman pursed her lips. "This winter has been too long already. They're all driving me crazy, wanting to get back out to the ranch and see the horses. Even the boys."

Sam gave a small chuckle. "Sure wish we had an indoor

arena so we could work with them during these long, cold months." She told Robin about the veterans and the possibility of working with them at the college in Miles City.

"That's awesome." Robin chewed on a fingernail, frown lines creasing her forehead. "You know what? I'll bet we could do something similar here in Billings."

Sam did a double-take. She'd never even considered that possibility. "Well, golly, I... That would be great, but I don't know how I'm going to work out the schedule with going to Miles and transporting horses and taking care of the ranch and the cows and..." Sudden tears welled and stung. "And Brad... he's in a coma in the hospital, and now he has pneumonia."

Robin's smile faded. "Oh my goodness, my dear. I'm so sorry. You do have a lot on your plate right now." She stood, came around the desk, and put an arm around her. "We can put that idea on hold until you're able to figure things out."

They sat in silence for a few minutes, while Sam attempted to control her runaway emotions. The counselor's presence soothed her, and her breathing gradually softened.

"Thank you, Robin. I needed this." Sam squared her shoulders. "And you know what, I'd like to see the kids. Are they all in school?"

"Most of them are, but Sapphire is home with cramps today. She would be absolutely over the moon to see you."

Robin led her down the hall, where the counselor knocked on a door. "Sapphire, honey. Are you awake? I have a surprise visitor for you."

A groan came from the room. "Um, okay."

Robin winked at Sam and opened the door.

"Hi, Sapphire." Sam stepped in.

The dark-haired girl who had been Electra's goth-look-alike last summer opened wide eyes and sat up, bouncing on the bed. "Sam! Oh wow! Sam!"

She sat beside her on the bed and gave the girl a hug. "I'm sorry you're not feeling well today."

"I'm not. For once, I'm glad I have these dang cramps. I get to see you!" She squeezed Sam in a choking bear hug. "What are you doing here? What's Electra doing? Is she here?" She scanned the doorway as if hoping to see another surprise visitor.

"No, not yet, but she is coming for Christmas. And we will be sure to visit you or have you come out to the ranch."

Sapphire squealed. "Ohmygosh, yes! Yes! Can we, Miss Robin, can we?"

The other woman nodded. "Of course. We'll make sure something like that happens."

After joining Robin and Sapphire for a soup and sandwich lunch, Sam left for home with a lighter step and a regained sense that things *were* going to be okay

CHAPTER FIFTEEN

Sam stopped at the Jersey Lilly and picked up a couple of burgers and a large order of fries. Punching in Horace's number, she told him, "I'm bringing supper. See you in a few."

"Great! I was just gettin' a little peckish."

At his place, she set out the food and he poured coffee. They sat in companionable silence for a few minutes while tucking into the food. Then Horace paused and peered into her face. "So... How was the trip to Billings? Get your shopping done?"

"Yeah, I did, and was feeling pretty proud of myself." She uttered a weak laugh. "But then, I stopped at the hospital..." Her shoulders slumped. "Brad has pneumonia."

Horace's eyes widened. "Oh, man, I'm so sorry to hear that. Poor guy. He can't catch a break, can he?"

"Doesn't seem like it. But you know what, I'm not going to let this get me down. This is a setback, for sure, but I know he's going to be okay. I feel it here." She put a hand over her heart.

Horace patted her other arm. "Yeah. I do too. And you're strong, little gal. You'll get through this. Like they say, 'This too, shall pass.'"

She rolled her eyes but responded with a nod. "Thanks."

Bolstered by the older man's support, Sam drove home and then curled up in her rocking chair with a cup of hot chocolate and her book. Warm peace flowed through her body, and she slept well that night for the first time in a long while.

***

December days marched forward, with blue skies and wind punctuated by blustery on-and-off snow flurries. Sam helped

Horace, and he helped her feed their cows, and she rode her horses when the temperatures moderated. Toby continued to heal, but remained skittish, not wanting to go into his stall, even when the thermometer hit single digits. Sam worked with him nearly every day, trying to win his confidence.

Phone calls with the Ashtons gave her little relief. The crushing, dark worry hovered in her periphery and threatened to take over her life, despite her resolve to remain optimistic. "Still in the coma," they said. "Still on the ventilator, but they think the antibiotics are working."

She drove to Billings every few days to see for herself and to give Brad's family as much support as she could muster. One day, as Sam tried to sneak into the ICU and the nurse stopped them, Melissa stood firm with hands on hips. "Listen, Samantha is Brad's fiancée, and she should be able to get in to see him."

Sam jerked her head back. *Fiancée?* Her pulse raced.

"Oh." The nurse's stern expression relaxed. "Oh, my dear, I'm very sorry. Of course you should be able to see him. I'll add you to the family list."

Sam stuck her left hand in her pocket in case the nurse questioned her lack of a ring. Melissa grinned at her. "Let's go see the boy."

Brad lay so still, swathed in bandages, connected to tubes, and the ventilator thumped and whooshed by his bed. Swallowing an involuntary sob, she took his hand. "Brad, it's Sam. I'm here. I'd sure like to talk to you. I have so much to tell you." She bit her lip.

Melissa held his other hand. "Hey, brother dear, you've just gotten engaged, so I think maybe you ought to come back pretty soon." She twinkled a smile at Sam who couldn't help but grin back.

"Yeah. We're arranging your life for you," she patted his arm, "and I know you can't be comfortable with that. So, I second the motion that you get your butt back here!"

Another nurse came up behind them. "His lungs and

breathing have improved a great deal, so doctor is thinking it's only a matter of a couple of days before we start weaning him off the ventilator."

Sam and Melissa exchanged glances. "That is great news, isn't it?" Melissa's eyes were wide and glistening.

She nodded, afraid to speak for fear of what childish noises might erupt.

Back out in the waiting room, Melissa relayed the latest to her parents. They all hugged, and then Sam headed back home, with hope and fear warring in her chest.

Electra and Alberta would be arriving a week before Christmas—only a couple of days away. Giddy with anticipation, she wrapped gifts and baked cookies. On her last trip to town, she'd bought a tree they could decorate together.

The morning of their arrival, Sam woke early with a fluttery stomach. *I can hardly wait!* She jumped up and dressed in a hurry, eager to get her chores finished before driving to the Billings airport. As she prepared the coffeemaker, she studied the calendar. December 17. Great-grandma Nettie's birthday. Sam smiled at the photo hanging on the wall of the cowgirl sitting so proud and erect on her horse. "Happy Birthday, G-G Nettie."

The horses kicked up their heels in the pasture next to the barn and came running when they saw her. "Hey, Apache, guess who's coming to visit! Electra will be here today." She rubbed his forehead and between his ears. "I'll bet you're going to be so glad to see her."

After chores and breakfast, she jumped into her old truck and sped down the road toward Billings. She patted the dashboard. "You know this road so well, I could probably take a nap and you'd get me there." A giggle traveled up from her belly, and she laughed out loud.

***

Sam spotted Alberta first, coming down the ramp from the exit gate. Behind her came Electra, dragging her carry-on case, black hair spiked high, a sullen frown on her face. Sam gasped.

Oh dear. She was dressed in all black again.

Then the teen looked up and saw Sam. Her face changed to a huge, beaming grin. "Sam! Sam! Sam! We're here!" She dropped her carry-on and rushed through the crowd to latch onto her with a crushing hug. "Oh, Sam, I'm so glad to see you, so glad to be here. Ohmygosh it's just been hell, how's Apache, is he okay, how are you, are you okay? Ohmygosh, I'm so glad to see you!"

Sam squeezed the girl. "Well, I'm glad to see you too! Apache is fine and so am I, now that you're here." She released Electra and held her arms out as Alberta came up to her, pulling both cases now.

"She's been insufferable the last few days, heck, the last few weeks," Alberta whispered as they hugged. "Gee, it's good to be here," she added out loud. "All right, Electra, let's go get our suitcases."

The teen grabbed Sam's arm and dragged her toward baggage claim. Sam gave her mom a wink over her shoulder.

"Oh, Sam, I can't wait to get to your place and see Apache and ride and play in the snow and..." The teenager kept up her nonstop chatter as they waited, while Alberta and Sam exchanged bemused looks.

Baggage claimed and loaded into the back of the truck, the women piled in. "Anything you need here in Billings before we head out? Last-minute Christmas shopping?"

"No, I think we're good. We'd better get down that road to see Apache before this girl detonates."

"Mo-o-m!" Electra bounced in the middle of the bench seat. "I can't help it, I've just missed Apache—and you too, Sam—so much, there's nothing in New York like this, and riding there is lame, and I don't have any friends, and..." Her voice trailed off, and she nibbled at chipped black nail polish.

Alberta rolled her eyes.

Sam's vision blurred.

The drive home followed much the same pattern, with Electra rattling on about horses or New York or whatever she saw on the horizon, punctuated with short, nail-chewing silences. Sam peeked at Alberta. The woman's face was drawn and pale, with more crow's-feet around her eyes than the last time she saw her. *She looks tired. Well, guess I can't blame her.*

As they approached the ranch, the teenager leaned forward, searching for a glimpse of the horses. "Where are they? Will Apache remember me, do you think? I can't wait to see him, I can't wait to ride him, I. Just. Can't. Wait!"

"Well, I guess we'd better find out first thing." Sam drove directly to the barn, where her little herd waited in the adjoining pasture, all four heads hanging over the fence.

"Oh, there he is! Oh, Sam, there's Trixi too, and there's Sugar, and oh yeah, your new horse! What's his name?"

"That's Toby. I've been working with him, because he had a traumatic experience in a vehicle accident and is still a little shy and skittish. But maybe you can help me with him, like you did with Apache."

The girl's eyebrows rose. "Yeah. I could do that." She pushed on her mother's arm. "Mom, let me out. I gotta go see Apache!"

"Okay, okay. But take it slow. It's been a while and you don't want to scare him." Alberta opened the door, slid from the seat, and let her daughter out.

The girl took a couple of running steps, and Sam called out, "Wait!"

Electra stopped in mid-stride.

"Here's a handful of cake pellets." Sam scooped a few from a bucket in the back of the truck.

The teen took them and stood in place for a moment, quivering. Then she walked slowly toward the horses, holding out her hand. "Apache. Hi, boy. It's me. Do you remember me?"

All the horses, except Toby, crowded the fence in anticipation of a treat. Sam and Alberta also grabbed pellets and approached.

Apache tossed his head and whinnied. He pressed his chest

against the wire. His greeting rumbled as Electra held out the treat. He sniffed her hand, took the pellets, and then nuzzled her arm as he chewed. "Oh, Apache. You do remember me, don't you? I'm so glad to see you!" She laid her cheek against his, and they stood like that for several long moments.

Sam swallowed around a lump and gave Alberta a big smile. The other woman's face had softened, and her eyes glistened. "She needed this." She took a visible deep breath. "And so did I."

Sam opened the gate for Apache to come into the corral. Electra went to the barn and came back with comb and brush. She stood by the horse, gently rubbing and brushing his neck and mane, moving to his withers and back.

Alberta and Sam gave the other horses their treats and petted them for a few minutes —even Toby had finally come forward to claim his.

"Well, I think Electra will be just fine here, so what d'you say we drive on up to the house and get you settled?"

"That would be great. I've been looking forward to kicking back for quite some time."

At the house, Sam led the way as they carried the luggage upstairs to the two tiny bedrooms. "I know this is cramped, but I hope it'll be okay for a few days anyway."

Alberta scanned the room. "It's perfect. Thank you."

"When you're ready, come downstairs, and I'll fix you a cup of coffee and some lunch if you're hungry. I'm sure Electra won't be interested in food for a while yet."

They both snickered.

Over coffee and sandwiches, the women began to catch up. "How is your friend Brad doing?"

Sam related the latest, about the pneumonia, her fears again scratching at her insides. "I'm really scared, Alberta, but there's nothing I can do. I feel completely helpless."

"Oh, my dear, I'm so very sorry. I know this is the hardest thing in the world to endure." Her eyes took on a distant look as she gazed out the kitchen window. "My son was in a coma for several weeks before he…" She swallowed hard and turned back to Sam. "But that was a different story. I knew from the beginning, there was no coming back." She patted Sam's hand. "But I do know what you're going through. And if I can help in any way, I'm here."

Sam blinked back tears. "Thank you. I appreciate it. You're a wonderful friend." She clasped the woman's hand and changed the subject. "But what about Electra—black again? Is she okay?"

Alberta sighed. "She's been going through a tough time. Her friends made fun of her when she got back to school and had no interest in going riding with her. So, she's gradually gone back to the dark Goth look and attitude, just to fit in again."

"Oh dear." Her voice dropped. "That's what I was afraid of when I saw her. But at least her face is fresh-scrubbed, not the white and black makeup."

"Yeah. That was just for you." Her friend stared out the window. "I don't know what we're going to do. I don't think going back to that school and those kids is a good idea."

CHAPTER SIXTEEN

After lunch, Alberta went upstairs to unpack and maybe take a short nap. Sam wrapped up a sandwich and took it out to the corral where Electra was still brushing and massaging Apache. Sam took in the sweet scene. "Gee, I think if he was a cat he'd be purring."

The girl's face glowed. "Yeah. Me too. Can we go for a ride?"

"Sure. I'm glad the snow has melted enough we can go. I'll get Trixi. Meanwhile, here's a sandwich. You need to keep up your strength." She got a bridle, went to the pasture, and whistled. The other horses grazed on dry tufts of grass a short distance away. Trixi raised her head and came trotting.

"Expecting another treat, huh? Golly, are you spoiled!" She rubbed the mare's face, gave her a cake pellet, and slipped on the bridle. Then she led her through the gate into the corral by the barn, where Electra sat on a log, gulping down the last of her sandwich.

They went into the barn, retrieved saddles, and tacked up their horses. Within minutes, the horses' hooves crunched in the snow and dried grass through the pasture, toward the large, flat-topped butte in the distance. At first, Electra seemed content with Apache walking, but finally, a lot more, before you go she nudged him into a trot, and then a canter. She squinted at Sam. "Race ya!"

Sam pressed her heels to Trixi's flanks, and the mare willingly joined the race. The cold December air bit at her face and ears, but she leaned forward, caught up in the exhilaration of the run.

Electra reined in at the base of the hill, laughing. "THAT was fun! Ohmygosh, I missed this SO much."

"Me too." Sam shivered and pulled her coat collar up farther. "I haven't been out as much as I should be, with the snow and cold and..." *Brad. Wonder how he is today.* A chill ran up her spine. She swallowed and forced a smile. "But now that you're here, I hope we can do this a lot more before you go back home."

The teen's grin faded, and she looked down at the frozen ground.

Sam studied her for a moment. "Electra?"

The girl turned her face away.

"Are you okay? What's going on?"

Electra didn't answer but nudged Apache and took off up the side of the butte. Sam followed. At the top, they stopped and slipped out of their saddles. Below them, the red and white Herefords gathered around the reservoir. Sam automatically counted to see that they were all there. Enough grass poked through the remnants of snow that she didn't need to feed them today.

"I... love this place." Electra sank onto a boulder and wrapped her arms around her middle. "I love Apache, and I love those cows... and I love you." Her eyes glistened.

Sam's chest cavity swelled. *Aww, how sweet.* She sat on the rock, put her arm around the girl's shoulders, and drew her close. "I love you too, honey." She waited a few moments, but Electra was uncharacteristically silent. "Did something happen back home?"

"No. Not really." She squirmed a bit on the rock. "But... it's a big city. There's too many people... and not enough horses."

Sam chuckled. "I can understand that. I don't think I'd want to live there."

"My friends... I guess I changed last summer. But they didn't." Electra swiped at her cheeks with her gloves. "They didn't like me anymore. They didn't understand me... and they didn't want to go riding. They made fun of me."

Sam's heart constricted. "So, you went back to being Goth, so your friends would like you again?"

"I didn't really want to." Electra picked at a clump of grass and stared out at the horizon. "B-but what else could I do? They weren't going to change. I don't have any other friends."

Tears trickled again. "I went to the stables a few times, but it... it wasn't the same! No galloping allowed. Sit up straight and hold the reins in two hands and be all prim and proper." Her voice raised in a mimicking tone. "The girls at the riding academy were all too snooty—they didn't want to be friends. And the horses... I couldn't relate to any of them." She looked at Sam. "They weren't Apache."

Sam chewed her lower lip. "I understand." Apache, the horse they had rescued together, on the verge of death from starvation. The teen and the horse had forged a bond like no other. Anyone who hadn't experienced that would have no understanding. But what could she do? Electra lived in New York. Boarding a horse would be astronomical, and Alberta certainly couldn't afford that.

"Well, honey, I'm sorry about all that. I wish I had a magic wand and could make everything better." She smiled. "But, you know what? We will just enjoy the heck out of the horses and riding and having the time of our lives while you're here. And then it'll be summer, and you'll be back again." Sam gave her a squeeze. "Sound like a plan?"

Electra wiped her cheeks again. "Yeah. You make everything better." She stood. "Let's go back. It is kind of cold up here."

The horses loped at an easy stride in and out of the low coulees, through the spicy sage, and back to the barn. Another brushing for Apache and Trixi, and then Sam and Electra ambled back up to the house, arm in arm.

That evening, after supper, Sam brought the fir tree in from the barn and set it up in front of the big window in the living room. Electra squealed as she opened the boxes of ornaments. "Oooh, come look, Mom! This is so cool." She held up a horse figurine and then a cowboy hat and a pair of boots. "Where did you get all these?"

"Oh, here and there." Sam hung the boot ornament on the tree, front and center. "A few have been gifts from friends who know I love horses and some I've found in little gift shops." She added a hat ornament and a gold garland.

Alberta brought in cups of hot chocolate with marshmallows and a plate of cookies. "Here's something to sustain us during our hard work."

"Thanks." Sam took a cookie. "You look a little more rested this evening."

"Yeah. I feel much better. This fresh air and the peace and quiet here are just what I needed." She picked up an angel ornament and added it to the growing bling on the tree. "I see you have a 'theme' area all over—cowgirl stuff here and angels there. It's lovely."

Electra exclaimed over every piece and asked the history of each—some were from Grandma Anna, reminding Sam of her German ancestry, others depicted milestone years of a happy childhood.

As she plugged in the glowing, multi-colored lights, a tender beam of affection enveloped her. "This is such fun. I'm so glad you're here to celebrate Christmas with me." A flash of Brad lying in that hospital bed, hooked up to the ventilator sobered her. "It's my favorite holiday and if you hadn't come, I might not even have put up a tree this year." She gave herself a little shake and sipped rich, steaming chocolate.

"We're happy to celebrate it with you too." Alberta came up behind her and wrapped her in a hug. Electra joined in. "Me too!"

Sam blinked back grateful tears.

The next morning, Sam awoke to the strong, earthy aroma of coffee. *Alberta's up already.* She stretched, eased out of bed, and put on her warm, fuzzy robe and matching slippers.

Alberta turned from the counter as Sam entered the kitchen and handed her the coffee she'd just poured. "Morning."

"Mmm. Mornin'. I could get used to this—someone else making coffee for me."

"I know, right?" She poured herself a cup. "Electra was up before the crack of dawn, and she's down at the corral already."

"Of course." Sam smirked. "Kind of what I figured. It's going to be hard to pry her away from the horses... not that we need to."

"No. This is so good for her, you have no idea. She's already a different girl and we've only been here a day."

"She and that horse... there's nothing like that special bond." She sipped her coffee. "Would you ever consider moving to Montana?"

Alberta whooshed a long sigh. "Believe me, I've thought about it. But I don't know how on earth that could happen. I need to work, we would need a place to live, and Electra needs to go to school." She gestured toward the window. "This is a wonderful, peaceful place, and I can see why you love it, but it's so far from... everything. What's the nearest town— Forsyth?—and that's how far?"

"Forty-some miles. Almost an hour from here." Sam nodded. "I know. That would be the closest for school and maybe a job."

"Well, can't think about that right now. I'm just going to enjoy the time I have here and worry about the future later."

"Sounds like a good idea." Sam swirled the dregs in her cup. But would Electra be able to readjust to New York life? So far it didn't look good. *Well, it's Alberta's decision, not mine.* She stood. "Bacon and eggs?"

"I'm going to gain ten pounds the first two days." Alberta giggled. "But yes, I'd love bacon and eggs."

After they'd eaten, Sam folded a fried egg and a slice of bacon in a piece of toast, and she and Alberta put on their coats to head for the barn.

As she approached the round corral, she stopped, her mouth open. Electra stood in the center, and Toby ran in circles around the inside of the pen. After a couple of laps, the girl waved her arm and the horse switched directions.

Sam blinked. *Oh my! She looks like a professional.*

"Wow. Where did she learn to do that?" Alberta's voice held a note of awe.

"I have no idea. I don't think we ever did that last summer." Sam walked to the fence to watch.

After several minutes and more direction changes, Electra lowered her arm and came toward the women. "Hi. I hope you don't mind. Toby looked lonesome when I was petting Apache, so I brought him in here."

The gelding stopped running, looked at Electra's retreating back, and after a moment's hesitation, came up behind her. He blew softly and then nuzzled her shoulder. The girl had a grin as wide as the horizon as she reached up and caressed his face.

Sam blinked rapid-fire. "I do not mind one little bit." Her heart seemed to have swelled to twice its size, and she could barely speak.

Alberta sniffled beside her and swiped a gloved hand across her cheek. "How did you know how to do that?"

"Watching 'Heartland' on TV." Electra was still grinning. "They're always doing that to acquaint themselves with a new horse or to calm one down."

"That's exactly right. You were doing just what Toby needed. You are amazing."

Electra ducked her head. "Thanks. It's fun. I like Toby. He's a good guy."

The days leading up to Christmas continued in that pattern, with Electra out in the corrals before Sam and Alberta were up. After breakfast, Sam drove out to the pasture. One day the three women caked the cows and the next, gave them a little hay. Back home and after lunch, it was back out to the corrals. Some afternoons, they all went for a short ride, bundling up against the cold. Electra rode Apache, groomed him, braided his mane, and lavished all the attention she'd apparently bottled up since last summer.

Then she and Sam worked with Toby. He still would not go into the stall in the barn but chose to spend his nights under the lean-to. "What's he going to do when it snows hard and gets even colder?" Electra brushed the bay's black mane.

"I've been worried about that too. But I have an idea we could try." She beckoned the girl to follow and behind the barn, collected several panels, which they set up in a wide passageway in the corral with both ends open.

Rubbing Toby's ears, Sam attached a lead rope to his halter. "C'mon, boy. Let's try something." She led him into the space, speaking softly. After hesitating at the entrance, he followed her through to the other end easily. "Good boy, Toby, good boy." She took him through again, with no hesitation.

Then, while Electra rubbed his neck and back, Sam narrowed the aisle. Once again, he stopped at the entrance, sniffed, and blew. "You can do it. C'mon now. C'mon, Toby." Sam rubbed his nose and stepped forward. One more fluttering snort and he followed. She and Electra praised him and caressed his neck and withers and back.

"Can I try this time?" Electra's eyes flashed.

Sam handed her the rope. Toby nuzzled her arm and followed her, pausing for just a heartbeat at the entrance. They went through a couple more times, and then she narrowed the passage once again, down to horse-width. This time, as they entered, the gelding planted his feet, blowing and snorting. "That's okay, boy. It's the same place. You know you can get out. You've done it before. C'mon now."

Electra quietly came in from the other end holding a cake pellet in her open palm. "C'mon, Toby, you get a treat if you come down here."

Sam continued to pat his neck and rub his ears until he seemed calmer. He sniffed toward the teen who had come within a few feet of them. He took one step inside. "C'mon, boy," she encouraged. He took another step and then another until he was within reach of the treat.

"Good boy." Sam praised him and rubbed his face. Electra backed up another few feet and held out another treat. He advanced slowly, took the pellet, and stood crunching. They continued in this fashion until they reached the end.

The budding young horsewoman threw her arms around his neck. "You did it, Toby. You did it. Good boy."

With Electra's treat encouragement, she took him through the narrow aisle several times more without a hitch. "I think we can let him relax for today. He's done very well. Thank you for your help. That was great, offering him the treats as an incentive. That gets him every time."

The girl ducked her head, face aglow.

When they went back to the house, Sam called Melissa to see how Brad was doing. "The doctors think he's doing better, and they're going to try weaning him off the ventilator, starting tomorrow, for about ten minutes. If that goes well, they'll try again next day, maybe a little longer."

Sam gulped. "That's a heck of a way to spend your Christmas. I'm sorry. But sounds like he's making progress."

"Yes, we're feeling rather hopeful." Melissa's voice sounded a note lighter than usual. "When they get him off the ventilator, then they'll gradually bring him out of the coma."

"Oh wow, I-I don't know what to say. I'm hoping and praying for the best outcome." She tried to match her tone to Melissa's.

"Thank you, we appreciate that. I'll call you tomorrow and let you know how it goes."

Hanging up, she leaned against the kitchen counter. Was it possible Brad would soon wake up? This was good news. Wasn't it? An anxious claw raked at her insides. But what if...? *No! Don't go there!*

Alberta came in and put an arm around her shoulders. "Everything okay?"

She told her what Melissa had said.

"That's great!" Her friend gave her a squeeze. "It sounds very encouraging. Doesn't it?"

Sam gave short, quick nods and blinked away the sting in her eyes. "Yes, it does. It really does." She forced herself to smile. "You know what? After supper, let's decorate those sugar cookies I baked."

"All RIGHT!" Electra rushed from the doorway and gave her a hug. "That'll be FUN!"

After the dishes were cleared, Sam brought out the cookies, mixed up a batch of powdered sugar frosting, and set out several small bowls and the food coloring. She brought out sprinkles, silver candy beads, and piping bags. "Okay, girls, have at it. Do your artistic best!"

She made hot chocolate, and they decorated Santas, reindeer, gingerbread men, and ornament shapes. Each held up their finished cookie, trying to outdo the other. Electra's creations grew wilder and more colorful. "Ohmygosh, this is so much fun!" she squealed.

"Some of these are too pretty to eat," her mom commented, "but some might be too gross." She pointed at the multi-colored cookie Electra had just finished.

"No!" the teen shouted, cramming a whole purplish Santa into her mouth and giggling.

Sam and Alberta erupted in laughter and crammed cookies into their mouths as well. "You have purple icing on your nose." Alberta smeared a blob of pink on Electra's cheek. Her daughter splotched green on her mom's nose and then turned on Sam to do the same. Sam beat her to it with blue icing on the girl's forehead.

The laughter and shrieks ricocheted through the little house and with the glow of the Christmas tree lights, Sam's home and heart were full of happiness, family, and hope.

CHAPTER SEVENTEEN

Snowflakes drifted lazily from a pewter sky as Sam and Electra finished chores the afternoon of December 24. The horses had been ridden, groomed, and fed, and the door to the barn left open if they needed shelter.

"This is perfect—snow on Christmas." Sam held the door open to the kitchen where cinnamon and yeast aromas greeted them.

Alberta straightened from the oven where she took out a tray of cinnamon rolls. "Yes, it does seem more like Christmas." She swatted a spatula at Electra who reached for a roll. "No, these are for tomorrow morning. We have other goodies for today."

"O-kaay." She giggled. "Sam, why is Christmas Eve at four o'clock such an important thing?"

"Well, it's a family tradition. That's when Grandma Anna and Grandpa Neil were married on Christmas Eve in 1948." She retrieved a china coffee pot from a glass-fronted cabinet, measured coffee grounds into it, and then poured boiling water over them to steep like tea.

"That's a weird way to make coffee." The teen cocked her head. "Why don't you just use the coffee maker like you usually do?"

"This is another family tradition." Sam smiled. "My grandparents made their afternoon coffee this way, and it's delicious."

Electra made a face. "If you like coffee."

"For you, we have cocoa. Do you want to get out all the

cookies and put an assortment on this plate?"

"Sure." The girl took out containers from cupboards and the refrigerator. "Mmm, we finally get to try them all." She arranged fudge bars, lemon bars, multi-layered bars, date-filled spice cookies, and the decorated sugar cookies. "Hey, why did your grandparents get married on Christmas Eve?"

Sam set her grandmother's dainty china cups on the table and poured the coffee and cocoa as Electra and her mom sat. "They met in Germany after the war. He was in the Army, and she was a nurse. When he went to visit a friend in the hospital, they met and became friends. Then a couple months later, Grandpa was shipped back to the States, and by the time he got home, he realized he'd fallen in love with this girl. So, he wrote her a letter and asked her if she'd come to the U.S. and marry him. And she said yes."

Electra took a bite of cookie, her eyes wide. "Wow. Cool."

"But it took her two years to get all the paperwork and visas approved before she could come. And Grandpa wasn't able to go back to visit her. But they wrote a lot of letters."

Alberta's eyes widened. "That must have been so hard."

"I think it would be." She pictured her petite but feisty grandmother. "I've always thought it took a lot of courage, to come to a new country where you didn't speak the language, to a different culture, out here in the middle of nowhere with the cows and horses and cowboys. And this country had just fought a war with Germany, so people still looked at her as the 'enemy.'"

Electra gasped. "Oh no. That's awful!"

"Yeah, I think she fought prejudice all her life." Sam sipped the rich, earthy coffee. "Anyway, she arrived here in November, and then in early December she got a letter that had been lost or rerouted in the mail for weeks, telling her that she still didn't have all the documentation she needed, her visa would run out on December 31, and she'd have to go home."

Electra paused in mid-bite. "What? Ohmygosh! How could they do that?" Alberta's brows were raised in a high arch.

"Well, you know, the government… So, they decided to get married before that deadline, and the pastor only had December 24 available because he was going on vacation the next day. It had to be at four o'clock since the kids' Christmas program was later that evening."

The teen's eyes were shiny. "Wow." She turned to Alberta. "Mom, isn't that the most romantic story? Married on Christmas Eve, so she wouldn't have to go back to Germany?"

"Yes, it is." Alberta blinked several times. "Your grandmother must have loved your grandpa very much to move out here." She stared out the window at the wide-open spaces. "I can see why you keep up this family tradition and why you want this ranch. You have a special history here."

After a light supper, Sam gathered her friends around the tree. "Another family tradition is to open gifts on Christmas Eve. When I was growing up, we opened the Moser family gifts at night, and then on Christmas morning, we had Santa's presents."

"The best of both worlds." Alberta smiled.

They took pictures of each other by the tree and then opened their gifts, one by one, each savoring the moment. "Another tradition," Sam explained. "We used to spend hours opening presents, carefully cutting the tape so we could save the paper for another year. And then at the very end, Grandma would pull out the box from Germany, and oh my, the treasures we found there—like special German chocolate, *Lebkuchen* cookies, and hand-crocheted items."

"Thank you for sharing these wonderful traditions with us." Alberta hugged Sam and her daughter.

Electra squealed. "Can we open them now? Can we?"

"Of course. Let's do it." Sam gave her the first box.

The teen started to rip the paper and then stopped and looked at Sam. "Do you want me to save this?"

Sam burst into laughter. "No, that's OK. I'm frugal, but I don't save paper like we used to. Well, maybe some of the pretty stuff. But you're a kid, you go ahead and rip."

"Oooh." Electra held up the light blue western shirt with dark piping and silver sequins. "Wow. I love this. This is so cool. Thank you!"

When Alberta opened her gift, she wore a broad grin, and her daughter squealed again. "Oh Mom, we got matching shirts! Ohmygosh! That is so awesome! I can't wait to wear them. Can we wear them tomorrow to the Bruckners'?"

"That sounds like a great plan. Thank you, Sam. This is perfect." Alberta hugged her again.

They oohed and aahed over each gift, and Sam's breath caught as she opened the one from her friends—a soft, turquoise, tooled leather handbag with a silver cross on one side and her initials on the other. "This is beautiful. It must have been expensive. You shouldn't have."

Alberta beamed a soft, tender smile. "Nothing is too good for such a wonderful friend. We appreciate everything you've done for us."

***

A light cover of snow greeted them Christmas morning, and after feeding and chores, the three drove to the Bruckners' for dinner. Sam brought the 24-hour fruit salad that had been such a big hit at Thanksgiving, along with a rum-soaked fruit cake she'd been basting for a month.

Horace joined the party, bringing a mincemeat pie he'd made. Sam gave him a hug. "My, I didn't know you were a pie-maker."

"I have a coupla kitchen skills." He winked. "But mostly I keep 'em secret."

The group lingered at the table laden with turkey, all the trimmings, salads, sweet potatoes, and then pies and cakes and cookies. Soft music and scented candles, laughter and friendship bathed Sam from head to toe in the warmth and spirit of Christmas.

As Sam drove them home later that evening, Electra and

Alberta were still chortling over the day, the food, and the gifts they'd exchanged. "This is the *best* Christmas I've ever had!" Electra declared.

Her mom smiled at Sam. "I think I have to agree."

They went inside, shedding their winter gear. Sam gestured toward the fridge. "Anybody ready for supper?"

The other two groaned.

"No way!" The teen draped herself over the couch.

"I don't think I'll have to eat for a week." Alberta lifted her daughter's feet and sat at the end of the sofa.

"Me too." Sam headed for her rocker and then stopped. "Oh, Melissa Ashton was supposed to call yesterday to let me know about Brad." She went back into the kitchen to make the call, her tennis-playing butterflies kicking off a match as the phone rang.

"Merry Christmas," she said when Melissa answered.

"Oh. Hi, Sam. Yes. Merry Christmas to you too." Her voice sounded subdued.

Oh-oh. Sam swallowed. "What's wrong, Melissa?"

"Well...they tried to take him off the ventilator for about five minutes yesterday and today, but it's not going very well." Her voice broke.

Sam trudged into the living room, chills racing through her body. Alberta took one look and bounded over to hug her, Electra following close behind. They held her for several minutes until she stopped shaking.

"Not good news?" Alberta peered into her face.

She shook her head.

"What's wrong with Brad?" Electra's face had paled.

With a heavy heart, Sam told them what Melissa had said.

"Come sit, Electra, would you make us some hot chocolate?" Alberta led Sam to the rocker. "Now, of course, I'm not a nurse, but I know these things take a while. Sometimes it doesn't work at first. He simply needs more time to heal."

Trying to will the optimism into her mind, she nodded.

Electra brought the cocoa. "I put marshmallows on top." She handed Sam a cup, a concerned look shadowing her face.

"Thank you, dear." Sam took a sip. "Mmm, good. This helps." She tried to smile at her. In spite of her own emotions, she couldn't help but notice how the girl's face had softened, how she'd lost the old Goth hardness.

Alberta took her chocolate, sat on the couch, and leaned forward. "Next time they try, it will work. I know it will."

Closing her eyes, Sam sat for a quiet moment. Then she looked at her friends. "Yes. I have to believe that. Thank you for being here with me."

"Why don't we go to the hospital tomorrow? It might help ease your mind to be with his family." Alberta patted Sam's hand.

"That's a good idea. Let's do that." Gratitude washed over her like a gentle spring shower.

After a restless night, where nightmare horses chased her, carrying a faceless, black-hooded specter, Sam rose early and headed to the barn. As she entered, she took in the musky smell of hay, leather, and manure. The horses, except Toby, were in their stalls, dozing or munching on whatever was left in their feed troughs. She stood still for a moment, taking in the hushed sounds—the soft blowing, crunching, gentle breathing. Peace settled over her. This was like being in church, the sounds creating a hymn. She focused upward, where a shaft of early morning sun beamed through a crack. *Thank you, Lord.* She couldn't think of how to pray for Brad, other than "Please let him be okay." She spoke aloud.

Sugar poked her head around the corner and gave her a soft rumbling greeting. Trixi whinnied then and Apache followed. The three horses came out of their stalls, each coming up to nuzzle her arms as if they knew she needed them. She leaned her head against Sugar's neck, one hand on Apache's head, the other entwined in Trixi's mane. She stood quietly and absorbed their peace and strength.

Sam wasn't sure how long she'd been there like that, the horses perfectly still, simply sending their love. Finally, she became aware of Electra's voice. "Hey, Toby, good morning, boy."

Blinking, she patted each beloved face. "Thanks, guys, I needed that." She went to the storeroom and grabbed a pail of cake pellets to feed them. "An extra treat for you today." Then she moved outside into the sunlight that sparkled on the light dusting of snow.

Electra stood, stroking Toby's face and neck, speaking in soothing tones. He stood quietly, apparently enjoying the attention. The girl looked up when she heard Sam approach. "Good morning! I brought you some coffee." She pointed to a large rock where she'd set a travel cup.

"Thank you. That was so thoughtful of you. I didn't even want to stop to make some this morning. Just needed to get down here with the horses."

"I know." She came over and put her arms around Sam, and they stood that way for several long moments.

***

On the drive to Billings, Sam tried to keep up a cheerful conversation with her friends, going over the wonderful Christmas they'd just celebrated, and reminiscing about past holidays with her family. She missed them greatly, but everyone had gone their separate ways, living so far away. Crippling debt had driven her parents to live off the grid in Alaska. *Just up and left. Abandoned me.* Even her aunt Monica was always either holed up researching and writing or off on another world-wide book tour. An ache occupied the empty spot in her heart.

But she shook off the ache, stole a peep at Electra and Alberta, and smiled. *Friends are my family now. And my horses.*

At the hospital, the other two opted to stay downstairs and browse the gift shop while Sam went up to the ICU waiting room. The three Ashtons were there, as if they'd become part of the furniture and fixtures.

Mrs. Ashton looked up first. "Oh, my dear, hello! I'm so glad to see you." She and Melissa rose from their chairs and gave her a hug. Mr. Ashton shook her hand, unconsciously pushing his wayward lock aside.

"Not a great Christmas for you folks, huh?" Sam swallowed past a lump.

"No, but..." Melissa's eyes glistened, "they just tried him off the ventilator again, and he went for the full five minutes."

"Ohhh." Sam's breath caught, and she closed her eyes. *Thank you.* "This is great news. That has to make you feel better, right?" Her own heavy tension lifted.

"Oh yes." Mrs. Ashton's face shone. "It's giving us hope."

"C'mon, do you want to go in for a minute and see him?" Melissa turned toward the door.

"Absolutely." Sam followed into the beeping, whirring, morgue-like ICU. The antiseptic smells sent a wave of nausea through her. *I can never feel comfortable in this place.* She took Brad's hand and gazed into his face. The bruises had faded to a light hue, and he seemed to have a more peaceful expression. "Hi, Brad, it's Sam. I'm here to wish you a Merry Christmas. Congratulations on your successful breathing exercise this morning. I'm rooting for you. You can do this. You *will* get better, or I'll never speak to you again!"

Melissa chuckled beside her. "I ditto that." She rubbed her brother's arm. "You *are* doing great!"

When they returned to the waiting room, Alberta and Electra were there, talking to Mr. and Mrs. Ashton. They'd brought up a small faux flower arrangement for Brad and a real one for the Ashtons to keep in the waiting room.

"Something to brighten your long days," Alberta said.

Sam embraced her friends and introduced them to Melissa, who hugged them. "Thank you all for coming and for being here for Sam, as she's been here for us."

Tears ran unchecked down Sam's cheeks.

CHAPTER EIGHTEEN

After they left the hospital, Sam settled behind the wheel of her pickup and exhaled a whoosh of air. Did she dare hope? Was this a sign Brad would get better? Beside her, Electra leaned closer and put her head on Sam's shoulder. She grasped the girl's hand and squeezed and then turned to meet Alberta's smile.

The other woman's eyes glistened. "Oh, Sam." She blinked hard.

"Yes. This is a good sign." Sam's voice came out raspy, and she cleared her throat. "You know what? Let's go visit the group home kids."

"Yeah." Electra raised her head and bounced in the seat. "I can't wait to see Sapphire. Let's go!"

"All right then." Sam started the engine and drove through Billings to the group home.

In the yard, several kids packed snow to build a snowman. "There she is. Let me out, Mom, let me out!" Electra reached across her mother for the door handle before Sam came to a complete stop.

"Wait just a second." Alberta gave her a stern look.

"Okay." Electra hung her head. But as soon as Sam parked, the teen bounced in the seat again. Alberta frowned and opened the door to let her out.

"Sapphire! Sapphire! It's me. Hi, Wendy, hi, Susie." She ran over to the girls, and they all shrieked and hugged each other, jumping up and down.

At the commotion, Robin opened the front door. "What...?

Oh, Sam, hello." She stepped onto the porch. "And Alberta. Good to see you. Sam said you were coming for a visit. Come in. I just made a fresh pot of coffee."

The women hugged and went inside, where the counselor poured the brew and set out a plate of cookies. Alberta groaned but took a chocolate nut bar. "I'm going to have to go to the gym three times a day when I get home."

Sam laughed along with the others. Then she told Robin about Brad's progress.

"That's great. I'm glad to hear it. You were pretty down last time you were here." She patted Sam's hand. "He's going to come out of this, I just know it."

After a couple hours' visit, Sam stood. "I think we'd better head for home… if we can round Electra up and pry her away from the kids."

"Let me call them in for a cookie. That should do it." Robin went to the door and before Sam could count to three, a whirlwind of laughing, shrieking teenagers blew in the door, shedding coats and mittens.

"All right. Settle down." Robin gestured to the table. "Have a seat, and I'll make you some hot chocolate."

The girls sat like demure young ladies, but all eyes went to the plate of cookies. Robin grinned as she added hot milk to the chocolate mix and served each a cup. "Okay, you can have a cookie."

"Yay!" "Thanks." "Mmm, I love these." They all spoke at once and grabbed for their choice.

Sam checked her watch. "All right, Electra, fortify yourself, and we need to get on the road."

"Aww, do we have to go? Can't we stay longer?" The teen's voice took on a little girl whine.

"Sorry, not today. We have chores to do and more work with Toby."

"Okay. But," she looked at Robin, "could the kids come out to the ranch to ride?"

Alberta gasped. "Electra! You need Sam's permission first."

152

"Oops, sorry, Sam. Would it be okay? We only have a few more days here and..." she sniffed, "I'd like to see my friends again and maybe ride with them?"

Sam stifled a smile. "Well... I suppose that would be all right with me, if—" she put a hand out to calm the girl who'd already started bouncing in the chair, "if it will work with Robin's schedule."

Electra raised huge, hopeful eyes to the counselor. "Please?"

Robin smirked. "I think we can work something out in a day or two."

"Yay!" All the girls squealed again and jumped up from the table, hugging and dancing around the kitchen.

Alberta blew out a breath. "We'll have our hands full with this group. But it's good to see Electra so bubbly and happy. I do wish..." Her voice trailed off and she shrugged. "Well, let's get going."

The drive home suffered no moment of silence as Electra regaled Sam and her mom with what the girls had done and who said what and who liked what boy and on and on. The women exchanged amused smiles.

Sam guided the truck down the road. *I do wish there was some way they could stay.*

Her cell rang. She glanced at Alberta. "Would you put it on speaker for me?"

Her friend answered, identified herself, and clicked the speaker button.

"Hello, Sam, it's Nick Seward, from the community college."

"Oh. Yes. Hello, Nick." She hadn't expected to hear from him so soon.

"I know it's still Christmas vacation and this is short notice, but I wondered if you might be able to bring your trick horse in, maybe tomorrow or the next day. Some of my board members would like to see what you do with the vets and your horse. It'll be a good time, with no students on campus, and Del and Garrett want to try riding again."

What? Sam's mouth fell open, at a loss for words. Several seconds ticked by.

"Sam? Are you still there?" Nick's voice came over the speaker.

"Uh, yeah. Yes, I'm still here. I'm quite surprised, is all. I wasn't expecting…"

"Well, like I said, it is short notice, so if you can't, I understand."

Beside her, Electra's head bobbed up and down. "Yes, yes, do it," she mouthed.

Sam blinked. "I think I can swing that. How about day after tomorrow?"

"Sounds great. We'll see you then. Looking forward to it." Nick clicked off.

Alberta raised her brow. "That sounds intriguing. And I want to see this too. Is it okay if we come along?"

"Of course. Electra, you can help me demonstrate. And, I hope Garrett will try again and won't fall off this time." She grimaced, remembering how helpless she'd felt. Her stomach fluttered. She still felt responsible for his injury.

***

When Sam rolled up to the Ag Center, several vehicles were already parked in the lot. Nick Seward met them outside the front entrance. "Good morning! I'm glad you could come on such short notice." He thrust out his hand.

She introduced Alberta and Electra who received another hearty welcome and handshake. "Where shall I unload Trixi?"

Nick told her to drive around the back to the outside pens and chute area.

Electra helped her unload the mare, and they led her into the indoor arena, where a group of men and women stood waiting.

Del rolled his wheelchair up to her. "Hi, Miss Sam. Thanks for doing this. We're so excited." He grinned and glanced at Garrett who had followed. "Right?"

His friend's Adam's apple bobbed. "Yeah." He gave a weak

smile. "Right."

He's still scared spitless. Sam's insides fluttered again. She shook his hand and spoke softly. "You don't have to do anything you don't want to."

His face softened, and he flashed her a quick nod.

"Ladies and gentlemen," Nick boomed, "I'd like to introduce you to Samantha Moser, her famous trick horse Trixi, and her friends Alberta and Electra." Polite applause, and he continued. "Sam will be demonstrating the kind of work she and Trixi can do to help disabled veterans. I hope to bring her on as a certified trainer, which I've already explained to all of you."

He gestured to Sam with a flourish. "Take it away, ma'am."

She gestured to Electra whose face shone and gave Trixi the signal. The horse kneeled and came to rest in a sitting position. Electra stepped into the saddle, gave another signal, and Trixi rose.

An audible "Ahhh" came from the group.

Electra rode the mare around the arena a couple of times, changing gaits, and came back to where Sam stood. She signaled again, the horse kneeled, and Electra dismounted.

"That's amazing." Nick applauded. "Something like this will be a great tool in assisting with the mounting process. Good job, ladies." He turned to Del and Garrett. "One of you want to give it a try?"

Sam gulped. Would they want to? Del propelled his chair forward, but Garrett stepped in front. "I'll go."

"Great! You've made such good progress." She held out a hand, which he hesitantly took. *He's trembling.* She paused to steady herself and led him to the mare who knelt again. "Okay, Garrett. Go ahead and get on." *Please let this go well.*

The group remained silent as if collectively holding a breath.

He stopped, leaned down to rub Trixi's neck for a moment, and then lifted his leg over the saddle.

Sam helped him place his prosthetic foot into the stirrup and grabbed him firmly by the belt. "Okay, clamp your knees against the saddle, put your weight on the stirrups and hold on to the horn."

He took a shuddering breath and finally nodded.

Sam motioned to Trixi. The horse rose to her feet.

Garrett stayed centered in the saddle. He flashed her a momentary grin. "Better?"

"Superb." She smiled back, releasing her own pent-up air, and led them around the arena. They were met with applause.

Dismounting from the kneeling mare without mishap, Garrett stood in front of the group. "I've only been to Sam's a few times, but I can tell you that she is a very patient teacher." He cleared his throat. "She never pushed me to do anything I didn't want to. She started me, and then Del, out with simply getting to know the horse, feeding her treats, and gradually beginning the grooming process."

Several people nodded, intently listening. "When I'm with this horse, it's…" his voice faltered, "…it's like a calm comes over me. I forget everything else… what happened…" he looked down at his prosthesis, "and all the demons I fight daily in the regular world."

Garrett stole a peek at Sam and continued. "With winter arriving, I've missed being able to do this on a regular basis. A program here at the center would be a godsend."

She had trouble swallowing. That was the longest speech she had ever heard from him. She bit her lip to keep her joy and gratitude from spilling out. *Oh my, I had no idea he felt this way.* All the hesitation, the stutters and starts, doubts and fears he'd had. *Heck, that we both had.* The work was paying off. She smiled at the veteran. "Thank you, Garrett. That means the world to me."

Del volunteered to ride next. Slow and painstaking, he maneuvered himself into the saddle—Sam hovering behind—and centered smoothly as Trixi stood. He flourished a bow from her back. The group whistled and clapped. Her head full with pride, Sam led him around the arena.

After his ride, he repeated Garrett's sentiments and ended

with a plea. "We need Miss Sam here to help us vets heal."

A couple of the onlookers asked to share in the experience with Trixi, and Sam happily obliged.

"Well, wasn't that something?" Nick beamed at the group. "I hope you will consider my proposal so we can bring Sam on board. C'mon over here." He gestured to her. "Let's give her another round of applause."

Her face heated and she couldn't help but grin.

As she stepped to his side, she glanced up. A dark-haired man stood at the back of the group, his arms crossed in front of his chest.

Jack Murdock! What's he doing here?

CHAPTER NINETEEN

"Wow, that went very well." Alberta reached across her daughter in the pickup and patted Sam's knee.

"Yeah, that was so cool." Electra chortled. "I love showing people what Trixi can do."

"Yes, I'm so thankful it was successful. I'm still blown away by Garrett. I didn't think he'd ever come back, that he'd probably be even more afraid of horses after he fell off and injured himself."

"That was amazing. You could have a future with this." Alberta beamed at her.

"Well, it all depends on the board and if they approve Nick's proposal."

"They will. I *know* they will. I can feel it in my bones."

Electra bounced in the seat. "And I want to help you. I want to work with the horses and the vets too! Can I, Mom? Can I? Please?"

Alberta grimaced. "I don't know, honey. How would it all work? You need to go to school. This is so remote—where would you live? Where would you go to school? And, I have a job to get back to in New York."

"Mo-om." The teenager huffed. "I can live with Sam, right, Sam? And I can... uh... I could home-school."

"Good grief, Electra." Her mother gave her a stern look. "That is so rude. You haven't even asked Samantha about this... or me. You can't be making assumptions about these things. There's so much more to it..." She trailed off, shaking her head.

Sam vacillated between wanting to break into a horse laugh

158

at Electra and shock about her abrupt declaration. Could she take in the teenager? She couldn't home-school her, though. She had too much on her plate already, with her job at Clyde's, working with the group home kids, and now possibly working with veterans in Miles City. And what about Jack Murdock? He didn't look like he was impressed with the demonstration. Being on the board, would he oppose her on this, like he had on selling the ranch to her? But why would he? Fears and what-ifs gathered into storm clouds and settled heavily on her shoulders.

She flashed a peek at Alberta whose face seemed to reflect her own overwhelming thoughts.

Electra's cheeks glistened with tears.

"We'll figure something out." *Now, why did I say that? Am I volunteering something I can't follow through on?*

Back at home after a silent end to the trip, Sam parked near the house. Electra went directly to the corrals, and Alberta walked to the house, her back rounded. Sam stood by the pickup, reaching into the bed to idly pick up stray wisps of hay. She braided them together, trying to make sense of the day… of her life… her future. The lunch she'd eaten after the event sat lumpish in her stomach. Her brain swirled. Brad still in a coma… Murdock's apparent disapproval… Electra's unhappiness in New York… *What am I doing? Do I even have a future here?*

An abrupt, shrill whinny broke the dark spell. In the corral, Toby reared up on his back legs in the narrow passageway just outside the barn door. Cold fear gripped her. *Where's Electra?* She took off at a dead run. "Electra!" *Oh, God, please, let her be all right!*

As she reached the gate, the girl's head popped up over the makeshift chute. "I'm okay! I'm okay!" She waved.

Relief weakened Sam's knees, and she nearly went to the ground. She forced herself to walk calmly into the pen. "What happened? What were you doing? You shouldn't be working that horse without me here."

"I'm fine, Sam. Everything's fine. You were right over there, and I thought... I-I just wanted to show you I could do this, that I could help Toby go into the barn." Tears streamed down her face.

"It's okay." Sam enveloped the girl in a hug. "It's okay," she murmured. "Thank God you're all right."

The teen gave a couple of shuddering sobs. "I want to work with horses so bad." Her voice was muffled against Sam's shoulder. "I want to stay here. I don't want to go back to New York. I'll *die* there!"

Sam blew out a breath. *Oh, man, what am I going to do now?*

Alberta's face turned pale when Electra confessed what had happened. Sam chewed her bottom lip. It only took a moment for trust to be shattered. Her friend would most likely think twice about allowing her daughter to come out again next summer, much less stay in Montana now.

She swallowed. "I'm so sorry, Alberta. I should've been watching closer. That's my fault. I was distracted by my own thoughts and problems."

The woman's face was a hard, angular plane, her lips pressed tightly together. "No," she said finally. "It wasn't your fault. Electra. You know better. If you have *any* hopes of coming back here, of working with horses, you *have* to be more responsible."

The girl blinked back tears. "I know, Mom. I'm sorry. I do know better. It won't happen again, I promise!"

"No. It won't." Her mother sighed. "I'm going to have to think long and hard about this situation. You may just have to wait until you graduate high school to follow this dream."

Electra's face reddened. "Mom. No. Please! Please, Mom."

Alberta shook her head, and the teen ran sobbing from the room.

Sam's heart felt like a two-ton boulder. "Let's give this some time. She does have great potential, working with horses. We all have to go through these experiences and hopefully learn from them." She peered out the window toward the corral. "I'm thinking maybe I need to sell Toby. Maybe he's not going to be redeemable after all."

"Oh, Sam. Don't do that. You work with him some more after we leave, and I'm sure he'll be fine." She mewed a tiny sob. "I don't know what to do... with Electra..." Pivoting, she headed up the stairs.

Sam sank into her rocker, her head in her hands. *I've messed this up too. Electra can't go back to that unforgiving Goth atmosphere. But I can't give up on Toby either. What are we going to do?*

The next couple of days, no one spoke of the incident, but tension thrummed between Alberta and her daughter like a high-voltage electric wire. Both were more subdued toward Sam as well. Regrets and worries lay heavy on her back.

She went about her chores, feeding the cows when needed, and half-heartedly trying to work with Toby in the round pen. He was gentle enough outside, but get him close to an enclosed space and he morphed into a snorting, pawing demon horse. Electra came to the corral to pet and groom Apache, but didn't attempt to help Sam, nor did she ask to go riding.

Clyde called to invite them to dinner and music the next night for New Year's Eve. At first, Alberta simply refused. "I don't feel much like socializing. Besides, we need to get packed up to leave on the second."

Sam grasped the woman's shoulders. "Listen. I think this might do us all some good. We've been skirting around this 'thing,' and it is like a heavy, wet saddle blanket over us, pinning us down. You only have a couple more days. Let's try to set this aside for one evening and enjoy ourselves a little."

"You're probably right. I'm just so worried about Electra going back to school there. I'm afraid... of her mental well-being. But I'm also afraid of leaving her here and the danger... That's too much responsibility, and I can't do that to you."

"Hey. Let's not worry about it right now. I've been praying for some kind of solution." Sam scuffed her toe on the floor.

"There is so much I need God's help with. I don't think I can deal with it all either."

Alberta patted her arm. "I know. And I'm sorry if my funk has put more pressure on you. I do not, repeat, do NOT blame you for this. You've been nothing but a wonderful friend and mentor to my daughter and to me, and I am so grateful."

Sam returned her friend's hug and pasted on a smile. "Let's all go for a ride. That usually helps me clear my cobwebs."

"Sounds good to me."

They found Electra leaning on the wood rails simply staring at Apache across the corral fence. Her eyes were red, face blotchy.

Sam put a gentle hand on her back. "Your mom and I are going for a ride. You want to come with us?"

The girl turned to her mother, eyes wide and pleading. "Are you? Can we?"

Alberta nodded.

Electra straightened and the corners of her mouth trembled upward. "Okay. Yes! I wanna go."

The three saddled their horses, pulled stocking hats down and warm scarves up around their faces, and set off toward the pasture. After walking sedately for a while, the teen looked at Sam, mischief dancing in her eyes. "Race?"

"You're on." Sam touched her heels to Sugar's sides, and they were off in a gallop, Alberta following more slowly behind.

They reined up at the base of the butte, laughing and whooping. "You beat me!" Electra yelled.

"Yes, I did, but not by much." Sam patted her mare. "After all, Sugar is a racehorse, you know."

They all laughed then, and after a short rest, headed toward home.

The Bruckners' ranch house was strung with twinkling lights, and several vehicles were there already when Sam, Alberta, and Electra arrived, carrying dishes with salads and dips.

"Hey, there you are!" a cheery voice greeted from the doorway.

"Teresa! I'm surprised to see you here. I thought you were still with your family." Sam hugged her friend.

"Nope. I'm back. But I do want you to meet someone." She gestured toward a tall dark-haired man. "This is my friend Allen Richardson."

His smile crinkled the corners of his blue eyes as he extended his hand to Sam, then to Alberta and Electra. "Good to meet you all. I've been hearing a lot about you."

Sam wiggled her eyebrows at Teresa as they entered the house. Her friend's face glowed.

Irene and Clyde Bruckner gave them hugs, and Irene took their dishes to the food-laden table. "Toss your coats in the bedroom there, and make yourselves at home," she directed.

Horace had unpacked his fiddle and was tuning it up in the living room, where leather chairs and a couch had been moved back against the walls, clearing a dance floor. Another neighbor had a guitar, and Clyde sat next to them with his. "Any requests?" he called out.

"Something we can dance to." Allen took Teresa's hand and led her onto the gleaming hardwood floor. Horace drew his bow across the strings and launched into an old Anne Murray song "Could I Have This Dance?"

Allen bowed and then swung his date into a waltz.

Another neighbor and his wife joined them. Clyde's baritone voice sang, "…for the rest of my life…"

Sam's chest ached with immediate thoughts of Brad. *He should be here. We should be dancing to this song.* She glanced at Alberta who had half-turned and was wiping her cheek. *Oh yes, she's also missing a partner.* She stepped to her friend's side and squeezed her shoulder. "Me too," she said. The two walked into the kitchen to pour themselves a glass of punch.

When the music turned to an upbeat tune, they went back out to watch. By now Irene had joined the men, playing the piano. Electra grabbed her mother's arm. "C'mon, Mom, let's dance!"

Alberta hesitated a moment and then put out a hand to Sam. "You too, c'mon. We can all flap our elbows to this one."

The three jitterbugged and jigged until they collapsed in chairs along the wall, laughing and breathless.

Electra giggled. "That was fun. But lots different from our dances at school."

"Oh, I don't know." Her mother tittered. "Seems like you girls all get out there and flop around together, just like we did."

"Mo-om," the teen sputtered. "Well, the music's different..."

"Yeah. That's for sure." Alberta rolled her eyes.

Irene stood from the piano bench. "Let's take a break and eat. There's lots of food, so help yourselves."

Sam, Alberta, and Electra piled plates high and found seats near Teresa and Allen. Alberta smiled. "You two are excellent dancers."

Teresa looked at Allen and elbowed him playfully. "That's one of the things that drew us together when we first met." She grinned. "My criteria for a man—that he's taller than I and can dance. Oh yeah, and easy on the eyes."

Allen laughed. "Well, I'm certainly glad I met those stringent requirements."

Teresa giggled. Then she turned to Alberta. "So, you're leaving us soon?"

The smile on Alberta's face faded. "Yes, I'm afraid we have to get on the plane day after tomorrow."

Her daughter bent over her plate in un-Electra-like silence. Sam's heart tripped. *Poor girl. She's definitely not looking forward to going home. And I don't want them to leave.*

Teresa apparently picked up on the teen's discomfort. "But, hey, you'll be back after school's out to help Sam again, right, Electra?"

The girl gave a quick, tight nod.

"Well, that's great." Teresa forged ahead. "That's only five months, and that'll go by so fast. Before you even know it, you'll be here riding and working with Sam's horses and the kids again."

A tear dropped into Electra's potato salad. She stood abruptly and rushed from the room.

"What did I say?" Teresa's eyes were wide. "Did I say something wrong?"

"No. No, you didn't. She hasn't been doing well in New York." Alberta's face sank into weary lines.

"Got back into the Goth thing," Sam added.

Teresa's mouth formed an O.

"She had her heart set on staying here, but the logistics are just not right for that." Alberta sipped her punch. "She's not happy with me at the moment."

Clyde sat next to them with his loaded plate. "So, what *would* it take for you two to move here to Montana?"

"Oh, not much, just a job and school for her." Alberta snorted a little laugh. "Both of which seem a tad out of reach from here."

Sam had trouble swallowing her bite of ham. *Yes, they certainly do.*

Clyde dug into a mound of potato salad and chewed thoughtfully. "You're an accountant, right?"

"Yes." Alberta cocked her head.

Sam stared at him. *What is he getting at?*

The rancher cut a bite of meat and again chewed for a long minute. "Well." He took a sip of his drink. "I could use a good accountant here. That would free up the missus to do what she prefers, cooking and baking and taking care of the guests."

Alberta's eyes widened, and Sam mirrored the surprise.

"Um... I..." Her friend stammered. "Wow... that's a very nice offer. I... I don't know what to tell you. It's—"

"No need to give me an answer right now. I know I won't be able to pay you what your New York firm does, but I'd also offer room and board." Clyde gave her an easy grin. "And, I'll bet most of the ranchers around here would give their best lariat to have a good, trustworthy CPA to do their books and taxes."

Horace slapped his knee. "You bet! I sure would."

One side of Alberta's mouth curved up. "Thanks, guys. But... there's still the issue of school for Electra. I mean, it's forty-something miles twice a day to Forsyth, and these roads out here when it snows..." She shrugged. "I just don't know how it would work out. I would love to, but I can't see how."

Sam slumped in her chair. Alberta had a point.

The first chords of "Tennessee Waltz" came from the living room as Irene and Buck started the music.

"Guess we'd better get back t' work, huh, Horace?" Clyde stood and deposited his now-empty plate on the counter. "Think about it, Alberta. I'm serious with my offer." The two men headed for their instruments, meeting Allen coming through the doorway.

"May I?" He extended a hand to Teresa who glanced at Sam with a twinkle in her eye. The couple danced away.

Alberta stood. Hope skittered across her face, followed by confusion. "I need to step outside and get some fresh air."

Sam got up to follow her, but she put up a palm. "I'll be right back."

Ambling into the living room, Sam leaned against the door frame to watch the dancers. Clyde's offer had stunned her, but then she shouldn't have been surprised. That was Clyde—generous and kind and caring—heck, that described most of the people in this neighborhood. *Getting Alberta and Electra to move here might take us all, but we'll figure something out.*

After a slow dance ended and the music jumped again, Allen and Teresa headed toward Sam. He put out a hand. "Would you like to dance?"

Sam looked at Teresa who nodded. "Go ahead."

"Okay. Sure." She followed the man onto the floor, and he swung her into a jitterbug. For a few minutes, she forgot the problems and worries that had plagued her for so long. When that song ended, Allen grabbed Alberta who'd come back inside and took her out for a dance.

"Whew." Sam fanned her face and lifted her long hair from the back of her neck. "That was fun. So nice of him to dance with us wallflowers."

Teresa giggled. "Yeah. He's a pretty good guy." She watched the dancers for a moment. "That's an awesome offer Clyde made Alberta, huh?"

"Yeah. But it still doesn't seem like that's the answer to keeping them here. School seems like the biggest obstacle."

Sam swore she saw gears churning in Teresa's head. When Allen brought a breathless Alberta back, Teresa grabbed her arm. "I know you guys have to leave tomorrow, but I'm going to do some scouting around town. There's got to be something in Forsyth for you and Electra."

Hope and excitement flared again in the woman's eyes. "Well, thank you. That's very nice of you."

CHAPTER TWENTY

At the Billings airport the next morning, Electra was inconsolable, mascara bleeding onto her cheeks as she dragged her carry-on down the ramp. Alberta threw Sam one last helpless look and a shrug as she followed.

Once again Sam watched the plane take off, carrying beloved friends away. She blinked back tears as she returned to her truck and headed for the hospital to check on Brad. When would this continual barrage be lifted? How could she go on like this? She bit her lip. *Grandma Anna and G-G Nettie wouldn't be wallowing in self-pity. They would simply forge ahead.*

"All right, Samantha Moser." She quickly scanned her sad face in the rearview mirror. "You can do that too. You are Moser stock and that means strong, independent women." She squared her shoulders and shifted gears. "So, cowgirl up!"

Sam strode into the hospital with a smile on her face. The phrase "fake it till you make it" flitted through her mind, and she giggled.

***

Melissa stepped through the double doors of the ICU as Sam arrived, her face shining. "Hey, Sam. I was just about to call you. He's breathing on his own!"

Hope soared inside like an eagle in a summer sky. "Oh my word, really?" She hugged the young woman.

"Yes. They took him off the ventilator early this morning and he's...he's..." Melissa's voice broke. "Oh, Sam, this is a milestone. It's huge."

"Can I go in?" The eagle wings flapped inside.

"Of course, yes." Melissa led the way into the room.

Sam took Brad's hand and peered into his face, the bruising now just a faint hue. His chest rose and fell gently. *Oh, thank you, Lord, thank you.* "Hi, Brad, it's me, Sam. You're doing very well. I'm proud of you, and I'm so thankful."

Melissa rubbed his other arm. "The doctor said he wants to see how he does today on his own, and then if all goes well, he's going to start gradually bringing him out of the coma."

A lump the size of an orange formed in her throat. She stared at the other woman through filmy eyes.

"It'll take several days. He said it's not like flipping a light switch and he comes awake immediately—more like a dimmer switch."

"Wow. I can't believe it. This is what we've been hoping and praying for." Sam swiped her cheek with the back of her hand. "I'm so glad for you."

"And for you." Melissa met her gaze. "I see how you look at him, how you've reacted. You really care about him, don't you?"

All she could do was nod. Yes, she did, and she hadn't realized how much until the accident. And yet, the question tickled her mind of what his feelings were, how he would react to her when he woke up. She swallowed hard. *Surely things will get back to normal. Won't they?*

She and Melissa went back to the waiting room, where Brad's parents enveloped them in a huge group hug. Dee Ashton's face shone with tears, and Paul's eyes misted as he appeared to fight to regain his usual stalwart expression.

As she left the hospital, Sam smiled broadly. *No faking it this time.* She climbed into her pickup and started the engine to warm it up. Then she grabbed her cell phone and speed-dialed Teresa.

"Guess what?" she blurted when her friend answered. She related the news of the day and Teresa's cheery laughter buoyed her even more.

The trip home seemed to take no time at all, and even a

couple of stray "what-if" thoughts about possible brain damage did not dampen her spirits. When she pulled in to Ingomar, she stopped to call Horace. "Hey, do you want a burger from the Jersey Lilly?"

"Sure." Her neighbor's deep chuckle reverberated over the airwaves. "I could use a bite."

"Okay. I'll be there in a little while. I have something to tell you."

***

Sam free-lunged Toby in the small corral, forcing him around and around, switching directions, back and forth. He responded like a champ and sidled up to her afterward, nuzzling her arm for a treat.

"Good boy." She smoothed his face and scratched behind his ears. "You love doing this, don't you? But... why can't I get you to go into the barn? Huh, Toby? Tell me. Why are you still so scared?"

Every time she set up the panels, she had to start practically at ground zero, coaxing him through a wider chute, gradually narrowing it. But as soon as she tried to get the exit close to the barn door, he rolled his eyes, snorted and bucked, contorting himself to turn around and get out.

"What am I going to do with you?" she murmured and shooed him back out into the pasture with the other horses.

Back at the house, her answering machine light blinked. Melissa and Teresa had left messages. She called Brad's sister first.

"Not much to report. Just wanted to keep you in the loop. The doctor is happy with the breathing and is going to gradually decrease the sedation meds, but he'll be keeping a close eye on Brad's progress. The waiting is excruciating."

Sam's stomach dropped. "I know. I'm trying not to think of... you know."

"Yeah. I do. We are being 'cautiously optimistic' as the staff around here likes to say." Melissa snorted a laugh. "But I'll keep you posted."

Expelling a nerve-laced breath, Sam disconnected and called Teresa. She related the latest.

"That's awesome! I'm so happy for you all." Her friend gave a whoop. "On another note, I've been checking around town, and there's only one accounting firm, Lund and Associates. I called David Lund, and he didn't sound like he was hiring right now, but he said he might be interested in talking to Alberta around tax season."

"Oh, okay. That might be good."

"The other possibility is the Rosebud County Treasurer. Again, no openings right now, but... you never know. Could I get Alberta's phone number? I'll call her and tell her about the options."

Sam gave her the number. "Sounds like Clyde's offer is the most concrete for right now though. But there's still the issue of school for Electra."

"Yeah, I know. The kids who come in from surrounding ranches usually board with relatives or friends. Sometimes the family will rent a house, and the mom comes in to stay during the week, going home on weekends."

A sigh rose from deep inside. "Sounds like a difficult way to live." Her grandpa Neil had told of boarding in a dormitory during the week, and Aunt Monica and Sam's dad had also done that during the 1960s and '70s. But Foster's dorm had shut down in the mid-1990s, the last public school dormitory in the United States. She raised her eyebrows. *That sure would be handy in this case.*

"Well, we'll keep thinking on this. Something is going to work out. I know it will." Teresa's cheery voice belied the seemingly insurmountable issue.

Sam hung up and wandered into the living room to stare out at the gently falling snow. *Sure hope Electra can stay strong until we figure this out.*

The next morning, Sam rose early and trudged through six inches of new snow to the barn to feed the horses. Toby

171

ambled out of the lean-to, and she scratched his neck, shivering as a gust of wind swept through. "You're going to freeze to death out here if you refuse to go in the barn, ol' boy." Shaking her head, she patted his back and climbed to the loft to throw down a couple of bales.

Hmm. She shifted her gaze from the stack of hay to the lean-to. Then she threw down several more bales.

Horace's truck ground up the hill, and he parked next to the barn. "Whatcha doin'? You didn't start the party without me, did ya?"

Sam shot him a grin. "Well, I just had an idea." She climbed down the ladder. "I want to build a wall of bales on the side of the lean-to where the wind blows in. That will give Toby some additional shelter—since you're too stubborn to go in the barn—" she raised her voice a notch toward the gelding. "That'll still give him two open sides, so he doesn't feel claustrophobic."

"Well, I'll be durned. You *are* a genius." Horace touched the brim of his hat. "I'll help you stack."

The hay wall went up quickly, and then they loaded the pickup to go out to the pasture and feed the cows.

"Are you going to keep on carin' for Murdock's cows forever?" Horace peered at her across the cab.

"I'd certainly rather be taking care of my own, or better yet, my herd of horses." A sour taste spread across her tongue. "I'm not sure what to think about him." She told her neighbor about Murdock at the ag college demonstration. "He sure looked like a negative Nelly."

"Hmmph. If that don't beat all." Horace shook his head. "I can't see any reason he'd oppose you workin' with the vet group. Especially since he's involved with them himself... I dunno, little gal. That's a head-scratcher, all right."

With breath-holding trepidation, Sam came out to the corrals the next morning and sneaked around the side of the lean-to. Toby stood by the hay wall, taking bites out of it. She laughed aloud. "You stinker, you. If it involves food, you're right there." He bobbed his head, chewing noisily.

She rubbed his face. "I may have to cover this with tarps, so you don't over-indulge. But at least a two-walled shelter didn't leave you out in the cold."

As January blustered its way through the next few days with intermittent snow showers and below-freezing temperatures, Horace and Sam continued to help each other every day. After feeding at her place, she gave him a hot lunch, and then they went to his place to complete his chores. By the time she took care of her horses again, it was evening, and after a light supper, she sank gratefully into her rocker by the stove with a book.

The phone jangled, rousing her from a doze. She strode to the kitchen to answer. Melissa's voice soared through the receiver. "Hi, Sam. Just wanted to update you. Brad is doing well with them bringing him out of sedation. It's a slow process, and he hasn't 'come to' yet, but he's responding to touch and stimulus tests."

Sam's heart beat a tattoo against her ribcage. "Oh, gee, Melissa. That is so great. Wow. I wish..." She gulped. "Do you think it'd be okay for me to come see him tomorrow?"

"Of course. Anytime. I know you've been nailed to the ranch with this snow and cold though. Are you sure you can get away?"

"I'll have to call Horace and make sure he can get someone to help feed, but if I can, I'm sure going to try."

She hung up, whispering a little prayer. *Oh, let him be all right.* Then she called Horace to see if he could get by without her. "Certainly! Don't you worry about a thing."

Picking up her book, she opened it to read but soon set it on the side table, unable to concentrate. Her feet twitched. She stood and looked out the window where the wind pelted snowflakes against the glass. "Darn. Why can't it quit snowing for one day, so I can go to town?"

She scrubbed her fingers through her hair, huffed a sigh,

and walked to the kitchen where she put on water to heat for a cup of cocoa. While she waited, she paced from one window to another, willing the snow and the wind to stop. *I want to be there when he wakes up!*

Despite the hot drink and a hot bath, Sam's mind fought sleep, churning through scenarios like movie previews. The wind continued to shriek, and snow scrabbled at the window like ghoulish fingernails.

She jerked awake to a dark gray dawn, sat up, and listened. The wind still howled, and snow had piled on the windowsill outside in drifts. She threw herself back against the pillow. There would be no trip to town today.

CHAPTER TWENTY-ONE

After a hot oatmeal breakfast and two cups of strong black coffee, Sam bundled up in her down coat, coveralls, and lined overboots. She pulled her wool hat low on her forehead and her knitted scarf higher over her nose. *I should be getting used to this after all this time, but I'm not!* Thankful she had remembered to string a line from the house to the barn, she followed it out to care for her horses. The wind gusted icy pellets against her, and she pushed her way through knee-deep drifts.

Toby, huddled in the corner of the lean-to, whinnied a greeting as she entered the corral. The makeshift hay wall had done a good job of keeping the snowdrifts out of the little shelter. She gave herself a mental pat on the back. Her idea had worked out well.

"Oh, Toby." Sam rubbed ice crystals from the whiskers around his mouth. "I swear you're half mule! You are so stubborn, you won't even go in the barn in this weather."

She climbed into the loft and threw down a couple of bales, gave Toby his flake, and then went into the barn. The musty, warm scent of leather, saddle soap, hay, and manure greeted her, along with the snorts and whickers of her horses. "You guys are the smart ones." Sam chuckled as she fed them hay and cake pellets and rubbed their necks with affection.

Taking a pail of pellets out to Toby, she held a couple out in her hand. "C'mon, Toby. Follow me into the barn, and you'll get your treats."

He came forward and lipped the cake from her palm. She held out more and moved back a few steps. He followed, crunching his treats, as Sam led him closer to the door. But when she stepped into the opening, he stopped short and blew, as if suddenly realizing what she was doing. Tossing his head, he whirled back to his corner.

This would take a lot more work. She fluttered her own lips in frustration.

Horace's diesel roared up the lane, the plow on the front pushing snow aside. After he parked, he lumbered out the door and into the corral. "Mornin'. Weather's pretty rough. You still plannin' to go to town?"

"No. I don't see that happening today. Do you think we can even get out to the cows?"

"We'll give 'er the ol' college try."

"I should've gone out yesterday and moved them closer." She shrugged. "But I really wasn't expecting this blizzard."

"Nope. I think the weatherman missed the mark on that one, as usual."

Sam climbed into the loft again and threw down bales for Horace to load into the back of his truck. Then she climbed into the cab, and Horace ground out toward the pasture in four-wheel drive, tires chained, plowing a path as they went. The wipers worked overtime to clear the windshield, pushing mini drifts to the side of their arc. Horace hunched forward over the steering wheel, squinting as he peered into the blowing snow. More than once he stopped, and he or Sam got out to get their bearings and check if they were still on the trail.

She chewed her lower lip as they clunked to a stop. "Are we stuck?"

Her neighbor shifted into reverse and moved the truck back a few yards. Then he winked at her. "Nope. Not yet." After studying the landscape, he steered around the spot and continued.

The wind and snow let up for a minute. Sam pointed. "There's the cottonwoods by the reservoir."

"Okay, good. The cows are prob'ly in that coulee there." He drove to a flat area between the pond and the wash that drained into it. They both got out to chop holes in the ice so the cattle could drink. Then Sam climbed on top of the bales.

"You sure you don't want to drive, let me do that?" he asked.

"Nope. I'd get us stuck, for sure." Taking off one mitten, she grasped her pocketknife, slit the twine on a bale, and threw flakes out onto the snow. Her hand quickly felt like a lifeless chunk of ice, and she put the mitten on again, repeating the process as Horace drove.

Pretty soon a head poked over the rim of the coulee and the lead cow sprinted for the hay. Sam called out, "Hey, bossies, here's the food truck. Come and get it!" The first cow was followed by another, then another, until the herd milled around the pickup.

Horace drove in a wide circle until she had distributed all the hay. Then she opened a sack of cake pellets and dribbled them out behind as he circled again. When it was gone, she thumped on the cab roof, he stopped, and she climbed in. The blast of heated air welcomed her, and she clapped her mittened hands together to restore circulation. She whistled. "Whew. That was fun."

He let out a belly laugh. "Just another day in paradise, huh, little gal?"

"Is that what this is?" Sam shot him a half-hearted grin.

"It's Montana. Gets snow and cold, what're we gonna do about it?"

"That's right. Kenny would never have survived here."

"Naw. He was a panty-waist." Putting the truck in gear, he drove back toward home. This time the path was easier to follow, although it was rapidly drifting in.

"I've got some stew in the crockpot. Let's go in and get warm before we tackle your place," Sam suggested.

"Stew sounds great. But let's wait till tomorrow to feed mine. I fed yesterday, so they should be okay until then."

A ping of guilt shot through Sam's insides. Horace had put her and her chores ahead of his. That wasn't right. "Are you

177

sure they're okay? I'm more than happy to help you this afternoon."

"Naw, they're close to the corrals and windmill. They'll be fine." He nodded to punctuate his declaration. "Now, let's go feed *us*."

***

The next couple of days repeated themselves, with home chores and feeding her and Horace's cattle. "I'm so glad it finally quit snowing." She helped load hay into her neighbor's truck.

"Yeah, me too." He stacked another bale on top. "At least the paths we plowed are staying clear, and that makes it easier to get out there."

"Since we fed your cows yesterday, if you don't need me, I'm thinking I'll try to get in to Billings to see Brad this afternoon."

"You go. We're good over at my place."

When they came into the house for lunch, the phone light blinked. The message was from Melissa to give her a call. Sam punched in the number with trembling fingers. *Did Brad wake up, and I wasn't there?* Each ring accentuated stomach flutters. *C'mon, Melissa, pick up.*

"Hi, Sam." Her friend's voice finally broke the tension. "Just wanted to check in with you."

"Yes?" Sam knotted her fingers in the phone cord. "Did he wake up?"

Melissa hesitated a moment. "Kind of."

Sam wanted to scream. *What does that mean?*

"He opened his eyes this morning and asked where he was and what happened. But then he went right back to sleep. I think he recognized us, but it was too short a time to tell."

"Oh wow." Sam's heart rode up her throat with spurs. "I'm coming in this afternoon, as soon as we get a little bite to eat. Hang in there. He'll be all right." This was as much for her sake as Melissa's. "See you in a couple hours."

"Sure. Drive safe. The roads might still be a little icy."

Sam replaced the receiver and slumped against the wall. Waves of fear and excitement alternately crashed through her.

"Did he...?" Horace stood in the doorway.

Her legs wobbled like a newborn calf as she pushed herself away from the wall. "For a couple of minutes, sounds like." She told him what Melissa said.

"That's a good sign, I'm thinkin'. So it's good you're going in today." He smiled. "Y'know, I haven't gone to church much in past years, but I'm a believin' man. And I been prayin' for Brad... and for you, little gal."

Sam's eyes stung. "Thank you." Her voice rasped. "Thank you so much." She faced the stove. "Stew okay again?"

"You bet. It's hot, it's filling, and it's mighty tasty."

The road stretched mostly clear and dry, but Sam watched for the hidden patches of black ice in the shaded areas as she tried not to speed her way to Billings. What would she find there? Fear that he would wake up but not remember her squeezed her insides. Her shoulders climbed toward her ears, and her fingers clenched around the steering wheel. "I'm coming, Brad. I'll be there soon." She kneaded her neck with one hand and forced herself to relax. "Hey, God, it's me again. I... don't know quite what to say to you, other than please help him, please heal him, and let him be all right."

Rays of sun beamed from behind a fluffy white cloud as she pulled into the hospital parking lot. *That's a good sign. I hope.* Slamming the pickup door shut, she strode as fast as she could across the icy pavement. The automatic doors sluggishly creaked open, and she strode across the lobby to the elevator. She stared up at the lit number that stayed on the top floor for endless minutes. As soon as the numbers showed the car's descent, it stopped again. She headed for the stairs and bounded up two at a time.

The Ashtons were not in the waiting room, so Sam opened the door to ICU, the drums in her chest nearly knocking her over. The beeps, whirrs, and whooshes of the equipment added

179

their pulsing beat. Brad's family stood around his bed. Sam stopped cold. *Is he...? No, he's not...* She expelled a sob.

Melissa turned. "Oh, Sam. I'm so glad you're here."

"How...? What...? Is he...?" Sam's voice choked.

"It's okay." The young woman put an arm around her and steered her to the bed. "We're simply waiting for his next waking moment. He woke up for another minute and asked again where he was and what happened."

Sam's tight ribcage welcomed a breath. Dee and Paul drew her into their circle. She grasped Brad's hand and stared at him. His head was still swaddled in bandages, but his face had a healthier rosy tint.

"Hi, Brad. I'm here. Wake up. I want to talk to you. I've missed you... so much." Her voice quavered.

Brad's hand squeezed hers. A jolt of electric hope ran through her. "Brad?"

His eyelids fluttered, opened for a second, and then closed. She squeezed his hand again. "Brad, are you awake? Can you hear me? It's me. Sam."

His eyes opened wide, and he looked directly at her. "Where am I?"

"You're in the hospital in Billings. You were in an accident when you were bringing Toby home. But you're okay now." Sam stroked the back of his hand.

"Sam...?" His voice grated like an unoiled barn door hinge.

"Yes, it's Sam. Hi, Brad. Welcome back." Her lungs seized.

He squinted at her. "Toby...?"

"Toby is fine. He wasn't hurt. He's at home with me."

"Accident... Mad?" His eyes opened wide.

"Oh no, I'm not mad at you." Tears tickled her cheeks. "I'm so glad you're awake."

He sighed and sank into the pillow, apparently drifting back to sleep.

Melissa pulled her into a hug. "He's awake, Sam. He knew you!"

Dee and Paul Ashton joined the group hug, laughing and

crying too. When they released her, Sam reached into her pocket for a tissue and blew noisily. "Y-yes. Oh, yes." She raised her eyes to the ceiling, tears still streaming. "Thank you."

She stayed the afternoon, alternating between the waiting room and standing by Brad's bedside. He awoke several more times, each time asking where he was and what happened. But then he looked at Sam and smiled. "Oh yes. Sam. Hi." Each time he seemed to be a tiny bit more aware and asked an additional question or gave an answer to her question how he was feeling.

Her heart soared as if on eagle's wings during his lucid moments, then dropped like a stone when he asked the same questions over again. She stared into Melissa's drawn face. "What is this? Will he ever—?"

A white-coated doctor strode into the room. "Hello, ladies. I'm Dr. Olson. How's our patient doing?" He took out a penlight, pulled Brad's eyelid back, and shined the light into his eye. Brad jerked and opened wide. "What...? Where am I?"

The doctor answered and explained in a quiet, soothing voice as he poked and prodded. Brad seemed satisfied and fell back to sleep.

"Is this normal?" Sam's voice was strained. "He keeps asking the same things every time he wakes up."

"Yes, it is common. He's still under a bit of sedation. It'll be a day or two before he's off entirely." Dr. Olson checked the bandages on Brad's head. "It's simply going to take some time before he stays awake and starts to remember. He had a concussion, which often affects short-term memory in itself, and remember, he's been under for over a month."

"So you don't think he has suffered... brain damage?" Sam's stomach folded in on itself.

"It's too soon to tell, but I'm encouraged by the fact that he recognizes you all when he wakes up." The doctor patted her arm. "Give him time. He has a long road of healing ahead." He slung his stethoscope around his neck and strode out of the room.

Sam's exhale was shaky. "Do you believe him?"

"Yes. I do. I have to, Sam." Melissa gave her a weak smile. "This doctor is supposed to be one of the best in his field, and I'm sure he's seen many coma patients like this."

Sam grasped her hand. "Okay. I'll keep hoping… and praying." *And I'll believe it when I see it.*

She called Robin to see if she had an extra bed for the night and then Horace to share the news and let him know she'd be home the next day. "I don't want to drive these roads in the dark. I'll leave early in the morning and will help you feed both herds. So don't start without me."

"All right, little gal. You hang in there. And drive careful, ya hear?"

"Come in." Robin welcomed her with open arms. "I have supper ready."

Sam gave her a hug and stepped into the bright, cozy kitchen, where the girls leaped from their seats and crowded around her. "Miss Sam. I'm so glad you're here for a sleepover." Sapphire chortled, and the other girls echoed her sentiments.

Robin set a steaming meatloaf, mashed potatoes and gravy, and a bowl of green beans on the table. "Okay, Wendy, it's your turn to say grace."

After a quick, mumbled, "Thank you for this food and for Miss Sam," the girls each grabbed a dish and offered it to Sam first.

Her chest cavity filled with the warmth and love that emanated from the group around the table. Her eyes stung, and she could barely speak. "Thank you. I'm so grateful… for… all of you."

With big grins, they dished up their plates, and the girls ate as if they were starving, giggling and jostling each other as they reached for butter or salt and pepper.

"So, Brad is waking up, huh?" Robin's eyes shone.

"Yes, very gradually." Sam filled her in on what she had

witnessed and what the doctor had said. "But I'm still... so scared. He doesn't seem to remember the conversation we had the time before. What if...?"

"No, no. You can't go there." Robin shook her head emphatically. "The doctor is right. Brad went through a lot of trauma, and he's been 'away' for nearly six weeks. He's not going to wake up, jump out of bed, and resume his normal routine immediately."

"No." Sam had to laugh. "You're right. I'm just a worrywart. I come from a long line of worriers."

Robin smirked. "We women seem to be wired that way, for sure. You need to be a warrior, not a worrier."

Sam slept hard that night and rose well before daylight to head home. She put on a pot of coffee and grabbed a cinnamon roll Robin had left out for her. After leaving a note of heartfelt thanks, she jumped into her pickup and was soon on the way home.

When she pulled into her place, Horace was already at the barn, throwing hay bales from the loft. "Hey you! You weren't supposed to start without me." She jogged to the ladder.

Her neighbor chuckled. "That's okay. Thought I'd get a little head start. Be ready when you got home."

Sam hooked a bale and positioned it in the truck bed, and soon they were grinding out to the pasture through the icy ruts of the path Horace had plowed during the storm. The cows heard them coming and ran to the vehicle, crowding around the first flakes Sam distributed. As soon as she threw down the next bit of hay, the lead group followed at a trot to get at the best morsels first.

After feeding, they chopped ice in the reservoir, and then after a quick hot bowl of vegetable soup and sandwiches, headed over to Horace's to repeat the sequence.

Violet shadows spread from the hills over the snow as Sam drove home that evening, cold and tired, but exhilarated by the work and the camaraderie with Horace. *He's good people. I'm so blessed to have him as a neighbor.* She couldn't help but smile.

The message light blinked furiously when she walked into the house. Shucking out of her overboots and coveralls, she hit the play button. A tearful voice greeted her. "Hi… Sam… It's Electra. I'm at the airport… in Billings…" A hiccup followed. "I don't know what to do… Can you come get me?"

CHAPTER TWENTY-TWO

Sam let out a long moan. *Oh, Electra, what have you done?*

The next message cued up with Alberta's frantic voice. "Oh, Sam, Electra is gone. I came home and she was... gone. She took my credit card and left a note that she was going to Montana to live with you. Have you heard from her? Oh, Sam, I'm so worried."

Another message followed from Electra, punctuated by sobs. "Sam, are you there?... I tried your cell... and your home... and... and... I don't know Robin's number... or the group home... name... I can't stay... h-here... The airport closes at... 10." Her voice wound down to a choked wail.

Sam closed her eyes. What to do? Electra didn't have a cell phone, and cell service at the ranch was non-existent, so she couldn't redial the number the girl had called from. *Think, Sam, think.* Which airline had they come in on at Christmastime? Or maybe she could call the airport. She grabbed a phone book and riffled through the yellow pages. *Maybe I'd better call Alberta first... Or maybe I should call the airport first and make sure she's still there.*

She found the number for airport security and punched it in. When a man answered, she identified herself and asked if he could page Electra. "Oh yeah. She's around here somewhere, pretty distraught, waiting for somebody. Hold on a minute."

Sam stared out the window into the darkness. Indecision loomed—another trip to Billings, and at night, on possibly slippery roads—*I really don't want to go again*—or call Robin and see if Electra could stay there? *Yeah, that's the best idea.* She blew out, fluttering her lips like her horses.

"Sam? Is it you? Sam, are you there?" A small high-pitched voice came over the line.

"Yes, it's me."

The girl broke into sobs.

"Electra. Electra. Listen to me. Calm down now. You're okay. I'm going to come and get you, all right?" She shut her eyes. *What did I just say?*

"All… all… right…"

"Take a couple of deep breaths and let them out slowly." She heard the girl comply.

"Okay, Sam. I'm okay."

"I'm going to leave now. It's going to take me a couple of hours or maybe a little longer, depending on the roads, so I should be there around 8 or 8:30."

"O-okay."

Sam tried to keep her own voice calm. "Have you called your mom? I had a message from her, and she's really worried about you."

"N-no." A sniffle. "She'll be… so… mad."

"Well, I suppose so. This was a pretty bone-headed stunt. I'm going to call her now and let her know I've talked to you. But you should probably call her too."

"Yeah… prob'ly should." More sniffles.

"I'll be there as soon as I can. Do you have any money to get something to eat in the café there?"

"Yeah."

"All right, you do that. Wait in the restaurant if you can, and I'm coming to get you." Sam hung up, her jaw muscles knotted. *Oh man! Whatever possessed her to do this? And why am I driving back to Billings tonight?* She punched in Alberta's number. *I'm such a pushover.*

"Yes?" The woman's answer was practically a shout.

"It's Sam. Electra's in Billings. I just talked to her, and I'm going to get her. She's fine, just scared and upset."

"Oh, thank the Lord! Good grief. I can't believe she did

this. She is going to be grounded for the rest of her life!" Now Alberta's voice shook with anger. "I'm so sorry this has fallen on your shoulders. I'm going to have to figure out what to do."

"It's all right. She's fine, and that's the main thing. I'll go retrieve her, and we can figure out what to do later. Just relax, get some rest. Things will work themselves out." *Or maybe not. What am I going to do with that girl?*

After Sam disconnected, she put a calming hand on her forehead. "Things will work out," she repeated, as she nuked a cup of leftover coffee, grabbed a couple of cheese sticks and granola bars, several bottles of water, and her purse. She threw her coveralls behind the seat with the extra blankets she kept there and hopped into the pickup.

The tires spun in the snow as she gunned the engine, and she stopped the vehicle. *Calm down, yourself, Sam. It's not going to do anybody any good to get stuck or slip off the road if you're in such an all-fired hurry.* She forced herself to sit quietly for several seconds, inhaling and exhaling in a slow rhythm. Then she left in a more sedate fashion, trying to hang on to the relaxed moment.

When she had cell service, she called Horace to tell him she was going to Billings.

"Oh golly. Is it Brad?" His voice held a note of concern

"No. It's Electra." She told him what had happened.

"Oh, for Pete's sake! Hey, stop by and pick me up. I'll go with you."

"I'm already on my way. Sorry. I'll be fine. See you tomorrow."

The road was mostly bare and dry, but she consciously drove below the speed limit, just in case. With little or no traffic, darkness engulfed the truck, the headlights narrowly pointing the way. Thoughts spun through her mind. If Alberta let her daughter stay… Maybe they shouldn't reward her for this stunt. But on the other hand, if she was so unhappy in New York… But how could Sam take care of this willful teenager and see that she got schooling?

She moaned and tapped her fingers on the steering wheel. *Oh Lord, tell me what to do.*

Finally, the lights of Billings winked on the horizon. She entered the city limits and drove up onto the rimrocks to the airport.

Striding through the lobby, she swung her gaze around, looking for Electra, and headed toward the Gateway Restaurant. Just as she opened the door, she was nearly bowled over with a jittery bundle of squeals and wails. "Sam! Sam! You're here! I'm so glad you're here! Ohmygosh, ohmygosh, ohmygosh." The girl buried her head in Sam's neck and sobbed.

Sam wrapped her arms around her and rubbed her back, murmuring and rocking side to side, trying to control her own anger. When the torrent finally subsided, she put an arm around the teen's shoulders and led her to the restrooms, pulling the suitcase behind. "Let's go wash your face. You're okay now."

When Electra was more composed, they headed outside to the pickup, loaded the suitcase, and Sam drove down the hill to the highway toward home.

"Did you call your mom?"

Rustling came from the passenger side as Electra fidgeted. "No." The small voice again. "I couldn't. I know I made a mistake. I shouldn't have done this. She's gonna hate me."

Sam chewed her lower lip and forced herself to speak calmly. "No, she's not going to hate you. Yes, she is upset and angry. But she loves you, and she was scared when she found you missing." She reached for her cell. "I want you to call her right now."

"Do I *have* to?" The little girl whine.

"Yes. Do it right now." Sam repeated in a firm tone. *C'mon, Electra. I don't want to have to deal with your attitude on top of everything else.*

As Electra made the call, snowflakes hit the windshield.

***

Flakes swirled in the headlights. Sam flipped on the wipers and the defroster fan. *Oh man. Just what I did not need.*

"But Mo-om…" the little girl voice whined from the other side of the cab. "I said I'm sorry…"

Sam couldn't hear Alberta's words, but judging from the raised voice, she was not happy.

"I know, Mom. I just couldn't…" Electra held the phone away from her ear while her mother ranted.

Peering through the mesmerizing whirl of snow, she blinked to keep from being hypnotized. She slowed the truck's speed and concentrated on watching the fog line on the highway.

"I can't, Mom. I can't go back there. Please…" She held the receiver out. "Mom wants to talk to you."

"Not right now. I'll call her when we get home." She hunched forward over the wheel.

"We're in a snowstorm, Mom. She'll call you later… Okay, 'bye."

Wind gusts whipped the snow into a frenzy. Sam tested the brakes. So far, it wasn't slippery. She mentally crossed her fingers. *I've got to get us home safe.*

Electra stayed blessedly quiet, also staring out the windshield at the falling snow. After a while, she moaned. "Geez, this is bad, Sam. I'm so sorry."

Clenching her teeth, Sam tried to hold back a sharp retort. "Maybe time to say a prayer." She smacked the steering wheel.

The girl moaned and bowed her head, mumbling.

Visibility seemed to clear a bit, and Sam forced her shoulders to relax. Then she saw the bright lights of a semi coming toward them. She clamped her hands around the steering wheel as the wind blast from the big truck rocked her pickup and blew snow across the windshield. *Stay straight. Stay on the road.* The vehicle slid sideways. Electra shrieked.

Keeping her eyes straight ahead, she steered in the direction of the skid and pumped the brakes rapidly. Eternal seconds stretched as the old pickup continued in its long swerve. Then as suddenly as it began, it straightened itself, and they drifted to a stop on the side of the road.

Electra panted tiny squeaks. Sam closed her eyes and lowered her forehead to the wheel. *We're not in the ditch. We're still on the road. Thank you, Lord.*

She sat upright and achingly opened her paralyzed fingers. "You okay?"

"Yeah," a mini voice replied.

"Good." Sam huffed a semi-laugh. "We dodged a bullet, that's for sure."

"Ohmygosh, ohmygosh, ohmygosh!" Electra's face glowed white in the dashboard lights. "I... I was so... scared. Ohmygosh."

"Well, we're all right. And it's only another forty-five minutes or so home. We're going to make it." Sam shifted into gear and eased the pickup back onto the road. The snow drifted now rather than swirling, and she was able to see the road in front of them.

With no further incidents, Sam pulled into the ranch yard at nearly midnight. They sat in silence for a minute, simply breathing.

"Th-thank... you... Sam." Electra's voice still quavered. "I've caused you so... much trouble. I-I'm s-sorry."

"Hey. We made it. We're okay." She squeezed the girl's arm. Let's go inside and make some hot chocolate."

Electra pulled out her suitcase, and they went inside. The phone message light blinked. Horace's voice held concern. "Sure hope you decided to stay in Billings tonight, little gal. Give me a call when you get this, no matter what time it is."

Alberta's message was equally tense. "Oh my, I hope you guys are all right. I didn't want to call your cell again if you were driving in a storm. Oh, I hope..." Her voice trailed off. "Call me when you get home. I don't care what time."

Sam took milk out of the fridge and the box of cocoa from the cupboard. "Go ahead and fix it. I'll make the calls." She punched in Horace's number first. When his sleepy voice answered, she said, "We're home safe and sound. Thank you for checking on us. Sorry I didn't call you, but I was a little busy with the roads."

"Yeah. When it started to snow, I kept picturing you in the ditch somewheres. You shoulda stayed in town. But I'm glad you're home."

"I know. I should have stayed. Didn't think it was gonna storm. Oh well. Go back to sleep. Sorry we worried you."

Alberta was apparently still awake, despite it being 2 a.m. in New York. "Yes?" Her tone high-pitched, expectant.

"It's Sam. We're home and we're fine."

A long, low sound soughed over the line. "Oh good. When Electra said you couldn't talk because you were in a snowstorm..." Another puff. "Golly, talk about feeling helpless."

"Yeah, it was a little hairy for a bit, but it's okay. We're going to have some cocoa, chill out a bit, and hit the hay. Can we talk more in the morning?" Now that she was home, Sam's limbs trembled, and she could barely stand.

"Absolutely. I'm going to have to figure out what to do with that girl. But you both get some rest now."

Hanging up, she slumped into her chair.

Electra poured two cups of steaming chocolate and sprinkled marshmallows on top. "Sam... don't be too mad at me. I'll make it up to you... somehow... I promise." Her wide eyes glistened with tears.

Sam forced herself to look away from the puppy-dog eyes and spoke in a stern tone. "We'll see what your mom has to say tomorrow."

"Do you think she'll let me stay?"

"I don't know. You'll just have to wait and see."

***

Although Sam desperately wanted to sleep in after the late night, she awoke to her alarm blasting at 6 a.m. With a groan, she dragged herself out of bed, shivering in the early morning chill. She put on her fuzzy robe and slippers and trudged up the stairs. She knocked on Electra's door. "Time to rise and shine!"

No answer. She knocked again, a little harder. "Electra! Time to get up."

This time she was answered with a moan.

"Are you awake?"

"Okay." The girl's voice was raspy. "Okay, I'm up." Rustling came from the room and finally, Electra opened the door. Her hair stuck out in all directions, and she blinked against the light in the hallway. "What time is it?"

"Time to get the chores done. If you're going to prove what you promised, you're going to have to work hard. Harder than you've ever worked before." She turned to go back downstairs. "Get dressed. I'll have breakfast ready in a few minutes."

She started the coffee and hot chocolate, and by the time Electra came down, she set a steaming bowl of oatmeal in front of them both.

The teen took a sip of the hot drink. "It's not even light out yet. How do we see to do chores?"

"It's getting light. We'll be fine." Sam gestured to the center of the table. "There's brown sugar and raisins if you want them on your oatmeal."

"Okay." As Electra reached for the dish of raisins, her sweater sleeve rode up, and Sam caught a glimpse of angry red marks.

"What happened to your arm?"

Electra snatched her hand back and pulled down the sleeve. "Nothin'."

Cold dread pooled in Sam's stomach. "Did somebody…?"

The girl shook her head and stared into her oatmeal.

Icy fingers clutched at Sam's insides. Had she gotten into a fight with her mom? *No. Alberta would never…* "Did the girls at school do this?"

A shrug. "No."

The chill crawled up Sam's spine. "Did you… cut yourself?"

Electra bent closer to the bowl. A tear dripped into the oatmeal.

Standing, Sam came around the table and put an arm around

the teen. "Oh, honey." What could she say? She'd heard of this thing, where girls cut themselves to take away emotional pain. She squeezed the teen's shaking shoulders. What on earth could she say? How could she fix this?

Electra stood abruptly. "I'm going to the barn."

"Okay. You can chop the ice in the tank and feed the horses some of their pellets. I'm going to call your mom, and then I'll be out to throw down some hay."

The girl slipped into the extra pair of coveralls Sam had set out, and left, head bowed, steps dragging.

The oatmeal sat congealing on the table. She had no more appetite either, so she picked up the phone and called Alberta.

"Good morning. You're up early. Things going okay?" The woman sounded tired but not as frantic as last night.

"Yeah. I figured I might as well give Electra a taste of the hard work she's in for... if you decide to let her stay." She swallowed. *How am I going to tell her?*

Alberta huffed. "I was awake most of the night, hashing this thing out. First, I was so mad I wanted you to put her back on the plane immediately. Then, I started worrying about how unhappy she is at this school. She has done a complete reversal to the way she was before... Oh, Sam, I just don't know what I should do."

"Well..." Sam swallowed. "There's something you should know." She told her about the cuts.

Alberta emitted a strangled sound. "No."

"Maybe it would be a good idea for her to stay, at least for a while." She wound the phone cord tight around her fingers. "Maybe she could talk with Robin—she's a counselor and deals with troubled kids. And I know Electra always makes a huge turn-around in attitude when she's here, working with the horses."

"Yeah. There is something healing about that. I feel it too." Her friend's voice was weak. "I... I'm going in to talk to my boss and see if I can take some more time off. I'll come out as soon as I can. I don't want you to take all this responsibility on by yourself."

Part of Sam felt a lift of relief, but down deep, she still harbored doubts. "I appreciate that. But I know it's hard for you to get away, and you're going to be entering your busy tax season soon. Why don't you give us a few days anyway, and let me see what I can work out here."

A pause. "Okay. That sounds good for now. But like I said…"

"We'll be all right." *Am I trying to convince her or myself?* "Maybe she'll confide in me, or if not, to Robin. I want to go back to Billings tomorrow anyway. Brad is gradually waking up, and I want to be there with him."

"That's wonderful, Sam. I'm so glad for you." Alberta was obviously trying to put a cheerful note into her voice. "Well, see how your day goes, and I'll call tonight to talk to Electra."

After she hung up, Sam poured coffee and the chocolate into travel mugs, grabbed a couple of granola bars, and headed for the barn. The ice on the tank was still intact. She set her shoulders and entered the corral. Toby whickered and came to meet her from his shelter. She stopped and patted his neck for a moment and then went into the warm, musty barn.

At first, she didn't see Electra, but then she heard muffled sobs from Apache's stall. She approached slowly. The horse stood quiet, his head and neck arched around the girl as if in a hug, while she buried her face in his mane.

Apache turned to look at Sam and rumbled a greeting. Electra jerked back. "Oh. Hi. I didn't hear you." She swiped a mitten across her cheek. "Sorry, I didn't get anything done yet. I only wanted to… to… see Apache." The last words came out in hiccupped sobs.

Sam stepped into the stall and wrapped her arms around the girl. "I know. That's exactly what you needed. And he knows that." They stood, entwined and rocking, for several long moments.

Then Electra eased back. "I'm okay. Let's get to work." She sniffled, reached into her pocket for a tissue, and blew loudly.

"All right then. If you want to give the horses some pellets, you know where the bin is. I'll go up in the loft and toss down a bale."

The teen looked at her. "What did Mom say?"

"She's going to give us a few days to work things out. She'll call you tonight."

An exhale lowered the girl's shoulders. "Okay."

When the horses were fed, Sam and Electra each grabbed an ax and chopped the four-inch-thick ice from the tank, throwing the chunks into a growing pile to the side. Electra hacked at the ice with more strength than Sam realized she had, as if she were beating down her demons.

CHAPTER TWENTY-THREE

As Sam lifted the last chunk of ice from the tank, Horace's truck roared up the driveway. Electra waved both arms at him. When he eased himself from the vehicle, she ran to give him a bear hug. "Ohmygosh, I'm so glad to see you, Horace. I missed you *so* much!"

"I missed you too." He gave Sam a wink.

"Well, I'm here to work... hard..." She stepped back and spoke with a serious expression. "I want to prove to Mom and you guys I can do it." Her eyes welled with tears. "I want to stay here... so bad."

"All right then." Horace swept an arm out. "Let's get to work. You can help me stack the truck."

Sam threw down the hay, and Horace showed Electra how to arrange the bales. He grabbed one end of the bale with a hook, the girl took the other, puffing and grunting as they maneuvered it in place. When the pickup was loaded, they all piled in, and Horace drove to the pasture, where the cows awaited them with eager white faces turned in the direction of breakfast.

"Okay, Electra, you come up top and help me distribute the hay while Horace drives." Sam cut the twine and tossed down a flake.

The teen threw herself into the job with gusto, dropping hay as fast as she could.

"Whoa. Slow down. A little at a time, like this." Sam showed her.

Electra relaxed into the task. "Look at those cows." She

laughed, pointing. "They take one bite and then run behind us to get the next one. It's like they're racing each other."

"Yup. Cows are greedy… just like people sometimes."

When the truck bed was emptied, Horace drove to the reservoir. Sam handed Electra an ax. "More ice to chop."

Again, the girl attacked the chore with all her might.

"Wow. She's turnin' out to be one heckuva worker." Horace raised his eyebrows.

"Yeah. She's trying. She's serious about staying here." Sam pressed her lips together. "I don't know what her mom is going to do, and I don't know how I'm going to handle this girl and her troubles."

"W-e-l-l, you've worked wonders in the past with her and the other kids." Horace peered from beneath bushy gray eyebrows. "I got faith in ya, little gal. Between you and the horses… and this hard work, I think she's gonna be all right."

"Thanks. I sure hope so."

When the ice was cleared from holes so the cattle could drink, they all piled back into the truck. Electra rubbed her hands together. "That's the only part of me that's cold." Her arms quivered, and her whole body shook with tiny tremors. "This is really hard work. You do this every day?"

"Twice a day." Sam grinned at Electra's shocked look. "About every other day when the snow's not too deep. Now, we go home for lunch, and then do the same thing at Horace's."

The girl's eyes widened. "Can I drive the truck this time?"

Horace guffawed. "I see right through ya, young lady. Nope, not this time."

***

When they got home that evening, Sam went into the kitchen to fix supper. Electra collapsed on a chair. "I can't raise my arms."

"You're probably going to be pretty sore tomorrow. You worked very hard today. I'm proud of you." Sam smiled. "We'll get a day to rest though. I want to go to Billings to see Brad. I

197

hope he'll be able to stay awake soon."

"Oh. Yeah. I hope so too. I miss his teasing."

"You do, huh? I remember when we first met him, you didn't like him at all."

The teen cocked her head to one side. "Well, neither did you, at first."

"That's true." Sam snickered." I thought he was in cahoots with those New York developers to take away our land and turn it into a big wildlife park."

"That was such a stupid idea." The girl scrunched her nose. "I'm glad he wasn't with them. I know you really like him... and I do too."

"I'm glad." Sam flipped burgers in one frying pan and stirred sliced potatoes and onions in another. Then she set ketchup, mustard, and pickles on the table. "Hungry?"

"Am I ever!" Electra scooted the chair up to the table and stuck out a hand to grab a napkin, slowing in mid-reach and wincing. "I'm sorry I didn't help with supper. I actually *can't* move my arms."

"You'll get used to it." Sam sat and dished up the food.

When they finished, she made hot chocolate and brought out oatmeal raisin cookies.

Electra took a bite and closed her eyes. "Mmm, so good."

Should I try to talk to her, or should I wait and have Robin meet with her? She cleared her throat. "Honey..." *Here goes.* "I know you've been going through some hard times lately."

The smile faded from the girl's face.

Oh dear. But I can't stop now. "I don't know what it's like to lose a brother and then having your dad leave." Her insides trembled. "But I do know how painful it was for me when my grandparents died. Grandma Anna and Grandpa Neil were so important to me while I was growing up. I really felt empty when they were gone."

Electra stared at the cookie in her hand.

"And now my whole family is far away, living off the grid in Alaska, and I hardly ever hear from them. Haven't seen them in about three years." Sam's insides roiled. "And my best friend, Jace, got into drugs and alcohol. We had a big fight over that at a party one night, and she got in her car, very drunk, and was hit by a truck. You know what happened—you met her. She's paralyzed for life." She closed her eyes a moment. *Forge on.* "I always blamed myself for not being able to stop her. We drifted apart, and our friendship withered and died. Until last summer when she came here."

The teen nodded but continued to stare at the cookie.

"It's not the same as what you've gone through, but..." she put a hand on the girl's arm, "I want you to know you can talk to me about anything."

Electra nodded again, her cheeks wet with tears.

Sam swallowed past the sharp rock in her throat, went to her young friend, and wrapped her in a long, warm hug.

After the supper dishes were done, Electra called her mother. Sam pretended to clean the countertops and put things away, so she could eavesdrop. Mostly what she heard was "Yeah." "No." "I'm fine, Mom." And "I worked really hard today, Sam can tell you... So can I stay?" Finally, the girl gave Sam the receiver. "Mom wants to talk to you."

Alberta's voice was subdued. "Did everything go okay today?"

Sam assured her it had and that, indeed, Electra had worked very hard.

"Well... I talked to her teachers and the school counselor today, and I'm going back in a couple of days. They're looking into setting up some kind of study program so she can keep up with her grade for a while... whether it's for a couple of weeks or the rest of the school year. That is yet to be determined."

"Okay. That sounds great. I'll make sure she keeps up with it."

Alberta sighed. "I sure don't want to stick you with this responsibility, but things are still up in the air with my job here. You don't have to be her teacher, just make sure she does the work."

"That's fine. She wants to stay, so she'll do it. I know she will." Sam gave Electra a wink.

"All right then. Thank you, Sam. I owe you bigtime. I'll do your taxes for free!" She chuckled. "Let me say goodnight to my daughter."

After Electra finished her call, she went upstairs to bed.

Sam called Melissa to check on Brad and tell her she was coming to town in the morning.

"Perfect timing. The doctor said this evening that he's going to take him off all sedation tomorrow morning and will see about moving him out of ICU if he responds well."

"Oh, that's great." Sam tried to breathe evenly. "I'll get in as early as I can." *Dear Lord, please don't let him have brain damage.*

She crawled into bed, the strength of renewed hope attempting to lift the boulder of dread from her shoulders.

The next morning, Sam popped in a couple of toaster waffles and spread them with peanut butter for a quick breakfast. "How are you feeling today?" she asked when Electra came down.

"Oh man. I could barely lift my arms to get my sweater on." She giggled. "I might not be able to help you chop ice today. I'm sorry."

"That's okay. Go ahead and finish breakfast, and then come down to the barn and feed the horses. I'll go ahead and open up the water on the tank." She shot the girl a grin. "But tomorrow, you're back on the job."

Electra spoke solemnly. "All right. I'll do it."

As quickly as possible, Sam finished the chores, and they headed for Billings.

"Did you talk to Brad's sister last night? Is he okay?"

Sam told her what Melissa had said.

"Awesome! Can I come and see him too?"

"I'm sorry, honey, but he's still in ICU, and they won't let anyone but family in. Melissa had to fib a little and tell the nurse I'm his fiancé so I could see him."

Electra widened her eyes. "Really? Do you think you and—?"

"No! It's way too soon for that. All I want right now is for him to have no brain damage." She leaned against the backrest. "So, while I'm at the hospital, do you want to visit Miss Robin?" Maybe the counselor could get her to open up about the cutting.

"Will Sapphire and the girls be there?"

"Probably not. It's a school day. But you and Miss Robin can talk…"

"Meh." Electra made a noncommittal sound. "I dunno." She swiveled to look out the window.

They sat in silence for a while, Sam shooting her daggered looks. Why was she being so uncooperative?

Finally, the teen asked, "So what about that program in Miles City with the vets? Are you going to do that?"

"I think so. I haven't talked to Nick for a few days, just waiting to hear if the board is all right with me getting started before I'm certified." A worried thought skittered through her. How would she be able to handle that, along with the ranch, and now Electra and Brad, and…?

"Well, if you do, can I help, like I did when I was here for Christmas? That was so fun." The girl's face lit up.

"I think so. We'd probably have to get permission for that too. But… I'm a little concerned about using Trixi too much for that. She is about twenty years old, still in good shape, but I don't know if all the up and down will eventually be harmful to her."

"Oh. Yeah, I hadn't thought about that." Electra shook her head. "That wouldn't be good." She sat silent for a couple of minutes. "Hey. I wonder if I could teach Apache to kneel?"

"Hmm. That's a good idea. Do you know how you would go about doing that?"

"Not for sure… but doesn't Miss Ellie live in Billings?" Her face opened in a huge smile. "Could I go visit her today? I could ask her how she trained Trixi."

"Yes, she is in Billings. I'll bet she would love to see you." Sam pointed at her cell phone on the seat between them. "Go into my contacts list and call her."

Miss Ellie was more than excited to see Electra, so Sam drove by the assisted living facility to drop Electra off. She went inside with her to say hi and double-check that leaving the girl was okay.

"Oh, honey, yes!" the tiny white-haired lady chortled. "This is going to be so much fun. Come here, dear, and let me give you a hug."

Sam left the two chattering with excitement and drove to the hospital. So, the kid had gotten one over on her, picking what *she* wanted to do. So much for being the "tough guy."

Her old tennis-playing butterflies were having a death match in her stomach as she approached the ICU. She stopped in front of the double doors, forcing her shoulders down. Then she pushed through to see the Ashton family gathered around Brad's bed. A doctor and a nurse leaned over him, taking vitals, poking and prodding.

Melissa turned to grasp her in a hug. "So glad you're here. He's starting to wake up, but he's fighting it."

"I can understand that." Sam swallowed. "I remember coming out of anesthesia for a minor surgery and not wanting to wake up. I was tired. I wanted to stay asleep!"

"Yeah, I remember something like that too," Melissa said.

Paul Ashton ducked his head in greeting, and Dee patted Sam's arm.

The doctor straightened and hung his stethoscope around his neck. "Vitals are strong. Everything looks good." He stood back as Mrs. Ashton took Brad's hand.

"Hi, honey. Are you awake, dear?"

Brad opened his eyes and blinked. "Mom?" He yawned. "What time is it? Am I late for school?"

She chuckled. "No, honey. You're not late. You're okay."

His brow wrinkled. "Why is everybody standing around my

bed?"

His dad took hold of his other hand. "Hey, son. Welcome back. You're in the hospital. Do you remember the accident?"

Brad frowned. "Accident?" He squinted at the group around him. "Oh. Yeah. Accident."

Sam gulped. Why didn't he remember the same conversation he'd had every time he woke up before? Did that mean...? Her heart was a leaden lump in her chest.

"Sam! Hi." Brad looked directly into her eyes. "I'm glad to see you."

"I'm glad to see you too. I... we've all been worried about you."

"Oh? No. I'm fine." He raised his head in an attempt to sit up but frowned at the casts on his arm and leg and let his head fall back onto the pillow. "Okay. I guess I'm... a little banged up."

"You are doing so much better now, honey." His mother leaned down to kiss his cheek and a tear fell on his pillow.

"I remember now... horse trailer..." Brad scrunched his face. "Yes. Trip to get Toby... blizzard... couldn't see... everything white..." He widened his eyes at Sam. "Oh... is... Toby... all right?"

Sam grasped his arm. "Yes, Toby is fine. He's at my place, eating hay and getting fat and sassy."

"Oh." He let out a breath. "I'm glad. I thought I dreamed it... the wreck... thought he was hurt..."

"Only some scratches and bruises, and he doesn't want to go in the barn, but we're working on that." Sam's grip tightened. "Maybe you can help me with him when you get out of here."

Brad bobbed his head and then cocked it to the side. "Were you... are you... mad at me?"

"Oh no. I'm not mad at you. I'm so relieved that you're okay." She blinked back tears stinging her eyes.

Melissa patted his hand. "Yeah, we're all glad you're back. You've been out a long time. Now you have to concentrate on getting better."

The doctor cleared his throat. "I'm pleased with your progress, Brad." Then he addressed the group. "We're going to move him to a private room, so I need you all to go back to the waiting room. The nurse will come get you when he's situated."

Paul Ashton put each arm around his wife and daughter, and Melissa took Sam's hand as they walked across the hall.

"What do you think?" Sam asked. "Is he...?"

"The doctor seems to think he's doing well." Dee had a hopeful look on her face. Melissa nodded.

"B-but... we just had the same conversation today that we've been having every time he wakes up." Even though the doctor said that was common, Sam couldn't let the hope inside just yet.

Brad's dad hissed air through his teeth. "I know. It's frustrating for us too."

"I know it is." She scrunched her mouth to one side. "I'm glad he's going to have a private room. That'll make it so much easier on you."

"And you too." Melissa looked into her eyes. "I know you've been worried, and I know you care. He's going to be all right. I feel it in my heart."

Swallowing past a lump, Sam patted the young woman's arm. "Thank you. Thank you for including me in your family. It means more than you can ever fathom." She fought back the ever-present threat of tears. "I think maybe I'd better be going. I don't want to overstay my welcome."

"No, no. Please stay. Come to the room for a while." Dee gave her a strong hug. "You are always welcome."

After two long, excruciating hours, the nurse came to tell them Brad had been moved and settled into a room down the hall from the ICU. "Finally!" Sam followed the Ashtons to gather around his bed. He opened his eyes and smiled. "Hey."

"Hey, yourself, son." His dad cuffed his arm gently. "You have a room of your own now."

Brad looked around. "Yeah. Good." His gaze settled on

Sam. "Thanks for being here."

She squeezed his hand. "I'm glad you're out of ICU." Was it her imagination or were his eyes brighter? She kept a big smile going as Dee and Melissa bantered with him for a few minutes. Then his eyelids drooped. He blinked them open and said, "Uh-huh," in response to something his mom said. Then they closed again. He tried several more times to continue a conversation, but sleep overcame him.

"I think the move tired him out. He probably needs to rest for a while." Melissa patted his arm and stepped toward the door.

The nurse met them in the hall. "He's doing very well. Doctor is quite pleased." Her face brightened. "I think he'll be getting the casts off in a day or two, and then we'll gradually get him up and doing physical therapy. The therapists have been manually moving his uninjured limbs to keep him from atrophying too much, but it's going to take some time to get his strength back."

Sam gulped. She hadn't thought about that. Lying completely still, in a coma, for more than a month would certainly take its toll. "Wow. It sounds like he still has a long road to recovery."

Paul Ashton nodded. "Yes, it does. But he's a trouper, a fighter. He can do this."

"And we're all here to help," Dee added.

"Absolutely. I'll be here as much as I can." Sam clenched her hands. "But—"

"We know. You have a ranch to run." Melissa patted her arm. "And now a teenager to take care of. You have more than your share on your plate. Just keep us in your prayers."

"I will… I am." Sam swallowed. "Keep me posted."

CHAPTER TWENTY-FOUR

The mid-afternoon sun slanted toward the horizon as she drove back to Ellie's to pick up Electra. Fear and frustration warred inside. Brad was still so fragile, not remembering what happened, the long recovery ahead from his injuries. Helplessness weakened her limbs.

Before she walked into the apartment, she stopped for a moment and pasted on a big smile. Tantalizing smells of cinnamon and sugar greeted her.

"We baked cookies." The teen held out a plate of oatmeal raisin delights.

Sam bit into one. "Mmm. Tastes wonderful."

"Is Brad okay?" Electra's eyes were wide.

"Yes. He woke up and visited a little while, and they moved him to a private room."

The teen let out a whoosh of air. "Oh, good. Then, next time I can go see him?"

"I think so. I'll check, but I'm pretty sure they'll let you."

"Yay!" Electra hopped from one foot to the other. "Miss Ellie and I have had so much fun today."

The older woman grinned from her recliner. "Oh yes, we sure have. Help yourself to some coffee and come, sit."

Sam poured a cup for Ellie and herself and eased onto the sofa.

Electra bounced beside her. "Miss Ellie gave me a lot of ideas for training Apache to kneel. She thinks I can do it. I'm so excited, I can't wait to get home and get started! Oh, it's going to be *so* much fun."

"Okay. Great." Sam glanced at the former trick rider whose

white curls haloed her beaming face.

"Oh yes, if anyone can, Electra can. With your help, of course."

Oh great. Another project. Sam pictured herself in center arena, trying to keep several chainsaws in the air, with more being thrown to her as she concentrated on not dropping any. Her head ached.

Electra chattered away about signals and if this, and what about that, continuing to test the couch springs.

When the girl paused, Sam took the opportunity to interject. "Well, yes, it sounds like fun. Miss Ellie, when the weather clears up a little more, I'd love to bring you out for a visit. I bet Trixi would be happy to see you."

The woman's eyes grew bigger. "That would be wonderful. I would enjoy that so much."

Electra continued her breathless litany as Sam drove them home. At least the girl wasn't as glum as she had been since she arrived. The visit with Ellie seemed to have ignited her spark again. Maybe this training thing would be good for her. And, if they could get another horse to kneel, that would solve one problem. One of many.

After chores and supper, Sam called Horace and then Teresa to bring them up to date on Brad and their day in town. Alberta called later to talk to her daughter, and then they headed for bed.

Sam stood at the window in her bedroom and gazed out at the moonlit snow. "Hey, God. Me again." She laughed quietly. "I'm kind of in over my head here. I'm worried about Brad... and Electra... and how I'm going to keep the ranch going... and work with horses and veterans and... the weather and feeding..." She shrugged and held her palms out. "I guess... I need some help... uh... if you're not too busy..."

She crawled under the covers. "Oh yeah... thank you... Amen."

***

Morning's early light gradually penetrated Sam's eyelids. She opened her eyes and stretched. Ahhh. She'd slept through the night without the nagging worries and nightmares of recent weeks. Easing out of bed, she put on her cozy robe and slippers and headed out to the kitchen to put on the coffee.

"Electra!" She called up the stairs. "Time to get up for chores. Feeding today."

No answer. That girl could probably sleep through an earthquake. She knocked on the door. Still no answer, so she opened it. "Electra?" The rumpled, unmade bed was empty.

Descending the stairs, she flicked a look out the window toward the barn. Electra and Apache were in the round corral, with Toby hanging his head over the poles. Sam laughed out loud. The girl couldn't wait to get started on training. Well, that was a good thing.

After she dressed, poured her travel cup of coffee, and grabbed a couple of granola bars for breakfast, she headed for the corral. She rested a foot on the bottom rail and watched quietly with Toby. He nuzzled her arm, and she smiled as she patted him and slung her arm over his neck.

Electra had Apache saddled, with only a halter and lead rope on his head. She spoke softly as she stood in front of him, putting pressure on the rope. The gelding tucked his head toward his chest and took a step backward. "Good boy." Electra kept talking to him and backing him. Then she brought the rope along her side and around to the saddle horn. She stood next to the stirrup and pulled back on the lead. Apache kept his head tucked and after a moment's hesitation, backed again easily. She released the pressure and repeated the exercise several times, each time rewarding him with praise and a treat.

Finally, she looked over at Sam with a shining face. "G'morning. Apache is doing *really* great."

"Well done, honey. You are so patient and good with him. I'm sure he will catch on quickly."

Electra led the horse to the fence, where Sam handed her the breakfast bar and gave Apache and Toby a handful of pellets.

"I 'spose we have to get the chores and feeding done now?" The teen caressed her horse's neck and gave her a wistful sidelong glance.

"Yes, ma'am. That's our number one priority." She spoke firmly to hammer home the point. "I see you chopped ice in the tank already. Thank you. So if you want to unsaddle him, we can feed them all some hay. Horace should be along any time, and we'll head out to the pasture."

"Okay. We'll do this some more later, Apache." She planted a kiss on his nose and led him to the barn.

Horace arrived in his usual fashion, cheerful and rarin' to go. "Mornin', ladies. It's a beautiful day in the neighborhood."

Sam squinted into the clear blue sky, the sun's golden beams reflecting from the snow. "Yes, it is." How could she not feel good today?

Electra trotted from the barn. "Horace! Hi! Guess what! I'm starting to train Apache to kneel, Miss Ellie told me all about how to do it, and she's going to come out and visit and help me some more when the weather is better, and now we'll have two horses to help with the vets in Miles City. Isn't that exciting?"

The old man raised his eyebrows. "Well, yes, I'd say it is. Very good, Miss Electra." He turned to Sam and grinned. "Let's get the truck loaded, and you can tell me all about Brad."

On the way to the pasture, Sam filled him in on the details and expressed her concerns about him not remembering the conversations they'd had before.

"W-e-l-l, I ain't no doctor, but with a head injury and him being in that coma for six weeks or so… He's bound to have trouble remembering. Give him time. He'll come around."

Acid churned in Sam's stomach. "I sure hope so. I know, I need to be patient. I really want him to be all right and get back to things… the way they were." She swallowed. Well, maybe not exactly like they were before. They weren't actually communicating, and he was mad at her for something she didn't understand.

After unloading the feed, Electra led the way to chop ice in the reservoir. "How's the muscles today, little gal?" Horace unloaded the axes.

She giggled. "Oh, I'm sore, but not as bad as yesterday and the day before. At least I can lift my arms again." She hoisted her ax high in the air to demonstrate.

Sam and Horace laughed. "We'll get you in cowgirl shape yet," he said.

Feeding and chores finished at both ranches, Sam and Electra came home, more than ready for supper and a quiet evening by the stove. The phone message light blinked as they entered the house. The first was from Melissa with an update on Brad. "He's doing better today, staying awake longer, and remembering more things. He asked about you. Still thinks you're mad at him for the accident. I know you're busy but come in when you can."

Relief lifted the worry cloud. "Sounds like progress," she told Electra.

"Yeah. I want to go see him next time, okay?"

"All right." The next message was from Nick to give him a call. He'd left his cell number, so Sam punched it in.

"Glad you called back." His voice was cheery. "Wanted to let you know the board is okay with you doing some work while you're training. You can get started with an online course—you have a computer, right?—and I was thinking maybe come in one day every two weeks or so, to start. Would that work for you?"

Sam's chest filled with anxious anticipation. Could she do this? "Oh, okay. Um… that sounds great. Let's give it try."

"Super! I'll email you the forms and link to the class and you can get set up. Of course you'll need to go for some hands-on training as well, but this will get you started. I'm excited about this program. It's going to be so good for these guys and gals, I know it is."

Sam hung up, feeling like a jackrabbit in a spotlight. *Oh my goodness, what have I agreed to?*

The following morning dawned as another cold, but sun-sparkling day. Again, when Sam got up, she found Electra working with Apache. "You need to eat a proper breakfast before you come out here." At the girl's crestfallen look, she handed her a protein bar, and then smiled at the pair. "He's making good progress."

"Yeah, he's so easy to work with." The teen flashed a broad grin. "So far, anyway. I guess I'll keep doing the backing training for a couple more days. Miss Ellie told me about putting a hobble on his legs to start the lying down process." She grimaced. "That's a little scary."

"I can see that it would be, but I'll help you if I can. And maybe if you can wait until Ellie comes out here, she'd probably have some more good tips for you."

"Okay. Good idea." Electra gestured toward the water tank. "I chopped the ice first and gave everybody some pellets but haven't fed the hay yet. Are we feeding the cows again today?"

Sam studied the hills, still covered by a coating of snow with maize-colored wisps of grass poking through. "I think they can get enough grass for today, but you and I can drive out and open up the water and give them some cake."

"Can I work with Apache and maybe Toby this afternoon again?" Electra gave her a hopeful, raised-eyebrow look.

"We'll see. I want to drive in to Ingomar and get the mail. Your mom said she'd mailed your books so they might be here by now."

The girl's hopeful look collapsed. "Okay. I s'pose I better be doing that or Mom won't let me stay."

"Yup. Hard work, keep up with your studies, and maybe you'll win her over."

As they drove to the pasture to chop ice in the reservoir, Electra sat quietly and then worked in uncharacteristic silence. What was going on in her mind? *Something about school, I'll bet.* She bit her lip. She needed to stay firm and tough with the girl, but she did feel the pain that radiated from her at times. "Tell you what. After we finish the chores, I'll treat you to a burger at the Jersey Lilly. How does that sound?"

That brought the big smile back. "Yeah! Can we? That'd be awesome!"

Clyde's pickup was parked in front of the café, and as Sam and Electra entered, he stood from his table near the window and waved them over. "Hi, ladies! Come join us."

Irene gestured to two empty wooden chairs. "How're things?"

Billy Cole took their orders, and then Sam filled them in on Brad's progress, the feeding chores with Horace, and the qualifying course to work with the veterans.

"Sounds like you've got your plate pretty full." Clyde sipped his coffee.

"Are you making time to simply enjoy yourself?" Irene's face held an expression of concern.

"Well… there *is* a lot going on, with running to Billings every couple of days too. But we do enjoy an occasional cup of hot chocolate by the fire with a good book in the evenings." She motioned toward Electra. "And this young lady has started training Apache to kneel, so Trixi can get a break."

"Oh yeah? I'll bet you're doing a bang-up job." Clyde raised his eyebrows at the teen, who blushed.

"I don't know yet, I'm just starting out, but Miss Ellie gave me a lot of tips and I'm trying to do it right and Apache is great to work with and he's doing great so far." She stopped, her face reddening, and glanced at the adults. "Sorry. I know I talk too much."

Billy brought their food, and everyone paused the conversation a moment to take their first bite.

"You're excited about this project, I can tell." Irene leaned over the table and patted the teen's arm. "I know how well you related to the kids from the group home and getting them used to the horses, so I have no doubt you'll do a great job at this too."

Electra looked down at her burger. "Thanks."

"And what about your mom?" Clyde pushed his plate aside. "Has she decided whether she's gonna take my job offer?"

The girl shrugged. "I don't know yet. I hope so."

"We've been talking with her almost every day, and her plan for now is to stay with her firm through tax season and then see what she can figure out about moving here." Sam fixed her eyes on Electra. "Provided, of course, that this horse-crazy young'un will buckle down. She's gotta keep up with her schoolwork and the ranch work too."

Electra's eyes grew wide in her earnest face. "I will, Sam. I promise. I will."

"I'll just bet you will." Clyde looked at Sam. "So, are you going to be too busy with everything to come back to work for me in the spring?"

"I'm trying to figure everything out, how to manage my time and this new opportunity, but I don't want to leave you in the lurch. I do want to continue to work with you."

"Okay. That sounds fine. Take your time. Maybe you'll want to come over part-time for a while." He waved his cup at the proprietor for more coffee. "And you still have my offer of setting up your business at my place. I do have the facilities."

Sam smiled through tears. "Thank you. I appreciate your patience with me while I try to decide what I want to be when I grow up."

The Bruckners laughed, and Irene got up to give her a hug. "Whatever you decide, we are there for you, my dear."

Sam sniffed and dug a tissue out of her jeans pocket. How did she get so lucky to have such great friends and neighbors? But that's what rural life was all about—just like with her great-grandparents and grandparents—neighbors were always willing to pitch in and help, no matter what. Just what she needed right now, a mental break from everything piling up on her.

CHAPTER TWENTY-FIVE

After Clyde and Irene left, Sam retrieved her laptop from the truck, downloaded the therapy course materials, and printed out a number of pages on Billy's office printer, just in case the slow dial-up at home wouldn't handle it. Then she and Electra walked over to the post office. Sure enough, there was a big box with Electra's name on it. Sam smirked. "Well, now we both have homework."

The teen made a face but then grinned. "Okay. As long as we can do it together."

"Let's head for home, work with the horses for a while, and then hit the books." Sam deposited the box behind the seats, got in the vehicle, and drove back to the ranch.

The horses lined the pasture fence close to the barn when they arrived, heads hanging over the wire. Electra giggled. "Look! They're waiting for us."

"They sure are." Sam got out and walked toward them. "I think they all need a short ride"

"Yay!" Electra loped to the barn to get the tack. Sam enticed the horses into the corral, and they saddled Apache and Sugar.

The afternoon sun warmed Sam's back, although the chill air reminded her it was still January. The snow was melting little by little each day, and she crossed her fingers that they wouldn't get another bad storm.

Electra trotted past her. "This is so fun!" Then she called over her shoulder, "Race you to the reservoir!"

The horses immediately jumped into the spirit of the run, and off they went, Electra whooping, and Sam nearly falling off in a fit of giggles. She felt like a teenager again.

She studied her bright-eyed, rosy-cheeked young friend. *Ahh, the good life. I wish every day could be like this.* She hoped the girl had the guts to keep going and not lose her enthusiasm.

They reined up by the pond, laughing, their mounts snorting and pawing the snow.

Sam patted Sugar's neck. "Okay, a little slower going home. Let them cool off a bit."

Back at the barn, they brushed down their mounts, and Electra took Apache into the round corral with her rope leads to practice backing.

Sam took Trixi out for a short ride and then eyed Toby. Not only was he afraid of enclosed spaces, but he was still jumpy and skittish of being ridden. Otherwise sweet and loving, he would most likely make a good saddle horse. She secured his halter rope to the fence, grabbed the brush, and worked on him, rubbing his legs and giving special attention to his back. He stood calmly, eyes half-closed, obviously enjoying the rubdown.

She smoothed a saddle blanket on his back, all the while talking softly. He flinched, but she kept caressing his neck and withers and rubbing his back under and on top of the blanket. After a few minutes, he relaxed again, his hind leg cocked as if ready to take a nap. Sam kept murmuring and stroking. Finally, she picked up her saddle and brought it to him to sniff. Instantly on alert, he snorted and blew.

"It's okay, Toby. You've done this before. It's not going to hurt you." Slowly and gently, she lifted the saddle into place, continuing her calm patter. His muscles tensed under the weight. She offered him a cake pellet, and he took it with his soft lips, his eyes on her. Sam rubbed his nose, up his face to his ears, and down his neck. He gradually began to relax. Still talking to him, she reached up and shifted the saddle a little. Instant tension. "It's okay, Toby. You're a good boy."

She repeated the actions several times and then buckled the cinch loosely to lead him around the corral. Again the tense muscles, the blowing and snorting. But when she held out a pellet, he eagerly followed her. They circled the corral, first one direction, then the other. Finally, she led him back to the fence and removed the tack. "Okay, boy. That's enough for today. Maybe next time you'll let me ride you, huh?"

Toby kicked up his heels and raced around the corral and through the gate she opened into the pasture. He lay down and rolled in the dirt as if to remove the feeling of the saddle weight, and then ran off, tail high and tossing his mane.

Sam grinned, watching him. He may have had only minor injuries from the accident, but his trust had definitely been damaged. She wished she had more time to work with him. Between winter weather, feeding, caring for Electra, and Brad's uncertain future… An ache grew inside. *I want to fix everything for everybody.*

She turned to the round corral to watch Electra with Apache. The gelding was so patient, backing and backing and backing again for his girl.

Electra glanced over at Sam. "Can I put a hobble on him, just to get him used to it?"

"Sure. I'll get one for you." She went into the barn and came back with a braided heavy cotton rope. A hobble was a restraint normally fastened around both feet to allow some movement while restricting the horse from running away. In training, Electra would use it to lift one foot, altering Apache's balance to try and get him to kneel.

"Miss Ellie said I need to help him get used to feeling the rope." The teen's eyes were wide. "I might need your help."

"Okay. First, let's see if he'll let you lift his leg."

Electra rubbed Apache's leg and murmured to him. Then she reached down and tugged at his foot. He willingly allowed her to pick it up and cradle it in her arm. She grinned.

"He's pretty used to having his feet worked on, so that's a good first step." Sam stood close by, also talking to the horse, and caressing his neck. "Now, just put the rope under his foot to cradle it."

Electra followed her instructions, and the gelding stood calmly, although watching the girl out of the corner of his eye. "Good boy, Apache."

She released his foot, repeated the exercise several times on that side, and then the other.

"I think maybe that's enough for the first time." Sam smiled at the pair.

The young girl's face glowed. "He's such a dream to work with."

"I'm so proud of you and what you've accomplished already. You're both doing very well." Sam hugged the teen whose body thrummed with the energy of a successful exercise.

"Well, I hate to be a killjoy, but now we need to go inside and do our homework."

"Aww." Electra made a pouty face. "I know." She gave the horse one last pat. "Be good, boy. I'll see you tomorrow."

***

Heart beating like a trip-hammer, Sam opened the door to Brad's room and motioned for Electra to stay back. None of the Ashtons were there today, and Brad, propped up in bed, stared at the TV. He tilted his head as she came in and his face lit up with a smile. "Hey, Sam. You came." He held out a hand.

She grasped it and sat on the edge of the bed. "You're looking pretty good today—sitting up and everything."

"Yeah. I was a little dizzy at first but doing better now. They're going to take off the casts tomorrow, I think." He stared at the plaster on his left arm and leg.

"That's great." She studied his face, pale and gaunt. He had lost so much weight. His hair was dark stubble, his wayward lock gone. "How do you feel?"

"Good, I guess." He drew his brows together. "Still trying to remember what happened. A snowstorm. They tell me I wrecked my truck and the horse trailer. And the horse... Toby? Is he okay?"

Sam's breath caught. *Oh dear.* The same questions...again. "Yes, he's fine. Still afraid of enclosed spaces, but we're working on that."

"Oh. I'm glad he's all right. Are you mad at me... for the wreck and...everything?"

"No, Brad. I'm not mad at you. I'm so glad you survived and are awake now. You're going to be fine." She forced a smile. "I'm really happy you're out of the coma and doing so much better." Her insides quivered. But would he ever regain his memory completely?

"Yeah." Then he looked toward the door. "Oh, hello. Who is with you?"

The teen came forward. "Hi, Brad. It's me...remember me?"

"Electra? Hi! Wh-what are you...?" A puzzled look scrunched his face.

"I'm staying with Sam for a while, helping her on the ranch with the horses and feeding and stuff."

"Oh, okay. Good." He looked at Sam. "I'm glad you have help. I guess it is winter, isn't it? You have a lot of work with the cows now, don't you?"

"Yes, it's been cold, and we've had some pretty good snows a couple of times, but Horace comes over to help, and we help him too. We're doing fine."

He nodded. "Mom told me I missed Christmas. We had a little party and opened presents yesterday." He glanced at the side table. "Um, thank you, um, for the wallet."

"You're welcome. I hope you like it."

"Yeah. I do." He looked around again. "I don't know where... Melissa must have taken it or put it away or..."

"That's okay. You'll find it."

Brad squinted toward her. "I remember... I heard you talking to me when... I was asleep, um, in the coma, I guess." He squeezed her hand. "Thank you for being here."

Electra gasped. "That's awesome! Wow!"

Sam's eyes stung. "You did? You heard us?"

"Yeah. I don't remember what you were saying, but I knew you were here." His face held an earnest gaze. "That means...

means a lot."

A nurse came in and bustled around the bed, taking his temperature and checking vitals. "And how are we feeling today?"

"Gmmph," he replied around the thermometer.

Electra elbowed Sam and they both snickered.

"Well, tomorrow your casts come off and then we'll see about starting physical therapy. Get you up and walking in no time." The nurse fluffed his pillow and smoothed his blanket. "Anything you need? More Jell-O?"

"No. I'm good. Thanks."

Sam moved closer and touched his hand. "Glad they're taking good care of you. Are you able to eat real food yet?"

"No. So far, just liquid. Stuff like Ensure and Jell-O." He made a face. "But I'm looking forward to a big T-bone at the Jersey Lilly with you two—soon!"

"All right. We'll hold to you that promise."

After a few more minutes of small talk, Brad's eyelids drooped, and he nodded off in the middle of a sentence.

"We better go, let you rest." Sam rubbed his shoulder. "Do you want me to let the head of your bed down so you can sleep?"

"Mmm-hmm." By the time she had lowered the bed, he was asleep.

She and Electra let themselves out quietly.

"He looks so…" The girl hesitated. "Not like Brad."

Sam swallowed. "I know. It's been so hard to see him with his head all wrapped up like a mummy and all the bruises he had. At least he has the bandages off, but of course they had to shave his head. And he's so thin, practically skin and bones."

"Like Apache was when we found him." Electra widened her eyes. "He was hurt bad, wasn't he?"

"Yes, he was. But he's alive and he knows us, and he remembered my voice when he was in the coma." Sam bit her lip, doubts and fear roiling in her stomach. *But he's still asking the same questions. Will the brain trauma allow him to be normal again?*

219

Sam hunched over her laptop, printouts nearby, looking through the course materials to become an equine therapist. The PATH (Professional Association of Therapeutic Horsemanship) program listed a credentialing application, compliance forms, First Aid and CPR requirements, and certification guidelines. She blew out a long breath that fluttered her bangs. This looked complicated. Would she be able to do it? She'd always trusted her instinct in working with horses and with the group home kids. Of course, flying by the seat of her pants hadn't worked so well with Garrett.

Across the kitchen table, Electra snapped her Algebra book shut with a groan. "This is too hard! I'll never get this stuff and I don't know how Mom and Mrs. Nelson thought I could do it all without classes and teachers and..." She huffed and stood.

Sam looked up from her work. *Oh-oh.* How was she supposed to encourage the girl when she had the same doubts? She reached out a hand. "I know it's hard, really hard, and I'm not sure how much help I can be. I didn't do all that well in Algebra myself."

Electra scrunched her face in a scowl. "Yeah. What was Mom thinking? She needs to be here to help me!" She strode to the wall phone and punched in a number. After a few seconds, "Mom? I can't do this! I'm stuck on Algebra and I need help and you need to come here and help me and..." Her voice broke with a sob.

Sam swallowed. She was right. How would this ever work? Was she doomed to failure with mentoring this teenager and with this equine therapy program and everything was just falling apart and... *Oh my word, I'm sounding just like Electra!*

She picked up the offending math book and retreated to the living room, trying not to eavesdrop on the phone conversation. The index listed Laws of Exponents, Multiplying Polynomial Formulas, Special Factoring Formulas, Quadratic Equation Formulas, Pythagorean Theorem. She grimaced. What did she even remember about the basics?

"...but, Mo-om!" Electra's voice rose from the kitchen. "I *want* to keep up with school..." "...No, I don't want to come home!" "...Please, Mom!"

The teen stomped into the living room, tears tracking her cheeks. "She wants to talk to you."

Sam stood.

"Please don't let her make me go back. Please!" Her face was crimson, and her lips trembled. "I'll do whatever it takes. I'll study more. I'll get this stuff. I promise."

Putting her arm around the girl's shoulders, Sam squeezed. "Let me talk to her. We'll see if we can work something out." She peered into the red-rimmed eyes. "Okay? Deep breath now."

Electra hiccupped another sob. "Okay. Please..."

Sam picked up the phone. "Hi, Alberta. We seem to be having a little trouble with math here at this end."

"Yeah. I was afraid of that. I don't know what to do, other than bring her home, maybe get her a tutor here. Maybe I could put her in a different school."

"Well, let's not make a hasty decision. She's been doing quite well with the other schoolwork. I don't remember a lot about Algebra either, but I can study with her and maybe both of us start from the beginning."

"No, no, no. I didn't want to dump the responsibility onto you, and there's no reason you should have to teach her this stuff. This is ridiculous. It's just not going to work."

Sam leaned against the kitchen counter. "I'd like to give it a try. And if I can't, maybe the tutor-thing could work from this end. Mrs. Bruckner does some of the bookwork for their dude ranch. Maybe she could help or maybe she or Teresa would know of someone nearby."

"Hmm. I don't know. I still don't feel very good about this." Alberta's sigh whooshed over the line. "Long-distance parenting... it's the pits."

"Let's see how it goes here for a while longer. She's been doing so well with the ranch work and training Apache. I think

Electra and I can do this together." Sam forced a confident note into her voice, trying to convince herself.

"All right. Let me say good night to her. I don't want to leave the conversation in the middle of upset."

She motioned to Electra who hovered in the doorway with a hopeful, wide-eyed look.

"Mom? I'm sorry…" She sniffed. "Okay. I'll work hard with Sam, I promise… okay, love you too."

With a smile she didn't feel, Sam patted the teen's arm. "All right. Let's crack this book. Help me remember the basics and then I'll see if I can help you with the more advanced stuff."

Oh, dear Lord. I'm going to need some divine intervention here if I'm to pull this one off!

CHAPTER TWENTY-SIX

Phone calls to Irene Bruckner and Teresa brought the same answers: "I took Algebra in high school, but I'd have to have a refresher to remember any of it now." Teresa suggested someone from the school, but that was in Forsyth, forty-five minutes away. No way could they make that drive every day or even a couple times a week.

Electra pouted. "Mom's not going to let me stay."

Sam opened the textbook at the beginning. Therapeutic equine certification would have to wait.

In the meantime, feeding cattle, keeping water open, and working with the horses took up the majority of her and Electra's time. Thankfully there had been no more snow to hamper efforts, but cold temperatures kept them from staying outside for long periods. Apache was getting used to hobbles, and Toby didn't flinch as much when Sam saddled him, but he still wouldn't go in the barn.

"I need to go see Brad tomorrow." She stripped off her coveralls one evening. "It's been several days, and Melissa says he has the casts off and has been getting physical therapy."

"Okay." Electra had been uncommonly quiet all week.

Most likely worried about her schoolwork and whether she can stay. Sam tried to encourage and joke with her, to prod her back to her old self. But while she prepared supper, the teen slouched on the sofa with her textbooks.

The phone rang after they'd eaten. Alberta didn't waste time on pleasantries. "I'm taking a few days off work and coming out there. I need to see what's going on."

Sam gulped. *Oh-oh.* Electra's heart would break if she had to go back to New York. And how would *she* deal with it if the girl left? She'd gotten used to having her around, despite algebra.

Tears streamed down Electra's face when she hung up. "She's not going to let me stay. I know it. She's not. If I have to go back there, I'll... I'll... just die!"

The following day, she dropped Electra at Robin's while she visited Brad, hoping the counselor could draw the teen out and alleviate some of her fears. Her own gut churned. Maybe she needed to talk to Robin herself. *I don't know if I can do this much longer.*

Brad was sitting up in a chair when she arrived at the hospital. Sam pasted on a cheery smile. "Hey. Good to see you up."

He didn't return the smile but grunted. "Yeah."

"What's the matter? You don't seem happy about it."

His face soured into a grimace. "Can't walk. Hurts. Wanna go home."

She rubbed his arm and sat on the edge of the bed next to him. "I'm sure it does hurt. But these things take time. You'll be able to walk again, and you'll be home soon."

"No use. I'm... a cripple. Can't do it."

Disappointment and frustration clogged her throat like a wedge of lemon. *What can I say or do?*

She stood, put her hands on both of his shoulders, and peered into his face. "Brad. Listen to me. You can NOT give up. You are stronger than anything life has to throw at you. I *know* you are."

He stared down at his lap.

"Brad. Brad, look at me."

He glanced up for a moment.

"I am here for you. Your family is here for you. We are going to help you get through this." She shook him gently. "Do you hear me?"

He nodded. A tear glistened in the corner of his eye.

"Hey. Just a couple of weeks ago you were in a coma. That's

where you've been for nearly two months. Nobody—not even Superman— is going to wake up, leap out of bed, yelling 'Look out, world, here I come.'"

One corner of Brad's mouth quirked up. He nodded again and shifted his eyes to hers. She squatted next to him. "So, you have a lot of work to do. But you know how to work hard, and you can do it, you *will* do it. And you have help, a lot of help. Okay?"

"Okay."

Sam forced herself to relax. "By the way, how good are you at algebra?"

He cocked one eyebrow. "Algebra?"

"Yeah. Electra's having trouble, and her being able to stay on the ranch hinges on keeping up with her schoolwork. And it's been so long, I've forgotten more than I ever knew."

Brad shook his head. "Me too, I'm afraid. Not gonna be much help there."

She huffed a laugh. "Well, I've been studying along with her. Talk about the blind leading the blind."

Finally, a chuckle. "I can just see you two. If it doesn't have to do with horses…"

She scrunched her face at him. "I know. I'm afraid you might be right. But we are going to give it a real hard try. Electra needs, no, *wants* to prove to her mom she can do it. And she's been a big help to me on the ranch. I don't know what I'd do if she had to leave." She blew out a breath. "I've gotten kind of attached to her."

"Yeah. I can see that." He smiled then. "I have too, sorta…"

Bemused, she tilted her head. The girl did grow on a person.

Sam stayed for a couple of hours, continuing to try to bolster Brad's spirits, telling him what they'd been doing with the horses, and how she was supposed to be training for the therapy program. He, in turn, encouraged her with that idea. She read to him from the newspaper, and they laughed and made snide comments about politicians and new laws and stupid crooks.

When she left, her spirit was buoyed. Brad had promised he would work hard at getting better, and she promised she'd be back soon.

Now, if only Electra got some of that bolstering from Robin...

During the next week, Brad moved to a rehab center and Melissa reported he was making good progress, although still had a defeatist attitude. Sam's jaw ached from clenching, not knowing what she could do to help.

She, Electra, and Horace continued their feeding and chores routine. Electra seemed somewhat more at peace after her visit with Robin but wasn't willing to tell Sam what they'd talked about. Although her inner butterflies still kicked up, Sam accepted the girl's wish for privacy. *It's okay, as long as she's talking to someone.*

But as Friday and Alberta's arrival approached, Electra's concentration on her studies wavered. She slammed her books shut. She paced. She ran her fingers viciously through her short hair, spiking it in all directions. She was impatient with Apache, and the horse refused to even back up for her.

Thursday late afternoon, her face held tight, Sam gathered their tack. "Let's go for a ride."

Electra nodded, eyes downcast. She saddled her horse, swung up, and took off at a gallop.

Oh boy, she's going to get him all lathered up. "Stop! Let him warm up," she yelled in vain after the retreating pair. With an exasperated groan, she followed. She so wanted to slap some sense into that girl. *Oh well. She needs to let off steam.* And Sam needed to figure out how to deal with this silent, sullen side of her.

At the top of a rise overlooking the reservoir and the few winter-bared cottonwood trees, Electra finally reined Apache to a stop. He blew and stomped as she slid off and slumped on a boulder nearby.

Sam stayed in the saddle for a few minutes before

dismounting. She sat next to the teen. "Okay. Tell me what's up."

Electra turned a wind-dried, tear-stained face toward her. "Mom's not going to let me stay."

"You don't know that."

"Yes, I do. She's not happy with me being here without her and not doing good in my schoolwork." Her chin drifted to her chest.

"Hey." She put an arm around the girl. "You and I have been working very hard on your Algebra, and I think we're doing much better. We'll get 'er done."

The thin shoulders raised in a shrug.

"Listen. Your mom misses you. And she's concerned about you. She just wants to come visit and see for herself how things are going. I get that. We have a lot of progress to show her— with Apache's training and that you're working hard on your studies." *And no longer cutting.*

"B-but Apache won't… he quit…" A sob broke.

Sam gave Electra a squeeze. "Apache is sensitive to your moods. He knows something is wrong. He wants to work with you, but you've been… maybe a *little* impatient with him lately?" She fluttered a breath. The girl did need to work on how her emotions affected the horse.

The teen buried her face in her hands and sobbed harder. Sam gathered her into her arms and patted her back, murmuring, trying to soothe the storm. "It's okay, honey. It'll be okay."

Finally, the crying subsided, and Electra pulled back. "I'm sorry, Sam." Lip quivering, she stood and walked to her horse standing patiently, watching her. "I'm so sorry, Apache." She rubbed his face and head and then leaned into his neck. "Please forgive me. I didn't mean to treat you bad." A hiccup. "I love you, Apache. I'm sorry."

The gelding encircled her with his head around her in a horsey hug.

Sam closed her eyes against the sting of her own tears. *She'll be okay.*

***

Friday morning, Sam and Electra stopped to see Brad for a few minutes before going to the airport to pick up Alberta. He had just returned from therapy, groaning and grimacing as the aide helped him into bed.

"I hear you're doing really well." Sam squeezed his arm.

"Meh. I guess." Then apparently remembering her last pep talk, he smiled. "Yeah. I am. I'm doing all right. At least that's what they tell me. But it sure is slow. And everything hurts."

"I'm sure it does. But you know the old saying, 'Slow and steady wins the race.'"

He huffed a laugh. "That's me, slow for sure." He looked over at Electra. "And how are you doing, young lady?"

"Better'n you." She poked his shoulder.

"Well, you just wait. One of these days..." He swallowed and gave her a half-smile. "I'll race you out to the pasture."

"But you won't beat me."

"We'll see about that."

"Betya!"

"You're on."

Sam grinned at their banter. So, these two were actually capable of being happy when they wanted to. "Well, sorry to break up this party, but we'd better go to the airport."

Electra's smile faded. "Okay. See ya later, Brad."

***

Sam spotted Alberta, clad in a dark blue puffy winter coat, at the baggage carousel. Beside her, Electra's body tensed as they headed toward her mother.

"Hey there," Sam called out. "Welcome back to Montana."

Alberta's face lit up, and she held her arms open. Electra hung back, her head down. Sam gave her friend a quick hug, and both turned to the teen.

"Sweetheart, come here," Alberta coaxed in a soft voice. She continued to hold her arms out.

Electra swallowed, looked up, and then ran into her

mother's arms, sobbing. "Mom. Mom... I'm so glad to see you... I-I... m-missed you."

Alberta glanced over her daughter's head, her eyebrows raised. She patted Electra's back and murmured. "I missed you too, honey."

At last, the tears and hiccups subsided.

She's so afraid her mom will take her back to New York. Sam rubbed the back of her neck. *Heck, so am I!* What would she do without the drama? But also without the laughter, companionship, and her help...?

Alberta grabbed her suitcase and linked her arm with Electra's. "Okay, ladies, I'm ready to head to the ranch. I need some peace and quiet."

Sam tittered. "Well... I hope you can find some."

Electra reverted to her usual bubbly self on the trip home. "Oh, Mom, I gotta show you what I'm doing with Apache, he's backing up, and I have him getting used to hobbles, and pretty soon I'm going to teach him to kneel down, and then we'll have another horse to work with when we go help the veterans learn to ride!" She gasped for air.

Her mom widened her eyes and spoke into the momentary pause. "Wow, that sounds great, honey."

"And Sam's been studying with me and helping me with my math and schoolwork and I think I'm doing okay now and I'm going to keep it up and I just... Mom..." The girl cocked her head in a pleading, puppy-dog look. "I just love it here and I love working with Sam and the horses, and I don't want to go back to New York... oh, Mom..."

Alberta put an arm around her and squeezed. "Let's not worry about that right now. I'm glad you're doing well." She peered at Sam. "How about you? Are *you* doing well?"

She waited a beat before answering. What could she say that wouldn't scare Alberta off? "Oh, yeah, I'm doing fine. I have the materials to study for my equine training certificate, and I'm going to the college Monday to start working with the vet program."

"You're a natural. I don't know why you have to be certified… well, yes, I do. It's good training, I'm sure, and it's also a CYA for the college."

"That's true. I certainly wouldn't want anyone to be discouraged by what I do or don't do. And I certainly don't want another accident like with Garrett when he fell."

"I'll still be here Monday, so I'd love to come in with you and see how it goes."

"Yay, Mom! How long do you get to stay?" Electra bounced on the truck seat.

"Gotta go back Wednesday. But we're going to enjoy every minute while I'm here." Alberta grinned. "I'm not even going to *think* about taxes for the next five days."

They chatted about Brad and ranch chores and neighbors for the rest of the trip, Electra punctuating their sentences with her exclamations and enthusiasm. Soon, they were all laughing to the point where Sam had to take a breath. "I'm going to run off the road if I don't settle down here. Hey, let's get a bite at the Jersey Lilly."

As they entered the café, Horace looked up from a table in the back and waved. "Hey there, ladies, come join me." After hugs all around, the women sat.

"Good to see ya, Miz Alberta. What brings you back to these here parts so soon?"

She picked up a menu. "Well, I was just missing my girl too much, so I decided to come for a short visit."

"I kin understand that. Good to see ya again." He took a sip of coffee as Billy brought his dinner and took the women's orders. "So, Electra, how's the horse training goin'?"

"Oh, it's so fun, I love it, and Apache is the most wonderful horse in the world, he's so patient and he's learning everything so fast." Her face glowed as she recounted, once again, everything she and Apache were doing.

Horace burst into laughter. "That's great, little gal. I'm proud of ya. And how's the schoolwork coming along?"

Electra's smile faded, and she shot a quick look at her

mother. "Well, I was having some trouble with Algebra, and Mom came to check on me. But Sam's been helping me, and I think I'm... well yes, I *am* doing okay. I *am* going to get it." She sat up straight in her chair. "I don't want to go back."

Alberta's face hardened into stern lines. "Yes, Electra needs to keep up with her studies and get good grades to be able to stay here."

Sam told her neighbor about her search for a tutor, with no luck, and that she'd been boning up on the subject, studying along with the teen.

Billy brought their meals. Horace leaned back in his chair. "W-e-l-l... You probably don't know this, but I went to college for a while when I was just a pup, and... I was a math major." His mouth turned up at one corner. "It was about a hundred years ago, but I'll bet I remember enough to be able to tutor you, young lady. Algebra was kinda my *thing*."

What? Sam's jaw dropped even as she saw Electra's mouth open in a huge O, and Alberta's eyebrows rose toward her hairline. They all stared, speechless.

Electra recovered first. She squealed, scraped her chair back, dashed to Horace's side, and threw her arms around his neck. "Ohmygosh, thank you, thank you, thank you! You are my angel, you're my lifesaver. Thank you, thank you, thank you!"

Horace gave the women a lop-sided, aw-shucks grin.

Still shell-shocked, Sam and Alberta exchanged a wide-eyed glance. *What on earth?* Of all the people she knew, the last person she'd think to ask would be Horace. Her lips quirked, and a chortle bubbled up from within.

Electra disengaged and stared with bright, saucer eyes at her mother. "Did you hear that, Mom? Did you? Horace can help me, and Sam's already helping me, and I'm going to keep up with my studies, Mom, did you hear that?"

Alberta sat silent for another moment. Then peals of laughter erupted. She stood and grabbed her daughter in a bear hug. "Yes, honey, I heard that. It's wonderful." She gazed over Electra's shoulder at Horace. "Thank you, kind sir."

He shrugged and scrubbed his fingers over his salty-gray crewcut. "W-e-l-l, let's see how much I actually remember." He guffawed, and Sam couldn't help but join in. Their laughter ricocheted around the room, infecting the other patrons and Billy behind the bar too.

CHAPTER TWENTY-SEVEN

When they arrived home, there was nothing doing but Electra had to show her mom what she and Apache had achieved. Alberta rolled her eyes at Sam but left her suitcase in the pickup and followed her daughter to the corral.

The teen attached a lead rope to the gelding's halter and put him through his paces, backing with his chin tucked toward his chest. Then she tapped his front shoulder and reached down to pick up his foot. Before she took hold, however, he lifted it on his own.

Sam gasped. This was something new. When had she done all that?

Electra supported the foot with the lead and ran the rope around the saddle horn. Apache stood patiently and quietly for several seconds, head down, leaning back slightly. She released the foot, patted his neck, and caressed his face. Giving him a cake pellet from her pocket, she murmured, "Good boy, Apache, good boy." Then she turned toward her mother and Sam, a glow lighting her face.

"Wow." Alberta released a breath. "Oh, my goodness, honey. I'm impressed."

"I'm so proud of you." Sam stepped forward. "When did you do this last bit? I had no idea."

Electra shrugged, her face aglow. "I dunno. Little by little. We still have a ways to go before I teach him to kneel though."

Her mom and Sam engulfed her in a group hug.

"You're doing great, daughter. I'm so, so very proud of you and what you've accomplished with this horse." A tear trickled from the corner of Alberta's eye.

"She is gifted, a natural." Sam gave the girl another squeeze. "Now, let's do chores and head on up to the house. You can show your mom what else you've accomplished with your schoolwork."

Electra scrunched her face in a mock scowl, but then her grin was back. "Okay!" She bounded off to the loft to throw down flakes of hay for the horses.

Alberta simply stood, rooted to the ground, shaking her head. "Wow, Sam. She is *so* much different here."

"Yes, she is. I can see a big contrast from when she arrived. She's still dealing with… things, and she's quite moody… but she did spend some time talking with Robin, the group home counselor, the other day. I don't know what they talked about, but I hope it helped."

Her friend emitted a strangled sound. "I hope so too. I can't believe I didn't know about her cutting herself."

"She doesn't seem to be doing that anymore."

"I'm so glad." Alberta chewed on her lower lip. "I can't see taking her back to New York. I just can't."

Hope and relief bloomed inside Sam's chest. She had known she didn't want Electra to leave but hadn't realized what a weight she'd carried from the possibility. She slipped an arm around Alberta. "I can't either. She's healing here."

Saturday evening, Alberta, and Electra joined Sam for supper at the Bruckners'. Irene met them at the door with giant hugs and a smile to match. "Come in, come in. We're so happy to see you!"

Clyde shook hands, his weathered face beaming. "Sure hope you've come to stay."

Alberta chuckled. "Well, not quite yet, but after April 15… It's a possibility." Electra stood behind her mom, nodding like a woodpecker on fast-forward, her face shining with hope.

They followed Clyde into the living room while Irene checked on the roast, which was giving off the most tantalizing aroma. Sam's stomach gurgled.

Shortly after, Horace arrived too, with more hugs, handshakes, and back-slapping all around. He winked at Electra and Sam. "Tomorrow okay for a math lesson?"

"You bet."

Electra bounced in place. "Sure!"

"Come and eat." Irene called them into the cheery country kitchen with blue checked gingham curtains framing the windows.

Around the large oak table, conversation and food flowed like warm rivers of honey. Sam wanted to curl up and purr like a kitten. Electra politely intertwined her bubbly conversation with the adults, and the worry lines on Alberta's face smoothed. She laughed and teased, along with Horace and Clyde. Sam clasped her hands to her chest with a happy realization. *Alberta really fits in here.*

After supper, while Sam relished her apple pie ala mode and coffee, Clyde pinned a more serious gaze on the accountant. "Well, my dear. I don't want to put pressure on you or nag you like an old lady, but…" Both chuckled, "… my offer of employment, room and board still stands. Are you considering it?"

Sam held her breath.

Alberta drew in a long draught of air and slowly blew it out. "Well, yes, this is what I'd like to do, but I need to finish my tax load and transfer clients to other CPAs in the firm, get the loose ends tied up… It would probably be the end of April, but I could make the move then. Does that work for you to wait that long, or do you need to hire someone sooner?"

"No, that'll work. We'll muddle through till then. Maybe I can send my taxes to you there."

"Of course. I'd be happy to do that."

He shook her hand. "It's a deal then."

"Thank you so much for this offer and for being patient with me." She threw a quick glance at Sam who wanted to do an "Electra" and jump up and down, squealing at the top of her lungs. And before her daughter could do just that, Alberta put a hand on her arm. "But, young lady, we'll have to see how your math tutoring goes first, along with everything else."

Electra's body vibrated, but she remained calm and quiet. "Okay, Mom."

It was taking everything the girl had in her not to erupt. Amused, Sam patted her young friend's shoulder. The teen beamed and gave her a quick nod as if to say *We can do this.*

The math lesson on Sunday was only slightly bumpy, while Horace refreshed his memory and reviewed the basics. Then he and Electra put their heads together over the book on the kitchen table and spent the afternoon talking fractions, formulas, and theorems.

Alberta gave Sam a cocked-eyebrow look, and they retired to the living room with their novels. Occasionally, Electra would groan. "Oh, this is *so* hard. I don't understand." Then later she squealed. "Yeah! I get it!"

Sam burst out laughing. "Sounds like they're making progress."

"I think that's going to be a match made in heaven. Who knew?"

Monday morning, Sam loaded Trixi into the trailer for their trip to Miles City.

"Could we bring Apache too? I can show Nick and Del and Garrett and everybody how well he's doing." Electra looked at Sam with pleading eyes. "And maybe do some more training at the same time?"

Sam scrunched her mouth to one side as she considered the request. Would the horse cooperate, with a group watching? Would he be too distracting to the lesson and work she'd be doing with the vets?

"Please." The little-girl voice broke in.

"Well… okay. We can try and see how he reacts. Maybe it would be good to get him used to being around more people while you're doing your thing."

"Yesss!" Electra fist-pumped the air, pivoted, and ran to the barn to get Apache.

Alberta chortled. "You're such a pushover."

"Yeah, I am." Sam giggled. "But this just might be good for both of them."

After the hour and a half drive, they pulled up to the chutes at the ag college, where Nick Seward met them. "I've got six vets here today, very interested in what you are doing."

Her stomach lurched. *Oh my. Six?* She'd only worked with a couple at a time before. Could she do this? She gulped and forced a smile. "That's great, Nick."

They unloaded the horses and brought them into the arena, where about a dozen people stood watching. Even more of an audience. Sam swallowed again and straightened her posture. *Here goes nothing.*

Nick introduced her, Electra, and Trixi, and she cleared her throat. "Good morning, ladies and gentlemen." She tried to keep the quaver out of her voice. "First, I'm going to demonstrate with Electra and Trixi what we can do for those of you who are unable to mount easily. After that, I'll let you meet the horses and get used to being around them. Then, if anyone would like to try to mount and ride, you are welcome to. But please don't feel pressured. If you are more comfortable just watching this time, that's fine."

She turned to Electra. "Are you ready?"

The girl gave Trixi the signal, and the mare bent her legs and knelt on the ground.

The audience gave a collective gasp.

Electra slipped onto the saddle, put her feet into the stirrups, and gave another signal. Trixi rose, and they trotted around the arena.

The audience clapped.

When Electra returned and dismounted, Garrett and Del came forward. Garrett told the group how much the lessons and riding had helped him with his fears and doubts. Then he nodded at Sam who signaled Trixi. When the horse kneeled, he swung his good leg over the saddle and eased his prosthetic foot into the stirrup. With a lump of fear in her throat, Sam made sure he was secure in the saddle—*don't want him to fall off again*—and then led them around the arena.

After Garrett's successful ride and applause, Del showed how well he could maneuver onto Trixi's back, even without legs. The audience again responded with enthusiasm.

Electra demonstrated how she was training Apache, with backing, lifting his leg, and leaning him slightly back.

"The next step is to train him to kneel, like Trixi, so we'll have two horses to work with here," Sam explained, relief washing over her. The gelding had reacted as docile as a lamb and gave a perfect demonstration.

"The next thing I'd like to do, is simply let you get acquainted with the horses. Do whatever you're comfortable with—petting them, feeding them, or just watching."

Two of the veterans came forward eagerly. A couple hesitated when they came close to the large animals as the horses blew and snorted and watched these new humans approach. A woman stopped several paces away, watching the horses warily.

"It's okay if you don't want to get close today." Sam offered each person pellets and spoke softly, trying to encourage them to go ahead and touch, talk to, and interact with the horses. The woman stayed back.

"Hi." She introduced herself and held out a hand to shake.

"Sondra." The petite veteran shook her head, a long brown braid flapping. "I faced the demons from hell back in the sandbox, but..." her eyes widened, "...horses are so *big!*"

Sam ruffled Trixi's bangs. "Yes, they are. But they are also very gentle, loving animals and quite intuitive. Mine always seem to know what my mood is."

"Hmm." Sondra continued to watch as Electra demonstrated how to brush Apache.

"Here's a treat." Sam handed her some pellets. "When

you're ready, just hold them out in your palm, like this, and the horse will take it without biting you."

The woman hesitated a few more seconds, and then stepped forward, holding out her hand to Trixi. The mare sniffed and gently lipped the treats from Sondra's palm. She drew in a sharp inhale. "Her mouth is so soft."

Trixi nuzzled the veteran's hand, and Sondra slowly stroked the velvety nose. "Wow." She glanced at Sam and continued to caress the mare's face. Trixi's ears were forward and after a moment, she rubbed her head against Sondra's arm. "Oh…" She breathed the word, almost a sigh, as she leaned into the horse, cheek to cheek.

Sam closed her eyes for a moment. *Thank you, Lord.*

She swiveled her head to watch Electra as she, along with Garrett and Del, encouraged the other veterans to try their hand at brushing Apache. *So far, so good.*

Then, out of the corner of her eye, she caught a glimpse of Jack Murdock exiting the door. The satisfied feeling fled, and her nerves jittered. *Why does he have to hang around every time?*

CHAPTER TWENTY-EIGHT

Sam shifted gears to climb a hill.

"You two girls are awesome!" Alberta's praise and enthusiasm warmed Sam's chill over seeing Jack. "You never cease to amaze me when you work with horses. You are so calm and patient, and you both have this instinct, or some kind of ability, to communicate with them." She put an arm around her daughter.

"Thanks, Mom." The teen snuggled against her mother. "I love them... and I love you."

Sam's throat constricted. She smiled back. "Thanks, Alberta. This girl is learning twice as fast as I ever have."

Electra grinned. "Does this mean I can stay, Mom?" She bit her lower lip and cast her eyes up and sideways toward her mother.

"For now, honey. I'm very pleased with your schoolwork as well, and now that you have Horace to help you with math, I think we can make it through this year."

"Seriously? Yay!" The girl bounced in the truck seat and threw both arms wide to hug her mom, nearly hitting Sam in the process.

"Hey, careful there." She hooted. "We don't want to run off the road."

"Sorry, Sam, but I'm so excited. Thank you, Mom, thank you, thank you, thank you! I can't wait to get home and work with Apache some more and Trixi too and maybe I'll learn more about her tricks, and when are you moving here, are you coming after tax season?"

"Take a breath, honey." Alberta cast a bemused look at her

daughter. "One step at a time, okay? You just keep up the good work with the horses and schoolwork. I'll also work very hard at getting here as soon as I can after I finish with my clients. But there's a lot involved with moving." Her face settled into a serious expression. "New York and Montana are two very different places, and I'll be taking a big cut in pay. Got to figure that out."

"I know that's a concern. However, Montana is a lot cheaper to live in than New York, and you will have free board and room... I have this gut feeling that it is going to work out just fine."

Her friend gave her a thumbs-up. "You're right, and with possible extra income doing other ranchers' taxes, I think it will."

That evening, as the purple shadows lengthened into darkness, Sam and Alberta washed and dried dishes while Electra dove into her schoolwork without being asked. Alberta raised her eyebrows.

"She's trying... really hard," Sam whispered.

When the phone rang, it was Nick Seward on the line. "Hey, Sam. You kinda rushed out of there this afternoon before I could talk to you."

Oh-oh, did I screw something up? She held her breath.

"I thought everything went quite well today."

Her breath released.

"And I heard very positive comments from the audience, which included some of the board members. They continue to be impressed."

Even Jack Murdoch? But she kept quiet. He had slipped out the door before they were even finished.

Nick continued. "The vets are excited, even the gal who seemed so afraid at first. She told me she can't wait to do it again."

Relief and warmth flowed like melted butter through Sam. "Oh. Well. That's great to hear. I wasn't too sure if she would be back. Fantastic."

"Garrett and Del have been talking you up, how much you've helped them both. I see a huge difference in them, especially in Garrett."

"I'm so glad. I was terrified he would be my first failure after he fell that time."

"Oh no. Not at all. In fact, I think after these six get done talking to their groups, you're going to see more students."

Her shoulders bunched. *I could barely deal with the six we had today. How am I going to handle more?* "Well, Nick, that's wonderful, but… I think we need to go slow. I can only do so much, and I want to spend time with each one. It's not an overnight process."

"Sure, sure. I know that." Nick's voice was reassuring. "We definitely will limit the group until we have an idea how the program is going, and until you get certified. We'll see about getting you some assistance too." He laughed. "Although you've already got a pretty darn good one with Electra."

Sam glanced back at the girl, hunched over her books. "Yes. Yes, I do."

***

The atmosphere was somber as Sam drove Alberta to the airport. Even Electra stayed quiet, hugging her mom's arm and leaning her head on her shoulder.

"Well, at least the sun is shining. No more snowstorms." Sam tried to lighten the mood. "You should have good weather for the trip."

Her friend gave her a half-hearted smile. "Yes, it is. I'm glad of that."

They drove on in silence, the miles stretching like a rubber band.

Electra sniffed. "Mom?" She looked up at her mother's face. "You're coming back here to live, aren't you?"

"That's the plan, honey." Alberta squeezed her daughter's arm. "Just a few more months. I'm going to try my hardest to make it sooner, rather than later."

"Time will go by super fast. You'll see. Spring will be here, with all the wildflowers blooming, green grass, and new calves being born." Sam tried to soothe herself as well as the other two.

Electra's face brightened for a moment. "That'll be cool. Can't wait!" Then she snuggled back against her mother.

After prolonged hugs, eyes blinking back tears, and last waves, Sam and Electra walked to the airport café for a hot drink and watched the plane pull away from the terminal.

"There she goes." Electra pointed as it soared into the sky.

Sam wiped her eyes, a little surprised at her emotions. *Being without your mom is hard.* The small, empty spot in her heart ached as she thought of how long she had been away from her family. *It's not like they don't care. They have their own life "off the grid" and that's their choice.* She probably should go visit them sometime, but then she had her own, very busy life here. She couldn't be away from the ranch and her work for very long.

The work. Like an endless ticker tape, her list of "to-do" items flashed through her mind. The cows, the horses, the training, the certification, the vets, the group home kids, her job at Clyde's, Electra. She drained her coffee cup. "Well, cowgirl, shall we go visit Brad? Or would you rather visit Robin?"

Electra stared into her hot chocolate cup for long seconds. "I dunno." She shrugged. "Robin?"

"Okay, that's fine. I'll drop you off there and go see Brad, and then pick you up."

"Wish today wasn't a school day so I could see Sapphire and Wendy and the others." The teen's mouth drooped.

"I know, honey." Sam checked her watch. Almost eleven. "Why don't we go see Brad, get some lunch, and then go back to the group home for a while. The kids will be home about 3:00, and you can see them for a short visit. We can't stay long though. Have to get home before dark and chores, if we can."

Electra beamed. "Yeah! Okay, let's do that, I want to see Brad too, and then I can see Robin and Sapphire and Wendy and everybody. Yay!"

"All right." Sam high-fived the teen. "We've got a plan."

They found Brad sitting in a wheelchair in the rehab center lobby, dozing in the sun.

Electra sidled up next to him. "Hey, Br-a-ad."

He jerked his head upright and his eyes flew open. "Wha...? Oh. Electra. Hi." He looked up and cleared his throat. "And Sam. Nice to see you."

"You too." She gently put her hand on his shoulder and then sat in a chair next to him.

"And how are my favorite ladies today?"

"We're good." Electra squatted beside him. "So, lazybones, what are you doing, napping in the sun like a kitty cat? You gotta get out to the ranch and ride some horses."

Brad chuckle-snorted. "Yeah." His thin face fell back into a sad grimace. "Like I could. Can't even walk real good right now."

"You will," the teen declared. "I'm waiting for that race. Besides, it's going to be spring soon, and you have to be out there for the flowers and the grass and the baby calves." She echoed Sam's earlier sentiment.

Sam laughed. "That's right. We're going to need your help about that time."

"Well..." Brad shrugged. "I guess." Then he smiled as if he remembered he needed to put on a brave face for them. "I'm looking forward to that. I'm workin' hard on getting outta here."

"You better be!" Electra grinned at him. "I'm gonna bring in a riding whip next time and go to PT with you."

That made Brad laugh genuinely. "Oh no. I don't want that! I'll do it, I promise."

"I'll be right there with her." Sam took his hand. "But really, I can't wait to have you come out to the ranch. That's the most healing thing I can think of right now."

He closed his eyes. "Yeah." When he opened his eyes, he

fixed his gaze on her. "I'd like to spend more time with you. Soon."

Hope fluttered on butterfly wings. "Okay. It's a deal." Would he be able to do it? He always seemed so discouraged. *We've got to get him out of here.*

At the group home, Robin welcomed them at the door with a big hug and motioned them into the empty hallway. "What brings you two here today?"

Sam's heart tugged as Electra's smile faded. "We brought Mom to the airport." She sniffled. "But she'll be back... I hope... by May."

Robin hugged the girl again. "Of course. I'm sure she will. We'll be thinking positive thoughts about that." She glanced at Sam. "You okay?"

"Yeah. We went to see Brad. But he's always so down and negative these days. He's discouraged about his progress, I guess."

Robin checked her watch. "Hey, Electra. The kids will be home pretty soon, and they're going to be so happy to see you. Do you want to come to my office and talk for a little while?"

Electra gave her a small, sad nod. "Okay."

"Coffee's on, and a plate of cookies. Help yourself, Sam. We can chat when the kids get home."

"Sounds good." In the kitchen, she poured a cup of coffee, grabbed a chocolate chip cookie, and sat at the large wooden table. Brad's downcast face haunted her. He only had a broken leg and arm, so why was it taking him so long to get back up and around? Of course, he'd been immobile for so many weeks. That had to take its toll. But he didn't seem to have that drive, that "want-to" she had always seen in him. She chewed the inside of her cheek. And there was that concussion too, a brain injury. Maybe that had affected him more than she realized.

She dunked her cookie into the coffee. Electra appeared to bring out some of the old humor and spunk in him, briefly. But what could she do to help him? She missed his smile and teasing. Maybe they needed to visit him more often. *I wonder how long he's supposed to be in rehab.*

The sound of the group home van out front broke into her thoughts, and before she could get up from the table, the kitchen filled with giggling girls. The boys grabbed cookies and ran back outside.

"Sam!" Sapphire's hand stopped midair over the cookie plate. "You're here. Is Electra...?"

"I'm here!" Electra scooted from the office. The girls shrieked and hugged and jumped up and down.

"Okay, girls." Robin's calm voice redirected them. "Get yourselves some cookies and milk and then go visit with Electra in your room. I'm sure you have lots to catch up on."

Sam caught the teen's attention. "Remember, we can't stay long. I want to leave by 4:00 so we can get our chores done before too late. Even at that, it'll be dark already when we get home."

When the horde had cleared the kitchen, Robin poured herself a cup of coffee and refilled Sam's.

"How do you do this? I'm so impressed by you. I only have one to deal with, and sometimes she leaves me at wit's end."

The counselor laughed. "Training, patience, and lots of prayer." She took a sip. "So, what's up with Brad? I can see something is troubling you."

"I feel like I should do something to help him. He seems depressed and not interested in getting back up and out." She poured out the thoughts and questions that plagued her.

Robin raised her brow. "I can see that this would bother you. Sounds like he's changed since the accident."

"Yes. He used to be so upbeat and funny and..." Sam swallowed. "I thought maybe we had something between us, but now, he's distant and cool, and never talks about before..." She related how he'd been angry at her for calling him "a friend" and his last voicemail with the ominous "We need to talk."

She stared into the inky depths of her coffee cup. "I've been afraid he wanted to break up, and now, his actions are contradictory, like a see-saw. He's supportive and kind one day and distant and negative the next."

"Do you feel like you could talk to him about that?"

Sam looked up at Robin. "No. I think he has too much to deal with right now, and... I don't really want to know... if it's bad news. This has been heavy on my mind for so long." She hung her head.

"Well, one of these days, you *will* have to address that concern. But in the meantime, are you in touch with his family? What are the doctors saying about his recovery?"

"I haven't talked to his sister Melissa for a while. I probably need to call her." She blinked against the sting in her eyes. "I feel so helpless. What can I do?"

Robin touched her arm gently. "You don't need to fix everything. He had an extreme trauma, a probable brain injury, and he's not the same person right now. I've not seen him, of course, but I'm betting he has PTSD."

She raised her eyebrows. PTSD. Her scalp twitched. She hadn't even considered that.

"Treat him firmly but with love and patience, pray, and simply give him time."

Time. Sam brushed a tear that escaped. *How do I do that? I want him to be well, the old Brad... now.*

CHAPTER TWENTY-NINE

Sam called Melissa who shared her concerns about Brad. "He'll only be in the rehab center for another week or two, I think. As soon as he can get around at least with a walker, they plan to release him."

"He doesn't seem to want to..." Sam's breath hitched. "I know he's not happy being in there, but... he's a different person."

A sigh wafted over the line. "I know. I'm seeing that too. The doctors think he's doing well, however, and that a brain trauma and being in a coma for so long does affect the personality—temporarily though, they say."

"Where will he stay when he gets out?"

"He'll go to Mom and Dad's for a while until he's able to function in his own place."

"It'll be good for him to be with family. I'm glad he won't have to be alone." She blinked against the sting in her eyes. "Well, Electra and I are going to try to come visit and encourage him as often as we can."

"I know he appreciates that and looks forward to your visits, even if he doesn't express it." Melissa tittered. "He does tell me about the funny things Electra does and says."

"Yeah, she seems to cheer him up a little. Heck, she cheers me up. We all need that right now. Well, you take care, and tell Brad we'll be back again soon."

***

The next couple of weeks were caught up in a whirlwind of chores, feeding, training, and study—Electra's schoolwork and

Sam's therapy certification. She hardly had time to worry about Brad, except when they went to visit him. He seemed to be progressing physically, although slowly. One day he met them in the corridor as he shuffled along on his walker.

"Hey, Brad!" Electra called out. "C'mon, I'll race you to the end of the hall." She touched him on the shoulder as if to signify he was "it" in a game of tag and took off powerwalking. When he didn't respond, she looked back. "Bra-ad. Come ON! We brought oatmeal-raisin cookies I helped bake, but you can't have one unless you win."

Sam couldn't help but laugh as he looked up at the ceiling, showing the whites of his eyes. "Oh, all right. Come back here. At least give me a chance."

"Okay. I'll even give you a running start." The teen giggled and took up a racer's stance about six feet behind him. "Go!"

He took off, scooting the walker and dragging his bad leg. Electra exaggerated her stride, slowing down to stay just behind him, sometimes catching up, almost passing, and then falling back again. She puffed and panted as if she was trying hard to beat him, keeping up a running patter. "Ashton's in the lead, now Lucci is gaining on him, they're neck and neck, oh no, she slipped on a wet spot, and Ashton surges ahead. Who's gonna win this hard-fought race? Will it be a photo-finish?"

Sweat beaded on Brad's forehead as he surged forward. Sam cheered him on. When he reached the end of the hallway, he stopped and grinned as Sam and Electra pumped their fists.

"Aaand, we have a winner! Mr. Brad Ashton!" Electra did a victory dance. Nurses looked up from their station and smirked.

He wiped his brow with the back of his hand. "Well, I know you let me win, but… I did get here first. So, pony up the cookies."

His mood seemed brighter, and Sam's step felt a smidgeon lighter as they left that day. In the truck, she sneaked a peek at Electra. "Hey, thanks for working so hard to lift Brad's spirits."

The girl shrugged. "He's hurting…" she put her hand on

her chest, "...in here. I know what that's like. And besides, I like him. I know I didn't at first. But he's still that fun and funny guy, just hiding it right now."

Sam cocked an eyebrow. *Wow. Where did that come from?* The little-girl flibbertigibbet had been replaced, momentarily at least, with this wise old soul. Her heart expanded, and she squeezed Electra's arm. "Thank you."

Their gazes met in a smile.

A couple of days later, they loaded Trixi and Apache, and Sam drove her team to Miles City for another session with the six vets at the ag college.

Garrett and Del met them at the chute, full of enthusiasm in the chilly but bright, sunny morning. "Can't wait to ride." Garrett's face was as relaxed as Sam had seen it. Nick came out to help unload and ushered them all into the arena, where the other veterans waited on the bottom bleachers.

Again, Sam talked about the horses, how intuitive they were to mood, and how, although they were huge animals, wouldn't deliberately hurt anyone. She held up a bucket of brushes and curry combs. "All right. Who's ready to groom?"

The three men immediately came forward with Garrett and Del, all around their late twenties or early thirties. Jimmy had a prosthetic leg. Linc was missing an arm, and the third, Al, Sam guessed had PTSD. *Heck, they probably all do.*

The petite but solid-built woman, Sondra, hung back. Sam walked toward her. "How are you doing today?"

"Okay." The woman's shoulders looked rigid beneath a gray USMC T-shirt.

"Do you want to brush Trixi?"

"Well, yeah, maybe. But... I'll wait till the guys are through."

"All right. That sounds like a plan." Sam spoke in a gentle tone. "There's absolutely no hurry for any of this. Whenever and whatever you're comfortable with."

She turned back to the group, where Electra demonstrated what Apache was learning. She pulled back on the lead until his weight shifted backward and then tapped his shoulder. The gelding lifted his foot automatically as he'd done the last time. Then he bent to where he rested his knee on the ground.

Sam gasped. The vets uttered "ohs" and "whoas." Garrett gave a low whistle, and they all applauded.

Electra's face shone as Apache stayed in place for a couple of minutes and then she slackened the lead and touched his shoulder again. He rose to his feet, and she slipped cake pellets from her pocket as a reward. "Good boy."

"That's amazing." Sondra's voice was a mere whisper.

Sam nodded to the woman beside her. "Yes, it is. I didn't even know he was doing that. He's going to be ready for you all to ride soon."

"Is it okay to give him some pellets?" Sondra's eyes were bright.

"Of course." Sam led her over to Electra and the horse. "Sondra would like to feed him. Is that all right?"

"Sure." The teen reached into her pocket again and offered the woman several treats. "Here you go. He's actually quite nice and won't bite." She demonstrated once again how to hold the palm flat.

Sondra took the pellets and held out her hand. Apache approached slowly, sniffed, and lipped the treats, almost smiling as he crunched. The woman gave a little giggle. "That's so cool." She offered him more and stroked his velvety nose. "Can I brush him now?"

"Sure." With widened eyes, the teen picked up a brush and guided Sondra's hand. "Like this, with the way the hair grows. Yeah, that's good."

Sam smiled too as she gestured to the guys gathered around Trixi. "Okay, who's ready to ride?"

The first rider, the man with the prosthetic leg, had a childish look of wonder on his face as Trixi rose with him on her back. Sam steadied him, and Garrett volunteered to lead the horse.

As they took their turns around the arena, her mind flashed

to Brad. He might have PTSD... These vets have PTSD. Horses have healing powers. Her nerves tingled. *Just look at how far Garrett has come. And now Sondra.*

She had to get Brad out to the ranch.

Higher than average February temperatures brought spring's promise with a spritz of green on the hills surrounding Sam's ranch, and fluffy sheep-clouds trotted across the sky. A warm wind had her and Electra shedding their winter garb for lighter jackets as they did chores and went for rides.

"We'd better enjoy this while we can," she told her young friend, "because we could still get a blizzard before spring is officially here."

"Really? Wow, that's weird. I hope not." Electra attached the lead to Apache's halter and then led him into the corral to continue training him to kneel. She rubbed his neck, talking to him all the while.

The teen was so much calmer than when she first arrived, and even her spurts of gushing monologues were fewer and farther between. An easy smile came to Sam's lips. She had seen no more evidence of the cutting, and Electra had thrown herself into her schoolwork every day after chores, as enthusiastically as working with her horse.

Toby came up to her, looking for a treat. She hadn't been able to work much with him for several weeks, with her veteran's program, study for the certification, and traveling to Billings every few days to see Brad.

Rubbing the gelding's face and ears, she spoke softly to him. "You're such a handsome fellow. Are we going to be able to get you over your fears? I'd sure like to be able to ride you."

He shook his head and snorted. She chuckled. "No, huh? Well, we'll see about that." While Electra worked with her horse, kneeling, mounting, and rising, Sam brushed Toby and massaged his legs and back. She put the saddle blanket on and led him around the corral. His back muscles tensed when she lifted the saddle on. Working slowly and speaking in a gentle voice, she took her time with the process. Giving him a treat and letting him relax between each step, she buckled the cinch and tightened it gradually. At first, he kicked at the leather encircling his belly but after a few minutes calmed down.

"Good boy. I know you've done this before. You were somebody's baby once." She led him around the corral for about fifteen minutes. Then she put one foot in the stirrup to test her weight. His head jerked around, and he sidestepped. "Easy now, easy." She stayed in that position for a minute or two and then swung her other leg over the saddle.

Again, he sidestepped and backed, shaking his head back and forth. His muscles bunched, and Sam tightened her knees to brace herself in case he decided to buck. "C'mon, Toby, you're not going to act like a bronc, are you?" She kept up an easy patter as she loosened the reins slightly and urged him forward.

He gathered his hind legs and gave a couple of crow-hops. Sam held on and kept her seat. "Easy, boy. Just quit that, okay?" Gradually, the gelding settled his nervous moves and moved forward in a walk, albeit still uneasy.

"Good boy, Toby, good boy." She patted his neck. "That's the way to do it." They took several turns around the corral with no further incident, and then she dismounted and unsaddled him. "That's enough for today. You did such a good job." She gave him more cake pellets, caressed his face, and rubbed him down. He leaned his head into her side and nuzzled her. "You really *are* a good horse. I know you are."

Electra applauded from the fence. "Hey, that was good. We're both making progress!"

***

Melissa called that evening and launched straight to the point. "I don't know what to do with Brad."

Sam frowned. "Oh? What's going on?"

"Well, he's been at the folks' now for two weeks, and I think they're at their wits' end." A sigh wafted over the line. "He's impossible to get along with. He's grumpy. Doesn't want to do his exercises. He complains about everything, and he just sits in the recliner all day."

"Oh my. I would've thought he'd be so glad to get out of the rehab center." Sam tugged at her ear. "Last time I saw him, he seemed to be doing better, more upbeat, and moving pretty good."

"Yeah, well... I think he's regressed. Oh, Sam, he's not the same Brad!" The young woman's voice ended in a sob.

Sam blew out her cheeks and released the air. "Gee, I'm sorry. Is there anything I can do to help? Do you want me to come into town and meet you for coffee or lunch? Sounds like maybe you need to talk to somebody."

"That would be great. Maybe Mom could join us. I know she's feeling as frustrated as I am. We don't know what to do."

Her shoulders sagging, Sam hung up and plodded into the living room. What had happened to her dashing, funny, up-for-anything Brad? Just like Toby, he was reluctant to face reality again. *I really need to get him out to the ranch to be with the horses.*

Saturday, Sam dropped Electra off at the group home to visit with the kids and Robin. She met Melissa and her mother at a local coffee shop and bakery near where the Ashtons lived. The cinnamon and spice aroma enticed her to pick out an apple fritter, and she took it and her coffee to the table where they were already seated.

"Thank you for coming." Dee Ashton gave her a weary but kind smile. "I know it's a long trip for you."

Sam shrugged. "I'm getting used to it. I think my truck knows the way, and I could probably take a nap." The women cracked up.

Melissa and her mom took turns venting about Brad's progress, or lack thereof, and his less-than-optimistic attitude. "Dad just threw up his hands, and he spends most of his time in his shop now."

Dee's face sagged. "His doctor doesn't seem concerned, just says his attitude is not unusual, and he needs time to heal from the concussion, the coma, and the trauma of the accident."

"He's probably right." Sam's thoughts jumped from Brad to the veterans. "Robin, the counselor at the group home, thinks he might have PTSD."

Dee tipped her head to one side, her brow furrowed.

"Really?" Melissa frowned.

"I was a little shocked at that too, because you normally think of veterans returning from war. She explained it can happen to anyone who has experienced a traumatic event, and I think it's safe to say Brad has." Sam sipped her coffee. "I've been working with a group of vets in Miles City, getting them acquainted with my horses, and I've been amazed at the change in a couple of them."

Dee nodded. "Yes, horses certainly do have a calming influence on some people."

"Well, here's an idea." Sam's outlook brightened as if a lamp had been switched on. "Why don't you guys bring Brad out to the ranch for a visit?"

"Oh." Melissa's eyes widened. "Yeah. We've all missed our ranch so much, and Brad grew up with horses, as he's probably told you."

The lines in Mrs. Ashton's face smoothed. "My dear, that is a wonderful idea! I would love it, and maybe Brad..." Her voice trailed off, but she retained a hopeful smile.

Sam stood. "I just had another idea. The weather has been so nice, and I promised Miss Ellie she could come visit Trixi. So, let me give her a call and see if she could come too."

"Sounds like fun." Melissa stood and hugged Sam, and her mother followed suit.

They all left the coffee shop with grins on their faces and a promise to see each other soon.

Sam opened the pickup door and climbed in. *Sure hope this helps.*

CHAPTER THIRTY

Ellie chortled when Sam proposed the visit. "Oh, honey, I've been chompin' at the bit to get out to see my Trixi! Yes. Absolutely. And I can come today."

"Great. Electra is going to be so excited. I'll go pick her up, and we'll be by to get you in about an hour, and you can spend the night."

At the group home, Robin ushered her into the kitchen. "Coffee?"

"No thanks, just had some." Sam told her of the plans to take Ellie today and for the Ashtons to bring Brad to the ranch tomorrow.

Robin's face lit up. "Hey! If I can get everybody organized, would it be okay to bring a vanload of the kids out too?"

Startled, Sam hesitated a moment, but then shrugged. "Why not? Let's make it a party!"

"Party? Where's the party?" Electra came through the door, Sapphire right behind.

When Sam told them the plan, squeals erupted, the girls hugged each other, and jumped up and down. "Let's go tell Wendy and the rest!" They were off before the women could say "jackrabbit."

Robin spread her hands in a gesture of apology. "I'm sorry about all that. I sure hope you don't mind this wild bunch invading your ranch."

"No, no, it's all right. The more, the merrier, right?" *Hope that proves true.* "I think they've all been cooped up for so long this winter, being around the horses will probably do them some good."

While she joked with Robin, her insides churned. Could she handle all these people? Maybe she should have waited, let Brad have his first time out with his family. *Oh dear, what have I done?*

Miss Ellie beamed as Sam pulled up to the ranch. "This is a beautiful place."

"Thank you. I love it here." Sam got out of the truck and unloaded the woman's overnight case, her walker, and a wheelchair. As she came around to get her out of the passenger seat, Ellie glanced up at her shyly. "Could I go see Trixi first thing?"

Electra quivered beside them, nodding rapidly.

"Sure, I don't see why not." Sam helped her into the chair. Electra jumped behind and wheeled her to the pasture, where the horses hung their heads over the fence. They whickered and flicked their tails in anticipation of a treat.

"Oh, my goodness. There's my girl." Ellie took the pellets Sam offered and held her palm out to Trixi. The mare leaned farther over the fence and nuzzled the woman's arm. "You remember me, don't you?" Trixi bobbed her head. The elderly woman gave her the treats and stroked the soft nose and face. "I've missed you so much."

She turned her face away, but not before Sam saw tears coursing down her wrinkled cheeks. Her chest cavity filled with the tenderness of the love between woman and horse.

Electra showed off what she and Apache had learned, earning cheers from Miss Ellie. "You're doing great! That's perfect."

After supper, Sam changed the sheets on her bed so Miss Ellie could stay on the ground floor and then moved her things to the second bedroom upstairs. As she crawled under the covers later, she smiled at the happy picture of the tiny woman seeing her Trixi again. They would have to do this more often. Then thoughts of tomorrow intruded, with the vanload of kids coming at the same time as Brad and his family. She rubbed the ache in her temples. *Why did I say yes to all those people coming? Dear Lord, I'm going to need some help.*

The next morning, Sam came downstairs to see Electra and Ellie already out at the corral, petting and feeding the horses. She poured coffee into a couple of travel cups and went out to join them.

Miss Ellie's white curls bounced as she greeted Sam and took the cup. "Oh, thank you, dear. I didn't want to take the time to wait for the coffee to brew. I just *had* to get out to see my girl."

"I can understand that." Sam warmed at the pair making a fuss over each horse. Both the young and the old showed their love of these animals in their faces and their body language. She wondered what had prompted Ellie to become a trick rider. Would Electra follow in the woman's footsteps, with the same horse? The possibilities were endless for this youngster.

The girl pirouetted to face her. "Hey... I was thinking..."

"Oh-oh. That's dangerous." Sam grinned.

The girl giggled. "Well... Miss Ellie trained Trixi, and they know each other, and... well, could we let Miss Ellie ride?"

What? Sam blinked. "W... I... uh..."

The older woman raised her eyes. "I would love to, if you think it's okay."

"Well, yeah, I suppose so..." Sam turned to Electra. "Go ahead and get Trixi's saddle and bring some of those extra straps so we can make sure Ellie doesn't fall."

"Yay!" The teen took off like a deer to the barn, returning in a couple of minutes with the gear.

Once the horse was saddled, Miss Ellie gave the signal, and Trixi knelt. Electra and Sam helped her into the saddle, and Sam secured her further with the straps. The mare rose on cue. Electra led them around the corral, with Sam walking beside them. She rested her hand behind the saddle, ready to catch the woman if she lost her balance.

Ellie laughed, a melodic tinkling sound. Her face shone, and

Sam imagined her for a moment as the young trick rider she had once been. She could almost see the wind in her hair, the speed and movement of the horse, the crowd cheering as the woman dipped and spun and stood atop her saddle.

When the older woman indicated she was getting tired, they rode back to the side of the barn, where Sam and Electra helped her off and back into her chair.

"That. Was. Wonderful!" Ellie's wrinkles had softened, her smile wide. "So special. You really made my day. Thank you." She gave each a hug.

Sam exchanged a happy look with Electra. *This is what it's all about. This is what I'm supposed to be doing.* Her heart filled to overflowing.

"Hey, what do you say we go bake those cinnamon rolls I got started before the rest of our company gets here?" She headed toward the house, and Electra pushed Miss Ellie back up the incline, giggling and chattering.

The Ashtons arrived about ten, and Sam stepped out of the house to greet them. "Hey there. So glad you could come."

"We're happy to be here." Melissa flicked her eyes toward Brad sitting in the back seat with a scowl. Dee and Paul exited the car and hugged Sam and then Electra who came running from the corral.

"C'mon up to the porch and have some coffee. It's warm enough to sit in the sun this morning." Sam gestured. "I have fresh cinnamon rolls too." She directed the last at Brad.

He finally gave her a smile. "Okay. Sounds good."

Desperately wanting to hug him, she opened the car door and forced herself to stand back. He eased out, using a cane to steady himself as they walked toward the house.

Miss Ellie pushed her walker onto the porch, and Sam introduced her to the Ashtons. "You remember Brad, don't you?"

"Oh, yes. I certainly do." Her face brightened. "You are the fine young man who made this all possible, to give my Trixi the perfect home. I owe you so many thanks."

Brad's cheeks colored, and he stared down at his boots. "No, you don't owe me anything." He looked up again and smiled back. "I was just doing my job. But it was also my pleasure."

Sam blinked back a sudden tear. He was such a dear man to do that. She turned away to hide her face and went inside to bring out the coffee and rolls. Dee Ashton stood at the porch railing. "Oh, my dear, this is such a nice place. I'll bet it's just lovely in the spring when everything is green."

Paul gazed toward the pasture with a half-smile. "Yup. A ranch is a lot of work, but I... I miss it." He faced Brad. "You too, son?"

"Yeah." He shrugged. "I guess so."

Sam chewed the inside of her cheek. She had truly expected him to be more excited to be there.

When the group finished their coffee, Dee and Melissa helped Sam gather the cups and plates and carry them inside to the sink. "Your house is really cute." Mrs. Ashton glanced around the kitchen and through the doorway into the living room.

"Thanks. It's small, but it suits me." Sam told the women about her grandparents living there and how she had found the place for lease and fixed it up, omitting the part about Kenny.

"What a great story." Dee's face lit up. "You've come full circle."

"Well, almost. I don't own it yet. But I hope to someday." Oh, how she yearned to make that happen.

As they stepped back onto the porch, the group home van roared up the drive. Electra gave a shout, "Woohoo! They're here!" and ran to meet them.

Sam peeked at Brad who scowled again. *Well, here goes nothin'.*

Robin, along with Jim, the other counselor, got out of the vehicle, slid the side door open, and the kids piled out. Electra hugged Sapphire and then gestured in a wide arc. "Come on down to the corral and see the horses!"

"Calmly now," Robin reminded in a firm but gentle voice. "Don't scare them. Walk slowly and don't yell."

"I'll go down with them," Jim volunteered.

"We'll be there shortly," Sam called after him. She helped Miss Ellie into the wheelchair and then followed the Ashtons toward the corral, where the girls were already petting and feeding the horses. A couple of new kids hung back with Jim by the fence and watched, one little guy peeking from behind the counselor's leg,

Brad shuffled slowly forward with his cane and sat on a rock nearby. Sam parked Ellie's chair, stood by his side, and rested a hand on his shoulder. "I'm sorry about the big group. I should have told them to wait and come another time."

He didn't reply.

Yes, a big mistake. She swallowed hard. "There's Toby." She pointed at the gelding who, like some of the kids, stayed off to one side. "He's doing great."

Brad nodded. "He wasn't hurt bad then."

"No, just scrapes and bruises. But he's still shy and skittish. I just got so I can saddle him, and finally got up on his back the other day."

"Hmm."

"Do you want to go in and see him?"

"Naw. It's okay."

Sam closed her eyes for a second. *Oh boy. This is not going well.*

They stood silent, watching the kids petting the horses, then saddling and bridling them. Electra helped the braver ones mount and walked with them around the corral. Sam's muscles tensed like a runner, ready to race in and help should there be trouble. But she relaxed a little as Electra conducted herself calmly and professionally. What a young lady she had become. Her mouth quirked. Well, sometimes, anyway. The teen still had her moments of "little girlhood" with her over-enthusiastic shrieking and talking a mile a minute. She was young yet. It would smooth out in time.

Toby approached the fence and poked his nose through the rails. He sniffed toward Brad who leaned forward slightly. The gelding blew loudly and then turned abruptly to run around the corral. Still skittish. She stood stock-still. Were they afraid of each other?

Several times, Toby came back and repeated his actions. Brad sat back on the rock with a dejected slump.

She patted his arm. "He'll come around. He still acts that way toward me sometimes." She took a couple of pellets from her pocket. "Do you want to offer him a treat? He's a sucker for food."

Brad stood. "Naw. It's okay." He limped back toward the house.

The excitement of the kids and horses faded. Sam's legs were weighted, her feet rooted to the ground. She sank onto the rock, so wanting to give in to her tears of disappointment.

CHAPTER THIRTY-ONE

Sam closed her eyes. *Dear Lord, please, I want to help Brad heal. But I don't know how to do that if he won't respond to the horses.* She visualized Brad turning around, coming back to the corral, feeding Toby, and petting him, the two becoming best buds. He should've seen Miss Ellie riding, even with her weakness and the crippling effects of her stroke. Why didn't he want to try? She sent her thoughts to Brad as if willing him to be strong, to "cowboy up."

When she opened her eyes, she glanced over her shoulder, almost expecting to see him limping back down the incline. But what she saw was Wendy pushing Miss Ellie toward the house. They stopped at the bottom of the steps, and Ellie motioned to Brad who sat on the porch. After a moment's hesitation, he rose stiffly and stood in front of her.

Sam saw the older woman gesturing, her white curls bobbing. How she wished she could hear what she was saying. Her pulse fluttered. Did she dare hope the woman would get through to him? *You tell him, Miss Ellie!*

But after several minutes, Brad shrugged and walked into the house. Ellie and Wendy came back to where Sam sat. "No luck?"

Ellie shook her head. "Poor boy. He's hurting so bad." She put a hand over her heart. "He blames himself for the accident and for Toby's fear. Says he 'ruined' your horse, and you'll never forgive him for that."

"What? Whatever gave him that idea?" Sam scrunched her face. "I sure hope I haven't said anything... I'm sure I didn't..." Tears threatened again.

"You didn't, dear." The old woman put a hand on her arm. "It's in his own mind. I know…" She took a breath. "I had a father who beat my mother, my sister, and me. I really, truly thought it was my fault, that I did things that upset him—like spending too much time with the horses and not enough in the house helping my mom."

Sam gulped. "Oh my dear Ellie!" Her stomach twisted. What an awful thing for a young girl to have to deal with.

"It's okay. He was arrested and later died in prison." The woman gazed into the distance. "Horses were my salvation. They helped me heal and to gain confidence in myself, and I realized everything wasn't my fault. Brad will come around. It may take a while, but he will."

A tiny sob choked its way out of Sam's throat. "I sure hope so." Her voice squeaked and she swallowed. "I want to help him, to *fix* him. I want him to be well and whole and happy again, like before."

"Patience, my dear, and prayer. It's not going to happen overnight. And he may not be exactly the same as he was before. But in some ways, he might actually be better." Ellie smiled. "You know the saying, 'What doesn't kill you makes you stronger.'"

She allowed a chuckle and put a hand on the older woman's arm. "Thank you. That helps… a lot."

As the afternoon sun slanted to the distant hills and the temperature dropped, Robin and Jim rounded up their charges and got them loaded in the van amidst tears and protests. "I don't want to leave yet! We were just getting started!"

As arranged earlier, Jim stowed Miss Ellie's wheelchair in the back and helped her into the front seat. She winked at Sam. "Hang in there, girlie. And thank you so much for letting me visit my baby… for letting me ride her once again."

Sam squeezed her shoulder. "Anytime. I'm serious. I hope you'll come back soon. You are an inspiration to us all."

"Yeah, you are *awesome*, Miss Ellie!" Electra's face beamed. A chorus from the back seats echoed, "Awesome!"

Ellie beamed and blew a kiss toward the teen.

Robin came around the vehicle, embraced Electra and then Sam. "Thanks for a great day. The kids needed this after being cooped up for so long. We'll be back soon too."

Sam and Electra waved as the van drove away, kids' faces pressed against the glass.

The Ashtons stood by their car, Brad already in the back. Paul shook Sam's hand and got into the driver's seat. Dee and Melissa gave their hugs, Melissa whispering in Sam's ear, "I know you're disappointed. Me too, but it'll be okay. It was a start. We'll be back."

Doubt and hope churned in her stomach. "I hope so." She squinted at Brad. "I really do."

She stepped to his window, and after a moment he rolled it down, still averting his gaze. Putting a hand on his arm, she whispered, "Please come back, Brad."

His glance flickered toward her but dropped again.

An empty ache formed in her chest as she watched the car drive away.

Electra slipped an arm around her waist. They stood, leaning into each other, for several long moments. The girl broke the silence. "Sorry about Brad."

She tried to swallow the boulder in her throat. "Me too." The words rasped. She rested her head against Electra's. "I made a mistake, and I don't know if it can be undone."

"Oh! No-no." The teen peered into her face. "There's always hope. You've told me that. You've shown me that. Don't give up on him. Don't give up on yourself."

Blinking against the sting in her eyes, Sam managed a weak smile. *This girl is turning my words back on me.* Pride won out over regret. Electra had been listening after all. She was maturing. "Thank you, honey. You are absolutely right. We can't give up, and we won't."

The morning after two days of mulling and stewing about how she should approach Brad, she set her coffee cup on the table with a declarative thump. "We're going to Billings today."

Electra's eyebrows shot up. "Really? All right!" She jumped up and gathered her dishes to carry to the sink. "Are we going to kidnap Brad?"

"Something like that." She laughed. "At least, I need to talk to him. He simply closed up when he was here."

"Yeah, it was kind of like a wall around him. He didn't even want to pet the horses." The teen's innocent face held a look of disbelief as if anyone could resist the animals' charms.

Sam's stomach knotted around her breakfast as they drove to town and doubts chased what-ifs through her mind. Maybe this wasn't such a good idea. What if he wouldn't talk to her? *Who am I to try to help him—I'm not a shrink or any kind of therapist. What if I just make things worse? But I'm his friend, and I care about him.*

As they approached Billings, she asked, "Do you want to go with me, or shall I drop you off to visit with Robin?"

"I'd like to come with you, if that's okay." The girl had been unusually quiet during the trip.

Probably having her own whim-whams. She'd had a lot to deal with, herself. "Yes, that's fine with me."

At the Ashtons' small gray-sided bungalow, she pulled into the driveway and took a long draught of air. "All right. Are we ready?"

Electra jumped out of the truck. "Yup!"

Dee opened the door with a wide smile of surprise and delight. "Hello, ladies. Nice to see you. What brings you here today?" She gestured them inside.

"I'd like to talk to Brad." Sam gave the woman a hug. "I'm not comfortable with what happened at the ranch the other day."

Mrs. Ashton's brow furrowed. "I know. He's being a stubborn little boy right now." She pointed. "He's in the living room. Good luck."

"We're gonna change his mind." Electra gave her a wink and strode forward.

Dee exchanged an amused look with Sam. "Make yourself at

home. I'll bring you some coffee." The woman moved toward the kitchen.

Sam shuffled down the hall, her feet heavy as if caked with gumbo mud.

Electra's voice trilled from the room. "So, *Mister* Brad, how come you were such a stick-in-the-mud the other day? I wanted to show you how I trained Apache to kneel, and I was even going to let you ride him. But you just turned up your nose and left. What's up with that?"

Sam peeked around the doorway. Whoa. Nothing like giving him both barrels!

Brad looked up from his chair in front of the TV and met Electra's wide-eyed stare. His face flushed dark, and his eyes narrowed.

Oh-oh. Is he going to yell at her? She stepped forward, clearing her throat.

But then Brad's posture relaxed, and his face softened into a grin. "Well, hello, *Miss* Electra. Nice to see you too." He pointed his nose in the air and sniffed. "Stick-in-the-mud? I resemble that remark!"

Her young friend giggled and punched his shoulder.

That was more like the old Brad. "Hey there."

His dark eyes settled on her. "Hey, Sam. Come, sit."

She sat on the couch next to his recliner. "Listen, I owe you an apology. I should never have allowed the whole gang to come out the same time as you. They can overwhelm anybody at the best of times. I'm sorry."

"You don't owe me an apology. It... it *was* a bit overwhelming, that is true." He shook his head. "But I... don't know... if I'm ready..."

Electra squatted beside him. "And when *will* you be ready? In a week? In a month? In a year?"

He drew his head back sharply. "Uh... I... don't know."

"How about now? Today." Sam moved to stand in front of him and grasped his hands. "Come back to the ranch with us and stay a few days. Take your time, enjoy the peace and quiet, and renew your friendship with horses... if you want to."

He stared out the picture window.

Sam bit her lip. *Maybe we're coming on too strong.* She kept holding his hands, squeezing gently. He sat without responding.

Dee entered the room, carrying a tray with coffee, Danish rolls, and a hot chocolate for Electra. She stopped in mid-track. "Oh." As she backed away, Brad switched his attention to her. "It's all right, Mom. C'mon in."

Then he looked from Sam to Electra and back. "Okay. I'll come out."

Electra squealed. "Yes!"

He glared. "But don't expect miracles."

Oh, but we will. Sam smiled, took a cup from Dee, and raised it to him in a salute.

The Ashtons waved goodbye with hopeful, raised brows. Brad stared out the passenger side window, his hands folded in his lap, while Electra squirmed in the middle. The old pickup ate up the miles toward the ranch as Sam drove, heart racing, neck tense, waiting for him to say something, anything. *What am I trying to do? I'm not a counselor. Can I fix things for him?*

She jumped when Electra finally broke the silence. "Hey, Brad?"

He turned his head toward her like an ancient turtle.

"So, what do you want to do first, when we get home?"

After several beats, he shrugged and looked out the window again.

Electra flashed her a look, mouth twisted to one side.

Doubt sat like a heavy weight on her chest. She forced a cheerful tone. "Well, what do *you* want to do, honey? Are you going to work with Apache today?"

"Yeah. I think he's ready for the vets to try and ride." The girl's face relaxed. "He's such a good boy."

"Yes, he is. Maybe I'll saddle Toby and see if he's over his crow-hopping by now."

The teen laughed. "I'd love to see you ride if he goes all

bucking bronc on you."

"Ha. No, you wouldn't, because you'd probably be picking me up out of the mud." Sam guffawed. "I'm not my great-grandma."

"Aw, I'll bet you could do it."

The two continued off and on with their light-hearted banter the rest of the way home, while Brad stuck to his silence.

This is going to get old, real fast. Downshifting, she drove up the rise to the house. Electra grabbed Brad's duffel bag out of the back. Sam set him up in her first-floor bedroom and moved her things upstairs once again.

They ate bowls of reheated stew and the brownies Electra had made for dessert. Brad grunted, nodded, or shook his head when they addressed him.

"All right, we're going to the corral and work with the horses." Sam stood and carried dishes to the sink. "Are you coming down?"

"No. I'm tired. I think I'll go take a nap." He eased himself from the chair like an old man and shuffled to the bedroom.

She closed her eyes and bit her lip to keep herself from chasing after him, grabbing his shoulders, and shaking him. She scrubbed her hands through her hair, snatched her coat off the peg by the door, and followed Electra outside.

"What is *wrong* with him?" The girl's voice raised in an exasperated tone. "He's worse than ever! Usually, I can get him talking, but not today."

"I don't know. I thought this was a good idea, but now…" Sam trudged to the barn to get Toby's tack and a handful of cake pellets. Thoughts skittered through her mind like mice in the hayloft. Maybe she should have encouraged him to talk to Robin or another counselor instead of bringing him here. Maybe she should simply leave him alone, not keep trying so hard.

She approached Toby with the treats, which he lipped happily, but shied away when she raised the bridle. "C'mon, boy." Tightening her eyes into a squint, she looked him in the eyes. "You and Brad. You are both stubborn men. What am I going to do with you two?" The gelding blew, and they circled for a few minutes before he came for more pellets, and she slipped the bridle on while he was occupied.

Murmuring to him, she ran her hands over his back and smoothed the saddle blanket on. She kept talking and caressing his neck until he stood quietly, then lifted the saddle. As usual, he flinched under its weight and sidestepped.

"It's okay, Toby. You know how to do this. You used to have someone who rode you all the time. Why are you acting like a green colt now?"

Finally, she stepped into the stirrup and swung her leg over the saddle, clenching her knees in anticipation of him trying to buck. He planted his front feet, his head strained downward, and his muscles bunched. Sam sat calmly and let him stand, quivering, for several long moments. Finally, his head came up. She pulled the reins to her right and guided his head around, urging him in a circle. 'Round and 'round they went until Toby relaxed. "Good boy." She slackened the reins and guided him around the corral in figure eights, walking, trotting, and loping.

"Would you open that gate into the small pasture?" she called to Electra. Riding the gelding into the larger space, she put him through his paces for the next half hour, talking to him, encouraging him, and patting his neck. A sensation of satisfaction and peace flowed through her. "You're doing such a good job. Good boy."

She returned to the barn and unsaddled him. If only she could do something like this for Brad. Electra brought Apache over and followed suit. "Toby did a lot better today."

"Yes, he did. Sure glad he didn't decide to dump me." Sam twisted her mouth to one side. "How'd Apache do?"

"Great, as always. I think he's ready. Tomorrow in Miles City?"

"Sounds good." As she turned toward the house, she saw Brad standing on the porch watching. A spark of hope flared. She and Electra headed that way, and the glimmer faded as he went back inside.

Brad came out of his room long enough to eat supper. Even though Electra tried to tease a response, he stayed silent. Sam's jaw clenched. It seemed as if he was trying to prove that being on the ranch wasn't going to help him.

"We're going to Miles tomorrow to work with the vets," she said. "I'd really like it if you came along."

He stood, gathered his dishes, and put them into the sink. Without a word, he shuffled back to the bedroom.

Electra looked at her with a saucer-eyed stare.

She shrugged, ran hot water over the dishes, and scrubbed each plate furiously, as if to wash away his pain and her frustration.

After dishes were done, the teen got on the phone with her mom, and Sam went to the living room to stare at her book, reading the same page over and over until she finally gave up and went to bed. *God, give me the strength, give me the words, give me some ideas. Please. I don't know what to do.*

The morning's weak sunlight woke her. She lay in bed, reluctant to face what the day might hold. Should she insist that Brad come with them or leave him alone? What would do the most good? She punched her pillow. *I don't know!* Finally, she stretched, rose slowly from bed, and went downstairs to start the coffee and breakfast.

Electra trotted down the stairs in a few minutes. "I'll go feed the horses and be back when breakfast is ready."

"Thanks, dear. I appreciate that." Sam poured a steaming cup of coffee, went to Brad's room, and knocked on the door. "Brad! Good morning. Rise and shine. I've got coffee for you."

A grunt.

She knocked again. "C'mon, Brad. Get up. Please."

"Go 'way."

"No. I'm not going away. If you don't get up, I'm coming in there to dump this coffee on your head."

Bedclothes rustled. Grunts and groans punctuated scuffing

sounds. He opened the door, his dark hair sticking up in all directions. "Thanks." He stuck his hand out for the coffee.

She pulled it back. "You have to come out to get it. I made pancakes. Chokecherry syrup."

He scowled and slammed the door.

Heat blazed inside her chest. Being kind and understanding hadn't worked. Even coffee and pancakes hadn't done the trick. She pounded on the door. "Brad. Listen up. Get dressed. You *are* coming with us to Miles City. No excuses. I'm serious."

She stalked back to the kitchen and slammed the cup on the counter, sloshing hot coffee on her hand. She couldn't force him to go, and if he stayed here all day and sulked, well... there wasn't much she could do about it. Her hands shook as she poured batter into the pan.

Electra came in and hung up her coat. "Brrr. It's cold out there. Feels good in here."

Sam put a plate of hotcakes in front of her and a cup of cocoa. "Here, this should warm you up." She forced herself to smile.

The girl's glance shifted toward Brad's room, but she said nothing, simply slathered butter on her cakes. Sam joined her at the table, but her stomach was rock-hard. No way she could eat this morning. She sipped at her coffee.

The door latch clicked down the hallway. She and Electra jerked their heads in that direction. He came out, dressed, but still unkempt, a two-day stubble dark on his face. She held herself still as if a sudden move might scare him off.

He sat. "So. Where's my coffee and pancakes?"

Electra giggled. "I knew the smell would get you up."

Sam's shoulders released. She stood, poured him a fresh cup, and gave him a plate.

He dug in and chewed, closing his eyes. "Mmm. Good."

"So, are you coming with us?" The teenager asked the question Sam was afraid to.

"Well... Thinking about it. If I can get another cup of coffee?" He gave them a weak grin. "Please?"

Relief flooded through her like a soft summer shower. *It's a step. One at a time.*

Brad remained subdued on the trip to town, Electra attempting to engage him in banter, Sam concentrating on the road. She silently repeated *one step at a time* until it became a rhythm in her brain.

CHAPTER THIRTY-TWO

Nick met them at the corrals behind the college and helped unload Apache and Trixi. Inside, Del wheeled up and clasped Brad's hand. "Hey, man. Good to see you again." Garrett greeted him likewise, and the two vets introduced him to the others. His response was terse, guarded, and he soon found a seat on the bleachers.

Sam went through the ground rules, as she did every time. Electra demonstrated Apache's new skills, and then Sam invited her students to come brush and give the horses treats. She spoke briefly with each one, to gauge how they felt about riding today. "You've seen Electra demonstrate how the horses kneel so you can mount, and Del and Garret have done it a number of times. But if you're not comfortable today, that's fine."

Sondra shook her head. "I'll watch."

The two men nodded. But Jimmy stood back, while Al stepped toward Apache and Electra. "I'll give it a go, if that's okay with you."

Del wheeled himself next to the man. "I'll be right here."

"And so am I." Sam gestured to Electra who gave Apache the signal. The gelding knelt and the veteran slipped his leg over the saddle. Del gave him pointers and encouragement. Although Al had no visible injuries, Nick had told her the man suffered from serious PTSD. She helped him get a firm seat and kept a hand on his back as the teen tapped the horse's shoulder.

He recoiled and gasped as Apache rose, but quickly cleared his throat to cover his reaction. He flicked his gaze toward her.

"I'm fine." His back remained rigid.

"Just take a deep breath and try to relax if you can," Sam said. "We'll stand here for a minute until you're ready."

His rib cage expanded and contracted several times. Then he lifted his head to look straight ahead. "Okay."

Electra led the buckskin around the arena, Sam walking beside. As they came back to the starting point, the young man flashed the group a grin.

"You want to go around again?"

He nodded.

Sam let Electra lead him around once more and turned her attention to the others around Trixi. "Anyone else ready to try?"

As Jimmy stepped tentatively forward, she glanced at Brad on the bleachers. Leaning forward, he watched with a new intensity. A bit later, Garrett and Del sat near him, talking with animation. *Hmm. Wonder what they're saying.*

After the horses were loaded, Sam steered the pickup and trailer toward home. "I think that went pretty well."

"Yeah." Electra's eyes danced. "Did you see what Apache did, Brad, huh? Isn't that awesome?"

He lifted one corner of his mouth upward slightly. "Yes, it was. I'm impressed with what you've done with him."

"So, are you going to try, now that you've seen how it works?" The girl peered directly into his face.

He shrugged. "I dunno yet. We'll see."

She sat back against the seat with a huff.

Sam patted her arm. "We actually got Al and Jimmy aboard today, and that's big progress." Her mind dug for other successes. "Sondra is coming along. She'll get there too." And maybe Brad…

The teen perked up again and launched into a recap of each veteran's ride, how they had reacted, and how the horses had been so patient. Brad stayed quiet until they reached home.

He stood by the pickup as Sam and Electra unloaded the

horses and then silently headed for the house as they did the evening chores. The teen rolled her eyes. "He's as bad as those vets. Maybe worse, cuz he used to ride. He grew up on a ranch. He knows horses." Sarcasm and frustration laced her voice.

"I know." Sam's heart hurt. "But like Robin told us, head injuries make people react strangely and can change personalities, at least temporarily. And I'm hoping this *is* temporary. We won't give up on him. He needs more time."

Her young friend frowned. "Yeah, that's right, I guess. He *was* watching everything though and seemed really interested in what everyone was doing."

"I think that's a good sign." Was she reading too much into his reaction? "Well, let's go on up to the house and get some supper."

That night as she drifted into sleep, thoughts of her and Brad riding together morphed into dreams of holding hands and gazing into the future.

The next morning, she rose with hope buoying her and stood on the porch sipping coffee as Electra headed for the barn. It was a new day and maybe it'd be a better one.

Brad joined them at the corral to watch them do chores. After they'd finished, the teen peered into the clear blue sky. "It's such a nice day. Think we could go for a ride?"

"That's a great idea." Sam looked at Brad. "Do you want to come with us?"

"No thanks. I'll stay here."

"But… it would be so easy for you to mount Apache or Trixi…" Electra held her palms out.

He turned away. The teen shot a fiery look at his back.

"Okay." Sam's hopefulness plummeted. Heading for the small pasture next to the corrals, she called in the horses. She fought the weight of disappointment as they saddled up, and the two trotted out into the rolling hills.

February had been unseasonably warm, the mud was almost dried, and the horizon held a faint tinge of green. The sun heated her back, and she relaxed into the rhythm of Sugar's gait.

"Do you think spring will come early?" Electra rocked easily in the saddle. "It almost seems like it's here already."

"You never know. It could stay this way, or we could have a snowstorm or two yet. As Horace likes to say, 'If you don't like the weather in Montana, just wait five minutes.'" Sam guffawed. "I've seen snow in July, in the higher elevations."

She snorted. Here she was, making small talk about the weather while her dream of a future with the man she loved was clogged like a beaver dam on a creek. Love? Really? Was that how she felt? She gulped.

"Wow. That's wild. Another cool thing about this country. In the city, winter is cold and icy, and the snow is dirty, not pure and white like here."

In spite of her desire to scream at the wind, she tamped down her warring feelings and simply responded, "Yes, it is beautiful, but it can also be deadly, and all that white gets dirty after we've been driving over it a while. You saw how muddy it was after the thaw."

Electra giggled. "Yeah, don't like the gumbo so much. But it does make you feel taller. Why is that?"

"It's clay in the soil. It sticks together and accumulates on the bottom of your boots until you do feel like you're on stilts." Sam smiled, remembering Grandma Anna who was only 5'2, holding up her foot and saying, "Now I'm as tall as Grandpa Neil." Her grandfather had towered over everyone at 6'4.

As they rode within sight of home, Sam reined in and motioned for Electra to stop. Brad stood inside the corral, with Toby eating from the palm of one hand, while he stroked the horse's face with his other.

"Ohmygosh." Electra's voice was hushed, almost a whisper.

Sam held a hand over the flutter in her chest. *Ohmygosh, indeed. It's another step. Thank you, Lord.*

They held still for several minutes until Toby swung his head their way and whinnied. Brad flinched and stuck his hands in his pockets. He leaned against the corral fence as Sam and Electra rode in. "Have a good ride?"

"Yeah, it was awesome! You shoulda—" Electra stopped. "It's a beautiful day, and I think it's going to be spring soon."

"Yes, it is a nice day."

Will he say anything about Toby? Should I say something? Sam finished unsaddling and handed Sugar's reins to Electra. Almost not daring to breathe, she walked to the fence to stand next to Brad. He remained silent, staring over the rails toward the house.

"Um... So..." she ventured, "Toby..."

The corners of his mouth creased in a momentary grin. "Yeah. I guess... he doesn't hate me."

"No! Of course not. Why would he hate you?"

"Because..." A shadow darkened his face. "Because I wrecked... hurt him... ruined him for you." He abruptly went to the gate, opened it, and limped to the house.

Sam fought the impulse to call after him, to run after him. Bending at the waist, she wanted to cry, scream, and rail at the heavens. *It's not fair!* One tiny step forward and two huge ones back. Would it ever get better?

"Are you all right?" Electra rushed up to her. "What's wrong? What did he do to you?"

"Nothing." She straightened. "He didn't do anything wrong, but he thinks he did."

"Just like my dad and his accident."

"I know, honey." Sam linked arms with her. "Let's go up and see if he'll join us for lunch."

Over tomato soup and grilled cheese sandwiches, Electra kept giving Brad glances from the corner of her eye. He remained stoic, periodically rubbing his forehead as though he had a headache and then forcefully scrubbing his hand through the stubble of his hair.

"That was a good thing with Toby this morning." Sam broached the subject again. "He really *is* a good horse, and I *know* he likes you. I kinda think..." she gulped, "I think maybe he has PTSD, like the veterans. And it will simply take a lot of time and patience..."

Brad cocked his head and his brow furrowed. "PTSD? A horse? I mean, the vets, sure. They went through some hellish stuff, so I understand that. But a wreck? Naw."

"Yeah. *I* think so." Electra leaned forward. "I don't know if you know about my dad. He got in a wreck, and it wasn't his fault. He couldn't help the ice and bad weather. But my brother Tommy died, and he blamed himself. He couldn't get over it and he—" her voice hitched, "he left mom and me. I thought I did something wrong to make him go away, that he didn't love me anymore."

Brad widened his eyes.

"When my mom brought me here last summer for that dude ranch 'vacation,' I was pretty messed up. I hated myself and everybody else. But then I met Apache." Her face held the tenderness of love. "I'm still kinda messed up, but he's been healing me, and I've been talking to Miss Robin, and... I think I'm getting better. Maybe if you give Toby a chance..."

"I'm sorry about your brother and your dad, and I can see a big change in you since last year." His gaze dropped to his bowl. "I dunno. Can't quite see it the same way for me... and Toby."

He rose, put his dishes in the sink, and went to his room.

A tear tracked Electra's cheek. "I tried. I-I thought maybe he could relate to my dad, and, and to horses and stuff."

"It's okay, honey." Sam put a hand on her arm. "You did try, and you never know. Maybe the things you said will sink in and help. Thank you." She wanted to join her and have a good cry. Instead, she stood and prepared to wash the dishes.

Brad stayed out of sight the rest of the day, and he didn't come out for supper.

Her eyes felt swollen, like a dam about to burst.

CHAPTER THIRTY-THREE

Later that evening, after Electra had gone up to bed, Sam sat in the living room alternately staring at her book and out the window into the inky darkness. Brad and Toby, what a pair. She'd made a little headway with Toby, but... *maybe I'm not being patient enough with Brad. Can you treat a guy like a horse?*

Footsteps in the hallway startled her. Brad shuffled into the room with his cane and settled on the couch.

A rapid pulse jittered in her throat. "Hi. Are you hungry? You missed supper."

"No. Not really. Been doing a lot of thinking today. I guess I'm kind of 'messed up,' as Electra put it." He stared at the cane by his side.

She searched her brain for something to say. *Yeah, you are.* But she couldn't say that to him.

"It's stupid, I know." Another long pause as Brad rubbed his thigh.

How could she encourage him? Leaning forward, she waited.

"I watched those vets with their prostheses, Del with no legs... and they're getting on the horses. But I... can't..." His eyes held glistening pain. "What's wrong with me?"

Tears needled. Sam got up from her chair and sat beside him. "You shouldn't find fault with yourself. First off, I've told you before, but I'll tell you again, I do NOT blame you for the accident. It was simply that—an *accident*. You got caught in a blizzard, for heaven's sake."

Brad's face sagged and his shoulders drooped. He appeared

so sad, she wanted to gather him in her arms and rock him like a baby. "And you didn't *ruin* Toby. He's coming along. Slowly, but we've made progress. Just like Toby needs lots of patience, you need to have patience with yourself."

He snorted. "I don't deserve it. I don't deserve you being so nice to me when I'm such a royal jerk. I don't deserve forgiveness... from you, or from Toby."

She squeezed his arm and leaned closer to peer into his eyes. "Yes, you do. Give yourself time to heal. You had a head injury, broken bones, and were in a coma for over a month. You don't come out of that and jump back into *normal* right away."

"I guess I think I should." His eyes shifted away. "With my leg not working so well and my arm so weak... and my brain... I'm not coming together like I should."

"You need more time, Brad. Listen, I like that you're talking to me about this. I want you to." Her heart swelled with a heavy ache. "But I think a counselor could help you a lot more than I can. Do you think you could talk to somebody—maybe Robin, or the one your doctor referred. Or maybe someone the vets use?"

He shrugged. "I dunno. I tried at first, and the whole process seemed... useless... like me..."

Wrapping one arm around him, she drew him close. "You're not. I need you back—my funny, irreverent, happy Brad."

He rested his head against hers, and his shoulders shuddered. Sam's chin trembled, and tears stung as they dripped down her cheeks.

They sat together in silence, hands gripping, for endless minutes. Finally, Brad stirred and shook himself loose. "Thanks." He pushed himself off the sofa and picked up his cane. "I mean it. Thank you. I've got some more thinking to do." He gave her a trembly smile. "G'night."

She stood and smoothed his forehead where the wayward dark lock once fell. "Sleep well."

The next morning, when Sam and Electra drove back from feeding, Brad stood in the corral again, brushing Toby. "Ohmygosh." The teen leaned forward to peer out the windshield. "He's out with the horse again. Ohmygosh!"

Sam lifted her eyes to the overcast sky. "Yes, he is."

This pattern continued for the next several days. While Sam and Electra worked with Apache and Trixi, Brad seemed content to simply stand with Toby as long as the gelding wanted to stick around, and then he either sat to watch them or limped back to the house.

"Do you think I should ask him if he'd like to try getting on Apache?" The teen's body quivered like a racehorse in the traces.

"No. Let him be. When he's ready, he'll tell us." It was almost more than Sam could do to not jump in and try to push the process along. But she forced herself to wait. She didn't bring up the subject over their meals, simply let him talk about whatever he wanted, when he wanted.

"He's beginning the healing process," she told Electra. "We can't do anything except be here for him, give him our love and friendship and encouragement."

"Yeah. I can see that." Electra pursed her lips. "It's kinda like working with a new horse, isn't it? At first, they're shy and skittish, but you have to earn their trust."

That brought a smile. Her wise little friend. *She's learning. And I hope I am too.*

Horace rumbled up in his diesel pickup one morning, stepped out near the corral, and stretched his lanky frame. Sam waved and finished throwing out hay flakes for the horses. Electra squealed and ran to give the older man a hug.

"Hey there, young'uns." He strode to the fence to stand beside Brad who nodded a hello.

"Good to see you, Horace." She hugged him too. "Everything going okay at your place?"

"Yup, fine as frog's hair." He took off his hat, ran a hand

over his iron-gray crewcut, and replaced the Stetson. "Nice to have good weather so we don't have to feed as often."

She stared out over the rolling hills. "Yeah, with a tiny bit of green out there, we're just supplementing with cake right now and some hay every few days."

"Might be a dry year though, if we don't get more moisture this spring."

The weather was always the number one topic for ranchers. She had come to realize more and more that farming and ranching were almost a bigger gamble than sitting down at the poker tables in Las Vegas. It all came down to Mother Nature—lack of rain, too much rain, no crops due to drought, good crops ruined by hail or grasshoppers. Or if there was an abundant crop, calf or grain prices went into the dumps because of excess supply.

She pushed back from the fence. "So true. C'mon up to the house. I'll put the coffee on and heat some cinnamon rolls."

The trio joined her in the short walk up the incline and settled around the kitchen table, where Horace quizzed Electra on her algebra homework. Soon the earthy aroma of coffee mingled with the fragrances of cinnamon and sugar as she served the snack.

Her elderly neighbor took a bite of the bun, rolled his eyes back, and gave an "Mmm" of appreciation. "You're a good cooker, Doris."

Electra giggled, and Sam burst into a laugh at his reference to an old TV commercial.

"So, how're you comin' along, son?" The old man peered over his cup at Brad.

He shrugged and scrunched his mouth to the side. "Slow."

"Guess that's the way the cookie crumbles." The rancher leaned back in his chair. "I 'member a feller a few years back, champion rodeo rider, horse smashed him up against the chute." He took a sip of coffee. "Broke five vertebrae. Paralyzed him. Docs said he'd never ride again, probably take him a couple years to learn to walk."

Sam tensed. Three pairs of eyes held their attention on the old man as he paused.

"Yup. Didn't look good for that young bronc buster." He reached for another cinnamon roll.

Electra jiggled her leg next to her. "Yeah? And…?"

Horace slathered the roll with butter, taking time to cover every inch. "Well, he was a champion. He weren't gonna give in or give up. He said 'Heck with you guys. I'm doin' this.'"

Brad traced a pattern in the crumbs on the table with his finger.

"Yup. He went to this physical therapy place, and he worked his butt off. Worked and worked and worked, hours ever' day. Blood, sweat, and tears, literally."

Wow. That took guts. Sam gave a slow wag of her head. *I don't know if I could do that.*

"So, did he walk again?" Electra's eyes were full moons.

The old man nodded. "He did, by golly. And not only that, but ten months after his smashup, he rode a bronc again."

"Wow! I can't believe it. Can you, Sam? Can you, Brad? Wow."

"That *is* amazing." She smiled. "Quite the story. With a happy ending too."

Brad brushed the crumbs into his hand and dumped them on his plate. "Yeah. Quite a story." He stared out the window.

"W-e-l-l, guess I'd better be skedaddlin'." Their neighbor pushed his chair back and stood. He put a hand on Brad's shoulder. "Just remember, you only need to ride one horse at a time."

As Sam got up to walk Horace to the door, she stole a peek at Brad. His face scrunched in a question mark. She held back a laugh. The old man's pithy advice apparently had him stumped.

After Horace drove away, she and Electra went back to the corral to finish chores.

"That was SO cool." The teen's face was still lit with astonishment. "Do you think that was a hint for Brad?"

Sam grinned. "Yeah. I think it was."

"You think he'll get it?"

"I hope so." *But I'm not going to bet the house on this one.*

When they went inside, Brad waited by the door with his duffle bag. "I'm going to go home for a while. The folks'll be here pretty soon to pick me up."

She felt her mouth go slack. She sagged against the doorframe and a wave of nausea rolled over her. *What?*

For a second, Kenny's image replaced Brad's, standing at the bottom of the stairs with his suitcase after that disastrous blizzard two years ago. Her heart and mind galloped in an uncertain race, spurred on by abandonment, loss, fear, guilt. Ice congealed her blood.

"What?" Her voice strained, high-pitched. She clenched her fists and jutted her jaw. "Are you giving up? On your recovery? The horse? Yourself? Us?"

After an initial gasp at Brad's declaration, Electra faded into the living room—a wise decision.

"Are you?" She stepped closer, probing his space with her forefinger. "Are you just like Kenny? Willing to give up all the progress, the experiences together, the relationship—just because things got tough for a little while?"

Eyes wide, he drew his head back.

Something inside snapped. Heat raged from her core into her face. "Well... Are you?" She jerked back, both arms in the air as if to say *I give up*. No. She wasn't giving up on him, not now, not ever. She stuck her face closer again. "You can't. I'm not going to let you do that!"

His Adam's apple bobbed several times. "I... I... No." He held up a palm. "It's not like that. Not what it looks like. No. No."

Sam cocked her head. "So, what *is* it?"

Pulling out a chair, Brad plunked into it. He motioned for her to sit. Pushing another chair aside, she sat across the table, pulse pounding. A great deal rode on his answer.

"The last few days have been... well, a lot. I've had a bunch of stuff thrown at me—you and Electra, the horses, the vets,

Horace's advice. My brain… I can't process it all yet."

She chewed on her lower lip.

"I'm not giving up, Sam. I… I care… about you… and your help and concern mean the world to me." He put his hand over his heart. "I *do* want to get better. Having Toby warm up to me, a little, and watching those vets overcoming their disabilities to ride… I know I have to try harder."

Her breath hitched. "Oh, Brad—"

He moved his hand to hers on the table. "I have a lot to think about. I just want to take a few days, go home, and let it cook a little." He pointed to his head and lifted one corner of his mouth.

"Okay…?" Her voice came out like a rusty gate hinge. *He's not like Kenny. He's not giving up.* Her hands trembled.

"I'm glad you're not giving up on *me*. I know I've been a royal butthead, and I'm sorry for that." His eyes held an unaccustomed shininess. "I hope you'll give me a little more time…. I would like to come back."

Do I dare hope? "Yes. Absolutely. You're right. You do need more time, and I can see how all of this has been overwhelming." She held his gaze. "But don't take too long, all right?" She flipped her hand over to grasp his.

He smiled then and gave a squeeze. "No. I won't. I do… miss you when I'm gone."

A small squeal brought their attention toward the living room.

"It's okay, Electra, you can come out now. I'm not going to bite anybody's head off… today, anyway." She grinned at the girl who wiggled into the room like a forgiven puppy.

"I'm glad of that." She hugged Brad. "And I'm glad you're not giving up and you'll be coming back and it better be soon because Toby is going to miss you and he might forget you if you take too long and…" She paused, "and I'll miss you too!"

Later, the Ashtons arrived, Dee with a tight, concerned look, and Paul pressing his lips into a firm line. They stood inside the kitchen door and stared at Brad.

"It's okay, Mr. and Mrs. Ashton. He simply needs a little time to process everything." Sam gave them a thumbs up. "C'mon, sit down and have a cuppa before you leave."

CHAPTER THIRTY-FOUR

February eased softly into March, soft breezes encouraging new green hues over the rolling hills. "Looks like March is coming in like a lamb," Horace quipped one day.

"I'm just glad I don't have to take care of any lambing." Sam chuckled. "But the end of the month we should be getting some new calves."

Electra danced on her toes. "Yippee! I can't wait."

She understood the youngster's delight. Calves frolicking in the pasture, clean, curly white faces against their reddish coats, were about the cutest thing she could imagine. Unless it was a colt. Would she ever see any of her own? That dream seemed to have drifted to the way-back burner. *Oh well. I have all this— my rescue horses, Electra... even Brad to an extent.*

The next couple of weeks, the two of them settled back into their routine, Electra doing her school work and Sam studying for her certification. They did chores, rode the horses, and worked more with Apache and Toby. Brad didn't call, and Sam tamped down her anxious questions about why, how he was doing, and if he'd be back. "Whatever will be, will be," advised a song Grandma Anna used to play. She tried to follow that advice and allowed her rides across the prairie to wash away conflicting thoughts. Electra's bright, bubbly companionship kept her spirits above the clouds, as well.

When the phone rang one evening, Electra dashed to answer. "It's probably Mom." A moment later, she stuck her head through the door, her eyebrows arched high. "It's Bra-a-d."

Sam's pulse tapped a rapid beat. "Really?" She dashed into the kitchen to pick up the receiver. "Hey, stranger."

"Hey. Sorry I haven't been in touch." He cleared his throat. "I… uh… I've been doing a lot of thinking…"

Anticipation stole her breath.

"…and I've talked to Del and Nick a couple times… and they recommended a counselor they work with in Miles."

"Okay…?"

His breath whooshed audibly over the line. "I'm thinking, if it's all right with you… I might come out again this week."

Relief flowed over her like a warm shower. "Of course. That would be great. We've missed you."

"Good. I… uh… I've missed you… guys too." Shuffling sounds. "Well, um, Melissa said she'd bring me out whenever."

"Super. We'll be looking forward to seeing you. Tomorrow?"

"Okay. See you then." Brad ended the call.

A wide smile wreathed Electra's face as she stood jittering in the doorway. "He's coming back?"

Sam nodded. Nerve pulses ricocheted in her stomach. What would this visit be like? She couldn't tell whether he'd made progress with his two weeks of "thinking," or if he was actually going to see a counselor, or what. *Time will tell, I guess.* "Yeah. Well, I suppose we'd better get things ready for our guest again."

Melissa and Brad drove up the lane late the next morning. Electra ran out the door and down the porch steps to greet them, Sam following more slowly behind.

Brad's sister got out of the driver's side and gave her a hug. "I bequeath him to you." Her mouth rose in a tiny smirk.

Sam laughed. "Let's get his stuff in. I hope you'll stay for lunch?"

"Oh, sure." Melissa giggled. "Seems like you're always feeding me and my family. But I love it out here. I'll stay."

Electra hovered nearby while Sam moved around to the passenger door. Brad eased out, steadying himself with his cane. "Hi. Glad you're back," she ventured.

He glanced up at her with a brief smile. "Me too. Thanks."

"My pleasure." She put a hand on his arm and squeezed.

The group tucked into stew and brown bread, Electra teasing Brad, and Melissa exaggerating stories about his childhood and how bratty he was.

He rolled his eyes. "No, I remember you being the instigator of all the trouble. And then you blamed me." He let out a rare laugh.

The sound of his merriment, even momentarily, gave Sam a glow of hopeful pleasure. *They say laughter is good medicine. We need to keep this up . . . if we can.*

As Melissa took the last bite of her cookie and sipped her coffee, she sighed. "Well, I suppose I should get back to town."

"Why be in a hurry?" Sam offered the dessert plate again. "Would you like to stay a while longer and maybe take a short ride?"

The woman's face lit up. "Oh. A ride. Yes! Yes, I would."

"Yay!" Electra stood up so fast she nearly knocked over her chair. "Oops. Sorry." She stacked the dishes to take to the sink. "I'll show you what Apache has learned and you know what Trixi can do and you can ride her or Apache or . . ." She trailed off, eyes flickering from Melissa to Sam and back.

"Any horse Sam says is okay."

"They're all very gentle." Sam grabbed a few carrots to put in her pocket. "C'mon down to the corral." She bit back an invitation to Brad. *Let him decide what he wants to do.*

Happy satisfaction bloomed when he limped along behind their little group.

As they approached the fence, Toby lifted his head and stared. Brad stepped to the railing. The gelding tossed his head and whinnied. Then he trotted to where Brad stood. Sam slipped him a few carrots and stood back.

Brad held out a palm with the treat. Toby sniffed, took it, and crunched happily. Then he leaned forward and rubbed his head on the man's arm.

Sam's heart squeezed, seeing the smile on Brad's face as he and the horse interacted. She stepped quietly to the side and motioned the women to where the other horses stood in the pasture, waiting for their own treats.

Melissa's eyes were owl-like. "Wow. That's different."

"Yeah, it is. They've made progress together." Sam's voice shook a little. "I didn't think Toby would forget, but…"

Electra's head whipped back and forth. "Oh no. I *knew* he wouldn't forget. I *knew*."

The women set off on their ride, leaving Brad with Toby. Melissa soon had her "horse legs" back and sat comfortably as Trixi trotted over the rolling prairie, dotted with silver-blue sage. "That sure looks promising—the thing with Toby and Brad."

"I know. They've been getting to know each other a little at a time, and Toby seems to be relaxing with him. Brad thinks Toby connects the accident to him and is afraid because of him. Says he 'ruined' the horse for me."

"Aw, geez." Melissa thinned her lips. "He's blown this all out of proportion. I don't think a horse carries a grudge. Not like a human."

"No, but he was traumatized by the accident, and they do carry a memory of things that hurt them. But I'm not sure that's all. Wish I knew a little more about his background. He was supposedly this woman's pet saddle horse, but she had to sell him when she moved, and he ended up in a kill pen."

Melissa adjusted herself in the saddle and raised her brows. "That could do it."

They topped the rise overlooking the reservoir, flanked with cottonwood trees beginning to turn a pale green. A small bunch of cattle grazed a few new shoots of grass nearby.

"Oh my." The young woman reined in her horse. "Brings back memories of the ranch at Livingston. It was a good place to grow up. "I pray this will bring healing for Brad."

"Me too."

When the trio returned to the corrals, Brad was limping slowly, leading Toby around by a halter rope, and stopping frequently to pat the gelding's neck.

After watching a while, Melissa gave her brother a hug, said goodbye to Sam and Electra, and climbed into her car for the trip back to Billings.

Brad sat on a rock to rest, and Toby rubbed the man's shoulder with his face.

"How's it going?" Sam leaned on the fence next to them.

"Pretty good. Thought I'd try leading him around a little. Can't go very far or very long though." He gave her a rueful grin. "But it's a start."

"Yes. It is. Small steps." She related how she had set up panels and gradually got Toby used to going through narrower spaces. "But he stopped at the barn door, and that was it. I haven't had a lot of time to work with him lately."

"That sounds like a good idea." Brad rubbed his leg. "I'm a little beat today, but could we maybe try that tomorrow?"

Hope lifted her like a fluffy cloud. "Sure. We can do that."

The next morning, Brad rode in the pickup to the pasture with her and Electra to check the cows, give them supplemental cake pellets, and make sure the water in the reservoir wasn't frozen over. After a quick lunch, Electra trotted ahead of them to the barn. "Want me to help you with the panels?"

"Yeah, that'd be great, thanks." Sam and the teen set up a chute that started wide at one end, narrowed in the middle, and led to the barn door.

Brad carried a small bucket with pellets and limped into the makeshift alley, stopped a few feet from the entrance, and rattled the bucket. Toby's ears pricked forward, and he stepped cautiously into the chute. Stopping to sniff the panels and blow, he raised his head to the sound of his beloved treats and took a couple more steps. When he reached Brad, he received a pellet, a pat, and a "Good boy," and then Brad moved into the chute farther away from him. They progressed in minuscule steps until they reached the narrower passageway.

Watching from the corral fence, Sam held her breath. Electra leaned forward, biting her thumbnail.

"C'mon, Toby," Brad's soft voice encouraged. "C'mon, boy." He rattled the cake again. The gelding swung his head back and forth, the barrier now only about a foot away from each side. His ears twitched, he sniffed the panels and snorted. Brad shook the pail. "It's okay, Toby, c'mon."

But the horse backed to where he could turn around and pounded out of the alley. He galloped around the corral, black mane and tail streaming as he tossed his head, blowing and snorting.

"Darn!" Electra expressed Sam's frustration in one explosive word.

Brad's body slumped. He leaned against the panel, staring at the ground.

She went to him and rested a hand on his shoulder. "It's all right. It's been a while since we've tried this, and sometimes we simply have to start from square one. He's come through it before. He'll do it again."

Brad squared his posture. "Okay. I guess so."

They left the panels up and called it a day, making their way slowly up to the house.

The next afternoon, Brad brought a step stool from the barn and sat just beyond the narrow point. With one hand, he sifted the pellets, letting them drop with tempting plunks back into the metal bucket.

Toby paced the corral, passing by the entrance to the alley several times. Then he trotted up to the side of the panels where Brad sat and reached his head over the low fence.

Sam snickered, and Electra giggled.

Brad let out a guffaw. "You smartypants, you!" He stood and walked back to the opening. "C'mere now. You don't get any treats until you do it right."

The horse stood, looking at Brad as if to say *What? You're not giving me a treat for figuring this out?*

"Nope. You don't get anything till you come this way." Brad remained still.

Toby shook his head and snorted. Brad rattled the bucket. The gelding blew out a breath.

Sam detected an air of exasperation in the horse's stance. She chuckled. Just like a little boy.

Finally, the gelding trotted down the length of the fence and just inside the opening. He stretched his neck toward the bucket. Brad laughed again. "All right, ol' boy, you can have a piece of cake now." He held out his palm. Toby closed the distance between them, lipped the pellet, and stood crunching.

Sam could almost see the horse smile.

Shaking the bucket, Brad walked farther down the lane toward the barn. The horse cocked his head, hesitated, and then followed him to receive the next treat. Brad praised him and caressed his face and neck. "You're a good boy, Toby. Good boy."

The gelding stopped again when the alley narrowed. Brad sat on his stool, running his fingers through the pellets.

After several long minutes of snuffling and pawing the ground, swinging his head back and forth, Toby flared his nostrils, sniffing the air, as if anticipating his reward. He took a step forward, then another. Temptation won out over fear of the narrow lane, and he shuffled up to the man and his bucket. "All right. Good job." Brad praised him, rubbed his nose and face, and then moved his stool farther away.

Again, the horse hesitated but finally moved forward.

Sam could barely contain herself. She wanted to jump and shout and cheer. She glanced at the teen whose body thrummed beside her. Electra mouthed "Wow," her face aglow.

"Yeah," Sam whispered, her own face warm with delight.

But when they reached the barn door, that ended the process. Toby turned around and trotted back through the lane, out to the corral. Brad shrugged, his palms out.

"Tomorrow's another day," Sam called out. "This was a really good start."

CHAPTER THIRTY-FIVE

The next day, after feeding and chores, Sam stood with Brad who studied the panels for several minutes. He ran his fingers over his hair, limped a few paces to view the makeshift alley from a different angle. "I wonder if we could set this up so it leads him into his lean-to."

Gee, she hadn't thought of that. "Oh. Yeah. That's a good idea. We can do that." He actually seemed to be getting into the project.

She and Electra rearranged the alley and stacked hay bales in the entrance outside the panels to prevent the horse from getting in any other way.

"Okay, Toby, come and get it." Brad rattled the bucket with pellets and walked into the alleyway. The bay followed without hesitation until he reached the narrowed neck. "C'mon, boy." Brad shook the bucket and continued with encouragement.

Again, snorting and shaking his head, Toby balked.

"C'mon. You know you want it. C'mon."

The gelding reached his head out, nostrils flared as he sniffed the air.

Brad rattled the pellets.

Slowly, Toby stepped forward until he reached his reward.

Brad moved into the shelter where he sat on a bale and sifted the cake through his fingers, speaking softly.

She swallowed. Would the horse go into his familiar shelter?

Ears forward, tail switching, Toby appeared to size up the situation. She chuckled again. It was like he was thinking things through—is it worth feeling hemmed in to get my treats? Do I trust this guy? What is he trying to do to me?

"C'mon, Toby." Brad kept up a soft, encouraging patter.

One foot moved forward. Then the other—slow, measured steps, ears twitching, withers quivering. Then he was in the lean-to, nuzzling Brad's palm for the cake.

Sam pumped her fist in the air in a victory salute. Electra clamped a hand over her mouth but bounced beside her. Brad looked over Toby's shoulder, a big grin splitting his face. Standing, he rubbed the gelding's face and neck.

"Ohmygosh!" Electra kept her voice low but couldn't contain her excitement any longer. "That is awesome."

"Yes, it is." Sam strode to the lean-to and spoke quietly. "This is a huge break-through, Brad. You did it."

He shrugged, the grin still in place. "Well, it's not the barn, but it's close."

That evening, he stayed in the living room with the women, more inclined to talk than before. He and Electra recapped the day with Toby, erupting into laughter when someone mentioned the looks on the horse's face and his body language.

"He loves his treats," Sam said. "But it's almost like he's a little kid—do I really *have* to do this?"

"Yeah. He does have quite the personality." Brad's face was more relaxed than she'd seen it in a long time. "Well, I think I'll call it a day. Gotta get up early for the session in Miles tomorrow."

"Good night, Brad," Sam and Electra chorused as he left the room and then gave each other high fives.

Sam woke early with a sense of bright possibilities, hoping Brad would have a good experience with the counselor. On the trip to town, he was quiet but not sullen as he'd been in the past. Electra chattered on about everything and nothing.

After they reached the ag college arena and unloaded the horses, Brad headed to the offices for his appointment with the counselor. "I hope that goes good." Electra's gaze followed him as he left.

"Me too." Sam turned her attention to the group of vets, all gathered around the horses, some more eager than others. But still, nobody hung back on the bleachers today. She greeted each one, touching a shoulder, shaking a hand, asking about their week.

Jimmy, always the more enthused of the group despite a missing leg, asked to ride first.

"All right. Let's go." She stood by, and her young helper signaled Apache to kneel. The other men gathered around Jimmy as he swung his prosthetic leg over the saddle, his buddies ready to catch him if he fell.

Smiling, she turned to Sondra. "What do you feel like doing today?"

The woman tucked her hair behind her ears. "Um... well..." She put a hand on Trixie's neck and finger-combed her mane. "Maybe I could... um... try...?"

"You want to get on her?" A surge of excitement rose in Sam's chest. This was the first time Sondra had expressed any interest in riding. She kept her face neutral although she wanted to applaud and shout, "Yay!"

"Okay. Here's how we'll do it." She explained the steps again, and when Sondra nodded, gave Trixi the signal to kneel.

The woman put her left foot into the stirrup, grabbed the horn, and lifted into the saddle. Her face pale, she shook her head. "Wait..."

"It's all right. You can just sit for a while before Trixi stands." Sam patted her shoulder. "And if you don't want her to stand up, we don't have to do that. You can get off."

Sondra swallowed several times. She squirmed in her seat and glanced down as she pushed her feet farther into the stirrups.

"Does it feel comfortable?"

"I... don't know..." Sondra flexed her thighs and rocked back and forth. "I... guess..."

Sam rubbed Trixie's neck. "Good girl. Just stay put a minute now, okay?"

After several deep breaths, the young woman cast big brown eyes at her. "Okay. I think... maybe..."

"You want her to get up? Are you sure?"

Sondra gave a series of quick, little nods. "Yeah."

As Sam gave Trixi the signal, she caught a glimpse of Jack Murdock at the back of the room. *That does it. I'm going to have to catch him before he leaves and find out why he's spying on me. What is he trying—*

Sondra's shriek jerked her attention back. As Trixi rose, the woman jerked her right foot out of the stirrup, trying to get down before the horse fully stood. Unbalanced, she slipped toward Sam. "Off! Help!"

Grabbing her around the middle, she stopped the fall before the panicked woman reached the ground. "Stop." She held her tight. "Calm down." When Sondra quit writhing, Sam spoke in a soft voice. "Okay. You're not going to fall. I've got you. Pull your left foot out of the stirrup now."

With high-pitched mews, she followed instructions and landed on her feet.

"You're all right." She let go and planted her hands on Sondra's shoulders. "You didn't fall. You're okay."

The woman panted in short gasps.

"Take a deep breath. Slowly let it out." Sam continued to speak in a low tone. "Another."

Finally, Sondra's gasping calmed, and her body relaxed.

"Let's go sit down." She guided her to the bleachers, motioning back the men who were hurrying toward them. She shook her head at Electra, and the girl corralled the vets back to Apache.

Reaching into her tote bag, Sam got out a bottle of water. "Here, have a drink."

Sondra gulped the liquid eagerly and then looked at her with tear-filled eyes. "I'm sorry. I... got scared."

"I know. I know. It's not an easy thing to do, to trust this huge animal who is moving under you. Your first instinct is to get the heck offa there." She grinned. "And that's okay. I was there to catch you."

Sondra drank again. "Did I scare the horse? Maybe I did something wrong."

"No, you didn't scare her. She stopped right away. She is so very gentle, and she knew something was not quite right."

"I don't know. I don't think I'm cut out for this." A tear trickled down Sondra's cheek.

Sam peered into the woman's eyes. "That's why we're having these classes. Take it as slow and easy as you want to. Please don't give up. Give it a chance. A cowgirl wasn't made in a day."

Sondra gave a shaky smile. "Okay."

With Electra's help, she finished with the rest of the group, loaded the horses, and stood by the truck, waiting for Brad to return. Then her legs nearly collapsed. She leaned against the hood and lowered her head into her shaking hands. *Oh my word.* She'd taken her attention away for just a second. That could have been a disaster. Sondra may *never* want to ride. Her job there might be in jeopardy. *Why did I get distracted by stupid Murdock?*

"Are you okay?" Electra put a gentle hand on Sam's back.

"Yeah, yeah. I'm fine." She straightened. "That took me by surprise. I wasn't watching close enough. It could've been bad, really bad." She wagged her head back and forth.

"But it wasn't." Her young friend rubbed the tight spot between Sam's shoulders. "You were right beside her, and you caught her."

Sam chewed her bottom lip. "It's not acceptable. From now on, you and I both need to be on high alert and have someone else with us to help spot the rider."

"Yeah. Good idea." The girl looked up as they heard Brad's halting footsteps on the gravel.

"Hi, ladies. Ready to head home?"

She forced a smile. "Yup, just waiting for you."

They all piled into the pickup, and she steered onto the road. After a period of silence, she addressed Brad. "How was the session?"

He cocked his head and shrugged one shoulder. "It was okay. I have some things to think about." After a moment, "How did it go with the vets?"

"Great!" Electra blurted but then threw a guilty look at Sam. Shaking her head, Sam sighed. "Not so great."

"You look a little pale. Something happen?" He peered at her.

"A near-accident." She told him how she'd seen Murdock, and in that moment, Sondra had nearly fallen, trying to get off the horse as Trixi rose.

Brad reached across the teen and covered her hand with his. "I'm sorry."

"What I still can't figure out..." Electra drew her brows together, "...is how these vets who have been in a war can be afraid of a horse."

"Well, it's not actually my place to figure out." Sam had wondered herself. "The fear issue is between them and their counselor. But I'm guessing this experience brings up something that happened to them, of not being in control, or maybe they're in a place where any challenge seems too much to take on."

"Yeah." Brad gave a slow, thoughtful nod. "I think I'm seeing that now. Looking ahead to what I have to do to recover from my injuries has been a mountain I haven't been able to climb."

"But you've already come so far." The teen quirked an eyebrow. "Look at what you've done with Toby."

He shrugged. "I guess you're right. That's kinda what the counselor said too. The ol' one step at a time thing."

"I know. We all want things to go fast and easy. Like praying, 'Lord, please give me patience, and I want it *now*.'"

Electra and Brad joined her laughter. *I need that patience... with the vets, with Brad, and maybe... even with myself.*

The next morning, when Sam got up, Brad was already outside. She and Electra walked quietly toward the corral, where he sprinkled little mounds of pellets on a path to the barn door. "What's he doing?" Electra whispered.

She motioned her to keep still. *What* is *he doing?* The panel alley was still set up to head into the lean-to, not the barn.

Toby watched from the far side, his ears pointed forward. Brad set the bucket in the doorway of the barn and went inside.

Sam and Electra crept closer for a better vantage point. Not far into the barn, Brad sat on a hay bale, his back to the entrance.

Toby approached the first pile of pellets and eagerly ate. He ambled on to the next couple and again lipped the treats. As he neared the last mound closest to the barn, he hesitated a moment, but the siren song of the cake called him forward. He stood crunching one at a time until they were gone.

The gelding reached his head toward the bucket sitting in the doorway, sniffed, and blew. He tossed his head, turned, and ran to the other side of the corral. Stopping for a minute, he then ran around the arena several times. Each time he passed by the barn door, he swiveled his head toward it and his stride hesitated, but he kept going.

Would this strategy work? Sam didn't dare move. Beside her, Electra remained still, her eyes and mouth in big "O's."

For what seemed like hours, the two watched. Brad sat, his back to the barn opening. Toby ran around and around but kept slowing at the doorway. Finally, he stopped... for a fraction of a second and then took off again like a shot.

Sam waited.

Electra fidgeted.

Brad sat still.

Once more, the bay approached the bucket in the doorway and cautiously sniffed as if it might hold a rattlesnake. He flared his nostrils. He blew. He sniffed. He tossed his head and tail. He sniffed again and took one step closer. Then one more. And another. He stuck his nose into the pail, grabbed a pellet, and ran.

Sam suppressed a giggle. She couldn't imagine how Brad

felt, not able to see what the horse was doing. But that was great strategy, being there but ignoring the horse.

Toby approached the "snake" bucket a second time as cautiously as the first, grabbed another pellet, and ran to the fence where he stopped and chewed. He repeated the sequence several times until the bucket appeared empty. The horse stood, his head inside the door, staring at Brad's back.

Sam exchanged a grin with Electra. *Probably wondering what this guy is up to.*

Then the gelding put a front hoof through the doorway. A pause. The second one followed. Sam gasped as Toby stepped all the way inside and stood, nuzzling Brad's shoulder. He stayed several minutes before he came out to run around the pen again. *A miracle!*

Brad's face glowed when he emerged from the barn and gave them a thumbs up.

"Awesome!" Electra whooped and ran to hug him.

Sam couldn't keep the grin off her face as she followed.

"Well, he didn't stay inside long." Brad shrugged. "But at least he went in."

"You can act like it's no big deal, but it is. It's *huge*." She threw her arms around him, and his at-first stiff body relaxed as she squeezed and then released him.

"Yeah. He's coming along." His smile momentarily erased months of tension and pain from his face. "Like me. Slow, but he's moving."

"Well, I'm so very proud of you." She patted his back.

"You're the man!" Electra danced around them.

Brad and Sam exchanged a bemused glance and then broke into laughter.

CHAPTER THIRTY-SIX

On the next trip to the ag center, only the men were there. Sam queried Nick with trepidation. "Where's Sondra?"

"She called and said she wasn't feeling well today."

A knot shimmied in her stomach.

"I saw what happened, and there was nothing more you could've done. It was one of those things. She panicked, but you caught her."

"Oh, Nick, I don't know. I feel like I need to do more. I don't want anyone to get hurt, and I don't want to discourage her either."

"It's okay, Sam. These vets have underlying issues that we can't see." Nick leaned against the arena wall. "Without betraying confidences, I can tell you that Sondra was a broken little girl when she went into the service, and what she saw and experienced there did not help her one bit. Her simply being here in this program is one giant step for her."

She picked at a hangnail. "Well, if you say so. I hope she'll be back."

"Oh, she will." He gave her hand a pat. "She will."

The session went well with the guys, Sam and Electra paying especially close attention when they rode. Each vet shook the women's hands when they were finished. "Thanks for doing this, ladies. We appreciate you."

Nervous tension eased when the rides were all done, the horses loaded, and they were on the way home.

"How did it go with the counselor today?" she asked Brad.

"Good." He gazed out the side window. "It was fine."

Electra nudged his arm. "Did you tell him about Toby and what you did? Huh, did you?"

He swung his head around. "Yeah, I did."

"And…?" She cocked her head.

"He thought my actions indicated good progress."

"Well, ye-ah. We told you that!" Electra continued to stare at him.

Brad grinned. "You know Rome wasn't built in a day. It takes time—for the horse, and for me."

The teen scrunched her forehead. "I guess. I just thought… he'd be more excited."

"I don't think counselors show their excitement." Sam laughed. "I think they're trained to remain calm and stoic."

Electra scrunched her mouth to one side. "Meh, whatever." Then her smile returned. "But *I'm* excited! And so is Sam. And that's what counts here, isn't it?"

"You bet it is." Brad patted her arm. "Thank you both."

That evening they sat in the living room after supper, enjoying a cup of hot chocolate and quiet reading. Brad shifted on the couch and cleared his throat. Sam looked up from her book, but he quickly looked down and flipped the page in his magazine. She went back to her story. He harrumphed and squirmed again.

Electra frowned from her end of the sofa. "What's up with you?"

"Nothing."

"You're making these funny noises and disturbing my peace."

He gave a little snort. "Well, sorr-ee, Miss Electra. I'll be quiet."

Sam set her book in her lap. "You have something on your mind. Go ahead. We'll listen."

"Mmm… I dunno… It's nothing… probably stupid and silly…"

"What?" Electra thinned her lips.

She shot a glance at the girl to hush her and then added,

"I'm sure it's not."

Brad stood and limped slowly to the window. "Well, um... the counselor suggested... maybe I should go to the scene... of the accident."

Oh wow. Her heart thumped. She raised her eyebrows.

Electra's mouth gaped open. "But, why? It's just a highway and a big wide-open prairie."

He leaned his back against the sill. "He says sometimes going back to the scene helps people... remember and um... be able to face the blockages... and... deal with what happened." He shrugged. "But I don't know that I need to do that. I mean, it's a long way, and like you said, Electra, it's just a spot on the road. Nothing there. It was nighttime in a blizzard. I probably wouldn't even recognize the place now."

Sam's chest constricted. The scene was a long way, and how would they find it? But maybe being there would help him.

She stood and walked to his side. "Do you want to? I think it might be worth a try."

His chocolate eyes peered into hers. "Would you take me? I know it's a big ask, but... maybe..."

"Of course I will." She put an arm around him and pulled him close.

He rested his head on the top of hers. "Thank you."

Sam lay in her bed, the events of the day replaying like a film loop—from Sondra's absence to the other vets and their progress to Brad's surprise request. Her stomach jitters were replaced by a warm fullness as she again felt his head against hers. She realized she had been missing that intimacy, that budding growth of a relationship, that possibility of someone to share her feelings and dreams and life with.

She awoke in the morning still buoyed by hope. People really did heal from great physical and emotional injuries. Just look at Jace, a paraplegic from a drunken accident, but now at peace with her life. Sam had never thought her childhood friend would forgive her for the fight they'd had before Jace raced off in her little blue Fiat. And she'd never thought she'd be able to forgive herself for not being able to stop her.

Shaking her head to clear the past, she dressed and went downstairs to fix breakfast. Last night she'd called Horace and arranged for him to keep Electra company, go through her algebra lessons, and help her feed the animals while she and Brad made what she hoped was a healing pilgrimage to Wyoming.

Brad seemed upbeat, if a little nervous, smiling but drumming his fingers on the table as he ate, and repeatedly scrubbing his hands over the dark stubble on his head, now growing back.

"Hey, even if we can't find the exact spot, this will be a great road trip, just you and I." She gently kneaded his taut shoulder. "It'll be fun."

He raised his gaze to hers. "Yeah. It will."

Gray wool clouds hovered above, creating an overcast sky as they got into the pickup. Electra stood on the porch and waved. "Have fun. Drive safe," she hollered.

Sam flashed her a thumbs up and put the truck in gear. "Well, here we go—Brad and Sam's Excellent Adventure."

He laughed. "Yeah, maybe I can travel through time and go back to before the accident." He scrunched his face and hmphed. "If only…"

"Sometimes I think that would be nice. But I don't know that I really would want to change things. I mean, yeah, I think about Jace and her accident, and if I could've stopped her, now she wouldn't be in a wheelchair for the rest of her life." A tender spot in her chest ached. "But then, would she still be an alcoholic-drug addict? Would she even still be alive?"

"Interesting thoughts. Yeah, I suppose that's true. If a person's life turned in another direction, how different things might be now." He stared out the window. "I guess there are trials you simply have to go through, to become the person you are at the end."

Sam cuffed his arm. "That's pretty profound, cowboy."

"Pffft. Yeah, Mr. Philosopher here. Enough of the deep thoughts." He flicked on the radio to an oldies country station. "Anyway, I never asked how your session with the vets went. From what little I saw, looks like they're getting more comfortable with the horses."

"They are, I think, although I'm worried about Sondra not being there." She told him what Nick had said. "I sure hope she does come back."

"Yeah. I believe she will."

She flicked him a glance. "Do you think you are getting close to trying to ride too?"

"I don't know. On one hand, I want to...." He licked his lips. "But on the other hand, I... I guess I'm a little scared. My arm and leg are still so weak and unpredictable... what if I can't do it? Here I am, raised on the back of a horse and questioning my abilities."

She patted his leg. "I know. I think that's perfectly natural. Boy, do I know. I question my abilities—all the time—especially in dealing with these veterans. And... I want to help you too, but I don't know how... what to do." She squeezed his thigh.

He put a hand on top of hers. "You do help me. You are. Simply being here and believing in me the way you do." He blew out a gust of air. "Man, I know how *difficult* I've been, how hard to live with. I can hardly stand to be around myself."

"It's okay." She swallowed, her throat thick and dry.

"No, it's not. Really. And I'm sorry." He laced his fingers with hers. "I do apologize. From my heart. I know I haven't shown it, but I... I care..."

Her pulse raced. *He cares.* For months she'd been questioning that: had he been about to break up with her, did he feel anything toward her, did they still have a relationship? Tears stung her eyes and she blinked to clear her vision of the road. *He cares.*

Sam navigated the pickup along the two-lane highway between Decker, Montana, and Sheridan, Wyoming, watching for the mile marker the accident report had given. Brad shifted and squirmed in his seat as he scanned the sides of the road. "We probably won't be able to find it," he mumbled. "This is a wild goose chase."

She flashed him a frown. "No, it isn't. We'll find it." She geared down and slowed the vehicle. "There's the mile marker. I think the accident happened between this one and the next."

He leaned toward her to peer out her window. "There. What's that?"

Deep ruts cut into the barrow pit. Sam pulled to the side and parked. "Think this is it?"

"Yeah." He pushed the door open and climbed out laboriously, using his cane as support. Together, they walked to the ditch. Brad stood in silence, staring at the disturbed earth where his truck and trailer had gone off the road and the wrecker pulled the rig out.

His chest expanded and his shoulders rose. He leaned forward, studying the tracks.

"Do you remember anything?" Sam broke the long silence.

"Just driving, and it's snowing…" His gaze shifted to the far horizon. "…and getting heavier… I can't see anything." He shook his head. "That's all, till I wake up in the hospital."

The tart taste of disappointment rose in her throat. She had hoped seeing the scene would trigger more memories. She trekked through the barrow pit and up the rise on the other side, scanning the rolling prairie, not knowing what she was looking for. She could imagine the whiteout—she'd driven through them herself—and the panicky, claustrophobic feeling of not knowing where you were. Not being able to see the road, knowing if you stopped, somebody could run into you from behind. And then, towing a trailer with a horse on top of all that. Her stomach contracted. Brad must have been worried sick.

A shift in the light and her eyes settled on a shiny object. Walking closer, she saw a piece of chrome partially submerged in the dirt. She pulled it out, waved it aloft, and headed toward him. "I found something."

Brad took the hub cap from her, turned it in all directions, peering at the front, then the back. "Looks like one from my truck all right." Bent, scratched, and dirty, this piece was the only thing left of his totaled vehicle. "Amazing that my pickup was so damaged but the trailer hardly scratched."

"It was a miracle." Sam smiled. "You saved your precious cargo at great cost to yourself."

He wrinkled his nose. "I didn't do a thing. In fact, I caused this whole mess, because I should've stayed in Buffalo or Sheridan. I know better than that." His voice rose.

"You never know when you're going to run into a storm on a trip. Bad weather can come out of nowhere. And does."

"No, I knew better," he repeated. "I did a stupid thing. But..." He stopped and stared at Sam. "I needed to get back... I wanted to get home... to you." His words choked.

She met his embrace and held him tight. Her heart made a funny little jump. He'd wanted to come back to her. Her icy fear loosened and melted into something soft and tender.

When their clutch relaxed, she stepped back and stared into his eyes. "I was afraid you were coming back to break up with me."

His face scrunched in a puzzled frown. "Why? Where did you get that idea?"

She huffed a chuckle. "Maybe I shouldn't remind you, maybe this is a memory best left forgotten... but when you volunteered to go pick up Toby, we had a little... disagreement, I guess, when I called you 'a good friend.' You got very upset and hung up on me." She swallowed. "And then your last voicemail was 'We need to talk.'"

"Hmm." Brad squeezed his eyes shut. "Oh man."

The warm hug erased, Sam couldn't move, couldn't speak.

He opened his eyes and rubbed his thigh. "I need to go sit."

When they were both back in the truck, she turned on the ignition to heat the cab. "Do you want to head home?"

"No, let's sit for a minute." His voice was hoarse. "I do

remember now. And no, I wasn't coming back to break up with you. In fact, the reason I was upset with your comment..." He cleared his throat, "...was that I wanted to be more than... just a friend."

Tears blurred her vision. All that time she'd wasted worrying about a break-up? "Seriously?"

"Yeah. When a guy is 'into' a gal, he doesn't want to hear the 'friend' thing. I mean, that indicates a dead-end road, as far as romance goes."

"Really." Her mouth dropped open. "Really?" She swallowed, stunned. "I had no idea. To me, being friends first lays down a good foundation for a relationship. I watched my grandparents, my parents, my aunt and uncle. They all had or have very loving relationships, and they all say that the other person is their best friend first and foremost."

"That makes sense, I guess. My folks feel the same way. I wasn't thinking clearly, and I felt frustrated with our long-distance arrangement. I know, the situation was my fault because I was on the road so much with work, but I didn't need to get mad at you."

"I guess that's why phone relationships are so hard." Sam blinked, trying to stop tears from flowing. "Sitting here talking and seeing each other's face and reactions... it's so much better..."

"Yeah." He slumped against the seat. "I don't know what I'm doing right now, much less what the future holds. I don't know if you'll be able to stand being around an old, grouchy cripple for very long, and I appreciate your patience with me so far."

The lump in her throat grew. *No. You are NOT going to cry.*

"Now I'm the one saying the 'friend' thing." He snorted a laugh. "But I think we need to take this slowly, see how I do, where things go..."

What? Where did that switcheroo come from? Clamping down on her thick throat, Sam shifted into gear and accelerated onto the road. *That sure sounded like a lead-in to a break-up to me!*

CHAPTER THIRTY-SEVEN

Gray clouds hovered, and the bleak landscape whizzed by as Sam drove, able only to concentrate on the broken yellow lines on the highway. Her mind refused to make sense of their conversation. First, he says he cares and wanted to come back to her, then he about-faces and says maybe they should just be friends... Was that what she'd heard? She caught a glimpse of him, sitting in stony silence beside her. *Say something!* Was he giving up on them, or was she? No! No way.

"Brad."

"Sam." They both spoke at the same time.

He huffed a laugh. "Great minds, huh?" He twisted to face her. "I... I get the impression I said something stupid... and now you're mad at me."

She flashed him a glare. "Yeah. I'm not making any sense of all this."

"I'm sorry. I sure didn't mean to complicate things."

"You were upset with me when I said the 'friend' thing." Her insides roiled. "Then you said you cared more about me than being 'just friends,' and then you said 'let's step back and see'... I don't get it."

He stared out the windshield into the darkening sky. "I don't either, Sam. I've been pretty confused and messed up, myself. I'm trying to figure out how to heal, and I'm feeling a little..." he fluttered air through his lips, "...insecure... about everything—my physical abilities, my mental state, our relationship."

She pressed a hand to her chest. *Aw, geez, I'm jumping to conclusions, making things more difficult for him, rather than helping him.*

And that's what she wanted to do, wasn't it, to help him? "I know, Brad. I think I'm feeling the same, in some ways. We're just a couple of messed up kids, huh?"

He smiled and covered her hand that rested on the gear shift with his. "If you can be patient with me a little longer, I promise I'll work hard at all this… stuff. I *want* to have a normal life again. I *want* to be well."

"Okay. I understand. I know you do." Hope ballooned and floated through her, and she sat lighter in the seat. "You *will* get better. You already are. And I'm here with you, every step of the way." She flipped her hand to lace her fingers in his and squeezed.

His chocolate eyes glistened, and the corners crinkled as he squeezed back. "Thanks."

A rat-a-tat-tat on the windshield startled Sam's attention back to the road. Sleet suddenly hammered the vehicle. "Yikes!"

Brad gasped.

She slowed gradually, testing the brakes to make sure the road wasn't slippery. The pickup rocked as the wind kicked up, and the sleet turned to snow, the world closing into whiteness around them.

"Oh, man." Brad grasped the armrest with one hand and the dashboard with the other, knuckles as pale as his face.

Sam peered through the window, trying to keep her bearings, her own hands in a death grip on the wheel. *No, no, no.* This couldn't be happening. He didn't need to go through another whiteout storm. She put on the emergency flashers and slowed the vehicle to a crawl, able to make out what she hoped was the shadow of the barrow pit on the side of the road. *Dear Lord, help me!*

Deep groans emanated from the passenger side. She bit her lip, not daring to steal a glance. Her heart pounded, her eyes stung from staring through the mesmerizing snowfall, and her breath dammed up behind a great wall of fear.

There was no stopping. If a vehicle came up behind them, it

could ram the pickup. But if she kept going, they could run off the road or into someone else who had parked along the side. She blinked, trying to focus on something other than the vortex in front of her. The truck inched along.

Minutes stretched like hours. She fought dizziness, tried to breathe. A thump jarred her. Were they headed for the ditch? No, still on the road. Must have been a dirt clod. Her gut was a solid block of ice.

There. Ahead. Was it? The road. The heavy, driving storm lifted minutely, and she could see a few yards ahead. Hunched over the wheel, she drove on. Yes, it *was* getting lighter. A dark shape ahead showed itself as a hill the highway cut through. Now the ribbon of road became clearer. The wind lessened and the snowfall slowed, and then, as suddenly as it had come up, it stopped. Lighter skies appeared.

Sam pulled over on the dry shoulder, gave a great, shuddering sigh, and unclamped her hands from the steering wheel. She swung her gaze to Brad who sat frozen in the seat, his eyes wide and wild.

Like an ancient tortoise, he moved his head to look at her. "Oh... my... gosh." His words stuttered out in short gusts.

"Are you all right?"

"I thought... I-I... Oh, man!" He buried his face in his hands.

"It's okay." She leaned over to put an arm around him. "It's okay. We're all right."

He looked up finally. "Yeah. We are. We made it." He popped his seat belt and returned the hug. They stayed that way for long minutes, simply breathing and letting the tension flow out like rivers of melting snow.

Sam squeezed her eyes shut against tears. Funny, how life was like the weather. It could veer out of control at any moment, and there wasn't a lot she could do about it.

The rest of the trip home was blessedly uneventful with no more snow squalls. Brad sat in thoughtful silence, and Sam replayed their stop at the accident scene and the terror of the sudden whiteout, wondering if this trip had helped or hurt his recovery.

She inhaled the fresh air of relief when she drove onto the dirt road from Ingomar to the ranch. "Home, sweet home."

As she parked the truck in front of the house, Brad turned to her. "Thanks for doing this, for making the trip. I still have a lot to process, and I hope you'll keep on giving me a chance."

"Of course I will." She cocked her head and gave him what she hoped was an encouraging smile. "Let's go in. I'm starved."

Electra and Horace greeted them at the door with great enthusiasm, and while they ate supper, Sam told them about the trip. Soon, her elderly neighbor regaled them with his own snowy adventures. Electra oohed and aahed and giggled, and Brad joined in the laughter and light-hearted conversation. Sam's tension melted like the butter on her roll.

For the next couple of days, Brad spent most of the time with Toby, petting, feeding, and leading him around the corrals. He repeated his barn-entering exercise until the gelding became more and more comfortable going into the enclosed space. Watching this process, a balloon of pride and hope swelled inside Sam.

***

On their next trip to Miles City, anticipation coiled in her belly as she approached the college arena. Would Sondra come back or had her experience turned her off from horses altogether? They unloaded the horses, Brad went off to his counseling appointment, and Sam went inside, her hands cold and clammy.

The men immediately surrounded them, eager to ride. She perused the bleachers. No Sondra. Her lungs deflated. That's what she'd been afraid of. She and Electra helped two guys mount, while the others walked closely beside in case of a slip.

As she gave Jimmy Trixi's reins and stayed by his side, she saw Nick enter the arena with a woman. *Sondra!* Her heart jumped. *She came back!* Sam waved at them and continued the lesson with Jimmy.

When he finished, she strolled to the bleachers to greet Nick and Sondra. "I'm so happy you came back. Are you all right?"

The woman nodded. "Yeah. I'm… working on… things. But I just want to watch today, if that's okay."

"Yes, of course. You take as much time as you want. I'll come back after the guys are done, and we can talk, if you'd like."

Nick followed her back to the group. "You're doing a great job here. With your online lessons almost completed, I think we'll soon be ready to send you for your certification training and testing."

Wings fluttered in her stomach. "Oh my. Really?" She raised her brow. "After that last fiasco with Sondra, I was expecting… I dunno, maybe to be fired?"

"Oh, heck no." Nick grinned. "On the contrary. You reacted appropriately during that situation, kept your cool, caught her, and calmed her. That's what we're looking for. And you've done wonders with the guys. They can't wait for 'riding day' to come around each week."

"Whew. I'm glad." She smiled back. "That means a lot. Thank you."

When the lessons ended and the other veterans stood around petting the horses and talking to Electra and Nick, she went back to sit beside Sondra. "So, what do you think about all this?"

"The guys are doing great." The young woman turned her big brown eyes on Sam. "I'm sorry I'm so slow. I'm way behind everybody."

"No, no. This is not a competition. Everybody has had a different experience to overcome, and everyone reacts differently to the horses. You have to move at your own pace. If you don't get to the riding part for six weeks, or months—or more—that's just fine."

Sondra's eyes glistened. "I don't want to give up. I want to do this."

"Good. I'm very glad. I'll be here every week. And when you're ready, you let me know what you want to do."

"Thank you."

As she headed back, Brad came into the arena and walked to where Electra and Apache stood. The men had unsaddled Trixi, but Apache was still tacked up. "Could I..." he glanced at Sam who came up beside him, "...could I have a go at it?"

Her mouth fell open, and the teen's face mirrored her surprise. "Yes! Yes, you sure can." She wanted to jump up and down and yell to the skies, but she forced herself to remain calm. "Okay, here's what we're going to do." She gave him the details, he nodded, and Electra gave Apache the signal to kneel.

Since Brad's left leg was the weak one, she suggested mounting from the right side. "Apache is gentle enough for that. He won't mind."

Brad slid his bad leg over the saddle, wincing as the muscles stretched. Sam and Electra stood on either side of the horse to give him a hand if he wanted help. He eased onto the saddle, squirmed to get his seat, and tucked his boots into the stirrups. His Adam's apple bobbed as he adjusted the reins and grabbed the horn. "I know cowboys don't hold onto the horn, but... I guess I'm as much of a greenhorn right now as anybody." He nodded at Electra. "Okay, I'm ready."

Apache rose. Brad gritted his teeth and hung on until the horse stood fully. Taking an audible breath, he touched his heels to the flanks, and the horse walked forward. His body relaxed, and he soon looked like his old self as they circled the arena.

Sam couldn't keep the smile off her face either. *Another miracle!*

"You da man!" Electra chortled as they settled into the truck and headed home.

Brad laughed, and Sam joined in, playfully reaching across the girl and poked his arm. "You did it, and I'm proud of you."

"Yeah. And now you can ride every day cuz we have Trixi

316

and Apache and you were awesome!" The teen's face beamed as though she'd won a prize. "Woohoo!"

"Well… I guess we'll have to see. Maybe…" He grinned. "Gotta admit though, it did feel pretty darn good to be up there again."

For the rest of the drive, Electra kept up her bird-like chatter, and Brad dished it back. A light spread its glow through Sam's insides, lifting her winter of doubts. Brad had ridden. The vets' group was progressing nicely. Nick was pleased. And Sondra had come back. *There may be hope, after all!*

When she parked at the ranch house, Brad eased out of the truck with careful movements, groaning as he put weight on his leg. "Ooh, boy. I'm gonna be sore now. I stretched things I forgot I had."

"You go on in and run a hot bath and soak while Electra and I do the chores," Sam suggested. "There's some horse liniment in the cabinet under the sink. That helps sore muscles."

"Sorry to bail on the chores." He grimaced. "But that bath and liniment sounds like the best route for now."

Brad was indeed sore, and he rested for a couple of days, doing some easy stretching exercises and hobbling out to the corral to give Toby treats and pats. "Man," he grumbled, "I knew I was gonna be sore, but this is ridiculous."

"Keep on trying. Rome wasn't built in a day, ya know." Sam winked.

He snickered. "Yeah, I guess."

Finally, one morning after feeding, he asked to ride Apache again.

"Yeehaw!" Electra bounded to the barn with glee, expressing the feelings Sam held back.

Brad slid onto a kneeling Apache, Electra mounted Trixi, and Sam joined them on Toby for a short ride in the pasture adjacent to the corrals.

The air was crisper than it had been, and Sam pulled her scarf higher on her face. Brad's face glowed, whether from the cold, or the exhilaration of the ride or both, she wasn't sure. The teenager urged the mare into a faster pace to lope ahead.

Sam inhaled. "It smells like snow."

"Hmm." His nostrils flared. "How do you know what snow smells like? It's a little late in the season, almost March, and we already have some green showing."

"I know. There's something about the air. It's colder, and... I dunno... feels different, I guess." She shrugged. "Probably just my imagination."

"Probably." He grinned and reached across for her hand.

She squeezed back through the layers of their gloves, hoping for more, wishing for skin contact, but accepting whatever affection he could manage.

CHAPTER THIRTY-EIGHT

Sam awoke to a dark gray light. She swung her legs out of bed into her slippers, grabbed a robe, and went to the window to look out at the white expanse. She knocked on Electra's door to wake her and hurried downstairs to put on the coffee.

The aromas of the brew and frying bacon soon had Brad shuffling from his room to the table. "Well, you were right. We're getting snow."

"Told ya." She winked and poured him a cup.

Electra thundered down the stairs. "It's snowing! Ohmygosh, it's snowing! Did you guys see it? Did you see?"

"Oh yeah, we saw it." Sam chuckled. "Eat a hearty breakfast now, we've got to get out to feed before it piles up."

"I'm so excited, I thought we were done for the season, but now it's snowing again, and I love the snow out here, it's so pretty!" The girl finally stopped to take a bite of pancake, her eyebrows still reaching for her hairline.

Shaking her head, Sam sat to eat. "I would have thought you'd be tired of it by now. It's been a long winter, even though we had some warm temps this month. I'm always glad to see the end. Snow makes for a lot more work."

"Yeah, but..." Electra spoke around another bite, "...we love our work, don't we? Taking care of the cows and the horses and the chickens and everything?"

The girl was right. Sam smiled. "We do. I do. I love it here, although those chores are simply a little easier to do in the spring, summer, and fall."

Horace called to ask if they needed help, but she reassured him they'd be all right and would be over to help him later.

The wind picked up and the snow started to drift as Electra and Brad helped her load hay. At the pasture, the hungry herd greeted them with loud moos. Brad drove in circles as the women distributed flakes of hay and then sprinkled cake pellets. Sam counted the cows to make sure they were all there. "I think we might be missing one," she said as Brad slid aside and she climbed behind the wheel into the warm truck. "That lop-eared cow. I didn't see her, did you?"

Electra shook her head.

"Let's go look for her." She steered the pickup toward the coulees that intersected the pasture. Snow fell harder now, propelled against the windshield by the wind. She switched the wipers on full as she maneuvered through the drifts, hoping she wouldn't get stuck.

"There! Something over there." The girl pointed.

Sam could barely make out a dark form ahead, but as they drove closer, the outline of a cow, hunched against the wind, came into clearer view. She got out of the truck and walked slowly toward the animal. Now she could see a mound under the snow next to the cow. "It's an early calf," she shouted to her companions, and then to herself, "Oh, Lord, I hope it's still alive."

"Oh no!" While Brad lumbered out the passenger door, Electra scooted out through the driver's side.

"Is it dead? Ohmygoshno! It can't be dead, Sam, can it? Is it?" Tears cascaded from the girl's eyes and froze on her cheeks. Without regard to the mama's warning moo, she hurled herself forward to brush snow away from the drift.

"Wait!" Too late, Sam realized what was happening. The cow stepped forward and butted Electra. The girl fell onto her side with a shriek, scrambling on all fours to get away.

"Hey!" Sam waved her arms at the cow. "You okay, Electra?"

"Yeah, I'm fine."

Brad grabbed a bucket with cake and shuffled toward the cow, rattling the pellets. She swung a glaring eye toward him.

"C'mon, bossy, c'mon." He rattled the bucket again, shoving it closer to her nose. The red and white heifer sniffed, moved her head toward her baby, and then back to the bucket.

The cow and the man continued their dance for several interminable minutes. Brad made half steps backward as she finally followed the lure of food.

With Electra on her heels, Sam dashed to the mound and uncovered the calf. "Is it...? Is it...?" The teen choked on her sobs.

Sam leaned close to its mouth, at the same time holding her hand on its ribs. "It's alive. Go get that blanket out from behind the seat."

Electra ran to the truck and back in split seconds.

"Now, scrape together the loose hay in the back and make a nest. We've got to get this baby home."

Brad continued to keep the cow occupied while Sam wrapped the calf in the blanket and snuggled it into the hay. "Okay, let's go." She opened her door.

"I'm riding back here," the teen declared.

"No! It's too cold." She gave the girl a push toward the truck. "Get in!"

Brad put the bucket in the back and sat on the tailgate. "I'll ride back here and keep shaking pellets so Mama will follow us." He pulled his body laboriously into the truck bed.

"You'll freeze!" Both women yelled at the same time.

"I'll be fine. Get moving." His face set in resolute lines.

Sam stripped off her heavy coat and threw it over his shoulders. "All right. But pound on the cab if you get too cold." She and Electra jumped into the truck, she ground it into gear, and headed for home as fast as she dared through the drifting snow.

The cow followed for a while, but they soon left her behind in the need to get the calf home and warmed. Snow blew relentlessly across the windshield, and she leaned forward to peer at the expanse of whiteness.

Electra twisted her body to look through the back window.

"Will the mama come do you think?" Her voice shuddered. "Will the baby be okay?"

"I hope so." Sam bit her lip as she drove, also hoping she wouldn't end up stuck in a drift, or worse, drive into a coulee. And, that Brad wasn't catching his death of cold back there.

Finally, she saw the dark shapes of the herd where they still picked at the remains of the hay and let out a breath of relief. Now she could follow the tracks back toward home.

She stopped the truck and got out. "How are you doing back here?"

"I'm fine. K-keep going." His words belied the chattering of his teeth.

"Get in and drive for a while. You can see where to go now, and it's not far. I'll stay back here."

"N-no, n-no, I'm fine. J-just h-hurry."

She lowered the tailgate and hopped into the bed. "Get. In. The. Truck." She grabbed her coat from him, shrugged into it, and put out a hand to help him up.

"S-Sam. D-don't d-do th-this. We'll b-both f-freeze if we s-stay h-here, argu-arguing."

"Exactly. So get in there!" She jerked on his arm. "C'mon, get up!"

At last, he gave in, shivers wracking his body. He got into the cab and drove.

She huddled in the corner next to the calf, hoping to keep them both warm the rest of the way.

Icy wind buffeted the truck, sending shards of frozen snow across the bed. Sam lay next to the baby, curling her body around it, out of the direct slam of nature's forces.

The mile back to the barn stretched like a wet lasso, but as she was just about to give up and pound on the cab, Brad pulled in next to the corral. He and Electra came around back and lowered the tailgate.

"You okay?" His voice was filled with concern.

"Still here." She tried a bit of levity around shaky words.

Electra jumped into the bed, gave her a hand up, and they

scooted the calf to the open end. The three carried it into the barn.

"Run up to the house, get a bucket of hot water, that jug of vinegar, and bag of rags from the broom closet." Sam motioned to the girl who took off like a shot.

"You need to get yourself thawed out," Brad admonished, as she pulled hay bales into a circle around the calf.

"This is doing the trick. There's a heat lamp over in that tack area. Would you get it for me?"

He brought it over, hung the chain from a hook in the ceiling, and plugged it in.

In a few minutes, Electra returned with the water and supplies. "What's this all for?"

Sam added vinegar to the hot water, dipped a rag in, and rubbed the calf. "This helps to draw the frostbite out of his legs."

The teen grabbed a rag and helped. Brad gathered loose straw to add to the nest around the baby. After she had rubbed and massaged the legs and body, Sam covered it with more straw and sat back on her haunches to survey her work. "It's breathing. We need to let the heat do its work now." She studied Electra's furrowed brow. "And pray."

She pulled the lamp closer to the calf and rose stiffly. "I don't know about you guys, but I could use some hot chocolate about now."

Brad held out his hand to help her. "That sounds like a great idea."

The three trudged through the drifting snow to the house, where Sam shucked off her heavy coat and coveralls and sank gratefully into a chair. Brad brought a blanket and tucked it around her shoulders, while Electra heated the milk for the cocoa. "It's past lunchtime, too." The girl looked at the clock. "Do you want me to heat up some soup?"

"That would be great." Sam sipped at the hot beverage. The warmth slid into her stomach, melting her frozen core. Her fingers tingled and burned as they thawed, and her teeth chattered.

Brad brought a pair of wool socks he'd heated on the stove in the living room, put them on, and gently massaged her cold feet. She smiled at him. "Thank you."

When she stopped shaking, she asked Electra to dial Horace and bring her the receiver.

"Hey there, little gal." His deep voice also sent warmth through the phone line. "Have some trouble in the snow?"

"A bit." She told him what had happened. "I'm sorry we're so late. We're getting thawed out and eating lunch, and then we can come over and help you feed."

"Oh, no-no-no. Not necessary. I went out and caked 'em up good, and they'll be fine till tomorrow. This storm'll be over soon. It's already tapering off."

She looked out the window. The wind had died down and the snow did seem to be slacking off.

"Do you need me to come over and help you with the calf or the horses?" Horace offered.

Her eyes misted. Such a wonderful neighbor. "No, Brad and Electra are here, and we've got it under control. But thank you, I appreciate it, and again, I'm so sorry we didn't get over there to help you."

"Not another thought about that. Just stay hunkered down, get yourself toasty, and stay that way." With another chuckle, he hung up.

Electra put bowls on the table, and they all leaned into the steam, dipping up the first hot mouthful of venison and vegetable stew.

"Thank you, my dear." Sam savored the soup. Her young friend certainly had "grown up" in the last few months. *She's being so kind, so helpful and giving.* Her heart swelled with pride.

"That Horace is a true gentleman." Brad buttered a hot roll.

"Yes, he is. I'm so grateful to have him as a neighbor. All the neighbors around here are so helpful, but he is the best." Sam slurped another spoonful.

"Yeah, he's a cool old guy. Like a grampa." The teen smiled.

Affection bloomed in Sam's chest, thinking of her own Grandpa Neil. The two men were a lot alike, quiet but wise and willing to give the last shirt off their backs to help someone. *I'm truly blessed.*

After they'd eaten, Electra volunteered to clean up the dishes, and Brad insisted Sam lie on the sofa near the stove. He brought another blanket, tucked her in, and kissed her forehead. "You rest for a while. We'll go out and check on the calf."

As much as she wanted to protest that she could do it herself, a sudden, powerful sleepiness overtook her. "Okay... thanks..." she murmured as she slipped into cozy oblivion.

Sam awoke to clanking sounds in the kitchen, sat up, and blinked. Dusk painted the windows violet. "Oh my goodness, I've slept all afternoon."

Brad came into the living room and handed her a cup of steaming cocoa. "Good evening, sunshine. You've had quite the nap."

"I can't believe I slept that long." A chill shot through her. "The calf! I need to check on the calf." She jerked upright.

"No-no, it's okay." Brad pushed her back on the sofa. "We've been checking all afternoon; just came back from the barn and doing chores. It's alive and beginning to stir. We tried feeding it a bottle, but it wasn't awake enough to get very much."

She exhaled. "Good. Mama never showed up?"

"Not yet."

"Well, it sounds like you two have it under control. I sure got chilled. Still can't believe I slept the afternoon away."

Electra's voice wafted from the kitchen. "Okay, love you, Mom. 'Bye." She sashayed into the room. "Hi. We need a wireless phone. You know, step into the twenty-first century?" She snuggled close to Sam on the couch. "You feeling okay?"

"I'm fine. Yeah, I suppose one day I should get one." Sam put an arm around the girl. "Thank you for taking care of the calf and the chores. I sure appreciate it."

"No problem. We make a good team, don't we, Brad?" She grinned.

"Yup. I have the know-how, and you do the leg-work."

After a supper of hamburgers that Electra fried, they all settled for a couple hours of reading by the stove. The wind had died down and a snow-muffled, peaceful feeling permeated the room.

Sam found herself yawning, despite her long nap. "I can't seem to keep my eyes open." She scooted to the edge of her rocker. "I think I'll head upstairs. The horses all okay…and everything?"

"Yeah, I'll go out and check them and the calf again in a bit. Last I saw they were all in the barn, even Toby." Brad helped her stand.

"Oh, that's great! Wow, what strides you've made with him." She turned to the staircase. "Be sure to leave the outer door cracked open some, so they can go in and out, if they want to."

"Okay, will do." He touched two fingers to his head in a salute. "Get some more rest. We've got it handled."

Sam curled on her side, pulled the cozy quilt up over her ear, and snuggled into the bed. Brad was progressing so well. She smiled with contentment, soon dreaming of baby calves bucking and frolicking in spring's green carpet, mamas grazing contentedly close by. Meadowlarks trilled melodies in the bright sunshine. Then a hawk's piercing shriek interrupted the serenade.

Sam sat bolt upright, listening. The shriek came again, only it wasn't a hawk. A horse's scream of terror, then another. She scooted across the frigid floor to the bright-as-day window.

The barn was ablaze with light, sparks shooting into the indigo sky.

Fire!

CHAPTER THIRTY-NINE

She shrugged on her robe as she ran from the room, slamming the door open against the wall. "Fire!" She smacked Electra's door as she raced by, half-stumbling down the stairs.

"Fire!" she screamed down the hall toward Brad's room. "The barn's on fire!"

Slipping her already sock-clad feet into rubber overboots, she grabbed her heavy coat and threw it on over her robe. *The horses. Oh, dear Lord, the horses!*

Their whinnies rose over the crackling roar. She ran, floundering through the snow to the barn, her arms windmilling to keep her upright.

Nearly skidding around the corner to the corral gate, she brought herself up short.

All four horses milled around the enclosure, wild eyes reflecting the terrible cherry-red flames. Toby reared up on hind legs, his piercing cry rending the air, and ran to the farthest corner of the pen. The others joined in, a macabre choir of fear-filled voices that spiked her heart.

She panted. *But they're safe, they're safe.* She opened the gate, another thought thudding in her brain. *The calf! Oh no, the calf. Oh, God, oh, God, oh, God, please...*

The entire barn was engulfed, the door swinging open to a fiery furnace. No way she could get in. The wind blew a tear across her cheek, freezing it in its track. She sank to her knees. *Oh no, oh no, oh no.*

Electra's shout brought her head up. "Sam! Look!"

A long, low moo came from behind her. She twisted to see

the cow standing at the pasture fence, her baby butting its head against mama's belly as it suckled.

Sam's body collapsed on itself. The animals were all safe.

Brad shuffle-hopped to her side, knelt, and gathered her in his arms.

"The barn... G-G's barn... We worked so hard to..." Petals of flame bloomed from the blackened rafters. Sparks streaked into the inky sky. No way could they save the structure now. Sobs erupted from her core, cries of anguish melded with whimpers of thankfulness. She buried her head in Brad's chest.

Electra huddled at her back, throwing her arms around them. Sam rocked with her two friends, souls locked together in grief. Tears mingled on adjacent cheeks as they watched the terrible, yet beautiful, inferno. Heat radiated, fireworks soared, timbers groaned.

The sound of a big diesel engine drew her attention away from the mesmerizing horror. Horace leaped from his truck. Behind him, another neighbor drove up, and then another. The men chopped ice in the tank and formed a bucket brigade, their efforts like a single drop of rain in the Sahara.

Finally, their frenetic activity slowed, and Horace slogged through the wet snow to Sam's huddled group, his head drooping. She gulped back her sobs. "Oh, Horace." She ran to her neighbor to embrace him. "Thank... you... for trying..."

"I'm sorry, little gal. I'm so sorry." He patted her back as her cries hiccupped against his smoke-infused coat. "I started the phone calls and came as soon as I could after Brad phoned."

She turned to watch the burning building again. "It was... already... gone... when I got out here." All that work she and Kenny had done to restore the barn to its former glory. Gone. Her chest ached. Then an incongruous smile came to her lips. "But, the animals all escaped. It's a miracle."

The group stared at her as if she'd flown in on angel wings. The men followed her gaze to the far end of the enclosure, where the horses now watched quietly, their withers and tails still twitching uncertainly, and to the cow nuzzling her calf.

"Well, I'll be…" A deep chuckle rumbled from Horace's belly. "Just look at that. You're right. It IS a miracle."

Sam strode to the horses and hugged their faces to hers, two at a time. "Oh, you dear ones. You're all right. Thank God, you're all right." Sugar rubbed her head on Sam's arm and Trixi blew softly against her neck. Electra was now with Apache, her arms wrapped around him, murmuring. Toby stepped cautiously forward when Brad approached and allowed him to scratch his neck.

Horace ambled over to where cow and baby stood. "Well, you saved this little one's life, and you got yourself a nice bull calf."

"I don't know that I had anything to do with it." She raised her eyes to the sky and breathed a "thank you."

When the building collapsed in a heap of sparks and the blaze began to die down, the heat dissipated. She looked down at herself, dressed in a robe, rubber boots, and a coat. Chills shivered through her. Electra and Brad were not clad much better, and the neighbor men's pantlegs were wet and frozen.

"Oh, guys, you must be freezing. Come inside and get warmed up." She threaded one arm with Brad's and the other in Electra's as they drifted toward the house, occasionally glancing back at the smoldering heap and then at each other.

Dressed in dry clothes, Sam brought hot cups of coffee to the men gathered around the stove in the living room. "Thank you all so much for coming." Neighbors helping neighbors. Angels in disguise. "You can't know how much this means to me." Gratitude flowered in her core, and her voice choked. "I'll fix you some breakfast." She pivoted and fled into the kitchen before they could see her tears.

Over hotcakes and bacon and more coffee, the men rehashed the fire.

"What d'ya think caused it?"

A niggling realization surfaced now, the germ of a thought that she'd shoved aside for the last several hours. "I… I think it was the heat lamp." She chewed her lower lip. "It was an older one, and I think I hung it too low…"

Brad's eyes widened. "And when the mama finally came to the barn, the calf was awake. He must have knocked it down, trying to get out of his hay bale nest."

Horace's weathered face creased in a frown. "That seems like the most likely explanation."

"Oh no." Sam gulped. "I caused this fire. I'm to blame. I burned—" A sob closed her throat.

Horace appeared instantly at her side, patting her upper arm. "It's okay, little gal. It wasn't your fault."

"No way you could've known." Brad put his arm around her. "It could've been mine. I was the last one out there to check. Maybe I should have—"

A deep chorus of "No, no, no's" erupted as the neighbor men protested. "It's nobody's fault." One of the men spoke out. "Just one of those accidents that spring up now and then when you're taking care of livestock."

Horace squeezed her arm. "Look't the bright side. The animals all survived."

Sam sniffled and smiled. "I'm so thankful for that. If any—" Her throat closed again around her words.

"It is purty amazing. Horses are usually so terrified of fire they won't go near it, even to get out." Horace ran a hand through his short, gray hair. "But that little calf's nest must have been far enough off to the side that they did."

Brad's eyes widened. "I'm so glad you reminded me to leave that door open. I propped up a hay bale to keep it from blowing shut." He let out a chuckle-snort. "I'll bet Toby was first in line."

"Yeah. I'll bet he was." Electra grinned.

The men all laughed when they heard the story of how difficult it had been to get the gelding to even step foot inside the barn.

Sam couldn't join in. *We'll probably have to start all over with him.* An ache dug a hole deep inside. *And a new barn.* Where would she get the money to rebuild? It would probably take everything she had set aside and more. How was she going to tell Murdock? All the hay had burned too. Would he let her stay, or would he try to break the lease again? Worry wormed into her gut. She couldn't blame him if he wanted to find someone more reliable and able to run the place.

She stood, gathering dishes.

Horace led the neighbors out to finish the mop-up. Brad and Electra volunteered to go do chores, and Sam stayed in to clean up the remains of breakfast.

She picked up one coffee cup and wandered to the sink, holding it while staring out the window opposite the corrals. She couldn't look in that direction. She lowered her gaze to the inky dregs of the cup. Cold. Black. Like the barn. She shivered. Grandma Nettie would be so disappointed. "I wanted to do something you would be proud of." The words echoed in the quiet kitchen. Sam dropped the cup in the sink and sank her head onto her arms, leaning against the cupboard as her tears dripped onto the floor.

That night, fiery horses chased Sam through the barn, their terrible whinnies like accusations. She raced from one end to the other, flames erupting all around. No door. No window. No escape. With great groans, the rafters collapsed. Her screams joined the horses' cries.

She jerked awake. A quiet, dark room surrounded her. No fire. No horses. But... no more barn. She rolled herself up in her blankets, trying to shut out the memory of the nightmare. And reality.

When the gray dawn finally lightened the window, Sam slipped out of bed and trudged downstairs to put on the coffee. With a hot cup of the java, she sat at the kitchen table, her cold fingers wrapped around its warmth. She stared into the brew. Options and questions swirled before her eyes. Call Murdock. Plead for mercy. If he wanted to break the lease, she'd have to find somewhere to go. With her four horses. With Electra.

What would she do? Horses were all she knew. This state, this ranch—*It's my home. It's in my blood. I can't leave here.*

Had her dreams gone up in smoke?

CHAPTER FORTY

The specter of the fire trickled its icy fingers through her as she sat, coffee growing cold in her unfeeling fingers. Her mind flashed back to the beginning when she and Kenny first leased the place and worked so hard together to fix it up. Then he gave up on her and their dreams and left. Now, when things looked hopeful for developing her rescue ranch, the barn burns.

Brad's shuffling step registered behind her. His gentle hand rested on her shoulder. She swallowed past the rock in her throat.

"Good morning." His low voice soothed. He kissed the top of her head and took her cup from her stiff hands. "You need a warm-up."

A tear spiraled from the corner of her eye. Brad. Did they have a future? Did he really care enough for her to stick by her—unlike Kenny? His injuries and PTSD were a mountainous obstacle, but despite those things, he was stronger than Kenny. He'd made huge strides already. To climb a mountain, a person only had to take one step at a time. *Listen to yourself, Samantha Moser! One step at a time.*

Brad set the hot cup in front of her and rested his hand over hers. They sat in silence as grief and doubt waged battle in her mind. She bit hard on the inside of her cheek, willing herself not to cry... again. But her hand trembled beneath his.

"I don't know if I can keep this up." Her voice matched the movement of her hand.

"What do you mean?" His face crinkled with concern.

"It's… it's all too much. I try so hard, work so hard…"

He gathered her icy hands in both of his, and his voice was soft. "Sam. Listen. You are exhausted. Things seem overwhelming right now, but you are strong, you are resilient. You've overcome so much and accomplished so much."

She stared down at their hands.

"Look at what you've done, practically single-handed—built up this ranch, rescued four horses and a little Goth girl, and turned the lives of six veterans around. And… you've helped me." He leaned closer until she brought her face to his level. "You've done more for me than any doctor or counselor. You believe in me. And I believe in you. You can do this." He let out a long exhale. "Please."

Her chest hurt as if her ribcage was laced too tight, and the sound of her own doubts hammered in her ears.

"Think of your great-grandma. I've read the books your aunt wrote. I can't even imagine the hardship Nettie lived through and survived."

She huffed. *Now he's playing the Nettie card.*

"And your grandma Anna. Living through the war, coming to a new country where she didn't know the language or the customs and didn't know anybody except a man she hadn't even seen for two years." Brad's voice rose to a higher pitch. "And then she beat cancer!"

And, the Grandma Anna card. She rolled her eyes to stare at the ceiling. Could she measure up to them, succeed in her dream? She *did* have their example to follow.

Brad persisted. "You are brave, the bravest person I know. Courage is doing the thing you think you can't do. And you keep doing that—all the time."

A cocklebur caught in her throat. She swallowed several times. "Well… th-thank you, Brad." She blinked away the blurriness in her eyes. "Thank you for believing in me. You're right, I am exhausted and feeling defeated right now. I won't make any hasty decisions, I promise." Weariness sat on her like a heavy weight. Brad was right. She had the Moser women's genes. Their blood ran through her veins. *I can do this.*

Through the fog of inner turmoil, she registered the sound of a vehicle pulling up outside. Brad cocked his head toward the window, and she slowly came back to the here and now. The clock said 7:30. Who'd be coming to visit this early?

A knock rattled the door. Brad got up to answer.

"Good morning. Sorry to bother you guys this early…"

Sam jerked upright. Murdock.

Her scalp tingled. How…? Who…? She hadn't even called him yet, didn't want to face the inevitable. But here he was, bringing the confrontation to her. *Oh, dear Lord, help me.*

Brad invited him in.

Words tried to come to the surface, but Sam couldn't will them out.

"I'm so sorry about the fire." The man removed his hat and held it over his chest.

"How did you find out?" Brad articulated what she couldn't.

"Well, you know, small-town grapevine. Word gets around quickly." Murdock leaned against the doorjamb.

Sam's insides trembled. *Here it comes. What can I say? What am I going to do?*

"I'd like to take a look around, if you don't mind. Why don't you guys get dressed and come out with me."

How could she do this? *He's going to rub my nose in this mess like a dog that pooped in the house.* She stood and slowly climbed the stairs as if to a hangman's platform. As she struggled to dress herself, every article of clothing seemed to have turned itself inside out and upside down.

After she moved down the staircase, one hesitant step at a time, Brad helped her on with her coat, and the three made their way to the wreckage of the barn. Wisps of smoke still rose here and there from the blackened mess. The charred stench brought bile to her throat. She faced away to take deep breaths of clean, cold air, willing herself not to vomit.

The men stood at the fence, staring at the remains.

"Um…" She cleared her throat, trying to make a path for

words. "I... uh... It was my fault... the heat lamp... the calf..." Complete sentences were impossible. All she could do was stutter.

"No." Brad stepped in. "If anybody is to blame, it's me. We were trying to save an early calf born in the snowstorm. I was the last one to check on things..."

"Brad. Stop." She shook her head violently and shifted her attention to Murdock. "I'm the one... you trusted... to take care of this ranch."

The dark-haired man remained intent on the ruins. "A shame. A real shame."

She turned watery eyes to him, that shame washing over her in an icy torrent. "And I let you down."

Murdock took a document out of his pocket. When he smoothed the paper open, the word "Lease" blared in bold letters on the top.

Her chest tightened. *This is it.* "I don't blame you for kicking me out. I'm so very sorry it didn't work. Just give me some time to figure out where to go——"

"Hey." His eyebrows shot up to his hairline. "Who said anything about kicking you out?" He put both hands on the paper and tore it lengthwise. "No. No. Absolutely not."

Sam scrunched her face, trying to wrap her mind around what he said. She stood and stared, dumbfounded.

"I've been watching you. With the vets. What you're doing with them is simply miraculous. They have nothing but great things to say what you've done for them. Nick and the board are quite impressed as well."

The vets? Question marks staggered through her brain. *What does that have to do with kicking me off the ranch... or not...?* "I don't... understand."

"Well," Murdock ran a hand over his face, "you've proven to them and to me that you have what it takes to follow through. And not only there, but here, on this place." He leaned forward, locking his gaze on hers. "You have taken excellent care of my cows and the ranch. You saved that newborn calf. I have to admit, I was skeptical at first—a young woman handling all this on her own. I didn't think you'd stick it out. I thought you'd be hightailing it back to Arizona in short order."

Sam snorted. *Of course, you did, and then you could have sold this place to the eastern developers for big bucks.* She stood tall. *But I proved you wrong, didn't I?*

"Listen. We've had our differences. But I've seen how serious you are about what you want and what you can do. And… if you want to buy the place, it's yours."

Sam's breath stopped. Had Murdock just said what she thought he said? The man who tried to sell the place out from under her to "The Big Open" developers? The man who wouldn't let her buy until the lease was fulfilled in three years?

She stared into his face. "Are you serious?"

"Yes. I am. And I'm going to accept what you've paid on the lease as a down payment."

Her knees turned to jelly. Dizziness overtook her. Electra jogged up and supported one side, as Brad took her arm on the other. *I must be dreaming.* "What's the catch?"

"No catch." A bemused smile formed. "You've proved yourself. Some people give up easily, on their first try at something. You didn't. You've defied the odds and improved this place and grown in the process. I'm proud of you."

The landlord swept a hand toward the barn. "I'll arrange for a load of hay to carry you through till there's enough grass, and I'll bring the papers in a day or two for you to sign."

Electra squealed. "Sam! Sam! This is AWESOME!"

Brad slipped an arm around her and squeezed.

She rubbed her brow, blinking, as she tried to make sense of the words swirling around her. Opening her mouth, she tried to speak, but no words came. She cleared her throat.

Behind them, the sound of several vehicles pulling up the driveway startled her. Horace got out of his truck, went around back, and unloaded a sack of feed cake. Clyde Bruckner did the same, and Irene came toward them, carrying an insulated casserole dish.

Sam covered a gasp with a hand over her mouth as another pickup arrived, and a second, then a third, the men all unloading sacks, the women carrying food. "Wha—?"

Irene gave her a one-armed hug. "It's what we do around here, bring food and show up to help when there's a tragedy."

Hot tears trickled down her cold cheeks, and Sam hugged Irene back. "Thank you." She faced the men. "Thank you." And to Jack Murdock. "Th-thank you." She couldn't get out any more words. Clouds parted above her, and the sunlight flooded her with gratitude.

CHAPTER FORTY-ONE

Throughout the next few days, neighbors came from as far away as Forsyth to help clear the barn wreckage. Wives continued bringing casseroles and pies and cakes, and that kept the work crew well-fed. Sam continued to walk around in a daze, not quite believing, first of all, what had happened with the fire and now, the generosity of friends.

Electra called her mom, breathlessly recounting the story with exclamations and embellishments. Alberta asked to talk to Sam. "Oh my dear, are you all right? Do you need me to come out for a few days?"

"No, I'm fine. I mean, yeah, if you want to come visit, that would be great, but... oh, Alberta, I can't believe all these people. And Murdock! A complete turnabout."

"Wow." The other woman's voice held a tone of awe. "I'm even more excited to move out there now. I can hardly wait until I get this tax season done. I'll be there the next day!"

"Well, we are so looking forward to having you join the family."

That evening, she sat on the sofa staring into the friendly flames dancing behind the glass door of the gas stove. With each flickering leap, she counted a blessing. She was here, in Montana, on her great-grandparents' ranch. It would soon be hers. Her horses were safe. She had so many good friends. Her neighbors were caring and generous. Her heart felt full.

Brad came into the living room and sat beside her, draping an arm around her. "You look contented."

She gave him a lazy smile. "I am."

"You know that I admire you."

She cocked an eyebrow.

"You've been through so much this year, and yet you've met it all headlong." He peered into her eyes. "And, along with all of your work, you've been my steady anchor, helping me get through my own piece of hell."

She shrugged. "Aw, well, I didn't do—"

He put a finger over her lips. "You did. You are my hero, my champion, and I care very much about you."

Anticipation curled through her, sweet and heady.

"I know I have a long way to go, but I want you to know I will be here for you, as long and as much as you want me to be." He leaned closer.

A warm, silky feeling crawled up her stomach to her chest.

His lips touched hers, and every doubt vanished with the heat, tenderness, and joy of the kiss.

***

The next morning Murdock drove up, followed by Teresa's SUV. She jumped out of her vehicle and ran to hug Sam. "I'm so sorry I haven't been here sooner. I've been in Denver for a Realtor convention. Just got home yesterday and heard what happened." Her friend held her at arm's length, peering at her as if to assess the damages.

"It's all good. I'm glad to see you."

Murdock strode up beside them. "Morning, Sam. If you have a cup of coffee to spare, I have some papers for you, and," he gestured toward Teresa, "a Notary to finalize things."

Butterfly wings fluttered inside. All her dreams had been leading up to this. They were meant to be. She heard echoes of Great-grandma Nettie and Grandma Anna cheering her on.

This place, with its rich heritage, would be hers. The legacy would continue.

Enjoy this book?
You can make a big difference.

Reviews of my books help bring them to the attention of other readers.

If you've enjoyed this book, I would be very grateful if you could spend just five minutes of your time leaving a review (it can be as short as you like) on the book's Amazon page.

Thank you very much!

Heidi

Next Book in the Rescue Series

Rescue Ranch Rising will be the third in the Samantha Moser series. Like a phoenix rising from the ashes, Sam struggles to build the dream ranch her great-grandparents once owned. Injured dogs, spooked horses, damaged veterans, troubled teens—they all find their way to Sam for nurturing and healing by her compassion and generosity. She sometimes wonders in the quiet of the midnight darkness if there will ever be anyone to love and nurture her and help her achieve her dream.

ABOUT THE AUTHOR

Heidi M. Thomas grew up on a working ranch in eastern Montana, riding and gathering cattle for branding and shipping. Her parents taught her a love of books, and her grandmother rode bucking stock in rodeos. She followed her dream of writing, with a journalism degree from the University of Montana. Heidi is the author of the award-winning "Cowgirl Dreams" novel series and *Cowgirl Up: A History of Rodeo Women*.

Seeking the American Dream and *Finding True Home* are based on her mother who emigrated from Germany after WWII.

Rescuing Samantha, and *Rescuing Hope,* the first two in the new "Rescue" series, continuing the fictional Moser family story.

Heidi makes her home in North-Central Arizona.